MURDER IN THE DRESSING ROOM

"I love *Murder in the Dressing Room*! What a fantastic read. . . . I couldn't put the book down until I found out exactly who the culprit was. . . . Every single character came to life in my mind. Holly is such an imaginative writer and storyteller. . . . I was hooked from the first paragraph. Through reading every page I was 100 percent invested and felt as if I were a drag queen detective myself. Call me Juju Misty Bee moving forward. I can't wait for the next installment of this one-of-its-kind story. The best drag show I've ever been to! I need more now!"   —Jujubee

"*Murder in the Dressing Room* provides all the comfort and entertainment of a traditional amateur-sleuth story, but from a wholly new and absolutely enthralling perspective. A page-turning mystery, larger-than-life protagonist, and a behind-the-scenes look at the glamorous and gritty world of drag. . . . What more could you want?"

—Mia P. Manansala, author of the Agatha, Anthony, and Macavity award-winning *Arsenic and Adobo*

"*Murder in the Dressing Room* is as bright and sassy as its cover. A witty, sparkly, cozy mystery that I lapped up with delight. I can't wait for more from Holly Stars!"

—Tess Amy, author of *The Confidence Games*

"The fabulous Holly Stars has burst onto the cozy-murder-mystery scene with the amateur sleuth I never knew I needed—drag queen Misty Divine is fierce, confident, and oh so glamourous. I loved this cast of characters and witnessing Misty come into her own to solve the murder of her beloved mentor, Lady Lady. Entertaining, touching, and a lot of fun, *Murder in the Dressing Room* was an absolute delight!"

—Ashley Tate, author of *Twenty-Seven Minutes*

"I loved it! A brilliantly plotted mystery and with characters I just wanted to hug, *Murder in the Dressing Room* is a huge-hearted novel and Misty Divine is a courageous, inspirational, and lovable heroine. She must surely be 2025's hottest new amateur sleuth! I got swept up in the glitter and the glamour, and rooted for Misty all the way as she became more and more determined to see justice for her friend and mentor. I loved Joe and Miles's relationship, and I am grateful to Holly for being so generous with her writing, for showing us the lives of characters we don't often see depicted in fiction. What a warm, humorous, and hugely important book this is! I am sure this has been said before, but I think we have a new queen of crime!"

—Emily Critchley, author of *One Puzzling Afternoon*

"A glittering whodunit debut. What Miss Marple did with tweeds and knitting, Misty Divine does with rhinestones and stilettos. A twisty, sparkly mystery with a huge heart."

—Jenny Bayliss, author of *A December to Remember*

MURDER
in the
DRESSING
ROOM

★★★★★★★★★★★★★★★★

HOLLY STARS

BERKLEY PRIME CRIME
NEW YORK

BERKLEY PRIME CRIME
Published by Berkley
An imprint of Penguin Random House LLC
penguinrandomhouse.com

Copyright © 2025 by Holly Stars
Penguin Random House values and supports copyright. Copyright fuels creativity,
encourages diverse voices, promotes free speech, and creates a vibrant culture. Thank you
for buying an authorized edition of this book and for complying with copyright laws by
not reproducing, scanning, or distributing any part of it in any form without permission.
You are supporting writers and allowing Penguin Random House to continue to
publish books for every reader. Please note that no part of this book may be used or
reproduced in any manner for the purpose of training artificial
intelligence technologies or systems.

BERKLEY and the BERKLEY & B colophon are registered trademarks and
BERKLEY PRIME CRIME is a trademark of Penguin Random House LLC.

Book design by George Towne

Library of Congress Cataloging-in-Publication Data

Names: Stars, Holly, author.
Title: Murder in the dressing room / Holly Stars.
Description: First edition. | New York: Berkley Prime Crime, 2025. |
Series: A Misty Divine mystery
Identifiers: LCCN 2024029843 (print) | LCCN 2024029844 (ebook) |
ISBN 9780593816714 (trade paperback) | ISBN 9780593816721 (ebook)
Subjects: LCGFT: Detective and mystery fiction. | Novels.
Classification: LCC PR6119.T434 M87 2025 (print) |
LCC PR6119.T434 (ebook) | DDC 823/.92—dc23/eng/20240705
LC record available at https://lccn.loc.gov/2024029843
LC ebook record available at https://lccn.loc.gov/2024029844

First Edition: January 2025

Printed in the United States of America
1st Printing

MURDER

in the

DRESSING
ROOM

Prologue

★★★★★★★★★★

DEAD.

There was no doubt about it: Lady Lady was dead.

She was dead and her wig had fallen off.

Misty had never seen a dead body before—the closest being a pigeon she had seen get run over by a taxi on Charing Cross Road last week; except the pigeon's death had been an accident. Lady Lady's death was clearly something more sinister. A *murder*, Misty knew instantly. *Lady Lady has been murdered.*

Misty had gasped in horror as she opened the dressing room door and discovered the body. She teetered on her high heels in the doorway for a second, unsure of what to do first. Her drag queen instincts were kicking in, and she desperately wanted to put Lady Lady's lavender wig back on, to cover up her exposed bald head, but she shouldn't. She knew she shouldn't touch anything.

Misty was dressed in too tight a corset to be running down corridors, but she ran anyway, back to the dressing room where the other queens were taking off their makeup and de-dragging after a splendid night of cabaret at Lady's Bar. Her stiletto heels clacked like horses' hooves against the tiled floor, and her left ankle wobbled beneath her. *Don't fall now*, she thought. *Must get help.*

Exploding through the door into the busy little room, Misty stopped and bellowed at the top of her voice, "Someone call an ambulance! And the police! Lady Lady has been *poisoned*!"

And it was true. It had been as plain as a Walkers' Ready Salted to see. Lady Lady's body was currently outstretched on her dressing room floor, her fingers clutching half a chocolate truffle, her mouth oozing thick white foam onto the soft pink carpet.

The room burst into commotion. Plimberley Walsh, a long-limbed lip-syncer in a bright blue leotard let out a startled scream as though she'd just sat her skinny buttock down heavy on a sharp pin.

"Poisoned?!" she screeched.

"I'm calling 999," said Moneypenny, a twenty-five-year-old stand-up comedian who performed as a hundred-year-old grandma. She lifted her phone to her ear, pressing it gently against her blue-rinse wig.

"Does she need help?" asked Amour, sparkling from head to toe in a beautiful deep green sari. "I'm a first-aider." Amour stood up from her makeup station and rushed past Misty out into the corridor.

Misty followed her, speaking quickly as they hurried back along the tiles to Lady Lady's room. "I went to check on her, I just opened the door and found her. She's dead, Amour, she's already dead in there."

Len and Den, the drag king double act who had closed tonight's show, emerged from the kings' dressing room into the corridor.

"What's happening?" asked Len, following Misty and Amour up the corridor.

They arrived at the door. A big brass star said *LADY LADY* in engraved italics.

There she was.

Lying on the floor, her foamy mouth wide open in a frozen wail—she looked tiny to Misty, no longer bursting with the giant and sparkling personality for which she was famous.

I can't believe it, thought Misty. *I can't believe she's dead.*

Dead.

1

****

WEDNESDAY—TWO HOURS EARLIER

T WAS A Wednesday night, hence the title of the chapter, and like every Wednesday night, Misty Divine was working at Lady's Bar, the glittering and opulent cabaret club on Old Compton Street in the heart of Soho. Later, she wouldn't be able to say precisely when she knew something was wrong, but there was something in the air, something Misty could feel in the pit of her stomach.

Misty was one of the bar's regulars, drag daughter and mentee of the owner, Lady Lady, and widely known as one of the best singers on the circuit. She had performed first, opening the show with three exuberant jazz numbers that ended with rapturous applause as she bowed, curtsied, and accepted a red rose from a table of gay men in the front row. She was tall and beautiful, and she knew it—a six-foot-one drag queen with bouffant blond hair, long legs, and exquisite makeup. Tonight, she was all in red: a red off-the-shoulder minidress with a sweeping neckline and hems so high she was more leg than skirt, red crystal jewelry that dripped from each ear and across her chest, and sequined scarlet heels so tall they were known affectionately in the business as "ankle breakers." Thankfully, Misty's ankles were still intact, despite stiletto-related injuries in the drag business seemingly at an all-time high.

After her performance she retreated to the bar at the back of the auditorium, choosing a high stool at the end of the counter from which she could survey the entire room. Lady's Bar was a stunning venue. A vast underground cabaret room decorated with velvet and gold leaf, it was *the* place to go to see the very best of the London drag scene, and all of it was hosted by Lady Lady herself, the sensation and living legend. There were a hundred cabaret tables, each one polished to perfection and adorned with a flickering candle and a vase of white flowers. Patrons dressed up for the occasion, and from the bar Misty could see customers in fabulous outfits ranging from black tie to rhinestoned tracksuits, served by waiters in bow ties and burgundy aprons as performer after performer took to the stage.

Was something off with one of the customers? Is that what had set her on edge? She looked from table to table as tonight's lip-syncer, Plimberley, brought the house down with a performance of acrobatic genius as she flipped and dipped and flicked her hair. But, no, there didn't seem to be anyone doing anything out of the ordinary in the audience, nobody who particularly stood out as problematic.

Maybe it's just a spot of anxiety, she told herself. *I'm imagining things.*

But still, she couldn't shake it.

When Lady Lady came back out onstage after Plimberley's lip sync, she looked sublime. She was dressed in a perfectly fitted bronze-and-gold gown, with a heavy crystal-encrusted train that dragged along the floor behind her, and her hair was the lavender purple she had worn for twenty years. Misty knew that up close, her hair smelled of lavender too. *Drag should be a delight for all the senses*, Lady Lady always said. She'd been known to ban drag queens from performing at the club if they showed up in stinking tights, which frankly, happened more often than Misty liked to admit. Drag could be a down and dirty business, and dirty tights were par for the course when you were gigging six nights a week.

In between each act Lady Lady would do a little stand-up comedy or sing a number or perform a lip sync, whatever she had prepared for the occasion. And every time, every night, she was faultless. Perfection. The finest cabaret host London had seen since Danny La Rue. Lady Lady was a tiny powerhouse. At five feet tall she was shorter than most of the other drag performers, but her stage presence was enormous.

"And let's hear a huge round of applause for . . . er . . . erm . . ."

"Plimberley!" shouted Plimberley from the side of the stage.

"Plimberley! Plimberley, of course!" laughed Lady Lady.

Misty stood up.

In the five years that Misty had worked with Lady Lady she had never, not once, heard Lady Lady "erm" or "aah" into the microphone. She prided herself on being an impeccable public speaker. And the fact that she had forgotten Plimberley's name was, quite simply, shocking.

Misty studied Lady Lady from the back of the room, the way she moved, the way she laughed. She was tense tonight, not as comfortable as she normally looked. Her shoulders were slightly raised, her teeth slightly more bared than usual, like an elderly Yorkshire terrier snarling at an unsatisfactory dog treat. Lady Lady had owned Lady's Bar for twenty years, and she hosted six nights a week. She was never tense. For most people present, it wouldn't have even been something they'd notice. A slip of the mind, a memory blip from a hostess who was otherwise dazzling. But to Misty it was serious. It meant that there was definitely something amiss.

The next act was Moneypenny, a stand-up comedian who told the stupidest jokes.

"Knock knock!"

"Who's there?!" cheered the audience in unison.

"Ivana!"

"Ivana who?!"

"Ivana let you taste my Battenberg, if you know what I mean."

Apparently, the audience did know what Moneypenny meant, because they rolled in the aisles with laughter. Misty didn't think it was very funny, but she smiled along.

Lady Lady stood at the side of the stage and laughed in all the right places, clapped with the audience, and smiled broadly at the crowd. But Misty watched her carefully. The laughs felt forced, like she was laughing slightly too hard, slightly too often. And the smile looked pained; it stretched all the way to her bejeweled earlobes and seemed hard and cold. She hadn't been like this during the first half of the show, had she? Misty tried to think back to before the interval, to whether Lady Lady had seemed off at the start of the night, but she didn't think so. No, this was something new. Misty was worried, concerned for her friend and mentor. This behavior was out of character for Lady Lady, who was usually confident and self-assured, hosting with an ease that was unmatched by other performers. Misty wanted to rush up, hold Lady Lady's hand, ask her what was wrong, and tell her that everything was going to be all right.

Maybe something's happened backstage. That must be it. It was rare, but not unheard of, to hear of a drag performer row in a dressing room. Drag performers were a feisty bunch: *Personalities like pythons*, that's what Lady Lady used to say. Misty sat back down, keeping her eyes on her drag mother, unable to look away as she crossed her long legs. She knew they looked glossy and elegant like Jessica Rabbit's, but the reality was they were sweaty and hot under three layers of tights and foam padding.

Misty tried to put her thoughts aside and enjoy the remaining performances, gasping along with the audience when drag queen Amour threaded a condom through her nostrils, and throwing her head back laughing at Len and Den, who tonight were playing bearded impersonations of Conservative British Prime Ministers Liz Truss and Theresa May in a hilarious and ridiculous set they had entitled *Primed Potatoes*. Misty had known Den for a long time, for years, since before she even put on a wig for the first time. It had in fact been Den who had encouraged Misty to get started in drag, during a long and serious conversation about their unfulfilling day jobs. She admired everything about him, especially his performance skills. And tonight, as he skipped across the stage in a blue suit, Misty reveled in his comedy talents.

When Lady Lady called all of the night's performers to the stage, Misty wound her way through the cabaret tables and stepped up, took an elegant bow, and enjoyed the applause. This was always her favorite moment of the night. Adulation. Was there any better feeling than adulation? Probably not. Everybody in the audience rose from their seats, a full standing ovation. This was usual, of course. At Lady's Bar there was a standing ovation every night.

Later, Misty handed the bearded barman, Jan, a drink token in exchange for a gin and tonic, sipping it as she watched Lady

Lady work the crowd. It was customary, and expected by Lady Lady, that the performers would stay in drag and have a drink with the remaining audience after the show, but Lady Lady's shoulders were tight, and she wasn't stopping to chat to as many people as usual. Normally Lady Lady would have congratulated each of the performers individually, always piling heaps of praise onto Misty, her protégé. This delighted Misty every time, giving her a powerful feeling of pride and achievement. But tonight there was none of that as Lady Lady hurried through the crowd like she had shit on her shoe and needed to get out fast. She did stop to have her photograph taken with a woman whom Misty recognized as a soap actor—Emma something—and the expensive-looking dress sparkled in the flash of the camera.

The more Misty looked at Lady Lady's dress, the more it seemed Lady Lady was uncomfortable in it. And it wasn't quite her usual style. Lady Lady normally had her pieces made by Florentina, one of London's most popular designers for drag artists, but this dress tonight, this bronze-and-gold feast for the eyes, looked like vintage. And it looked like it must have cost an absolute fortune, the sheer amount of crystals of all shapes and sizes. Lady Lady pulled at the sleeve as she had her photo taken, as though she wanted to take the dress off immediately, like it was too tight or digging in somewhere. Misty knew the feeling well. Drag wasn't an art famed for its high levels of comfort.

AFTER THE SHOW, Misty was in the Queens' Room sitting at a makeup station next to Amour. The dressing rooms at Lady's Bar were a stingy affair. There were three: the Queens' Room, the Kings' Room, and the Lady Lady's Room. Her room was bigger than the other two put together. She even had a fridge-freezer in there and freestanding rails of costumes that glided on wheels across the floor whenever she was deciding what to wear. Luxurious.

It was time for them all to de-drag, to end the individual fantasies that had been created, and to become their regular day-to-day selves. Everybody has their own process for this, what products they use, which part of the face they attack first, and Misty always began by taking the lashes off, even before the wig. But today, she didn't want to. She wanted to keep it on as long as possible, to stay Misty for a few extra moments before becoming Joe again, a hotel accounts assistant who spent their empty evenings binge-watching noughties crime shows with their boyfriend Miles.

Don't think about it now, she told herself. *Don't think about the day job.*

The job at the hotel was as bleak as a picnic in a graveyard. And as much as Joe loved curling up with Miles on the sofa to plow through six episodes of *CSI: Miami*, they loved something else more: drag.

Drag, to Misty, was freedom. Freedom to wear whatever she wanted, to perform whatever she wanted, to *be* whoever she wanted. It was a superpower. She felt like one of the older drag queens on the scene, at the ripe old age of thirty-four. Like sprinters or figure skaters, a lot of London drag performers retire before the age of thirty. Then they might abandon the capital and move to Margate or some other queer-friendly seaside resort, where they get jobs in marketing and adopt Hungarian rescue dogs. Only a few stick around, and fewer still continue performing until the ripe old age of forty. A rare treasure indeed is the successful middle-aged drag queen or king. Youth, in the drag business at least, is a prized commodity.

But with age comes experience, and with experience comes higher performance fees and the confidence to host a room and control a crowd. Misty knew that while some of the younger performers might dismiss her as being past her prime, she was on a path to success, thanks to Lady Lady's guiding hand. She'd started drag five years earlier, at the age of twenty-nine, out of a desire to change something, to burst through the dirge and repetition of their daily work. And ever since she'd started working with Lady Lady, she'd been more inspired than ever to rise through the ranks of the London drag scene and become a performing star, just like Lady Lady herself. She had seen potential in Misty and had helped her discover a life outside of the nine-to-five that was exciting and magical. Her thoughts drifted again from Lady Lady to the next day, to going to the windowless hotel office and processing invoices all day. *No, not yet.* She pushed down the thoughts of her non-drag work life and focused instead on Lady's Bar: the beautiful place she called her second home.

Moneypenny and Plimberley were on the other side of the room gossiping, so Misty turned to face them, procrastinating. She desperately wanted to talk to Lady Lady, to ask her what was the matter, why she had been behaving so strangely during tonight's show, but Lady Lady didn't like to be disturbed in her dressing room right after a performance. Misty studied Moneypenny instead, watching as she sipped a drink and chatted with Plim, waiting for the right moment to talk to her mentor. Under the gray wig and grandma makeup Moneypenny was nerdy-looking with a handsome face and a strong jaw. Misty knew Moneypenny was extremely intelligent, and if Misty had been single, and ten years younger, she would have probably been her type.

"Did you see the guy with the diamond Rolex?" shouted Plimberley. "Bought me three gins."

"Three gins?" replied Moneypenny. "There's no way that was a Rolex, Plimberley, don't mean to burst your bubble."

"It was from Argos, Plim!" shouted Len from the Kings' Room across the corridor.

"He wishes he could afford Argos," snarked Moneypenny.

"All right, all right," laughed Plimberley, "maybe it wasn't a Rolex, but he was nice, you know."

"Three gins kinda nice," said Misty. "Not bad, Plim, not bad."

Plimberley grinned, her glossed lips reaching upward to reveal a set of teeth that were bright white. She was young. Twenty-two. And Misty knew she had a difficult life: unsupportive family, not much money, no stable accommodation. Moneypenny had taken Plimberley on like a sister and was helping her out a lot, but Misty felt sorry for her. She had, on a few occasions when the fallings-out with her family had been serious, slept on Misty's sofa, and Misty had listened to Plimberley crying late into the night about her viciously homophobic father.

"Oh my God," said Plimberley, suddenly remembering, "did you hear Lady Lady forget my name? My fucking name!"

"Sshhh, Plim," urged Moneypenny, lifting a finger to her lips, "she'll hear you."

It's true the walls of the dressing rooms were thin, and Plimberley was certainly not holding back.

"Did one of you lot have a row with her tonight or something?" Misty's spidey-senses were tingling as she thought back to how Lady Lady had seemed off since the interval.

"Not me" was the muttered consensus from the queens.

Misty got up. "I'm just going to ask her."

"You can't!" gasped Amour, laughing. "You nosy fucking bitch."

They all laughed raucously as was tradition when insulting one another in the dressing room. For the others, Misty knew that the idea of knocking on Lady Lady's dressing room door was an impossibility, a privilege allowed to very few. For Misty, however, Lady Lady's drag daughter, it was permitted—even welcomed.

"Don't tell her I was slagging her!" said Plimberley, panicked.

"I'll tell her about Mr. Three Gins," laughed Misty. "She'll love hearing about the Rolex."

MISTY WALKED UP the long, narrow, and pristine corridor to Lady Lady's room. The door was closed, and Lady Lady's name glistened in swirly writing. Misty thought in passing about how she barely knew Lady Lady's non-drag name. In the drag circuit, you could be best friends with someone for years and never know what was on their birth certificate. But Misty liked it that way; it was freeing. And it would be so strange now for any of the kings or queens to call her Joe. She was Misty here, always Misty.

She was about to knock on the door when, from behind it, she heard hushed voices arguing inside the dressing room.

"We don't have any other choice, Mandy," Lady Lady was saying. "We are all out of options now."

Misty was intrigued. Her inner nosy neighbor was well and truly peeking through the net curtains. She pressed her wigged head closer to the door to hear better.

"Yes, but this is dangerous, Lady," replied Mandy, the club's co-owner and Lady Lady's business partner of twenty years. Misty would have recognized her Scottish accent anywhere.

Oooh, an owners' quarrel! Like a lovers' tiff, it wasn't something that should be eavesdropped on by a curious drag queen, she knew, but she just couldn't help herself. She readjusted her hair and listened again.

"Get out of my dressing room," said Lady Lady. "I need to get out of this fucking dress."

"You'll regret this, mark my words," snapped Mandy. Her voice sounded hard and cold. "We'll all end up regretting this."

Suddenly the door swung open, and Misty found herself face-to-face with Mandy White. She had tears in her eyes, and her face was like a bright tomato behind her excessively large glasses. The thick black rims always reminded Misty of prison bars.

"Were you listening?" she asked.

"No, listening to what?" said Misty.

"You nosy fucking bitches," muttered Mandy as she walked away to the club's office in the room next door. "Can't even have a private conversation behind a shut door."

No sooner had Mandy disappeared into the office, than Lady Lady burst out of the dressing room after her, strutting straight past Misty, shouting out into the corridor between the Kings' and Queens' Rooms.

"Okay!" she shouted. "Who's been in my dressing room?"

Misty trotted quickly behind her, careful not to step on the jewel-encrusted train of the elaborately decorated dress. The queens and kings gathered in the doorways and looked at one another in confusion. Everybody knew that nobody was supposed to go into Lady Lady's room when she wasn't there, and nobody did. Ever.

The performers braced themselves to feel the wrath of Lady Lady for this apparent dressing room invasion when she unexpectedly broke into a broad smile.

"Thank you for my chocolates," she said.

"Chocolates?" asked Moneypenny.

"One of you left chocolates in my dressing room, right?"

"Not me," said Plim.

"Nor me," said Den.

Everyone else shook their heads.

"Well," announced Lady, "whoever did it is absolutely marvelous." She lifted up her hands and revealed to the room a beautiful red box that looked as though it were covered in silk. The top was adorned with a giant black bow. Nobody was under any illusion that Lady Lady would share them.

"Lovely!" said Misty. "And there wasn't a note?"

"Nope! Just the gorgeous chocs sitting on my dressing table."

"Well, enjoy them, mawma," said Plimberley, in an American accent that was more terrible than amusing.

"That's exactly what I'll do," said Lady Lady. "Now get your slap off and go home, the lot of you."

Lady Lady walked away, and Misty noticed how quickly her smile dropped from her face as she dragged the crystal-covered train of her dress down the corridor back to her room.

"Does she seem okay to you?" asked Amour quietly so the others wouldn't hear.

"You noticed it too?" replied Misty. It was a relief to know she wasn't going crazy.

"Forgetting Plim's name," said Amour. "That's not like her."

They were interrupted by a thud on the other side of the wall, followed by the sound of a glass smashing. It was loud enough to raise the alarm, as though somebody had picked up and dropped a chair on the floor.

"Ooh, she's mad tonight," said Plimberley, nodding toward the wall that separated the Queens' Room from Lady Lady's room.

Misty rushed back down the little corridor. She took a deep breath and knocked on Lady Lady's door. There was no response.

"Lady Lady?" called Misty.

She knocked again and the door swung open a little way. She pushed it farther and poked her head into the room.

Lady Lady was lying on the ground, her heels swapped for fluffy pink slippers, her face contorted in a silent scream. Dead.

2

★★★★★★★★★

T WAS LESS than ten minutes before the police and paramedics arrived. Misty and the other performers, along with Mandy, Jan the barman, and the rest of the club's staff sat in the auditorium in small groups. The performers had stuck together. They weren't allowed to finish de-dragging, weren't allowed to collect their things and go home. Not yet. They were all required to give statements.

Misty thought she must be in shock—she didn't even feel like crying. Plimberley was inconsolable, sobbing and sniffling, and Amour and Moneypenny were all over their phones as word was already spreading on social media.

"Christ, it's on all the *Drag Race* fan accounts already," said Amour.

"And Reddit," said Moneypenny. "How did they find out so quickly?"

A bubble of snot burst on the rim of Plimberley's left nostril, and she wiped it away with the back of her hand.

The only person Misty had been in contact with was her boyfriend. Miles would be waiting for her to get home safely, so she'd needed to let him know she might be late. At least she was with friends.

Or was she?

A sneaking voice sounded an alarm somewhere in the back of her mind. *The chocolates must have been left by somebody who had access to the dressing rooms.* She looked around the table at Amour, Moneypenny, Plimberley, Len and Den. *Could one of you . . . ?* Misty and Miles were halfway through a rewatch of the American FBI series *Criminal Minds*, and Misty tried to think the way the profilers of the show's Behavioral Analysis Unit thought. One at a time she studied her colleagues' faces, their behavior, the micromovements of their hands and bodies to see if any of them might give away the fact that it was them, that they had left the chocolates. Could one of them really be a killer? Could it be Plimberley, the hard-done-by kid who went from sofa to sofa? Could it be Den, one of Misty's oldest friends? What about Amour, community icon and activist? Surely not. But it *could* have been . . . it could have been any of them. One of her friends. Her stomach turned at the thought of it.

None of them seemed to be showing signs of being a crazed murderer, but then what would that look like? Anybody who had the cool mind and cold heart to leave a box of poisoned chocolates might very well be extremely calm under pressure. Oh yes, a poisoned-chocolate murderer was a cruel murderer indeed.

ABOUT HALF AN hour later two detectives in suits arrived in a hurry. They both looked tired, as though they'd been busy elsewhere or had been called back to work, having already finished for the day. Their suits were cheap and shiny from being over-ironed at home instead of dry-cleaned. One of them introduced himself to the group as Detective Inspector Davies. He was a broad man who looked to Misty to be in his early forties, scruffy, and a little tired-looking, as if this were the end of a very long day. The other detective said her name was Detective Sergeant Linda Hughes—she seemed friendlier and had a patch of dry skin on the back of her hand that made Misty's own hand feel itchy.

"Performers," said DI Davies, in a sort of sneer, "you won't be able to go back to the dressing rooms tonight, so I'm afraid you'll be going home in your . . . costumes. We'll arrange lifts for you all. I realize that you've been waiting for a little while already, but you'll be here a bit longer as we look at the crime scene. Once we've done that, DS Hughes and I will come back and take your statements, and then you can be on your way." He was matter-of-fact, plain as day. They would simply have to sit and wait.

Misty felt relieved by the thought of going home, of seeing Miles. She didn't want to be here anymore. In this room, in this bar. She was longing for fresh air and to feel the night breeze on her face. She thought about Lady Lady's face, tight and twisted and foaming. It was horrible.

"Oh my God," said Plimberley, annoyed and still crying. "Can't we just tell you what happened now? She was given some chocolates by someone. She ate one and she fucking died. That's what happened. What else do you need to know?"

"Plim, no," said Moneypenny quietly, putting her hand on Plimberley's. Moneypenny was good for Plimberley, Misty thought. Since Plim had moved into Moneypenny's flat in World's End, she'd been more professional, had shown up on time, had been ready on time. Moneypenny's calmheadedness was clearly rubbing off on the younger queen, and it made Misty warm to her greatly. Seeing her now, taking care of Plimberley like a younger sibling, gave Misty a lot of respect for Moneypenny.

But she could be Lady Lady's killer, said the quiet voice. *Either of them could be.*

"Will we be here long, DI Davies?" asked Misty, trying to brush away the uncomfortable feeling that one of her friends might be a murderer.

He tutted and looked toward the dressing room like he couldn't wait to get away from them. "It's difficult to say. It'll take the time it takes." He was dismissive, as though their time was irrelevant.

"Well, can I at least get a blanket or something? I'm freezing like this." Plimberley was wearing a low-cut, high-hipped leotard and nothing else. Not even her wig to keep her head warm.

DI Davies performed an exaggerated roll of the eyes. A blanket for near-naked Plimberley was a huge personal inconvenience apparently.

"We'll see to it," said DS Hughes.

DI Davies and DS Hughes walked away toward the dressing rooms and left the performers alone again.

"I want to go home," said Len.

Den took his hand and squeezed it.

Misty looked at the others one at a time: Shivering, sniveling Plimberley. The calm assertiveness of Amour. Moneypenny was still in her grandma costume. Len and Den still sported their drag too, beards and prime ministerial wigs still on.

Could one of them have really left the chocolates? Why would anyone want to poison Lady Lady, of all people?

Across the room, Mandy White was crying hysterically, and her short aggressive bob bounced with each heave of her breath. *You argued with her*, thought Misty as she looked at Lady Lady's business partner. Jan the barman had his arm around her shoulders, with the bar staff all sitting together in their little bow ties, like a table of penguins, and the security guards, with head bouncer, Tess, sitting separately again.

One of you might have killed Lady Lady. One of you could have done this.

By the time DI Davies and DS Hughes returned from the dressing rooms it was nearly 11:30 p.m. and Misty was tired and ready to go home. Misty was interviewed first, in the bar's big open-plan kitchen. She supposed she was first because she was the one who'd found Lady Lady dead, but she didn't like it. Everybody had watched as she walked through the bar with the officers, like she was responsible. She felt worried about going into an interview with the police. Should she have a lawyer? Did she need one? Should she ask for one? All she could think about in this moment was *Criminal Minds*, and she doubted that the highly dramatic methods of a group of renegade profilers with their own private jet bore any similarity to how the Metropolitan Police operated when confronted with a poisoned drag queen.

I don't want to do this, she thought as she sat down in front of Davies and Hughes.

"What's your name?" said DI Davies, tapping a pen against his knee.

The tap, tap, tap instantly set Misty on edge. "Misty Divine," she said without even thinking.

"No, your real name," said Davies.

"Joe . . . Joe Brown." It felt strange to introduce herself as Joe while in drag. There was a clear mental divide that happened when she put the drag on—Joe wasn't there. Joe was away taking a break somewhere until the wig came off.

"Joe," said DI Davies, "tell us what happened tonight. Start at the beginning."

Misty felt irritated that he had called her Joe. Not that this conversation didn't warrant Joe's presence, but because DI Davies had made the decision for her. He thought he could be the one to decide, and that pissed Misty off. It stank. It was a fleeting irritation but one she registered in a new mental log about her dealings with the police.

"Well, after the show, I went to see that Lady Lady was all right, and I overheard her arguing with Mandy." As soon as she said it, she regretted it. She shouldn't have mentioned the argument to the police—Mandy might not have done anything wrong.

"Mandy White? The owner?"

"The co-owner," said Misty, "yes."

"Now, did you hear what Ms. White and Mr. Fulton were arguing about?"

Mr. Fulton!

"I'm sorry, DI Davies, but nobody called Lady Lady Mr. Fulton. She hasn't used that name for decades and, honestly, it feels disrespectful. But, no, I didn't hear what they were arguing about. I arrived just as Mandy left." She wished she could go back in time two minutes and keep Mandy and Lady Lady's argument a secret. This DI Davies was clearly an asshole.

"And then what happened?"

No apology, Misty noted.

"Lady Lady came out asking who had been in her room. Somebody had left those chocolates for her, and she wanted to say thank you."

"So, Mr. Fulton brought the chocolates to the group dressing rooms?"

Misty felt her chest prickling with sweat. She was annoyed. "Yes, *Lady Lady* brought the chocolates to the dressing rooms."

"But he didn't offer you one."

"No. *She* just said, 'Thank you,' and then went back to *her* room. Then we heard a thud and a glass break, and when I went in to check on her, she was already on the floor. She had a chocolate in her hand and was foaming at the mouth. It looked like she'd been poisoned."

"Did you touch anything in the room?"

"No," said Misty. "I just called for help and then the others came. Moneypenny called the ambulance."

"And Moneypenny's *real* name is?"

"I don't know," said Misty. It was true. But the way DI Davies had used the word "real," as if drag identity and persona were somehow *un*real, or didn't exist. Moneypenny was as real a name as Misty was. Misty had DI Davies's number now, and she didn't like it.

DS Hughes leaned forward in her chair. "What was your relationship like with Lady Lady?" Hughes was a softer presence and certainly seemed more approachable and understanding. Misty instantly felt more comfortable talking to her than to Davies.

"We were close," said Misty to DS Hughes. "She was my drag mother."

"Drag *what*?" scoffed DI Davies.

"She was your mentor?" asked DS Hughes, ignoring Davies,

but answering his question at the same time. "I've watched a bit of *Drag Race*." She smiled, and DI Davies rolled his eyes.

"Yes, my mentor," said Misty, shifting in her seat so she was facing Hughes more than Davies. "And we've worked together for years. I don't know how anyone could do this."

"Do you know where Lady Lady gets her costumes?" asked Hughes.

"Yes, from a designer called Florentina, mostly. She specializes in drag custom pieces."

"And is that where she got the dress she was wearing tonight?" asked DS Hughes. "From Florentina?"

"I don't know," said Misty. *What did the dress have to do with anything?* "Maybe. Probably not. Florentina normally makes everything herself, and that one looks vintage."

"Did she tell you anything about the dress she was wearing?"

"No, nothing. I mean, it looked expensive. All those crystals and sequins. I told her it looked nice. But she didn't tell me anything else. But what does that have to do with anything?"

"When and where did you first see the dress?" asked DI Davies.

Misty frowned. "Maybe seven o'clock, when Lady Lady came out of her dressing room wearing it."

"Today? And you'd never seen it before today?"

"No! What's so interesting about the dress?" Misty asked, feeling frustrated by the line of questioning.

"Do you know anybody who would have reason to want to harm Mr. Fulton?" said DI Davies, changing the subject.

"No," said Misty, still wondering about their extensive interest in the dress but glad they were finally asking something that related to the murder.

DI Davies sighed. "So, there's nobody you can think of with

an axe to grind? Nobody who would want Mr. Fulton dead? Lady Lady . . ." He said her drag name like he was holding back a throatful of vomit.

"She got along with everybody," said Misty. "Well, except Auntie Susan. But she hasn't spoken to her in years."

"And who is Auntie Susan?" said Davies.

"You know who Auntie Susan is," said Hughes, shocked at her partner. "Remember? Lady Lady's TV partner from the nineties. From breakfast telly."

Before she opened Lady's Bar, Lady Lady had been part of a famous television comedy double act with fellow drag queen Auntie Susan. They'd interviewed celebrities, presented the weather together, and performed comedy sketches. Misty remembered seeing them on TV when she was little, and though she'd only been working with Lady Lady for the last five years, it felt as if she'd always been part of her life. Lady Lady and Auntie Susan had been a huge hit until they fell out, privately and famously. Lady Lady went on to invest in the Old Compton Street bar with Mandy and became a huge cabaret success, while Auntie Susan vanished into obscurity and now operated a run-down pub on an even more run-down street.

Thoughts of these moments ran through Misty's brain. *A life thoroughly lived*, she thought, *but one that shouldn't be over already*. Lady Lady had meant so much to Misty: a childhood inspiration, a queer icon, and then a personal friend. *She should still be here*. Tears brimmed in Misty's eyes and she tried her best to hold them back—a drag queen instinct to protect the lashes.

Davies shrugged, somehow, almost impossibly, having never heard of Auntie Susan at all. "And you said Lady Lady had some sort of problem with this Auntie Susan?"

"No," said Misty. "I said they hadn't spoken in years."

Misty didn't like this DI Davies one bit. He was arrogant, and now it felt like he was putting words in her mouth.

"Can I go now?" she asked. "I want to go home." She wasn't comfortable in this room anymore, in this small space with this horrible man, and she didn't have the strength to deal with him tonight, not so soon after losing her friend.

"Yes, fine," said Davies. "We need to talk to the others anyway."

Misty sighed heavily as she walked toward the door.

"We'll come to visit you tomorrow," said DS Hughes, "to take a more complete statement. Is there a time you'd prefer?" It seemed that DS Hughes was kinder than DI Davies, genuinely caring. There was a hint of something in her eyes that suggested she was annoyed with Davies, too, but that she was hiding it well. Misty almost felt as though she could trust her, but not quite—not after the way Davies had just behaved.

A more complete statement? she thought. She wasn't sure what else she could possibly tell them and didn't relish the idea of seeing them again, but hopefully they'd seem less like dickheads in the fresh light of day.

Misty told DS Hughes that she'd prefer the evening, after work. *Am I really still planning on going to work tomorrow?* Hughes pointed her in the direction of a police officer who would drive her home. Dazed, that's how she felt, dazed. So much had happened, and her emotions were racing to catch up with her brain. She needed to take off her corset. She felt trapped by it, as if it were squeezing the energy out of her with every second that passed. But she would wait until she got home for that.

As she stepped out of the club onto Old Compton Street, she suddenly found herself on the edge of tears. The coffee shop across the road was where she and Lady Lady would go before a show. Balans, the twenty-four-hour restaurant down the street, was where they'd head for postshow midnight dinners, always with Lady Lady buying champagne for the table. Now, standing on the pavement in her drag, about to step into a police car, Misty realized that all that was over.

She'd really never see Lady Lady again.

3

****

BY THE TIME Misty got home it was after midnight. She lived near Russell Square in a small one-bedroom flat with her boyfriend, Miles, and it wasn't a long drive from Soho, but one during which she seemed to have plenty of time to think, to start to process the loss, the realization that her friend and mentor was gone forever.

When she opened the front door of the apartment she saw that the kitchen light was still on. *He's waited up for me. Of course he has.* The kitchen door swung open and Miles threw himself into the corridor, giving Misty a tight hug with arms that went on forever. His hugs always reminded Misty of a stretchy-armed Hulk Hogan toy her mother had given her as a child.

"I'm so sorry," said Miles.

"I'm hungry," replied Misty. She truly was. And she didn't have the energy to talk about any of it until she'd eaten, that much she knew. A drag queen is a beast who must be fed after a show, especially when there's been a murder in the dressing room, it seemed.

"Come on, I'll make us some eggs." Miles broke the embrace and took Misty's hand, leading her to the flat's little kitchen. "Do you want to take your drag off first?"

"No," said Misty. She wasn't ready to be Joe just yet. "I'll eat first." Being Joe meant returning to the reality of Lady Lady being dead: their friend, their mentor. The reality was one of their friends could have been the killer, and Misty wasn't ready to face that as Joe. Joe was more emotional, introspective, thoughtful. For now, as Misty, she had a barrier up to the world, to the grief.

Once in the kitchen Misty sat down at the small table, and Miles began pottering, taking eggs from the fridge, a pan from the cupboard. Misty played with her fingernails, tugging gently at a hangnail, finding the focus irresistible to break from.

"Do you want to talk about it?" he said.

"I'm not sure," said Misty.

"We don't have to if you don't want." Miles started cracking eggs into a glass jug, glancing at Misty over his shoulder, checking that she was okay. He added milk and whisked with a fork until the contents of the jug were a smooth light orange color.

"I just can't believe she's gone," said Misty.

"I know," replied Miles. "She was such a big personality. It's strange to think of life without her." He sounded sad, as Misty expected a lot of people would over the coming days. Lady Lady was an integral part of the cultural landscape, and losing her was going to be hard for a lot of people. "I feel really cut up about it," he said. Though not a drag performer, Miles was well known as being Misty's partner, and over the years, he'd become firm friends with many of the people on the scene. He and Lady

Lady had known each other for as long as Misty and Lady Lady had.

"Someone killed her, Miles. Can you believe that? Someone *killed* Lady Lady. On purpose."

"What happened?" asked Miles, tipping the scrambled egg mixture into a hot frying pan. From across the little kitchen his eyes looked watery, and Misty wasn't sure if Miles was crying or if it was the steam from the eggs.

"Nothing and everything," said Misty. "Someone left some chocolates in her dressing room, and it seems like they were poisoned. I went to check on her and found her on the floor. Dead."

They were silent for a moment, and Misty's thoughts turned to Lady Lady on the dressing room floor again: the vein in her forehead, the contorted face.

"I can't stop thinking about it, Miles," she said. "About her dying like that. About what she looked like."

They ate their food quietly, the sound of crunching toast and slurping tea the only noise for a while. Misty found she couldn't finish hers. She had been hungry, but now, confronted by a plateful of egg, she felt sick. She pushed her plate to the center of the table.

"I need to get out of this drag."

In the bathroom Misty looked at herself in the mirror. Her makeup tonight had been perfection. Her eyeliner was pristine and swept up from the outside corners of her eyes into sharp points on her temples. Her lashes were long and fluffy and her lips expertly lined and glossed. Her wig was big and long and blond and the height of glamour.

She peeled off her lashes, then raised her hands and unpinned her wig, tucking her thumbs under the lace. She lifted it up off her head, revealing a wig cap wrapped in a tight bandage to hold it in place. And as the wig came off, Misty went away, for now.

Looking back from the mirror was Joe. A plain, brown-haired thirty-four-year-old in a red dress with a full beat. Joe took a wipe from the cupboard and started removing their makeup, and as they did, they started to cry.

4

THURSDAY

UNSURPRISINGLY, JOE DID not sleep well. They kept waking in the night, their dreams filled with images of Lady Lady's dead body on the dressing room floor. At 4:13 a.m., according to the alarm clock on the bedside table, they made the mistake of checking their phone. Through sleepy eyes in the dark bedroom Joe read hundreds of notifications and messages from nosy drag queens and kings who wanted to know what happened.

When their alarm went off at 7:30 a.m., Joe did not feel ready to be awake again. Their eyes were swollen and sore from crying late into the night, and Miles was already up, so the bed felt empty. They lay in and listened to Miles whistling in the kitchen, a cheerful sound on what was otherwise a very uncheerful morning.

Joe couldn't help but think about the first time they met Lady Lady; it was one of their first times out in drag. They had performed a few times, mostly in unpaid open mic slots, before they saw a competition advertised on Instagram: Lady Lady's Star Search, a talent contest at Lady's Bar for new and upcoming drag artists. She had been running it once a year for ten years. It was one of the best reputed drag contests, and winners would see their bookings increase overnight, along with their fees.

With Miles's encouragement, Joe decided to enter Misty. They'd been so anxious at just the thought of it, and without a gentle shove from Miles and some drag tips for beginners from Den, they'd have never had the guts. Putting Misty out there, in front of judges, was a big deal. A first tentative step away from the Empire Hotel. For the first round of the competition Misty performed an Adele song, one of the big belters. She'd felt anxious to perform at Lady's Bar; the place had a reputation for booking only the biggest and best performers, and though she was there as a contestant, it was still her most significant stage to date. Misty's song went down well with the judges: a panel of bigger, more established drag names and Lady Lady herself. But they said Misty's look had let her down. She'd worn a simple black dress and a straight wig that she'd bought on Amazon for fifteen pounds, and the judges said she didn't look sophisticated enough, not *draggy* enough. They said she was clearly a talented performer but too early in her career for the competition. Needless to say, she didn't win.

That night, coming home from Lady's Bar was difficult. Joe felt embarrassed. They got out of drag as quickly as they could and drank whiskey in the kitchen with Miles. But the next day, hungover and eyelashes clogged with yesterday's glue, Joe received a text from a number they didn't recognize.

Misty, I think you have more potential than you realize. I'd like to invite you to come and have a coffee with me at

Lady's Bar one day. Let me know when
you're free. LL. X

Joe could hardly believe their eyes. A message from *the* Lady
Lady. And she thought Misty Divine had potential! Joe replied
with haste, and before they knew it they'd arranged a meeting
with Lady Lady for a few days' time.

MILES OPENED THE bedroom door, interrupting Joe's reminis-
cence, and they were suddenly snapped back to reality.
Lady Lady was dead.

"I'm making porridge, if you're hungry," said Miles.

By the time Joe had showered and dressed, Miles was sitting
at the kitchen table eating his porridge, a bowl waiting for Joe
next to him. They ate in an uncomfortable silence, and Joe knew
already what it was about. But before they could say anything to
preempt it, Miles spoke up.

"I don't think you should be going to work today," he said. "I
think you need to text Jane and explain what happened and then
rest today. You've experienced a trauma." Miles was caring, always, and though his high-flying job at a big marketing agency
was much more corporate than Joe's job at the Empire Hotel,
Joe knew it was a more compassionate environment. At Miles's
work, Joe would have been given a whole week off for finding
Lady Lady's body. Sadly, the same could not be said for the
hotel.

Joe could have called in sick, they supposed. But they felt
very much like they should go to work. Even though they hated
it, they hated taking days off more. For the last couple of years

they'd been getting enough gigs as Misty to cover their monthly outgoings, and a little more, but instead of giving up the hotel and focusing full-time on the drag, Joe was burning the candle at both ends, working long days and then performing four or five nights a week. The security of the regular hours, the regular income, was hard to break away from, they supposed. They hadn't yet found the courage to quit. And today there was something ever so appealing about returning to work, stepping out of Lady Lady's world before the rotted DI Davies was due to come over to take his "more complete statement." Joe couldn't bear the thought of him and his cheap shiny suit.

Joe thought for a second, swallowing hot porridge. They didn't want to have an argument. It was too early in the day and they were already feeling on edge. "Miles, I love you," they said, "and I appreciate your concern. But honestly, I think the best thing for me today is to have something to focus on. Even if it's spreadsheets."

"Do you need to talk about it? About what happened? I'm worried about you, Joe, because I know how much Lady Lady meant to you. How much she meant to all of us."

"I'm fine," said Joe.

"You can't be fine," said Miles, taking Joe's hand across the table. "You've given yourself no time to process it or even think about it. You got out of drag and went straight to bed, and now you're going to go straight to work. It's going to hit you sooner or later, and it's going to be hard."

"Honestly, I just can't sit still today. I know that will be worse. Going to the office is for the best."

Miles made a face that said he clearly didn't agree but that he was giving up. "Okay, well, you know where I am if you need me for anything. And I mean anything. You call me, okay?"

"Okay," said Joe.

"And I'll make sure I'm home in time for the police coming over. I won't stay late at the office tonight."

"Thank you," said Joe. "I love you."

"I love you too."

Miles left for work and Joe washed the dishes, thinking about the day that lay ahead. There was something cocoon-like about the windowless office that might feel comforting, they hoped. On the windowsill in front of the sink sat DS Hughes's business card, the one she'd given to Misty last night.

Are the police really going to be able to help? Joe wondered as they looked at the crisp white card. They weren't so sure. The police were already a somewhat controversial presence in the drag community, and somebody like that DI Davies barging in like a bull in a china shop was hardly going to encourage people to open up. Joe thought back to the interview in the kitchen of Lady's Bar, to the many questions that DI Davies had asked about Lady Lady's outfit. It had seemed as though he was more interested in Lady Lady's dress than he was in Lady Lady her-self, so he had surely started off by looking in the wrong di-rection.

Perhaps Joe had watched ten thousand too many episodes of *Without a Trace*, but to have put the chocolates in the dressing room, the killer must have had access to the corridor that night. And that meant the prime suspects were all people Joe knew. The murderer was surely one of Misty's friends or colleagues.

Maybe I'll *find out who did it*, said a voice somewhere in the back of Joe's mind. *Maybe I could catch the killer.*

Standing at the sink, they felt that surely they could get to the bottom of it. They'd seen enough *CSI* and *Criminal Minds*, for Christ's sake, and the drags were much more likely to confide in Misty than they were in that fetid pustule DI Davies.

Lady Lady deserved better than DI Davies; that's what Joe thought. She was an icon, a legend, a community leader. And she had changed Joe's life in ways they couldn't begin to quantify. Suddenly Joe was furious at whoever had left those poisoned chocolates. Who could have done such a terrible thing? And why?

It seemed impossible to Joe that anybody would want to kill her for any reason.

Joe knew that they needed to solve it, for Lady Lady.

5

****

WHEN THEY ARRIVED at the office, Joe discovered that it wasn't going to be the comfortable day they had planned. Instead of feeling like a cozy and distracting hug, the windowless office felt like a coffin, and Joe's thoughts quickly turned to Lady Lady, to where she might be now—in an industrial refrigerator somewhere or lying on an autopsy table with her insides all on show.

Joe had worked at the Empire Hotel since they were twenty-two and had started there pretty much as soon as they finished university. The job at the Empire was supposed to be a stopgap, a pause on the way to stardom as a serious actor after a degree in theater studies, but of course, life had other ideas. The truth was, Joe was a much better singer than they were actor, and so they had never really succeeded at that. An early reviewer of Joe's acting, from a university production of *Romeo and Juliet*, described it as "wooden as a pirate's teeth," which had stuck with Joe ever since.

In a strange way though, the Empire Hotel had been what

led to Joe discovering their drag alter ego. One of the night receptionists was the drag king, Den, of the Len and Den double act. Joe originally knew Den under their work name, Francesca. And Francesca worked four nights a week, twelve-hour shifts, covering the reception desk of the small hotel throughout the night. Joe would see Francesca early in the morning, and they often had coffee together as Joe was settling in for a day of invoices and spreadsheets.

"Have you ever tried it?" asked Den one morning when he was telling Joe about his new partnership with Len. "Drag, that is. Have you ever tried it?"

Joe hadn't, but they'd thought about it. There was something appealing about the idea of the costumes, the sparkle, the opportunity to perform again, something they hadn't done since university. And though they'd worked through their relationship with their gender and were fully comfortable being nonbinary, there was perhaps more exploration to be done, always more to uncover. Joe was certainly tempted.

"I think you should try it," said Den. "I reckon you'd make a gorgeous drag queen."

And that conversation lit a spark, a yearning to try something new and dangerous and exciting. *Drag.* Eventually Joe took a trip to Superdrug, investing a whole forty-five pounds in makeup, not really knowing what they were buying or what the different products did. They started playing with them, learning how to contour, how to paint perfectly neat eyebrows, watching hundreds of YouTube videos late into the night. And that was how Joe discovered Misty and what led Misty to Lady Lady's Star Search.

After the competition, Lady Lady's guidance had been a revelation: in confidence, in self-expression, and in acceptance. In the drag community Joe had found their queer family, people who supported one another no matter what. Of course, there was gossip and backbiting and sniping about smelly tights, but when it came to the crunch, the drags had one another's backs. If it wasn't for Misty's rise in popularity in the nightlife scene, Joe wasn't sure how they'd have coped, stuck in the nine-to-five. And today, thinking about how unexpectedly Lady Lady met her demise had left Joe feeling their own mortality more intensely than ever before. With only a limited number of hours, days, and weeks on Earth, did they really want to spend five days a week doing the administration for a two-star hotel and, in winter, barely getting a glimpse of daylight? Surely it was time for a change.

The newspapers strewn around the hotel reception all had headlines about Lady Lady. Of course, Joe's boss Jane had already seen it in the news. Who hadn't? It was the hot topic du jour. And once word got around that Joe had been the one to find the body, they found themself grilled by the receptionists, desperate for an inside track on today's top story. Joe retreated to the office and tried to concentrate on a stack of invoices, but to no avail. Instead they turned to Google, looking at articles and headlines about Lady's Bar and the murder.

TV DRAG QUEEN KILLED IN LONDON

TELEVISION'S LADY LADY DEAD IN DRESSING ROOM

MAN MURDERED IN SEEDY SOHO CLUB

The last one was from the *Daily Mail*. Joe tutted.
"Joe. Joe. Earth to Joe," sang a voice behind them. It was Jane, Joe's line manager. Joe found her irritating. She was all

fake smiles and boxy suit jackets—the kind of person who shops at Aldi and carries it home in a Waitrose bag.

Joe quickly shut the internet browser on their screen and turned around to face Jane.

"Sorry, Jane, I was just . . ."

"You were reading the internet, Joe, 'surfing the net.'" She performed big air quotation marks around the last bit with her fingers and Joe cringed inside.

"I was," Joe admitted, knowing where this was going. Jane was a micromanager. She wanted to know everything: what you were doing, where you were going, how long you were spending on bathroom breaks.

"Well, Joe," she said, a hideous smile revealing her coffee-stained teeth, "I've seen the papers this morning, and the receptionists are all saying you were at that club last night, so I know you've had a bad night . . ."

A bad night! thought Joe.

". . . but if you're going to be here today, I really need you to actually do some work and not spend away the hotel's internet budget reading articles about your personal life."

"Yes, Jane," said Joe meekly, kicking themself mentally for not telling her to go screw herself like Misty would.

"Good," said Jane, and she turned on her chunky Clarks heel and walked out of the office.

A S SOON AS Jane was out of sight Joe reopened the internet browser, turning back to the articles about Lady Lady. There wasn't much in the articles that Joe didn't already know. Most of them called Lady Lady "he," and they all referred to her birth name, Sean Fulton, which felt strange to Joe, foreign somehow.

They were reading Sky News's take on the murder when a red banner popped up on the top of the screen.

BREAKING NEWS: LADY LADY WEARING STOLEN DRESS

What?

Joe clicked on the article; it was short, as though it hadn't even been finished, as though the writer had received some information and posted it immediately before the full story was even available.

LADY LADY WEARING STOLEN DRESS

Drag queen Lady Lady, murdered in her own cabaret club last night, is at the center of a new mystery today as it is reported that the dress she was wearing at the time of her death is the one stolen last month by the criminal known as the Kensington Catburglar. A press conference is expected to begin shortly.

So this was why DI Davies was so interested in the dress!

Joe was now one hundred percent distracted from work. Thoughts of Jane were quickly forgotten as Joe became enthralled in thinking about the Kensington Catburglar. They tried to remember what they knew about it. It was the most talked about criminal mystery of the year: a thief operating in Kensington and Chelsea who was targeting rare valuables. The owners of the missing items were so rich and powerful that the failure to capture the Kensington Catburglar had even been raised in the House of Commons.

Joe tapped "Kensington Catburglar" into Google. The first article that came up, one of the most recent it seemed, was from a few days before the murder: a detailed rundown of the case.

The Catburglar had taken, among other things, a rare diamond-encrusted Montblanc pen, a crown called the Sunbeam Tiara, and a giant ruby called the Red Egg, just two weeks earlier.

And here was something else. An article from an independent fashion magazine about the dress theft. There were no details about the dress itself, just a photograph of the shop the cat burglar had targeted—a fancy boutique in South Kensington called the Dress Collector—and a brief profile of the owner, a Mrs. Anna Bowman. The boutique looked very expensive, and not the kind of place Lady Lady would have shopped—the dresses in the window were elegant, stunning, the type of dresses that models wore. Lady Lady's outfits were normally more costumey, more camp. That was one of the things that had struck Misty about the vintage gown she'd died in—it wasn't her usual style.

Could Lady Lady have been the Kensington Catburglar? Joe wondered. They couldn't imagine her breaking into Christie's to steal a tiara or a diamond pen. She was always working anyway. When would she have had the time to plan a series of perfect thefts?

If Lady Lady wasn't the Catburglar herself, perhaps she knew them. Maybe that's how she got the dress. Or she was given the dress by somebody. Or maybe she bought it not knowing where it had come from. Oh, how Joe longed to be able to ask her.

And did this mean that the Catburglar was the killer? Had they graduated from theft to murder?

JOE'S PHONE VIBRATED on the desk in front of them. A Whats-App message from Amour.

Have you seen the news? About the
dress?! What the fuck??

And then another message from Miles.

Hey Joe—hope you're ok. Thought you
should know there's a story in the news
about Lady Lady and the dress she was
wearing last night. It was stolen! Look it
up when you get a chance.

Joe sat at their desk and thought about that first coffee with
Lady Lady five years ago, after the Star Search competition. Joe
had gone to Lady's Bar on a Tuesday afternoon and found Lady
Lady already in drag. They'd later learn that she spent most of
her time in drag, in the same way many people spend a lot of
their time in suits. Joe and Lady Lady sat at one of the cabaret
tables in the empty auditorium, and Joe tried not to think about
the judges' comments as they looked at the stage.

"Who do you want to be, Misty? What kind of drag artist?"
Lady Lady asked.

"What do you mean?"

"Well," Lady Lady continued, "there are many types and
styles of drag. Do you want to be a queen, a king, a thing, a
monster, a fashion queen, a camp comedy queen? The possibili-
ties are endless. You know, where do you want to take Misty
Divine?"

"I guess . . . I want to be glamorous," said Joe. "A glamorous
singing queen. Is that really basic?"

"Not at all! But you've got work to do, my love." Lady Lady
laughed. "The talent is all there—the singing is spectacular. You
just need to invest some time and money in hair and makeup.
You need to elevate the look."

"Thank you," Joe said, "for the compliment on my singing.

As far as the look goes, I'm still feeling very new and I'm not sure where to begin."

That was an understatement, as evidenced by the dreadful showing she'd made at the drag competition. *Wooden as a pirate's teeth* came to mind.

"Well, that's why you're here, dear. If you'd let me, I'd love to help you."

It was an offer Joe couldn't refuse.

"Of course I'd let you. You really want to help me? Why?"

Lady Lady took a sip of cappuccino and smiled. "Because I've been doing this a long time. I know potential when I see it. And maybe there's something about you that reminds me of me."

"Really?" asked Joe.

"Really. I've been in the limelight for centuries but there was a life before that, before the television gigs and cabaret clubs. I was starting out once, just like you, and your voice is so good I think you could be huge."

"Well, thank you," said Joe. "I really appreciate it."

"First things first," said Lady Lady, businesslike. "You need new hair. Consider it urgent. When you get home after this you're going to put that Amazon straight-out-the-bag wig you wore the other night in the bin. Nobody needs to see you in that again." She shook her head as though remembering something as grave as a fatal car accident. "Just terrible . . ."

"Wow, okay," replied Joe, shocked by the bluntness of the instruction.

"Do you have a hundred fifty pounds available to you to spend right now?"

Joe thought for a moment, trying to recall the last time they'd checked their savings. They had enough. "Yes," they said.

"Good. Then you'll go to this website." Lady Lady wrote a web address down on a Lady's Bar napkin. "And buy a styled wig. Doesn't matter the style as long as it's big. Should be as wide as your shoulders."

"Erm . . . okay."

"It's all about creating an illusion, you see, if glamour's what you're after. You need shape and style. It doesn't really matter how cheap your outfit is for now. If you've got good hair and good shoes, you can carry it off. And of course, this is drag, Misty. Nothing's obligatory and nothing's forever. Experiment. Try things out. Have fun!"

New hair. New shoes. A mental list was forming.

"How many songs do you have in your repertoire?" asked Lady Lady.

Joe guessed, "Maybe ten."

"Good," said Lady Lady. "That's good. Then I'll book you."

"What?" Joe could barely believe their ears. A booking from Lady Lady. A booking at Lady's Bar! Joe's thoughts immediately turned back to the competition, to what a disaster it had been: the cheap wig, the judges' comments . . . "But do you really think I'm ready? What if I'm not ready?"

Lady Lady tutted. "When are we ever truly ready to take the next big step in our lives?" she said wisely. "But I'm not here to gently massage you into it. I've made you an offer, and you can either accept it or not. It's now or never, Misty, sink or swim."

Joe felt hesitant, anxious, but knew they couldn't turn it down. It was the opportunity of a lifetime.

"I'll do it," they said. "Of course I'll do it. Thank you."

Lady Lady smiled. "Good. That's what I needed you to say. Once your new hair has arrived let me know and I'll book you to sing three numbers. The fee's two hundred pounds, so you'll make back your wig money and a little extra. Does that sound okay to you?"

"Okay?" Joe replied. "It sounds amazing!"

Joe's thoughts were interrupted by the computer, by the Sky News website, where a live video feed had appeared at the top of the page. Kensington Catburglar Press Conference LIVE was the headline. The video started. Joe put in their headphones to listen. There were a couple of minutes of nothing, of background noise and a shot of a Metropolitan Police press wall. Eventually, a man appeared onscreen behind the bank of microphones: DI Davies.

"Good afternoon, and thank you all for coming. I'd like to make a short statement on developments in the Kensington Catburglar case. Last night officers were called to a suspicious death at Lady's Bar on Old Compton Street, and I can now confirm that the performer known as Lady Lady, Mr. Sean Fulton, was murdered in his dressing room.

"At the time of his death, Mr. Fulton was wearing the evening gown stolen from the Dress Collector boutique by the Kensington Catburglar last month. This is of course an important development in both cases, and we are pursuing every possible line of inquiry to bring the perpetrator to justice.

"Posts on various social media platforms have shown Mr. Fulton wearing the dress in question, so today we will be announcing details of the garment that had previously been held back from the press to protect the integrity of our ongoing investigation."

Joe leaned forward on their elbows, fascinated, desperate to hear more about the bronze-and-gold gown that Lady Lady had died in. DI Davies continued.

"As was reported at the time of the burglary, the dress was taken from the Dress Collector boutique in South Kensington. The dress had been recently purchased at auction by Mrs. Anna Bowman, the owner of the Dress Collector. As far as we are able to establish from the dress's records, the only time it was worn in public before last night was in 1953, when it was worn by performer Judy Garland on the red carpet of a fundraising gala in Los Angeles. Given this provenance, it is a highly valued collectible, insured for £250,000. The dress is being held in evidence and will be forensically examined over the coming days."

A quarter of a million pounds. For a dress!

That was definitely the kind of money someone might kill for, but how would she have got such a thing? Did she know what it was when she wore it?

Joe had a million questions.

"DI Davies," shouted a journalist from behind the camera, "how did Lady Lady obtain the dress? Do you believe that she might have been the Kensington Catburglar?"

"Our investigation into how Mr. Fulton came to be in possession of the dress is still underway."

Joe listened as DI Davies answered a couple of questions about Lady Lady and the murder, avoiding giving any actual detail in his responses. Then a third reporter spoke up.

"Gregory Fletcher, *Kensington Chronicle*. DI Davies, is there anything you'd like to say to the people of Kensington and Chelsea who are so worried by these unsolved crimes?"

DI Davies shifted behind the microphones, and Joe was sure they could see him sweating, even on the tiny video.

"Of course, Gregory. To the people of Kensington and Chelsea, I would say that finding the Kensington Catburglar and returning *all* of the stolen items is our number one priority."

Joe ripped out their headphones and slammed them down on the desk. They felt furious, angry like they hadn't felt in a long, long time.

Number one priority! Returning the stolen items is Davies's number one priority?

What about Lady Lady? Didn't she deserve to be the top priority, over some stolen jewelry? Shouldn't the murder of an actual human being, an icon to her community, be the most important thing Davies had to focus on?

Joe's phone vibrated against the office desk. A WhatsApp from Amour. They opened it.

Did you see the press conference?
JUDY GARLAND?!

I can't believe it, Joe replied.

It's true that Lady Lady was a Judy Garland fan. She could quote all the old movies and regularly performed songs from even her most obscure musicals. But surely she wasn't enough of an obsessive to steal one of her dresses. It seemed impossible.

Have a look on Insta, Amour texted. It's gone crazy.

Joe opened up Instagram and flicked through people's stories. There were lots of memorial posts: people sharing their photos of when they'd met Lady Lady or seen her perform. And then there were a few of the same new posts, all showing a photograph that Joe had seen being taken last night: a photograph of Lady Lady with her arm around Emma Chalmers, the *East-Enders* actress. They were both smiling for the camera, though Joe knew Lady Lady's smile had been forced and unnatural. Joe thought about how they'd sensed something was wrong even then, remembering how Lady Lady had tugged on the dress sleeve like she wanted to get it off. The photograph of Lady Lady and Emma Chalmers was posted side by side with a photograph of Judy Garland on a red carpet in 1953. There was no doubt about it, they were wearing the same dress.

This didn't feel like the Lady Lady Joe knew.

And Joe had known Lady Lady for a long time.

J OE?" ASKED JANE. "Joe? Are you there?"

Joe snapped back into the office with a startled jump. Their heart was racing. "Sorry, Jane. I was miles away."

"Joe," said Jane, with a tone so patronizing Joe could hardly bear it, "I've just been talking to Nick," the hotel manager, "and we can see on the system that you haven't done enough today, despite me coming to talk to you earlier."

I haven't done anything at all, thought Joe.

"I'm sorry, Jane. After last night I'm . . . distracted."

"Well, I hate to say it, Joe, but you're going to have to stay late until you've finished the reports for Nick."

"I . . . erm . . . I can't stay late, Jane. I need to get home."

The thought of staying late in the windowless office was claustrophobic, and Joe felt as though the walls were already beginning to close in. Miles was right, as usual—the office had been a bad idea. Joe should have listened.

"I can't just ignore this, Joe," said Jane. "You can't expect me to pay you to sit here and read the World Wide Web all day. Who's going to do the petty cash?"

Joe glanced at the stack of receipts on the edge of their desk that they were supposed to have processed this morning, and just as a pang of guilt was about to kick in, they remembered Lady Lady's face, twisted and poisoned and dead as a dodo.

Joe stood up, suddenly repulsed by Jane, repelled by the hotel and its windowless offices. There was something else they needed to do, something much more important than staying here to finish reports for Nick. Their insides churned, and they felt sick at the thought of standing up to Jane like this. Normally, at work Joe kept their head down, did what they were told when they were told. There was safety in following the rules, even Jane's rules, in following instruction instead of taking initiative. Misty was the opposite: impulsive, loud, in control. That was the magic of drag, they supposed.

"Do you know what, Jane?" Joe said, channeling their inner Misty. "I probably shouldn't have come in today at all. I'm really not feeling very well. I'm going to have to take this afternoon as a sick day."

Jane flustered, her dry lips wobbling against her yellow teeth. "But the reports . . . for Nick . . ."

"I'm sure Nick can cope without the reports today," said Joe, picking up their jacket from the back of the chair and shrugging it on quickly. They handed Jane the stack of petty cash receipts, and she took them breathlessly. "I'm sure you'll manage."

JOE LEFT THE hotel and stepped out into the warm July day, taking a deep breath of polluted London air. Their brain felt full: full of Jane and Nick, DI Davies and Judy Garland.

They pushed thoughts of Jane and Nick to one side and tried to focus instead on everything they'd learned about Lady Lady, running through DI Davies's statement in their mind. It had been clear from the press conference that he was only interested in finding the Kensington Catburglar and the stolen items, and it felt to Joe as though Lady Lady's murder was an afterthought, a small part of a bigger investigation rather than a case in its own right. It wasn't just. It wasn't fair.

But now, having escaped the confines of the Empire Hotel for the afternoon, Joe remembered washing the dishes before work—the little voice they'd heard telling them that they might find the murderer. And standing outside the hotel with the rest of the day stretched out before them, they knew they had a new plan, one that didn't involve reports or petty cash. They were going to find out who killed Lady Lady.

6

****

FIRST THINGS FIRST, thought Joe as they sat on a bench around the corner from the hotel. *What would they do on* Criminal Minds?

First, the FBI profilers would have flown to Soho on their FBI private jet and visited the scene of the crime. Joe would have to settle with walking to Soho, but thought that if they really were going to try to find the killer, a visit to Lady's Bar might be the best place to start. A visit to the scene of the crime.

They put in their headphones and set out to walk to Old Compton Street. If the bar was no longer a sealed-off crime scene, they could say they had come to collect their drag bag and maybe see if they noticed anything out of the ordinary inside. If the bar was still closed off, perhaps they could talk to the police there, see if they gave anything away. The farther they got from the hotel, the more determined Joe was to find out the truth. DI Davies had clearly only been interested in the Judy Garland dress from the beginning, and his press conference was even further proof that he didn't care a jot about Lady Lady.

They walked through Russell Square, and the little park in the center was busy with tourists and people relaxing in the sun. Overconfident squirrels approached Joe to ask for snacks, but they didn't have any to share today, so the squirrels scattered swiftly at the sight of Joe's empty hands. Joe thought about their desk, about how they had handed Jane the stack of receipts, and felt not a tinge of remorse for taking the afternoon off. *The mental abuse of capitalism*, that's what Miles called it. He'd once said in an argument that Joe had been conditioned by capitalism into believing they needed a regular job to survive, and that's what was holding them back from making Misty their primary career. Joe didn't think that was necessarily the case, and that the comment was a bit rich given Miles's career in marketing for big brands; the hotel was just the backup plan in case the performing didn't work out. *But at what point does the backup plan just become the plan?*

The pavement got busier as they approached Soho, and they turned up their music to block out thoughts of Lady Lady choking to death on her own mouth foam and pressed onward to Old Compton Street. Joe couldn't get the image of DI Davies out of their mind, sweating onscreen, telling the world that finding the Kensington Catburglar's stolen items was his number one priority. Joe's brain somersaulted with rage and they walked even faster.

Old Compton Street was Joe's favorite street in London. It wasn't always the gritty, sexy place Joe had seen in films about London in the sixties but was now a bit more family friendly. In the daytime it wasn't so much a destination for those looking to experience London's sleazier side, but a great place to go to get a coffee and a croissant shaped like a bagel. Over the years the prices had gone up, forcing some of the independents out and allowing the chains to set up shop, but it was still unapologetically queer. Every other building had a pride flag hanging outside, creating a sea of rainbows that warmed Joe's heart. Joe felt they could fully be themself here, no holds barred.

Joe arrived outside Lady's Bar and found that the crime scene tape on the outside of the club had been removed. It looked normal, and people walked by without a second glance. Lady Lady, Queen of Soho, seemed to have passed away unnoticed. The world carried on. Soho kept on turning. If it weren't for a police car parked outside, you'd never even know anything had happened there at all. But though the bustling streets of Soho might have forgotten Lady Lady already, Joe hadn't, and they were going to make sure her killer was brought to justice.

JOE SWUNG THE door open wide and descended the narrow staircase to the auditorium. A police officer was standing at the entrance to the main club space. Joe felt surprised by the police presence—after the press conference Joe had kind of expected them to have moved on already, to be looking for rubies and tiaras instead.

"Can I help you?" she said.

"I'm Misty Divine. I was one of the performers working last night. I wondered if I could collect my bag from the dressing room."

"I'm afraid not, sir. The dressing rooms are still being processed."

The word "sir" rankled them. In this space, they were most definitely Misty, even out of drag, and Misty was not a sir. Joe didn't feel like they were a sir either, not in the binary sense, but that was a more complicated topic, and not one they had brain space for today.

Joe looked around the police officer at the door and saw another one outside the dressing room corridor. The corridor was still taped off, and yet behind the tape, there didn't appear to be anything happening. Joe couldn't see any movement back there. No trench coat detectives, no CSI types, no FBI profilers pacing back and forth quoting deep works of literature to one another—nobody. But Mandy was there arguing with the police officer guarding the corridor. She was a squat figure of a woman, a powerlifter, her thighs thick and muscly, and her arms bulging in her tight black T-shirt. Her hair was chopped into a pointed bob, and she wore thick-rimmed glasses that wouldn't have been out of place on an eccentric film director.

"I need to get into my office," she was saying to the officer. "It's urgent."

The officer shook his head and explained, for what looked like the fifth time, that Mandy was not allowed to go to the club office. The corridor was the crime scene and it was out of bounds.

"Shit. Fuck. Well, who else can I talk to? Let me talk to that guy who was here last night. Davies. I just need to grab something from the office." She sighed in defeat and shrugged her shoulders, walking away from the corridor, muttering, "Shit, shit, shit . . ." She let herself in behind the bar and poured a very large brandy in a very large brandy glass.

Joe walked past the officer at the door and into the auditorium, passing through the cabaret tables until they reached the bar. "Hi, Mandy," they said.

"Can you believe it? They won't even let me in the fucking office." She was stressed and angry. She brushed her fringe back off her forehead. "Sorry, Misty, love. What are you doing here?"

Remember why you're here, Joe told themself. *To find the killer. And maybe you're standing right in front of her.*

"I just stopped by to get my drag bag. I wondered if the dressing room corridor was open yet."

Ask her, willed inner Misty. *Ask her about the argument with Lady Lady.*

But before Joe had plucked up the courage to ask anything, Mandy spoke first.

"Nope, you're not getting anything out of there anytime soon." She finished the brandy in a big gulp and then gasped and belched like she might be about to throw up. She looked at her watch. "Sorry, Misty, love, I have to go." She wrestled a handbag onto her shoulder with what seemed like far too much effort and headed to the door. Joe noticed a shiny layer of perspiration across her forehead as she passed, and she was chewing her bottom lip with such vigor she was surely at risk of biting right through it. Mandy walked straight past the police officer guarding the entrance to the auditorium and made her way up the stairs to the street.

Joe wasn't so caught up in the mystery of Lady Lady and the cat burglar that they couldn't spot what was going on right in front of them—it was blindingly obvious that something was going on with Mandy. Something happening right now. Mandy hadn't even mentioned Lady Lady, and whatever it was she needed from the office, she wanted it urgently. Maybe this had something to do with what she and Lady Lady had been arguing about. About being out of options. About something dangerous.

You'll regret this, mark my words . . .

Before they even had time to think about whether or not it was a good idea, Joe found themself running across the bar and up the stairs, following Mandy out of the club into the streets of Soho. If the police weren't paying attention to Mandy's suspicious behavior, someone had to.

They were five or six people behind her as they walked down Old Compton Street. *Am I really doing this?* Joe thought. *Am I really just following her like an absolute creeper?*

But she's up to something, something's wrong.

Something's wrong with you.

They nearly lost her as she headed up Dean Street and passed through a crowd outside a pub, but Joe caught up with her soon after thanks to the bounce of her bob making her easy to spot. There was a moment Joe panicked that she might have spotted them as she turned to look over the road before crossing. Thankfully Mandy's gaze didn't seem to quite meet Joe's, and she seemed none the wiser that she was being followed.

You are being an absolute creep right now, Joe told themself, hearing Miles's voice of reason in their head.

Mandy stopped at a cash machine and Joe stepped into a shop doorway a few buildings down. They watched as she went through bank card after bank card, taking out piles of cash at a time and stuffing them into a brown envelope.

Okay, I was right. She really is up to something.

Why could she possibly need all that cash?

Once Mandy had expired her wallet of cards, she pushed the brown envelope deep into her handbag and bustled on up toward Tottenham Court Road. She took some twists and turns and ended up on a fairly residential road near Charlotte Street.

Joe hung back far enough so that they weren't obvious. And then Mandy stopped. She stopped right in her tracks at the end of a little alley.

What is she doing?

Behind her, a man emerged from the alley. From the distance they were away, Joe couldn't make out a face, just a wiry body type in a navy tracksuit with a denim baseball cap. Mandy pulled the envelope out of her bag and waved it at the man. He snatched it off her and looked inside before thwacking it against Mandy's head and giving it back to her. Whatever was going on, it was clear Mandy had brought nowhere near enough money. The man leaned in close to Mandy and pointed threateningly in her face. And then she ran off, stowing her cash back in her handbag as she went, the man retreating into the alley.

Joe had a decision to make. Follow Mandy or Baseball Cap.

Or I can give up this folly and go home and watch Netflix.

Miles would tell them to go home right away, to pack in this weird extreme nosiness that had gripped Joe's interest. But it was too late for that, Joe knew. Through whatever curiosity had led them to follow Mandy, they felt part of this now. The police had turned a blind eye to Mandy this afternoon, and here she was, up to something! Something strange and deadly was going on, and Joe was, maybe, about to find out what.

They had to admit, it was a little exciting too. A lot better than being at work in the hotel. A lot better than moping around the house feeling sorry for themself.

Joe decided to leave Mandy and follow Baseball Cap and set off for the alley. As they got to the spot where Mandy's altercation had taken place, Baseball Cap was already at the other end, about to come out on Charlotte Street, and Joe rushed after him. Then Baseball Cap turned left, and Joe had to burst into a sprint to catch up, only for Baseball Cap to step back into view, looking right at them.

"Are you following me?" he said. He had a strange scar on his cheek as though he'd once been stabbed in the face with a fork. Three little scars all in a line. He stepped up close toward Joe, and they could almost feel the heat from Baseball Cap's chest against theirs. He was a couple of inches taller than Joe and glared down into their eyes. His gaze was cold, violent, and maybe sexy in the way a Marvel supervillain might be. He was close enough for Joe to smell his breath: beer and cigarettes.

"No," said Joe, quietly, heart pounding, sweating instantly. "Why would I be . . . ? No, of course not."

"Good," said Baseball Cap. He edged even closer, his face almost touching Joe's. "On you go, then." And he stood with his arms folded, his eyes boring into Joe's nosy soul. Joe couldn't move. They were fixed to the spot.

They wanted to ask something, everything: Who are you? Why is Mandy giving you envelopes of cash in back alleys? Does this have anything to do with the Judy Garland dress, with Lady Lady's murder? But they couldn't ask anything. Baseball Cap was too scary. Joe thought that if they tried to ask anything, they might literally piss their pants. It had been a long time since Joe had felt this intimidated by someone. Thoughts of their stern grandfather and his strict dinnertimes flashed through Joe's mind. Joe wanted to escape.

Look where you've got yourself, worrying about pissing your pants in front of a stranger on Charlotte Street. Go home, Joe.

"Sorry. I, erm . . . I think there's been a misunderstanding. I'll just be on my way."

Joe walked hurriedly past Baseball Cap out of the alley and onto Charlotte Street, rushing through throngs of people to get quickly across to Tottenham Court Road, their heart pounding, their forehead sweating. They didn't dare look back to see if Baseball Cap was still standing there, but they knew that he was. Arms folded, standing in the same spot until Joe was well and truly out of sight.

Fuck. What am I even doing? This could be dangerous. Go home, Joe. Go home and forget all about this.

7

✶✶✶✶✶✶✶✶✶

B Y THE TIME Miles got home Joe was feeling incredibly foolish
for their Miss Marple moment. They shouldn't have done it,
and they'd spent all afternoon regretting it. Firstly, it was creepy
to follow someone. Secondly, it was obviously dangerous. Not
only had Mandy argued with Lady Lady, but she was also clearly
involved in some kind of illegal activity.

Joe told Miles what had happened and was met with an astonished face.

"So, you're telling me you followed a nightclub owner to a
shady deal in an alley and then got threatened in the street?"

"Yeah, pretty much."

"What on earth did you think you were doing? Some Sherlock Holmes nonsense? This is real, Joe. Real and dangerous.
Lady Lady was murdered last night. *Murdered.* And today you're
following Mandy around to cashpoints all over the West End?
You shouldn't be interfering in a police investigation—that's really serious!"

Miles was probably right. Joe should probably leave DI Davies to do his job, but they just didn't trust him, especially after his announcement that Lady Lady wasn't his top priority.

Miles got up to wash the dinner dishes, and there was a knock on the front door.

"Who's that?" asked Miles, jumping at the knock.

"How should I know?" Joe replied.

"Well, I don't know, you're the detective all of a sudden."

Joe tutted and got up from the sofa to open the door.

Standing on the doorstep were the two officers, DI Davies and DS Hughes. *Of course*, Joe remembered, *they said they'd come this evening.* In the wake of everything that had happened with Mandy, Joe had completely forgotten. In the flesh, DI Davies looked even more tired than he had the night before, as though he'd worked nonstop. Joe thought of the press conference, of his "priorities," and they felt that somersaulting brain sensation again as the rage kicked itself to the surface. They looked away from Davies, unable to bear the sight of his unmoisturized face a second longer. DS Hughes looked slightly fresher, and Joe found themself resisting the urge to look for the patch of dry skin on the back of her hand that they'd spotted last night.

"Misty, Joe?" said DS Hughes. "I'm not sure which you prefer."

"Mr. Brown, may we come inside?" said DI Davies.

Mr. Brown. Mister *Brown.*

This guy is an absolute asshole.

"Call me *Joe*, please," they said.

"May we come inside for a few minutes, Joe? We just need to run through your statement again to make sure we've got everything. Would that be okay?"

Miles made a pot of English breakfast tea and placed it on the kitchen table in front of Davies, Hughes, and Joe. He then offered his excuses and headed to the living room, closing the kitchen door behind him.

Joe didn't like having DI Davies here. Not at all. There was an intimidating air to him that Joe didn't want in their home, invading their space. That, and he stank of Lynx Africa, an assault to any homosexual nostril.

DS Hughes started the questioning, and unsurprisingly, most of the questions were about the dress: Could Joe remember having seen it before? Where do queens normally buy vintage or used dresses? Was Lady Lady a big Judy Garland fan? Did she have a penchant for rare or collectible costumes?

Joe felt annoyed and they could feel it in their chest. They were hot and shaky and didn't want any of Miles's tea. Hughes and Davies were clearly more interested in finding out about the dress than they were about the murder. Perhaps they thought the two were intrinsically connected, that the Catburglar and the murderer were one and the same. Or perhaps they were just more interested in finding a rich woman's dress than solving Lady Lady's murder . . . Joe felt uncomfortable with them and uneasy. Something stank, and it wasn't just the Lynx.

Eventually they moved on from the dress, and Joe was relieved they were finally showing some interest in something else: the actual murder of Joe's friend and mentor and not just what she'd been wearing. DS Hughes asked about the other queens and kings who had been there last night. Who liked who? Who had beef with other queens or kings on the scene? Who had ever had an issue with Lady Lady? Late payments, nonpayments, personal disputes, that kind of thing. It felt thorough, Joe supposed. And probably the police were thinking the same way Joe had, that the murderer must have been someone who had access to the dressing rooms. But even though DS Hughes was nice and respectful, the way DI Davies was behaving set Joe on edge. He had sat silently through most of the conversation, staring at Joe. Their gut told them not to trust either of them.

I should tell her about what happened with Mandy, thought Joe. *About the guy with the baseball cap. Maybe it's a lead they could follow.*

But the quiet voice inside kept them from doing it—Joe wanted to find out what was going on first. It felt like something they definitely *would* tell the police. Just not now. They didn't want to risk another run-in with Baseball Cap, and they didn't want to get Mandy in trouble if she hadn't done anything wrong. They should speak to Mandy first, confess about the following, and ask what was going on. Then, if it still seemed suspicious, they could talk to the police once they had some evidence. That seemed like a reasonable thing to do.

Everyone stood up, the questioning over. DI Davies tutted as though the visit had been completely useless, as though Joe was a complete waste of his precious time.

The detectives were about to leave when Davies spoke for the first time. "What were you doing at Lady's Bar earlier today?" he asked. His question was heavy, loaded with accusation.

Joe panicked and felt sick suddenly, even though they knew they hadn't done anything wrong. "Erm . . . I, erm . . . I just stopped by to collect my drag bag from the dressing room."

"Right," said Davies, as though he'd made a decision about Joe that they weren't being let in on. The room shrank and the atmosphere was crisp and awkward.

DS Hughes interrupted. "You can collect your belongings from the bar tomorrow. Everything's been gone through and processed and photographed, so don't expect it all to be exactly as you left it."

Joe nodded and thanked DS Hughes for coming, and she went out through the front door. DI Davies didn't turn back to say goodbye. He just left, heading straight for his car.

"What did they ask you?" said Miles, bursting into the room as soon as the front door closed. "What did they say?"

"Pretty much the same as they asked me last night but with a lot more questions about the bloody dress. Where could it have come from? Had I ever seen it before? That kind of thing."

"You didn't tell them about Mandy, did you?" Joe wasn't sure if it was an accusation or not, but there was certainly a hint of something in Miles's tone.

"No, I didn't. It didn't feel right."

"*Why*, Joe?" Miles was annoyed. "What are you doing? Mandy's giving cash to guys in alleys, and you didn't tell the police? You're annoyed that they're not looking into the murder properly, but you're not giving them all the information."

"I don't trust him," said Joe, "that DI Davies. And if I'd told him about Mandy, I'd have had to explain that I was following her, which makes me look weird."

Miles shook his head. "So, what are you going to do?"

"I don't know."

"Just promise me, no more Sherlock Holmes."

"I promise," said Joe. But they had a feeling it might be a promise they would go on to break.

A FEW SECONDS later, their phone starting ringing. *Amour.* As Joe saw her photo flash up on the screen, a thousand thoughts ran through their mind: *Amour might be the murderer*, being the first one. She had access to the dressing rooms, she was trusted by Mandy and Lady Lady. Trusted by everybody. But not by Joe, not now. Everybody was a suspect, or that's how it felt. If they were going to talk to Amour, they needed to surely ask her if she had been questioned by the police, if she'd had any problems with Lady Lady, if she knew anything about what Mandy was involved in.

Joe didn't know if they had the nerve though. Not to interrogate Amour, one of the drag scene's most beloved performers. Not right now, on the phone . . . Out of drag Amour worked as a banker in the city and had done very well for herself. She was regularly included in lists and articles about South Asian inclusion in the city and was a vocal advocate for trans rights. Joe truly couldn't imagine her being a murderer. But until they could prove who was guilty, they felt as though anybody could be a suspect.

Joe took a deep breath, picked up the call, and pressed the phone to their ear. Joe and Amour talked about their days, sharing how they had each been plagued with images of Lady Lady. Amour had also tried to go to work and had also left the office after lunch, taking the afternoon to think and to begin processing what had happened.

"Did the police question you again?" asked Joe, trying to steer the conversation toward the investigation.

"Yes," said Amour. "They were asking a lot about the dress. Seemed like it was all they were interested in. I just couldn't believe it when I saw the breaking news earlier. *Judy!*"

"She did love Judy," said Joe.

"Well, that's the thing, right?" said Amour with conspiracy in her voice. "Makes me think that she knew it was Judy's when she put it on, that she must have known the Kensington Catburglar."

"I don't know . . ." said Joe, thinking aloud. "It would be a bold move to wear a famous stolen dress in front of hundreds of people like that."

"I guess," said Amour. "Maybe you're right . . . You knew her better than me. Still, the whole thing is weird."

"Did you know anything about the dress?" Joe asked. "Did she mention it to you at the club?"

"No," said Amour, "nothing. Though I was surprised to see her wearing vintage. She's usually a custom gown kinda gal. Or she *was*, I should say."

"And what about this Kensington Catburglar? Have you ever heard anything about that? Anything on the drag scene any-where?"

"Nope," said Amour, "but the police sure are obsessed."

"Did you see the press conference? With that DI Davies? He had the nerve to say that finding the Catburglar's stolen items was the police's top priority. Imagine saying that right when Lady Lady has been murdered. What a scumbag." Joe felt so annoyed just thinking about it again that they almost forgot that Amour was still a potential suspect, not just their good friend.

"You steal off enough rich people and you're going to be the number one priority, that's what I think." Amour sighed. "It was a beautiful dress though."

"So, who do you think might have left the chocolates?" Joe asked. They felt nervous asking this, like it was the first time they'd tried to investigate anything, their first proper interview question. "Did you see anybody go to Lady Lady's room last night?"

"Only you when you went to check if she was okay."

Shit, thought Joe. They hadn't thought about how it must have looked to the others, about what they would have said to the police. But Misty had gone to Lady Lady's dressing room before the chocolates were found, and that's what everybody saw.

"And you didn't see anyone else? Nobody else went up the corridor?"

"Not that I noticed, but I wasn't paying attention. You know how these things are. I had my head in my phone for most of the night." Amour gasped. "Ooh, do you think it might have been Jan?" Jan was the club's barman, a tall hairy bear with a thick Polish accent. "Jan looks like he could be a murderer."

Jan, thought Joe. It's true he did look like a murderer in a cartoony way—his face was all dense black beard and ice blue eyes. Jan's job running the bar meant that he occasionally came up the dressing room corridor to go to the office, so it was possible that he could have done the same last night. Nobody would have paid a blind bit of difference.

But Joe had never seen anything unusual or tricky between Jan and Lady Lady, no signs of disagreements or arguments of any kind. And they definitely didn't see him backstage last night.

"Did you see Jan in the corridor yesterday?" asked Joe, wondering if perhaps they'd been too busy Misty Divining to have seen him.

"No . . . but as I say, I probably wouldn't have noticed," said Amour.

"Do you know if Jan had any trouble with Lady Lady?"

"Nothing I've ever heard about."

Joe paused, thinking for a second about what to ask next.

"Have *you* ever had any fallings-out with Lady Lady?" Joe asked, trying to sound casual but realizing as soon as they'd said it that they didn't sound casual at all.

"Misty . . . what do you mean?"

Joe was suddenly hot, sweaty, the iPhone slick in the palm of their hand. "Erm . . . I was just wondering if . . ."

"Hang on—what's with all the questions? You're not seriously asking if *I* might have murdered Lady Lady? Misty, come on."

Joe laughed but knew it was awkward now. Amour was insulted, offended. "No. No, of course not," said Joe. "I just . . . I'd never heard of her falling out with anyone. I just can't imagine it, you know."

"Well, for the record, no, I didn't *kill* Lady Lady, and no, we never had any falling-out. The thing is, Misty, the police are never going to hear whether or not she had a falling-out with *anyone*."

"What do you mean?"

"Nobody will want to talk to them, not now they've put that rotter DI Davies in charge of the case. He's been asking questions in all the wrong ways. Everyone's been talking about it. He's not going to get a foot through a door if he carries on like that."

Amour was right, Joe knew. If word was already spreading that DI Davies was a man not to be trusted, and if someone as well established and respected as Amour was involved in those conversations, then the police weren't going to get far in the drag circuit.

"They need to put someone else on the case," Amour was saying. "That Hughes woman seems better, but I think they're all cut from the same cloth, to be honest . . . All they're interested in is the dress. The dress. The dress. And why? Because the dress was stolen from a rich straight lady who lives in South Kensington. And the dress is connected to the other stuff that Catburglar's stolen, which belongs to more rich straight people

who live in Chelsea. I bet they won't find Lady Lady's killer because they're not interested in us. They're only interested in *them*.
That's why they can't even get the basics right."

Amour's right, thought Joe. *The police are only interested in the
Catburglar. But what if Lady Lady's killer is someone else? What if
they're looking completely in the wrong direction? That's why* I *have
to find the killer.*

"Amour," said Joe, interrupting her ranting, "what about
Mandy? Do you think there's something going on with her?"

"Mandy? I doubt it. She's mega-professional. One of the best
venue owners in London, if you ask me. Can't imagine she'd
have had anything to do with it at all."

That's exactly what Joe would have said two days ago as well.
But now, having been led by her to Baseball Cap in the alley, Joe
wasn't so sure.

As Joe finished on the phone with Amour, Miles shut his
laptop in the kitchen and returned to the living room, joining
Joe on the sofa.

Miles took a sip of tea. "I take it you're not going to work
tomorrow?"

"Do you know what, Miles? I don't think I am."

All Joe could think about was Mandy White, Jan the barman, and everyone else who had access to the dressing rooms.
And the dress, the stolen dress. And the killer.

*Somebody murdered my friend, and I'm not going back to work
until I find out who.*

8

★★★★★★★★★

FRIDAY

THE NEXT MORNING Joe woke up and immediately sent a message to Jane at the hotel, explaining that they weren't coming in and needed to take two weeks' annual leave. Bam. Just like that. They were well owed some time off. They'd barely taken a day off for the last three years and had accrued massive amounts of holiday. Jane replied quickly: a short but succinct email agreeing that it was a good idea for Joe to take time away. Joe thought about her quivering micromanagy lips as they'd handed her the petty cash receipts. She'd been fuming. But this morning, Joe didn't care about Jane in the slightest.

Two weeks off. It was that easy. Two weeks off to do whatever they wanted—to catch a killer. The whole day stretched out in front of them, and there was so much they could do with it. They had a gig tonight at the Royal Vauxhall Tavern and thought that they would probably still do it and that maybe they could use the opportunity to ask some of the other performers about Mandy, whether anyone else had noticed anything icky at

Lady's Bar. They should also ask the others about the dress, because maybe someone knew something but hadn't wanted to confide in DI Davies. Yes, a plan was forming for tonight's dressing room conversations.

Joe felt stronger today. Emailing Jane had been a victory. And now they were determined to make good use of their day off.

I'll go to Lady's Bar to collect my things, they decided. *And maybe I'll see if I can find anything else out about Mandy while I'm there.*

Joe walked the same route as they had done the day before, feeling ever so slightly more aware of men in baseball caps than they usually would. It wasn't as sunny today as it had been yesterday, and fluffy white clouds floated overhead. This time they had remembered to bring a bag of peanuts to share with the squirrels in Russell Square, and they spent a few minutes standing on the lawn by the fountain feeding the little creatures.

When they arrived at Lady's Bar, the club door was closed. Joe pressed the buzzer and a voice sounded back.

"Yes?" Short, abrupt, Scottish. It was Mandy.

"Hi, Mandy, it's Misty. I've come for my drag bag."

The door clicked loudly and Joe headed inside, down the stairs, and across the auditorium. They thought about how filled with life this space had been just a few days before, about people cheering and clicking their fingers in the air to Lady Lady singing Bette Midler. It felt cold in here. Empty. They walked through the rows of cabaret tables to the dressing room corridor. The crime scene tape was gone now. The door of the club office was open, and Mandy was sitting at her computer behind a desk piled high with papers and empty Tesco meal-deal wrappers. She looked like a cartoon character with her thick glasses and her pointy bob.

Joe wondered whether it was normal for the crime scene to be released so soon after a murder. They didn't know anyone they could ask—maybe something to google later. But normal or not, two days still felt very quick to just let Mandy back in to do whatever she wanted.

"Hey, Misty, love." Mandy sighed. "Sorry about rushing off yesterday. I had an appointment."

Is this it? they thought. *Is this the moment I tell her I followed her?*

"I can't believe she's gone." Mandy looked grief-stricken. She had loose bags under her eyes that said she'd been crying non-stop, and aside from the puffy eyes, she was pale, like she hadn't slept. "We worked together here for almost twenty years, you know. I don't know how I'm going to do it without her."

And that gave Joe an idea. An idea that would have completely horrified Miles but that might lead to finding out what Mandy was up to and who killed Lady Lady.

They could use some of their new time off work to help Mandy at the club. Get close to her. Isn't that what detectives are supposed to do? Get close to the suspects? Certainly there had been episodes of *Criminal Minds* where the detectives went undercover. Yes, getting close to Mandy was surely the best first next step of their detecting.

You're not a detective, Joe, said Miles's voice in Joe's head.

Maybe so. But there was a limited group of people who had access to the dressing rooms, and apart from Misty, Mandy was the only person anybody saw in Lady Lady's room. She and

Lady Lady had argued. *You'll regret this . . .* she had said. She also had whatever was going on with Baseball Cap and the cash. Out of everybody, Mandy was surely suspect numero uno.

Offer to help, thought Joe. *Perhaps you'll find out what's going on here.*

And before Joe knew it, they were making a proposal they hoped Mandy wouldn't refuse. "Well, if there's anything I can help with, let me know. I'm not working this week, so I could come and be of assistance if you need it. Don't mind doing emails, invoices, whatever."

Miles will think I've gone completely mad.

And maybe I have gone completely mad. Mandy might well be a murderer.

But there's only one way to find out. Keep your friends close . . . and your suspects even closer.

"Oh, that's very kind of you," said Mandy. "Maybe I could offer you some cash to do some emails for me if you're serious. I'm swamped with messages about bookings and reopening and questions from the press about Lady Lady. It would be great if you could help me clear the inbox. If you really don't mind."

Her face seemed to tighten and her eyes scrunched, then filled with tears, and her mouth went all stiff and weird. She was about to do an ugly cry. Joe handed her a tissue from a box on the cluttered desk.

"I'm already fucking everything up," she sobbed, her lips gurning uncontrollably. "How am I going to do this without her?"

She whipped the tissue from Joe's fingers and dabbed it to her eyes.

For a moment Joe forgot all about Mandy's shady dealings

and her argument with Lady Lady, and just saw a friend, somebody they'd known and worked with for years. They put their arm around her.

Seeing how upset she was seemed at odds with Joe's suspicion that she might be the killer. Would the murderer really be this upset? A chocolate poisoning wasn't a spur-of-the-moment kind of murder; it was premeditated, planned out in advance. That kind of killer would surely have a cold, collected demeanor, not be sobbing in a corner like a baby who just let go of a balloon.

Joe consoled Mandy for a while longer, but eventually she stopped crying and they both got to work. Mandy set Joe up on a laptop and opened Outlook.

So much for a day off . . . they thought.

They spent a couple of hours silently replying to messages, occasionally checking responses with Mandy to make sure they were written how she wanted. Turns out, Mandy's email style was as blunt as her haircut:

No, they didn't know when the club would reopen.

No, they didn't want to elaborate on their statement about Lady Lady's death.

Yes, Plimberley, you will still get paid.

A T AROUND LUNCHTIME the buzzer for the front door sounded. It was Len and Den, who had come to collect their drag bags. Without their elaborate costumes and makeup, they looked so different: no beards, no sharp perfectly painted contours.

"I hate this," Den announced as Joe greeted them in the auditorium.

"What?" asked Joe. "Being here?" They gestured to the club.

Den sighed, and the heavy-looking ring that hung between his nostrils wobbled from side to side. "All of it."

Len caught Joe's eye and shook his head, as though to say, *Don't ask any more.*

"Leave it, Den," said Len. "It doesn't matter now."

"It does matter," said Den, irritated. "Everyone's going to think I'm the murderer, and I'm not."

Think he's the murderer? What?

"Why would anyone think you're the murderer?"

Den looked like a steaming pipe just waiting to hiss with relief, like he was bursting to let something off his chest. He paused as if he were building up to it and then let it all out.

"The police think I did it," he said hurriedly, "because I had a row with Lady Lady."

"A row?" Lady Lady hadn't mentioned anything about an argument with Den, and Amour hadn't mentioned anything about it either. "What was it about?"

"It was about her bookings, her lineups. I confronted her for not putting enough kings on the lineups. I'd seen a couple of shows with only one king, and it felt like tokenism. So I called her out for it. But it was weeks ago!"

Joe knew nothing about this at all, but they were eager to know more. They supposed Lady Lady had thousands of conversations that she never told them about, and perhaps this one just didn't register as something she should discuss with Misty.

"And they think you killed her because of that?" asked Joe.

"Yeah, seems like it. I have to go to the station tomorrow to do another interview."

Interesting, thought Joe. *If they suspect Den because of an argument with Lady Lady, surely they're looking into Mandy too?*

Unless they know it's Den already but can't prove it.

Joe was desperate to ask more, to find out every detail about this argument with Lady Lady, but Den clenched his fists and clammed up, turning the conversation to gigs, to what everyone had coming up. Len was on the same lineup as Misty at the RVT tonight, so they promised to see each other later and parted ways with tight hugs. Joe told themself that they'd quiz Len this evening, see if he could give them the inside scoop.

Len and Den collected their drag bags from the kings' dressing room and went on their way, so Joe went back to the office and made Mandy a cup of tea. Their mind was abuzz with what they'd learned. *Den* was the police's prime suspect? But what about Mandy? Misty had told DI Davies that she'd heard Mandy and Lady Lady arguing, so surely, if a disagreement was enough to put Den in the firing line, that would be enough for them to suspect Mandy too.

"Have the police asked to question you again?" Joe asked Mandy as they stirred two sugars into Mandy's tea.

"Nope," said Mandy. "They questioned me after you on Wednesday and then came to my flat yesterday morning for more detail, but they don't want to see me again. Not that I've been told anyway."

The police must know something else, thought Joe. *Something that either exonerates Mandy or strongly points to Den.*

And it's true that if the police were considering the killer and the Catburglar to be the same person, Den was a more likely candidate than Mandy. Mandy was always at the club.

Joe thought back to Den encouraging them to start drag for the first time, to their morning chats at shift handover time at the Empire Hotel. That Den, that supportive, loving, funny friend and colleague—surely he couldn't have killed Lady Lady?

But Joe's hackles were up. If Den had really had an argument with Lady Lady, that put him in the same place as Mandy in their mind: top of Joe's suspect list.

9

★★★★★★★★★

IN BETWEEN WRITING emails, Joe's brain was obsessed with thoughts of Lady Lady. Could she have known that the dress had belonged to Judy Garland? What was Mandy up to? Who was the guy in the baseball cap? Could the police *really* believe that Den had murdered Lady Lady over a tiny disagreement? Did they also suspect Mandy? Maybe it was time to tell the police about Baseball Cap, about the envelope full of cash. Perhaps that wasn't the kind of thing Joe should keep a secret. Was Miles right?

Just as Joe was thinking of Miles, they received a text from him.

> Hey, Joe. The Guardian just published
> an obituary for Lady Lady. Thought you
> should know. x

Underneath the message was a link and a preview of the article. Lady Lady's face popped onto the screen, a glamorous shot of her taken at a photo shoot a couple of years earlier. Her purple hair was in bright contrast to a gold backdrop. She was a knock-out. Joe felt a pang of grief rising up in their chest.

They clicked on the link.

CABARET ICON TAKES DRAMATIC FINAL BOW
Obituary: Lady Lady
Written by Jessica Gethyn

As a nation we expect a lot from our drag queens. We expect glamour, comedy, talent, and costumes that whip off to reveal other costumes. We want the drama they bring. Well now, television and cabaret icon Lady Lady has taken the drag queen dramatics to stratospheric levels by dying in the center of her very own murder mystery.

Everybody born before the year 2000 will remember Lady Lady and Auntie Susan from morning television. Their regular double act appearances on breakfast TV made sure the nation started its day in hysterics. But who was the real Lady Lady?

Born Sean Fulton in 1965, Lady Lady was raised and, later, publicly disowned by her mother, Jeanette. In an article published in the *Sun* in 2001 she stated, "No son of mine will go around dressing like a tart."

Lady Lady quickly responded by selling T-shirts with the word "tart" on the front from a stall in Covent Garden Market.

In 2005, after an acrimonious split with TV partner Auntie Susan, Lady Lady opened Lady's Bar, a luxurious cabaret venue in the heart of Soho. Giving up television work in favor of living the cabaret high life, Lady Lady hosted drag, comedy, and burlesque performers from all over the world. Many of our most beloved comedians performed alongside her and found it difficult to keep up with her fast wit and razor-sharp reflexes.

She famously came out of television retirement to host the *Royal Variety Performance* in 2010, where she sang a duet with Jason Donovan and received a standing ovation.

This week Lady Lady took to the stage for the last time.

On Wednesday night she performed "the best show of her life," according to *EastEnders* actress Emma Chalmers, who was in the audience. But it was a photo with Chalmers that has gone viral this week when it was discovered that Lady Lady was wearing a dress last worn by Judy Garland in 1953, which just happened to have been stolen by a London thief known as the Kensington Catburglar. After the show, and the now infamous photo in the dress, Lady Lady is said to have retreated to her dressing room, where she was murdered. Details surrounding the cause of death are yet to be released, but at the time of writing there have been no arrests made.

A mystery worthy of an episode of *Midsomer Murders*.

Detective Inspector Davies of the Metropolitan Police said, "We are closing in on the Kensington Catburglar and look forward to questioning them about the sad death of Lady Lady as soon as we can."

Sad death? thought Joe. *Sad death!*

It was more than a sad death—it was a murder! The murder of someone beloved and central to the London queer nightlife scene. Joe wanted to grab DI Davies by the shoulders and shake him until he rattled.

"What do you make of this Kensington Catburglar business?" Joe asked Mandy across the little office, wondering whether she might be able to shed some light on the situation.

"I have no idea," said Mandy. "I'd barely been paying attention to the news recently, so I didn't know much about it until the police started asking. And I don't know where Lady Lady got that dress."

"Strange, isn't it?" Joe muttered.

"Very strange," Mandy replied, taking a revolting-sounding slurp of tea. "But she did love Judy."

If the police were so certain that the Kensington Catburglar was the murderer, maybe that's who Joe should be looking for. Maybe someone who was in the dressing rooms that night *was* the Catburglar.

Don't be ridiculous. Give this up, Joe. It's complicated and dangerous and it's almost definitely illegal to be keeping secrets from the police. How would you *catch a cat burglar anyway, you plonker?*

Joe turned back to the computer. Alongside the obituary there were screengrabs of condolence tweets from Denise Van Outen and Liza Tarbuck.

"Of course they had to talk about Auntie Susan. She'll be loving this." Mandy had appeared behind Joe and was reading the obituary over their shoulder. Her Scottish accent was so thick, it was almost a growl.

"Auntie Susan will? You know," said Joe, "Lady Lady never told me what happened between those two. Always said she didn't like to discuss it. Do you know why they fell out?"

"I do. It was a whole lot of fuss. A dispute between friends that never got resolved. They stopped working together and haven't spoken since." Mandy tucked the pointed end of her bob behind her ear.

"But that was twenty years ago. Surely they could have put it behind them by now?"

Mandy shrugged. "Not my place, not my fight. That's what I

always said. What those two wanted to do with their own resentment was up to them."

She shuffled on the spot and fiddled with the pen she was holding.

Joe couldn't quite put their finger on how, but they knew Mandy was lying.

What is going on here? they thought. *Lies about Auntie Susan on top of everything else . . .*

"You don't think, Mandy, that Auntie Susan could have had anything to do with what happened to Lady Lady?"

"Ha!" scoffed Mandy. "She's a scoundrel but she's ancient history. Forget all about it, Misty, love."

L ATER THAT AFTERNOON, Joe excused themself from the office, saying goodbye to Mandy, and went to the dressing room to collect their things to take home to get ready for this evening's show. In spite of everything that was going on, they were excited for the gig tonight. They didn't often perform at the Royal Vauxhall Tavern, but it was a special venue indeed, and they'd never have got a first foot in the door there without Lady Lady's mentoring. Missing tonight's show would have felt like Joe was besmirching her memory. With one of the richest and best-documented histories of drag in the capital, it was a place in which Misty/Joe felt connected to their queer ancestors, to the drags who came before. They had passed many an hour watching YouTube videos of the RVT in the sixties and pondering how even more radical it was to be a drag performer then and what that must have been like. Every time Misty stepped onto that stage she felt as though she were following in the footsteps of legends.

They decided to get into drag early. Sometimes, it was nice to do the makeup process leisurely, over a couple of hours, with plenty of breaks. *That's what I need today*, thought Joe. *To take it easy. Easy, breezy, beautiful, CoverGirl.*

Getting into drag was a long and, frankly, irritating process of many small steps, and many techniques and tools that need to be learned. From knowing which brush to use to identifying the right products for your skin type, it was something that had taken Joe a long time to get comfortable with. The first time they'd got into drag they'd been a hot mess. A pig in a wig with wooden teeth. Photographs of the occasion reveal patchy Primark foundation and thin red lips that should never have been allowed out of the house. They hadn't cared at the time. There was a feeling of empowerment about drag that overrode any anxieties they might have had about their beginner makeup skills, and they'd gone out that night feeling absolutely banging.

That top lip's too thin, Lady Lady had told Misty later. And it had never been that thin since.

Once home, Joe shaved their face in the bathroom and thought about the mystery that was unfolding in front of them. They thought of Matthew Gray Gubler, the star of *Criminal Minds*, how his character would have solved it by now with his super memory. Joe tried to recall the details one at a time, a knockoff Gubler impersonator in their own mind. Somebody put the chocolates in Lady Lady's dressing room, and only a limited number of people had access to the corridor. Mandy was up to something. Maybe in debt? Maybe being blackmailed over something? Who knew? She'd also clearly been holding something back about Auntie Susan. *Could Auntie Susan be a suspect?* wondered Joe. Could she have hated Lady Lady enough to have arranged for someone there that night to plant the chocolates?

Or had something new happened to reignite their feud? The police thought Den was the killer, but Joe just didn't think that could be right. They'd known Den for years. Surely they'd have had an inkling that there was something seriously wrong if he was the murderer.

Tonight they would see Len and Moneypenny again, as they were both on the RVT lineup alongside Misty. Joe knew the dressing room would provide the perfect opportunity to ask them some questions. Perhaps they knew something about Mandy or the Catburglar. And hopefully Len would share a bit more about Den's row with Lady Lady.

Once shaved, Joe moved to the dressing table in the bedroom and laid out their makeup and brushes. They always started with the eyebrows—the fiddliest part in their opinion and the easiest part to get wrong. But, oh, how Joe loved to see a wonky eyebrow. The curse of the wonky eyebrow could strike even the most talented of drag makeup artists, without warning and without mercy.

Joe took out a glue stick—the kind used by primary school children to make dreadful collages—and started applying the glue to the hairs of their eyebrows. They used a thin metal comb to brush the hairs flat and then applied more glue, layer after layer, until the eyebrows were fully flattened. While they waited for the glue to dry Joe thought more about Mandy. Was it really a good idea to be working for her, knowing she might be a murderer? Wouldn't it be the sensible thing now to tell the police that they saw Mandy's weird deal gone wrong with Baseball Cap? Probably. And that's almost certainly what Miles must be thinking. But while Mandy's behavior was certainly suspicious, Joe had known her and worked with her for years. She had been Lady Lady's business partner for two decades. Joe certainly didn't want to get her into any trouble if she didn't have anything to do with the murder.

No, the best thing to do is to find out for myself what she's involved in, and then make a decision from there.

Once the eyebrows were dry Joe covered the rest of their face in a generous serving of a creamy primer that smelled like marshmallows. This was probably their favorite part of the process, besides the final moment of transformation, using their fingers to massage the sweet-smelling cream into their freshly shaven skin. They found it soothing. And after primer came foundation and powder, and then the fiddly work on lips began.

Joe was halfway through the makeup when Miles arrived home from work. Joe made them both a gin and tonic in the kitchen, a preshow tipple to calm the butterflies.

"So," said Miles, taking off his jacket, "how was your day off? What did you get up to?"

"Actually, it didn't end up being much of a day off."

"What do you mean?"

Joe explained to Miles what had happened—going to collect their bag, offering to help Mandy, staying all day to answer Lady's Bar emails.

"You mean to tell me you've swapped one windowless office for another on your first day off in months?"

"It felt like the right thing to do," said Joe. "I think Mandy really needed the help."

"Mandy's trouble, Joe. Whatever it is she's involved in, carrying round envelopes of cash, it's not something you want to touch."

Joe felt annoyed, defensive. "Well, I'm not touching anything. I'm just doing emails. Something was going on at the club, Miles. Lady Lady and Mandy were involved in something, and maybe I can help Mandy out with emails and find out more at the same time."

"So, you're helping Mandy in order to spy on her!" Miles shook his head.

"Yes and no. I'm helping her because she really needs help, and if I find out what's been going on, then it might satisfy my curiosity while I'm there."

"You're spying," said Miles, taking a sip of gin.

"Okay," said Joe, smiling. "I'm maybe spying a little bit."

"Just be careful, Joe." His voice was soft, caring, protective. But Joe knew it was also hiding some judgment: that Joe shouldn't be keeping secrets from the police, that they shouldn't be investigating Lady Lady's murder on their own.

"I'll be careful," said Joe.

They returned to the makeup and used a brown eye shadow with a wet brush to paint over the high, sweeping eyebrows that reached deep into their temples, making them as symmetrical as they could and fading them from white in the center to dark brown on the arches.

As Joe concentrated on makeup, Miles sat on the end of the bed and talked about his day, telling Joe the ins and outs of a pitch for a new client that he'd been working on. He was very good at his job, by all accounts, and had been promoted a few times over the last three years. Joe liked listening to him talk about work—he was so into it, so passionate about it. It was always a joy to hear him. By the time he'd finished his very thorough debrief of his day in the office, Joe had finished their makeup. They went to the wardrobe and stepped into a pair of hip pads and a padded bra and then asked Miles to tie them into a corset. Miles was good at this, having had much practice since Joe had started drag.

Joe already knew what Misty was wearing tonight: a royal blue sequin minidress and a canary yellow high ponytail. Miles zipped Joe into the dress, and they lifted a polystyrene head from the shelf. The yellow hair was glorious. Joe returned to the mirror and placed the wig atop their head, using spirit gum to glue the edges of the lace down, making the wig blend into their makeup.

Joe disappeared. Misty had arrived.

10

★★★★★★★★★

MISTY WALKED THROUGH the RVT doors and felt so confident she could have burst. She headed straight upstairs to the dressing rooms. She was ready to perform and to get some answers.

The acts for tonight's show were in the biggest room, all together, in a large dressing space that made Soho's dressing rooms look like shoeboxes. Misty noticed Len and Moneypenny across the room and was suddenly in sharp investigator mode. She couldn't help but think that the last time they were all in a dressing room together, someone was murdered. She was unable to tear her eyes away from them, watching them talking, looking for any sign one of them might be a killer. *Time to ask you some questions*, she thought.

"Misty!" shouted The Australian, a nonbinary drag artist who was currently dressed as a robot in a homemade gold-and-silver cardboard outfit that was seriously impressive. The Australian thrust themself toward Misty and threw their arms around her in a light hug. "How are you? We all heard about you finding Lady Lady. Are you okay?" The twist to The Australian's drag name was that they were not actually Australian and spoke with a heavy Liverpudlian accent.

Everyone in the room was looking at her.

"I'm okay, thanks," said Misty. "It's been a bit of a shock." *Understatement*, she thought, *of the year*.

Len the drag king, wearing an amazing blue beard, spoke up next. "A bit of a shock? It was awful." Misty looked at him. His costume was fabulous, a sky blue suit that was covered in silver embroideries. Len couldn't be the murderer, right? By day Len was a charity events fundraiser, managing teams of people running the London Marathon to raise money for poorly donkeys or something.

"We're going to do a minute's silence for her tonight, love, and a charity collection in her memory," said The Australian, interrupting Misty's thoughts of lame donkeys hobbling across the marathon finish line.

"That's nice," said Misty. "She'd have liked that."

"I just can't believe she's gone. And *murdered*. Totally crazy."

The Australian was animated, excited, desperate to talk about it. An insatiable gossip.

"I think we should talk about something else," said Misty in an attempt to shut down The Australian. She didn't want to talk about Lady Lady like this, like she was a scandal to be whispered about backstage. What she wanted was to ask Len and Moneypenny about her suspects.

"Yeah, of course, sorry," said The Australian. "But who do you think did it? You know, who poisoned the chocolate?"

"How do you know it was a poisoned chocolate?" asked Misty, remembering how the news article from earlier said the details hadn't been released.

"Everybody knows," chirped Moneypenny. "It's the worst-kept secret on the drag scene."

"The police think it was Den," said Len.

"I was so shocked to hear that," said Misty, snatching the opportunity to dig a little deeper. "I hadn't heard anything about this row between him and Lady Lady."

She moved away from The Australian and sat down next to Len in front of a messy makeup station.

"Oh, it was something and nothing," said Len, touching up the crisp contour lines on his cheeks and chin. "Den was annoyed that Lady Lady had been booking more queens than kings and thought she should be setting a better example. So he called her out on it, and rightly so I say."

Now Misty was intrigued, and it seemed Len was opening up. "What did Lady Lady say?" she asked.

"She agreed that she needed to book more kings, but she said she didn't like Den's attitude, the tone of his messages. She said he was arrogant, that she'd been booking lineups for twenty years. But all of this was months ago, it's crazy that the police think it could have anything to do with the murder."

"How did the police find out? About the argument that is? Did you tell them? Or Den?"

"Wasn't me or Den, that's for sure. Not sure who told them, but someone must have."

"So, who else knew about it?" asked Misty.

"No idea," replied Len. "Maybe Den told people, but I didn't."

Len looked frustrated and Misty knew she had asked too many questions, but she was a dog with a bone.

"How come Den isn't here tonight?" asked Misty. "Don't you always perform together?"

"Not always," said Len. "With everything that's going on, Den wanted to take a break for a few days. Get out of the drag scene for a little bit."

"That's understandable," Misty supposed.

"There's no way Den's the killer," said Moneypenny, looking up from her mirror. "That's ridiculous."

"Well, who do you think it was?" Misty asked Moneypenny.

"I don't know"—she put down the brush she had been using to paint deep old-lady wrinkles onto her cheeks and around her mouth—"but Lady Lady must have been involved in something dodgy to have ended up with that Judy Garland dress. Maybe she knew someone shady and got on the wrong side of them somehow."

Moneypenny was right. How well did Misty really know Lady Lady? Clearly not as well as she'd thought. From arguments with Mandy to fallings-out with Den, Lady Lady obviously had a life that Misty had only seen part of. She'd been private, holding things back for all this time. Thinking of this caused an uncomfortable shift in Misty's brain, like a loose Jenga block breaking free. For years she thought she'd known Lady Lady, and now it seemed her mentor, her idol, could have been keeping enormous secrets from her. Misty hated the thought of it. Having always been completely honest with Lady Lady, discovering that honesty hadn't been reciprocated was like betrayal.

The Australian gasped dramatically. "Maybe it was Auntie Susan! Now that would be a twist, can you imagine?"

"Auntie Susan, pfft," tsked Moneypenny. "She's a scammer, but I don't think she's a murderer."

"A scammer?" asked Misty.

"You know, the gigs she offers at The Plough," said Len.

"That *is* bad," said The Australian.

"I feel like I'm completely out of the loop here. What's going on at The Plough?" asked Misty.

The Plough was Auntie Susan's East London pub. And in stark contrast to the mostly gorgeous East London queer nightlife scene, The Plough had a reputation for being rough and ready. It was the kind of place where your shoes stuck to the floor and the performers took to the stage with their life in their hands. And Auntie Susan herself had the most fearsome reputation of them all. She was an infamous tough cookie, one not to be messed with.

"She's been booking new drags for 'open mic slots' and not paying them," said Len. "It's exploitation."

Moneypenny leaned forward. "And do you know what the hosting fee is over there? Twenty quid. That's what she offered me to host a whole show."

Misty was shocked. Of course there were venues all over the place paying drag artists a pittance, and many of them felt obliged to take the low-paying gigs to build a name for themselves. New drag artists were easy pickings for greedy promoters, but someone as established as Auntie Susan should know better.

"Right," said The Australian, "we're nearly at curtain up. Let's run through the running order."

Misty was frustrated; she wished she had had more time to talk with the others, to ask about Mandy, but the show must go on. She tried to shake herself into show mode.

The Australian pulled a sheet of paper from a folder on their dressing table and read through it out loud, telling each and every performer the precise time they were onstage and for how long. Misty was opening, which she was glad about. Lady Lady had once told her it was best to perform first on a big lineup, to set the bar for everyone else instead of following in their wake. Misty liked it that way too, because it meant she could do her bit and then sit back and enjoy the show.

As they all descended the narrow staircase from the RVT dressing rooms to the main space, clomping down them in big heels, Misty wondered more about Auntie Susan. Surely, after so many years, the feud couldn't still be strong enough to end up in murder. Perhaps Lady Lady got wind of the dreadful exploitation situation at The Plough and had a word with her. That wouldn't have surprised Misty. If anybody knew anything about what had gone on between Auntie Susan and Lady Lady, it would be Mandy. She'd been Lady Lady's business partner for over twenty years. But Mandy had been holding back, lying about what she knew about Auntie Susan. Misty made a note that the next time she saw Mandy, she was going to push for the truth.

The Australian performed a number to kick-start the show. A robot interpretation of Kim Petras mixed with clips of *Come Dine with Me*. It didn't make any sense at all that Misty could grasp, but it was very funny. After the sexy robot, The Australian introduced Misty. Sometimes, as Joe, they thought that their drag wasn't as creative or fun as other people's. Jealous, perhaps, not to have the crafting skills and imagination of performers like The Australian, but she knew that what she could do, she did better than anybody else.

Misty stepped onto the stage, took hold of the microphone waiting for her, and began to sing.

A FTER HER PERFORMANCE Misty joined Miles in the audience and sat to watch the other acts. Miles whispered to Misty, "Well done, you were fabulous."

"Thank you," she replied.

"Have you seen who's behind the bar?" said Miles quietly.

Misty turned to look, straining her neck to see beyond the crowds waiting for a drink. Then she saw him, Jan, the Lady's Bar barman with the beard and scary eyes.

"What's he doing here?" Misty whispered back.

"He must have picked up some shifts here while Lady's is closed," said Miles.

Seeing Jan busy at work in the RVT reminded Misty of what Amour had said about him. He *did* look like a murderer, it was true. Well, a caricature of a murderer in any case. He was tall, maybe six five, and his beard was long, stretching down from his chin to between his nipples, which were very much visible through his black T-shirt. His eyes were piercing, and even from the other side of the room Misty could see how blue they were.

I need to talk to him, she thought. *I need to ask him about that night. Thank God I'm here as Misty.*

She didn't think she'd have the courage to speak to Jan as Joe. He was scary, with his big beard and nipples. But Jan would talk to Misty—they'd known each other for a long time, though not closely. And as Misty, she could do anything. She knew that while the show was on he'd be too busy to talk but that if she stayed, the bar would quiet down very quickly once the show ended. That would be her moment to pounce.

Miles and Misty watched the rest of the cabaret, and it turned out that it was the welcome distraction she didn't know she needed. Misty laughed hysterically at Len's drag king act. He performed a stand-up set that was sidesplittingly hilarious and then sang a parody lyric version of "Tale as Old as Time" from *Beauty and the Beast*, the words changed to "Male as Bold as Rhyme"—a series of rhyming couplets about cishet mans-plaining.

Misty loved drag kings.

After Len was Moneypenny, her act not unlike Catherine Tate's Nan character. She performed a twerking, thrusting dance to "Wet Ass Pussy," and the juxtaposition of her long pleated skirt with her explicitly sexual dance moves was a delight.

Lady Lady would have loved this, thought Misty. And there she found herself, in a room full of strangers' laughter, with tears running down her cheeks. How she longed to talk to her one more time. She laughed through her tears as Moneypenny humped a microphone stand with wild abandon.

After Moneypenny's act, The Australian returned to the stage. They had a grave look on their cardboard-covered face. They took to the microphone.

"We're going to take a short pause in tonight's show to talk about something serious," they said. The audience went quiet. You could have heard a pin drop. "This week, the UK drag scene suffered one of its greatest losses—the death of Lady Lady. I'm sure you've all seen in the news, Lady Lady was murdered in her dressing room at Lady's Bar on Wednesday night. Many of us worked with her and knew and respected her, and we want to honor her tonight with a moment of silence. If you'll please join me in a moment of quiet reflection."

The whole room fell still. People put down their drinks. Heads bowed. And there was silence. Misty closed her eyes and tried to think of Lady Lady, of the happy times they'd had to-gether, but her mind wandered, thinking only of the people who were in the dressing rooms that night: her friends, Mandy, Tess, Jan. And one of them a murderer.

Once the long minute of group reflection was over, The Australian announced that they would be collecting money in Lady Lady's memory for Terrence Higgins Trust, the HIV charity that Lady Lady had long supported. Charity buckets were passed from table to table and people looked to be very generous. Misty saw paper money going into the collection tubs: ten- and twenty-pound notes. Lady Lady meant a lot to a lot of people. Her legacy stretched broadly, and Misty really saw that as she watched somber-looking patrons pulling out their wallets without hesitation. Witnessing this outpouring of love and respect for Lady Lady made Misty put aside thoughts of her secrets and instead ignited a burning desire to find the truth, to find justice for Lady Lady.

After the show most of the audience left pretty quickly, so Misty headed straight for the bar to talk to Jan the barman.

There were only three or four people waiting for drinks, and Misty saw a gap just in front of the beer pumps. She hustled through the crowd and placed the empties down. Jan came straight over, his chest like a barrel.

"Great show tonight, Misty," he said.

"Thanks, Jan!" She smiled. "How've you been? Since Wednesday and everything . . ."

Jan leaned on the bar and looked Misty in the eye. "It was very, very sad for me, you know. Lady Lady meant a lot to me." His voice was soft and genuine.

"Don't suppose you saw anyone? In the corridor that night?" she asked.

"I didn't go down to the dressing rooms on Wednesday," he said. "I was at the bar the whole time."

"You didn't go to the office at all on Wednesday?"

"Nope. We were rammed at the bar. I said the same to that policeman, they can check the CCTV. I was serving all night."

So Amour's suspicion was wrong—Jan was not the murderer. Misty knew that the police would have indeed checked the CCTV, and so could she. And besides, she had an instinct, a gut feeling that said Jan was telling the truth.

"And you didn't serve anyone who seemed suspicious at the bar?"

"No, it's just like I told the police. Seemed like a totally normal night to me, until the end, all that screaming from the dressing rooms as we were clearing up."

"What about Den?" Misty asked. "Have you ever seen any trouble with Den at the Club? Any signs of a falling-out with Lady Lady?"

"No, nothing," said Jan.

"And Mandy? Have you noticed anything strange going on with her?"

"No. But what is this, Misty? You sound like that policeman who came to see me." He laughed, but she could tell Jan was starting to get a little annoyed with her. His mouth had tensed up in the corners. Misty knew she wouldn't be able to ask much more without pissing him off.

"Sorry, I don't mean to. I'm just trying to get my head around what happened."

"I understand."

One more question, she thought. *It's worth pushing one more time.* "In all your time working at Lady's Bar, have you ever suspected that anything . . . criminal . . . might be going on?"

Jan sighed and then leaned forward. He looked conspiratorial, like he was ready to divulge a secret. Misty felt a flutter of excitement. "Not criminal, but there was one weird thing recently," he said. "A couple of weeks ago, when Tess the bouncer was off work—she wasn't off sick, she'd been *suspended*. I didn't hear what it was about, but she was very upset."

Tess? Tess was a middle-aged mother hen who fussed over all the performers and took great care of the bar. She'd been the head of security at Lady's Bar for a long time, Misty knew, though she didn't know how long. At least ten years. What could have prompted Tess to be suspended? Tess and Lady Lady were like sisters.

"Did you tell the police? And you didn't see her fall out with anybody else?" Misty asked Jan. "None of the bar staff? Mandy?"

"No, and I didn't tell the police about Tess. Didn't want them to think she was the killer if she wasn't. She was very upset. Besides, it looked like a one-off. They'd been friendly since. Tess was back to work, and that policeman is an asshole," he replied. "Listen, I'd better get back to work. Can I get you a drink?"

Misty ordered drinks for her and Miles and headed back to the table.

"You looked like you were interrogating the poor man," said Miles.

"Well, I was, kind of."

Miles lifted his glass up in the air as though to start a toast. "To Detective Misty Divine!"

"Oh, stop it! You're drunk."

"You don't really think you're going to find out anything that the police can't. Do you?"

Maybe I already have.

Tess was suspended.

A falling-out with Den.

An argument with Mandy.

Mandy's mysterious money dealings.

"Maybe I already know quite a lot," she said.

And she was going to find out more.

11

★★★★★★★★★

S O, WHO DO you think it was?" asked Miles as they walked across Russell Square toward home. "What are your detective instincts telling you?"

"I don't know," said Misty, wondering whether a few Friday night drinks had helped Miles warm to the idea of her investigating this behind the police's back. "Everything's pointing at Mandy so far. I still think she's my top suspect. But then there's Den and now Tess. And possibly even Auntie Susan."

"Auntie Susan? Really?"

"I have to consider it. She and Lady Lady had a very serious falling-out, and according to Mandy they never made up. Perhaps she still had a motive all these years later."

"Well," said Miles, "the newspapers would love it, but I just don't see it. And it can't be Den. We've known him for years. We'd surely know if he was a murderer."

"I don't know," said Misty. "Seems people are good at keeping secrets. Lady Lady certainly was."

Maybe I didn't know her at all.

They walked past a big white round building tucked behind the Brunswick Shopping Center. Miles's office. It was out of place in Bloomsbury, Misty thought, this giant egg of a building, but the insides were fancy. Miles had a swanky job title to match his standing desk: accounts director. Which basically meant he kept his own schedule and spent a lot of time running around London meeting his clients, who were some of the UK's biggest household brands: detergent companies, food brands, soft drinks. There was no limit to his selling skills.

"Thank God it's the weekend," said Miles, looking at the office doors.

"Thank God we're nearly home, my feet are killing."

MILES AND MISTY'S flat was only a five-minute walk from his egg-shaped office, and as they walked Miles talked a little bit about his work, his voice only slightly slurring from the gin.

"Chris thinks I'll be promoted again by the end of the year," he was saying as they climbed the outdoor staircase to their first-floor flat. "He says the work I did on the Douglas account was my best yet."

"Miles, that's amazing!"

"Probably a pay rise too, maybe even my own office. It'd be big." Miles was excited, Misty could tell. While Joe couldn't give a flying fig about promotions and offices (there were no offices to be had at the Empire Hotel), Miles's career meant a great deal to him. He worked hard and Misty knew he deserved this.

Misty was about to ask more when Miles stopped in his tracks. "Shit."

"What?" said Misty.

"The door."

Misty looked up and saw what Miles had already seen. The front door to their flat was wide open.

MISTY'S HEART POUNDED and she felt panicked instantly. A burglary? Had someone broken in? Her computer. Her jewelry. "Shit."

They raced forward to the door and stopped outside. The lights in the little apartment were all off. The place was in darkness.

"What do we do?" asked Miles.

"We go in, see if anything's been taken."

"We can't go in! What if there's somebody in there? We should call the police," Miles protested.

But Misty was already on the move. She took off her stilettos and raised one above her head, heel first, ready to defend herself if necessary. She stepped into the dark hallway, Miles close behind. "Hello?" she called, switching on the lights. "Is anybody here?"

Silence.

She entered the living room and looked around. Her laptop was sitting on the coffee table, along with her Apple Watch. Not a burglary, she guessed. She rushed across the living room to the bedroom and flung open the door, shoe still raised ready for defense, but there was no one in the bedroom or the little bathroom.

"There's nobody here," she said to Miles.

"Computers are all still here," said Miles. "Let me check the kitchen. My work bag."

Miles hurried past her to the kitchen, and Misty opened the

passport drawer to check they were still there. They were. Then she checked her jewelry, her photo albums. Everything valuable or sentimental to her was where she'd left it.

"Weird," said Misty.

"What do you mean?" asked Miles, emerging from the kitchen.

"It's just weird, isn't it? The door being open but nothing missing."

"I guess we just didn't close it properly or forgot. We left in a rush to get to the RVT."

But Misty wasn't so sure. Thoughts of Baseball Cap rushed to the front of her mind and then the Kensington Catburglar. Was this a warning? A warning from the killer to stop looking into the murder, to stop asking questions and following people?

"What if it's something to do with . . . you know," she said.

"Now you're being paranoid," said Miles. "Nothing's been taken, everything's just as we left it."

"Hmm . . ." said Misty, unconvinced.

Miles took Misty's hands in his and squeezed her fingers gently. "You've had a shit week, and you've got a lot going on, but I think we just didn't shut the door properly on the way out. I don't remember locking it, do you?"

Misty thought back to leaving the flat. She didn't remember locking it either. "No," she said, "I don't."

"See?" said Miles. "If anything, we're lucky we *weren't* burgled, leaving the front door wide open in Central London."

"Lucky . . . ?"

"You know what I mean."

"Yeah, sorry, it's been a shit week, you're right."

"Hungry?" he asked, smiling.

"Always," said Misty.

THEY DIDN'T TALK much while they ate. Misty was tired, ready to take off the drag and have a shower. And she was preoccupied, thinking about the Kensington Catburglar and the open door.

Once she'd de-dragged and become Joe again they took a long shower, scrubbing their face and neck to remove every last trace of foundation. They put on some light pajamas that Miles's mum had bought them for Christmas. They were pastel yellow with a bold blue trim, and though Joe thought they looked a little like an IKEA staff uniform they were exceptionally comfortable.

Pajamas on, Joe slid into bed and unlocked their phone. They decided not to look at social media before bed, but their mind was whirring and they wanted to know more. They wanted to know everything there was to know about the Kensington Catburglar. If the police were paying so much attention to them, then maybe Joe should be too.

Like all the best detectives, they started with a Google search.

It was a huge case, and there were hundreds of articles, the most recent ones being about Lady Lady and the Judy Garland dress. Joe scrolled until they found an article called The Kensington Catburglar: What We Know So Far. It was from an internet crime blog that Joe had never heard of: CrimeTime. It appeared to be a site for internet sleuths trying to solve real-life cases, no doubt inspired by the thousands of true crime podcasts and documentaries that seemed to be everywhere. Joe read eagerly.

According to the article, the Kensington Catburglar had committed twelve burglaries to date.

Thirteen if you count my flat, thought Joe.

Each of the burglaries had taken place in Chelsea or Kensington and had targeted one specific item at a time: a diamond Montblanc pen, the Sunbeam Tiara, a rare ruby called the Red Egg.

The victims were all exceptionally wealthy business owners, and as a result the case had received a lot of press coverage and police resources. The Kensington Catburglar had even been discussed by MPs in Parliament.

The cases were connected by a calling card. A literal calling card: a plain white business card left in the place of the missing item. The CrimeTime article cited an unnamed officer in the Metropolitan Police: "The twelve Kensington Catburglar calling cards have undergone the most thorough forensic examinations I've ever heard of in my time on the force. It's a complete waste of money if you ask me."

Joe understood now why the police had been so obsessed with the dress. The pressure to solve the case and catch the Catburglar was high. But it made Joe unhappy to read, to think that Lady Lady's murder investigation had been subsumed into an investigation into a stolen pen rather than being investigated in its own right. The fact that DI Davies was responsible for both cases spoke volumes about how the police were prioritizing. *Trash*, thought Joe.

Joe wondered about the calling cards and racked their brain thinking about Lady Lady's dressing room. There definitely hadn't been a card on her body or on the chocolates. Lady Lady herself had said there was no note. Did that mean it *wasn't* the Catburglar? The whole thing felt complicated, like there were too many questions Joe couldn't yet answer.

AND COULD THE Kensington Catburglar have really broken into their apartment?

If it was the Kensington Catburglar, why didn't they take anything? Or leave a card?

No, thought Joe, it didn't fit the Kensington Catburglar pattern. Bloomsbury was way out of their operating area, for starters. And Miles and Joe had nothing mega-valuable to be stolen.

If it wasn't the Kensington Catburglar, could it have been the guy who Mandy met? Or someone connected to him? Was the open door a warning that Joe should stop poking around?

Whatever it was, it cemented Joe's urge to find out more about the Kensington Catburglar, about the dress, and where it might have come from.

But then maybe Miles was right. Maybe they'd simply left in a hurry and not closed the door properly. That was the most likely answer, surely.

Surely.

It took Joe a long time to get to sleep.

12

★★★★★★★★★★

SATURDAY

THE NEXT DAY Miles and Joe slept in late. Joe woke first and lay for a while listening to Miles's gentle snoring. Their thoughts turned to the open door and then to Lady Lady. Of course they did. It had only been three days since the murder, and Joe had lost one of their closest relationships. Lying quietly, they felt sad for fixating on the murder and trying to solve it rather than spending more time processing the loss. Should they be crying more? Were they supposed to be a grieving sobfest like Mandy? Maybe that just wasn't them. Or maybe Mandy wasn't crying because she was grieving but because she was guilty. Perhaps she was overwhelmed with the guilt of killing Lady Lady and couldn't contain it.

Joe thought about everything they'd learned so far. Mandy was clearly the most obvious suspect for the murder, though given her working hours Joe didn't think she could have also been the Kensington Catburglar. Jan was off the suspect list because of the CCTV and so, Joe thought, was Amour. She'd been genuinely horrified at the suggestion she could have had anything to do with it, and Joe had believed her. That left Tess, suspended for something by Lady Lady. Den, who had argued with her. Then there were Moneypenny, Plimberley, and Len, who all had access to the corridor too.

Was any of this connected to Auntie Susan?

And how did Judy Garland fit into it?

The bloody dress. It felt like the elephant in the room. A great big giant clue that Joe just couldn't work out yet.

It's time to find out more about the dress, they decided.

H AVING HAD A night's sleep Joe was much calmer about the front door incident. And probably Miles was right that they had just left it open while leaving in a rush.

I'm being paranoid, Joe thought, remembering how they had fallen asleep half convinced that the door had been left open by the Catburglar.

They picked up their phone from the bedside table and opened Instagram, looking at all the posts Misty had been tagged in after the show at the RVT last night. There were beautiful photographs and video clips of Misty onstage and of Misty posing with people after the show. Legs like a Beverley Callard workout video.

Joe was working through the notifications, replying to every one of them, when a text message from their mother arrived via WhatsApp.

Hi Joe. I saw in the news about your
friend and wanted to let you know I was

thinking of you. Figured you'd call when
you're ready but wanted to remind you
that I'm here if you need me.

They reread the message and then tapped out a speedy reply, hoping that they sounded reassuring, that everything was okay and that they'd give her a call soon.

They put the phone back on the bedside table and turned over, wrapping their arms around Miles and closing their eyes.

WHAT SHALL WE do today?" said Miles, stirring a pot of porridge with blueberries.

Joe was sitting at the kitchen table, their hands wrapped around a mug of coffee. "Well, I was thinking . . ." they said, worried about what Miles might think of their plan for the day.

"Sounds dangerous already," laughed Miles.

"Oh, don't!" And they both laughed. "I was thinking, if you'd be up for it, we could go to Chelsea."

"And what's in Chelsea, on this fine Saturday?"

"I want to visit that dress shop, the Dress Collector. You know, the one where Lady Lady's dress was stolen from?"

"What for?" asked Miles, pouring purple porridge into two bowls.

"Well, I thought I could talk to the owner, see if they know where Lady Lady might have got the dress. This stuff with the Kensington Catburglar is the most confusing bit of it all. I thought it might help to talk to the dress's original owner."

"You're really dead set on investigating this thing, aren't you?" Miles sighed.

"I am. I need to, for Lady Lady."

"I don't know, Joe . . . this feels like a *really* bad idea. I know we like our *CSI*s and all that, but you know we're not CSIs. You're not a detective, Joe, and this could get you into really big trouble."

"Then come with me, to the dress shop," said Joe, pleading a little, longing for Miles's help and support. "You could come along, and if you think it's all going wrong somehow, you can let me know. Two heads are better than one and all that."

Miles thought for a second, and Joe wondered whether he was about to argue, to protest Joe's insistence in trying to catch the killer. But then he said, "Okay. I'll come with you, but on one condition."

"What's that?"

"If we find out anything that the police need to know to properly solve the case, we *have* to tell them."

"Deal," said Joe. "So, you'll really help me?"

"Yes. Maybe I'll be able to stop you from getting into any more trouble. But we're not going to chase dodgy guys up alleys, okay? No more danger."

Joe thought of the open front door, of the way their stomach had flipped when they saw it unlocked. *Danger*, chimed a little voice in the back of their head.

Miles poured himself another coffee and said, "If we're really going to do this—I can't believe I'm saying this—but if we're really going to look into it a little bit, maybe we should make a list of everything you know so far. Perhaps we can narrow down the suspects."

Joe smiled. They loved Miles so much right now. "Okay, hold on."

Joe got up and went to the living room, where they knew they had a brand-new Moleskine notebook in the cupboard under the television. They took the notebook and found a pen and returned to the kitchen filled with energy and enthusiasm for working this out with Miles.

"So, let's get it all written down," said Miles. "How should we do it? On a timeline? Or a list of suspects?"

Joe wondered. There was a lot of information to get down. "Let's start with a list of possible suspects."

Joe wrote down the names of everyone who had access to the dressing rooms, leaving space between each one to make notes where necessary. They talked Miles through it as they wrote.

"Mandy, Den, and Tess seem to be the only people with motives so far."

"How so?" asked Miles.

"Well, Mandy's up to no good, and she had an argument with Lady Lady on the night of the murder. The police think it's Den because of his falling-out with her over the lineups. And Tess was suspended from work, but we don't know why yet. That's three people who had access to the dressing rooms, all with something going on with Lady Lady."

"What about the others?" asked Miles. "The others who had access to the dressing rooms?"

"It wasn't Jan. He didn't leave the bar and the CCTV would have been checked to prove it," said Joe. "And I don't think it was Amour. That would leave Plimberley, Moneypenny, and Len, but truly, I can't imagine any of the drags having done it. It just doesn't feel very . . . draggy."

"Murder by poisoned chocolate while wearing Judy Garland's dress is pretty camp though," said Miles.

"That it is."

"Is there anyone else?" asked Miles.

"The Kensington Catburglar," said Joe. "If Lady Lady had

the dress maybe she was involved in something more sinister. Perhaps she got on the wrong side of the wrong people. And the Kensington Catburglar seems to be able to get in anywhere."

Joe added the Catburglar to the list.

"There's also Auntie Susan, Lady Lady's ancient nemesis, but now I've slept on it I feel like that's a long shot."

Miles thought for a second and tapped his fingertips on the table. "The police think the Catburglar and the killer are the same person, right?"

"I think so," said Joe. "That's what it seems like from all their press statements."

"So, do you think any of your suspects could be a mastermind cat burglar?"

Joe thought for a second, running the names through their mind. They tried to imagine each of their suspects weaving through a labyrinth of laser beams like Catherine Zeta-Jones. "I don't know," they said. It seemed so unlikely that Mandy, Den, or Tess would be the Catburglar, but they were clearly the prime suspects.

"So, where do we start?" asked Miles.

"Well, I think I need to talk to everybody on the list, to ask them face-to-face what they remember about that night, like I did with Jan last night. Perhaps one of them will reveal something. I especially need to talk to Den and Tess. I'll see Mandy again on Monday."

"I guess you'd better text them," said Miles.

Joe snatched up their phone off the table. "Very well," they said, tapping out messages to Den and Tess, asking them each if they had time for a coffee.

"We also need to know more about what's going on at Lady's Bar," said Joe. "Maybe we could speak to Moneypenny and

Plimberley, see if they know anything about it. They're also on the possible suspect list, so it would be good to hear their accounts of Wednesday night."

"Why don't you invite them over?" said Miles, maybe getting into it a little bit now that they'd started.

"Here?"

"Yeah, we could invite them over for a drink and see what they know."

"Good idea," said Joe, smiling at Miles's newfound interest in the investigation.

Joe texted Moneypenny to see if she and Plimberley were around to come over for coffee that afternoon.

As they were sending the message, a reply arrived from Tess.

"Tess can meet me tomorrow morning at her house."

Let's see what you know, Tess, thought Joe. *But first, I've got a rich lady's dress to investigate.*

13

★★★★★★★★★

ONE SHOULD ALWAYS dress nicely when going to Chelsea, that was Joe's rule. So Joe wore a light, white linen shirt and a pair of smart shorts. Nice. Smart. Summery. Miles wore a black shirt and a pair of beige cotton cigarette pants. He was always so stylish. Timeless.

They arrived just before lunchtime and headed straight to South Kensington to the dress shop that had, just a few weeks before, been targeted by the Kensington Catburglar.

The Dress Collector was the kind of expensive shop that Joe would normally never even dare go inside. It was fancy. Joe had been to fancy places for Miles's work, posh product launches and Christmas dinners in five-star hotels, but this little shop felt *too* fancy. A place that was out of their world completely. They wished they had come as Misty: she wouldn't have thought twice about going in.

The outside of the boutique was painted an ivy green, and the front doors were adorned with bushes in pots that had been trimmed into perfect spheres. There was a short patch of red carpet running over the doorstep, and it was immaculately clean, like it had been recently washed or newly purchased. The window display had three mannequins, each wearing a beautiful jewel-encrusted dress. They were the kind of dresses that Misty could only dream of. Her budget, and likely her morals, would never allow it.

Joe thought about Lady Lady and how she had glittered in that Judy Garland dress. She had been aesthetic perfection that night, even if her performance had been off. Thinking about her brought back the lavender perfume of her hair, and Joe's senses were suddenly filled with the scent of it.

"Ready to go in?" asked Miles.

"I think so," said Joe.

"Okay, Detective Divine, let's go."

They pushed open the door.

T HE INTERIOR OF the Dress Collector was as plush as the little bushes outside would have you believe. The carpet was so luxurious that it was like walking on a duvet. It was a small store with one wall of clothes rails, a large seating area, and a little reception desk with a marble counter. There were no customers to be seen, and a brass plaque on the counter said, By Appointment Only. Joe supposed that with dresses worth £250K they needed very few customers to keep the lights on.

A woman with short spiky hair stood behind the desk. "Do you have an appointment?" Joe was surprised by her accent. Like Mary Poppins but posher. Joe didn't think there were people who really spoke like that.

"Erm . . . no, sorry . . ." Joe stuttered. "We . . . erm . . ."

They suddenly felt stupid—for coming here, for thinking they could catch a murderer, for all of it. They'd be better off at home watching TV instead of dicking around like this, talking to "suspects."

"We'd like to talk to Mrs. Bowman," said Miles boldly. Joe felt relieved to have Miles by their side. His cool confidence was worlds away from Joe's own low self-esteem, and they were so glad he had agreed to come with them. Standing in the fancy shop, Joe realized that they couldn't have done this on their own.

Mrs. Anna Bowman was the name of the woman who owned the shop and the Judy Garland dress. Miles and Joe had looked her up before they left the house, and this receptionist with the spiky hair was certainly not her.

Spiky Hair shuffled uncomfortably on her feet behind the reception desk. "Mrs. Bowman isn't talking to any more journalists."

"Oh, we aren't journalists," said Miles. "Are we, Joe?"

"No," said Joe, Miles's encouragement giving them a boost. "Not journalists. But we would like to talk to Mrs. Bowman about the dress. We're from Lady's Bar, where the dress was found."

"I see." Spiky Hair hesitated a second longer before making a decision. She picked up a telephone and held it to her ear. "Anna, it's Sylvia. I've got two gentlemen here to see you. They're from Lady's Bar."

Gentlemen, noted Joe.

Sylvia put down the telephone and said, "She'll be a few minutes, but she'll talk with you. Can I get you some tea while you wait?"

She gestured to the seating area opposite the opulent changing room. Two small sofas and an armchair and a coffee table that looked as though it might have been more expensive than the entire contents of Joe and Miles's apartment.

"Tea would be lovely, thank you," said Miles.

Joe and Miles sat down on the sofas, and Sylvia disappeared into a back room. Miles whispered to Joe, "The tea means we can stay for longer. Nobody kicks a person out before they've finished their tea."

"I'm nervous," whispered Joe.

"Don't worry," said Miles reassuringly, "we're just here having a nice cup of tea."

A few moments later Sylvia emerged with a teapot and two cups and saucers on a tray.

"I'm so sorry about your colleague," she said. "Lady Lady, wasn't it? A terrible business."

"Yes," said Joe, mustering the courage to ask their first question, "very sad indeed. Did you ever meet her? Lady Lady that is? Did she ever come into the shop here?"

"Not that I'm aware of," said Sylvia, "but I'm not here every day. Asking Mrs. Bowman is your best bet."

"And what about the dress? Did you get it back now?" asked Miles.

"Oh, I'd rather not discuss anything about that without Mrs. Bowman being here," said Sylvia.

Sylvia excused herself and made her way back to her reception desk where she shuffled papers and clicked too loudly on her computer mouse. Moments later a woman Joe recognized from the internet as Anna Bowman walked into the store through the front door. She was a tall woman, spidery. All long skinny arms and legs and hair that was dyed blond to within a millimeter of its life. She was wearing a brown silk dress with a brown scarf, and Joe couldn't help thinking that she looked like she'd dressed up as the poo emoji.

She walked over to them. "Hello, I'm Anna Bowman. You wanted to see me?"

"Hello, I'm Joe Brown, and this is my partner, Miles. I work at Lady's Bar."

Anna sat down on the armchair, completing the seating area. Up close, the brown dress was much prettier, and Joe noticed deep chestnut embroidery running along the hems. "I'm sorry about your friend Lady Lady. Did you know her well?"

"I did, actually," said Joe. "She was my drag mother—my mentor."

"Well, I'm sorry for your loss." Her face seemed soft, genuine, as though she truly sympathized.

"We were wondering," said Miles, "did you know Lady Lady? Did she shop here maybe?"

"I'm afraid not," said Mrs. Bowman, "and I told the police the same thing. To be honest, I had never heard of her until this week. I suppose we moved in *vastly* different circles."

There was something snooty about that last comment, something condescending in her tone that didn't appear intentional, just a deep-rooted superiority. Joe had heard that kind of tone before—people from the non-drag world who had the idea that drag was seedy, less-than, somehow dirty. Anna Bowman hadn't seemed like the type. *Takes all sorts*, they thought.

"Perhaps she dealt with you under her other name, Sean Fulton?" asked Joe.

"I'm sure she didn't," said Mrs. Bowman. "The police

asked me that too, but I'm afraid I really have never heard of her."

"We're trying to work out how she might have ended up with your dress," said Miles. "Before it was stolen, was there any interest in it from potential buyers?"

Mrs. Bowman sighed. "While it's been lovely to meet you boys, I'm afraid I don't have time to sit around chatting all afternoon. I really must be getting on."

She got up to leave, wafting a cloud of sweet perfume across the room as she moved.

"Please," said Joe. "We'd really appreciate if you could help us."

She sighed. She was cold, hard, bristly like a hedgehog. But she gave in quickly, talking more as they began walking as a group toward the door.

"The truth is, I hadn't had the dress for very long. Only a couple of weeks. It arrived from a collector in the States, and two weeks later it was stolen. There were a few potential buyers interested, but nobody serious or remarkable, just my usual customers. There have been more inquiries since, of course."

"What do you mean?" asked Joe.

"Well, now the dress has a mysterious history. Owned by Judy Garland, then found on the body of a murdered drag queen in a Soho cabaret club . . . Macabre as it sounds, the dress is more in demand than it ever would have been before. For a collector it's a dream story."

A S THEY LEFT the store, Joe felt lighter, encouraged that they had conducted a successful first interview. Matthew Gray Gubler would be proud.

"She seemed nice," they said to Miles.

"Did she?" laughed Miles. "I might be getting sucked into this now."

"What do you mean?" asked Joe.

"I've got a theory. I think Anna Bowman could be my new prime suspect."

14

★★★★★★★★★★

Y OU SEE, SHE could have coordinated the whole thing—staged the initial theft and then sent Lady Lady the dress and the chocolates. She said it herself, the dress is worth loads more now than it ever was before."

"So you think she could have murdered Lady Lady to increase the value of the dress?"

"It's a possibility. It's a motive."

"I think it's pretty unlikely," said Joe. "It's a lot of effort. And besides, she'd still have to have had someone plant the chocolates, someone who had access to the dressing room. Surely it's more likely to have been one of the people there that night."

"People do all kinds of things for money," said Miles.

They crossed Fulham Road and continued heading south. They passed designer shop after designer shop. They walked by a family coming out of an exclusive-looking children's clothes store, and Joe watched as the mother gave the baby a piece of chocolate. They thought of the text they'd received this morning from their own mother and how they should really call her.

"I had a text from Mum this morning," Joe said.

"She'd heard about Lady Lady, I suppose?" said Miles.

"Yeah, she's worried, I can tell."

Joe grew up in Croydon, in South London. They'd had a happy childhood, for the most part. Joe's parents had been young when they had them—in their late teens. Photos of them from the eighties revealed stripey tights, facial piercings, and what must have been dangerous amounts of hair spray. In those days, when a seventeen- and eighteen-year-old had a baby it wasn't impossible to get a council house, so that is what they'd done. They hadn't had much money, but Joe's mum and dad always made sure Joe had enough to eat and a new school uniform every year. They were kids themselves, Joe always thought, working out the parenting thing as they went along.

At school, the other kids called Joe's parents "hippies," and maybe that's what they seemed like from the outside. Joe and their parents were regular attendees at antiwar protests, antinuclear weapons protests, and they'd taken Joe to London Pride every year. Something now that Joe looked back on as a fairly radical act—taking your kid to Pride at the height of the Section 28 era, when homophobic politics and headlines were rife and the law of the land forbade teachers from even discussing queer issues with students. Joe's parents knew better. Joe had fond memories of getting their face painted and holding their mother's hand as they watched the parade. Later, in their twenties, Joe had asked their mother why they'd gone, why she had taken them.

"There was always something magical about you, Joe, from the day you were born. And maybe this nonbinariness is it. I wanted you to know that whoever you were, whoever you grew up to be, that you were safe."

Joe thought about this moment as they and Miles continued their walk through Chelsea. All their mum had ever wanted for Joe was safety, and they knew that the murder at Lady's Bar would have her worried. But they didn't want to call her yet, didn't want to worry her further by talking about everything that was happening before the killer had been caught.

J OE'S PHONE RANG in their pocket just as they were about to reach King's Road. It was a London number, but not one Joe recognized, and they were snapped out of thoughts of their mum.

"Who is it?" asked Miles.

"Not sure," said Joe. All sorts of thoughts flashed through Joe's head about who it could be: Baseball Cap the horrible policeman.

They picked up the call.

"Am I speaking with Joseph Brown?" asked a deep, well-spoken voice.

"This is Joe," they replied.

"Excellent. My name is Colin McDermott, I'm the solicitor acting for the Sean Fulton estate."

"Okay . . ."

"I'm calling to let you know that you have been named as a beneficiary in Mr. Fulton's will."

Joe was gobsmacked. "What do you mean?"

"Exactly that. You've been named to receive something from the estate. As such you're invited to the reading of the will on Monday morning at ten a.m. I'll email you over the details this afternoon."

Joe gave the solicitor their email address and thanked him for the call, turning to Miles. "Apparently Lady Lady left me something in her will!"

"Wow. What do you think she left you?"

"I have no idea. Maybe her costumes? Her makeup? I guess I'll find out on Monday."

"I guess so," said Miles. "Maybe it'll be a new lead in the investigation."

"Ooh, yes," said Joe. "Maybe the will reading will even reveal a prime suspect!"

15

✶✶✶✶✶✶✶✶✶✶

MONEYPENNY AND PLIMBERLEY arrived just after lunch. Moneypenny burst through the door and greeted Joe with extravagant air-kisses.

Mwah! Mwah!

She was good-looking out of drag—a bit geeky but cute. She had a sprinkling of freckles across her cheeks and floppy brown hair that reminded Joe of the French teenagers they'd met on school exchange visits.

"My loves," said Moneypenny. "Thanks so much for the invitation!"

Plimberley thrust forward a plastic carrier bag that clinked as though it had far too many bottles in it.

"We brought booze," she said. "We were both meant to be performing at Lady's Bar tonight, but seeing as it's closed . . . let's get messy!"

Plimberley was a tall string bean of a human. Her limbs were long and limber. Out of drag she had a mop of dark brown tousled hair and a few spots that were likely just hangovers from adolescence. The spots were covered in a light layer of foundation that was only visible up close; Plimberley was an excellent makeup artist.

Miles looked at Joe and grinned. It was so nice to see them, and felt so normal, Joe had to remind themself that they had invited them here to investigate, that there was still a chance Moneypenny or Plimberley was the murderer.

"Right, what are we drinking?" said Moneypenny. "It's Saturday afternoon, let's have a gin."

Miles took the carrier bag of drink and whisked it away to the kitchen, where he set about making four gin and tonics for the group.

"It's great to see you," said Joe.

Unless one of you murdered my friend.

"T HE DRESS IS the big mystery of the whole thing," said Moneypenny, curling up her legs onto the sofa beneath her and taking a large gulp of gin. "You don't think . . . you don't think Lady Lady was the Kensington Catburglar?"

Joe smiled. "I don't think so," they said. "She really wasn't the cat-burgling type."

"That's true," said Moneypenny. "Well, it's a mystery to me. And she never told you? Where she got the dress, I mean."

"No, nothing. I didn't know anything about it until I read it in the news," said Joe.

"I reckon she robbed it," said Plimberley.

Moneypenny laughed. "I can imagine her now, breaking and entering with her purple hair."

"I'm serious!" insisted Plimberley. "How else do you get a *quarter-of-a-million-pound* dress? She might have been rich by drag queen standards, but she wasn't that rich."

"That's true," said Miles. "Unless Lady's Bar is the most successful drag bar in London."

"How rich do you think she was?" asked Plimberley. "Like, do we reckon she was a millionaire?"

"I doubt it," said Joe. "She didn't behave like a millionaire."

Moneypenny wagged her finger. "But you never know, do you? People keep all kinds of things secret. Especially when it comes to money."

Joe thought of Mandy, her head bobbing through busy Soho streets with her envelope of cash.

"Have you ever noticed anything weird about money at Lady's Bar?" asked Joe, keen to get started on their stealth interrogation. "Late payments, nonpayments, anything?"

"I'll give her this," said Plimberley, "she paid her invoices on time."

"Bang on time," said Moneypenny. "Every time."

"What about Mandy?" asked Miles, leaning forward, getting in on the action. "Have you ever noticed anything unusual going on with her?"

"You're starting to sound like the police," laughed Moneypenny. "That's what that prick asked me."

So, the police are *asking about Mandy too . . . maybe they're following up on what I told them about the argument in the dressing room.*

"Sorry," said Miles. "Didn't mean to grill you."

"Mandy's always been great with me," said Moneypenny. "I've never seen anything unusual at Lady's Bar at all. It's always been one of my favorite places to perform."

"I need a fresh gin!" Plimberley announced.

MILES AND PLIMBERLEY chatted in the kitchen, making fresh gins for the group and leaving Joe and Moneypenny alone in the living room.

"I just can't believe it's real," said Moneypenny. "That she's really gone."

"Me neither," said Joe. "What do you think about this theory that Den did it?"

"I don't know . . ." said Moneypenny. "It's hard to believe."

"Why?"

"I just don't think any of the drags would have done it." Moneypenny took off her glasses and inspected the lenses before cleaning them on her T-shirt. "So, it must have been someone else who was there that night. My money's on Mandy."

"Mandy, why?" asked Joe, curious, thinking of Mandy's dodgy dealings and wondering if Moneypenny knew what was going on.

"Well, firstly, the police can't be asking about her for no reason. They must be suspicious, right? And don't they say that it's usually someone close to the victim? Mandy was closer than any of us—except for you, Misty!"

"Right," shouted Plimberley, entering the living room with fistfuls of gin glasses, "drinks up."

Joe's heart sank. They felt like they were just getting into it with Moneypenny. It was useful hearing her perspective and interesting that she suspected Mandy too. Joe wanted to ask her more.

"Jesus, that's strong," said Joe, taking a sip of Plim's gin.

"Don't blame me," said Miles, winking at Plimberley.

"Plimberley's special measures, is it?" said Moneypenny. "We're in trouble . . ."

———

THEY WERE INDEED in trouble. Plimberley's special measures saw them get through a bottle of gin and half a bottle of vodka in no time at all.

"What was I supposed to be asking them?" Joe whispered to Miles in the kitchen, fully aware that their voice was slurred.

"I can't remember," Miles laughed. Then Joe started laughing.

And they laughed until they cried, both of them doubled over in the kitchen.

"Sshhh . . ." hushed Miles through teary eyes.

"What's going on in there?" called Moneypenny from the living room. "We can hear you giggling."

"We've got the giggles, Money," chuckled Joe.

BY THE TIME they'd finished the vodka Moneypenny could hardly sit up straight, and Plimberley had given up sitting altogether and was sprawled across Miles's lap in the armchair.

"Right," said Moneypenny, drunk as a skunk, leaning forward toward Joe. "I don't care what anybody says, right, *I* don't think you did it."

Plimberley lifted her head. "Money!"

"I don't though," said Moneypenny, "I don't think it was Misty."

"What do you mean?" asked Joe, their brain taking a second to catch up. "Who's saying I did it?"

"Everyone . . ." slurred Plimberley. "'Cause you went to the dressing room. You were the only one."

"That's crazy," said Miles. "Surely everyone knows how much Lady Lady meant to Misty."

"Yeah, that's why. Being close to the victim and all that," said

Moneypenny. "But what I'm saying is . . . what I'm saying is, *I* don't think you did it."

"What about you, Plim?" asked Joe. "Do you think I did it?"

It hurt Joe to know that people were suspecting them of murdering one of their closest friends. Lady Lady had been more than a friend. She'd been the type of family that sticks by you through thick and thin. It stung that anyone thought they could have killed her. But then again, Joe was suspicious of everybody too.

"I think it was Den," said Plimberley, playing with the hair on Miles's arm with her fingertips.

"Really?" asked Joe, surprised to hear this and instantly eager to know more. "Why Den?"

"He just always looks . . . shifty, doesn't he?" said Plimberley, her eyelids drooping shut and then reopening suddenly as though she were trying to keep herself awake.

"Shifty?" asked Joe. "What do you mean? When have you seen Den looking shifty?"

"I don't know . . ." Plimberley rolled her head back over the edge of the armchair and looked at the television upside down. "He's just shifty, isn't he? I don't know how to explain it . . ." Her eyes flickered shut and she let out a snort of a snore.

Joe's thinking was foggy with gin and vodka, and they wanted to ask more but Plimberley had fallen asleep.

"Plim," they said. "Plim!"

Moneypenny laughed. "She always does this. Pours the strongest drinks then can't hold her liquor."

OKAY," SAID MONEYPENNY, "that's enough murder talk for one afternoon. Put *The X Factor* on."

"*The X Factor* ended ages ago, Money," said Miles.

"I mean on YouTube, on your big telly. Put the old auditions on. Me and Plim watch them all the time at home. Don't we, Plim? Plim? Plim?"

Miles obliged, reaching for the remote and switching on Joe McElderry's now ancient-looking first audition.

Plim's tired eyes reopened and she gazed upside down at the television. "Aww . . . bless his little socks," said Plimberley, gazing at Joe McElderry.

"He was good, wasn't he?" said Moneypenny.

And everybody nodded in agreement. He was good.

THINGS TOOK A turn, and not for the better, when they opened a bottle of whiskey that Miles had been given as a gift by a client.

"We shouldn't drink any more," said Joe, holding themself up against the kitchen counter. "We're really, really, really drunk."

"Then this isn't going to make a blind bit of difference, is it?" said Miles, giggling and popping a cork out of the bottle.

"Quick, come back in, ladies," shouted Plimberley, now on her second wind. "Leona Lewis is on!"

As Joe stepped into the living room they felt a sense of relief, to be around friends again, to feel like themself again. After the stress of the last few days it was nice to let loose a little, to relax. Through the boozy haze they tried to switch back into investigator mode, to think through whether they'd learned anything from Moneypenny and Plimberley, but their brain couldn't latch onto a clear thought. They'd have to ask Miles in the morning. For now, Joe was quite content sipping their whiskey and watching Leona Lewis.

TWO TUMBLERS EACH of whiskey later and Moneypenny was throwing up in the bathroom. When she emerged through the kitchen her glasses were wonky and her French hair disheveled. Her chin was wet from where she'd rinsed her face.

"I'm wasted," she said.

"I think we all are," said Joe.

"I think I should go home," said Moneypenny. "Come on, Plim, let's get a taxi."

But Plimberley was out for the count, her skinny arms tucked under her head on the living room floor. She didn't even stir when prodded.

"She can stay here," said Joe. "I'll send her back in a taxi tomorrow morning."

"Let me call you an Uber," said Miles to Moneypenny.

"Thank you."

ONCE MONEYPENNY WAS safely stowed into the back of a car home, Joe and Miles gently woke Plimberley and lifted her onto the sofa, spread a throw over her, and tucked a pillow underneath her head.

"Misty," whispered Plimberley.

"Yes, Plim?"

"I like you."

"I like you too. Now good night, my love."

Joe turned off the living room lights and joined Miles in bed.

16

★★★★★★★★★

SUNDAY

JOE WOKE UP with a headache and a dry mouth. They took a sip of water from the bottle on the bedside table and it tasted refreshing and pure. Each mouthful was like a smooth glass marble soothing their parched, hungover throat.

Miles rolled over and groaned.

"We shouldn't have had that whiskey," he said, rubbing his eyes.

"Big mistake," said Joe.

Miles put his hand on Joe's chest and his head on their shoulder. "I don't want to get up."

"Me neither," Joe replied.

They lay in comfortable silence for a while, enjoying the sounds of Sunday morning London floating up through the window.

"What have you got on today?" asked Miles.

"I'm going to see Tess this morning," said Joe, "and then I've got a brunch."

"Aah, the investigation continues." Miles smiled with tired eyes. "Where's the brunch at?"

"Dalston Superstore."

Dalston Superstore was a small, cool venue in East London. It was a hub for the LGBTQ+ community, and a nice brunch venue, where the shows often spilled from inside onto the pavement. Joe looked forward to performing there.

"Oh my God, Plimberley's still here," said Miles, suddenly remembering the previous night's antics.

"I'll make her a coffee," said Joe, swinging their legs around out of the bed.

"I'm staying in bed until she's gone," said Miles. "She's too loud for my headache."

"Understood," laughed Joe, heading out of the bedroom to the kitchen.

Plimberley was already awake and had switched on the television. She was watching an episode of *Bad Girls* on a down-the-list Sky channel and eating a piece of Miles's apple pie that she'd helped herself to from the fridge.

"Misty, I'm dead sorry, I had to eat the pie. I needed carbs urgently," she said.

"Don't worry about it, Plim. Eat away. Can I get you a coffee?"

"Yeah, please!"

J OE PLACED DOWN a pot of coffee and two mugs on the living room table.

"Did you sleep all right?" they asked. "Hope the sofa was okay."

"Oh my God," said Plimberley, full of apple pie, "slept like an absolute log." She forked a huge lump of pie into her mouth. "I love a sofa, me."

Joe rubbed their temples. "You're not hungover at all, are you?"

"Nope."

"You bitch. Wait till you hit your thirties."

"I'm enjoying it while it lasts."

ONCE THE *BAD Girls* credits were rolling Plimberley stood up. "I'd better get going," she said.

"Before you go," said Joe, thinking of the previous evening's conversations, "last night, you said something about thinking Den was shifty, and I wondered what you meant by it."

"Oh God, is that what I said? I was steaming, Misty."

"But why would you say that? Have you seen him do something? Heard something?"

Plimberley thought about it for a second. "Yeah, I guess. But it might not be anything really."

Plimberley was smart—smarter than she let on. She had spent the last few years sofa-surfing and building up a career for herself at the same time. And she was doing pretty well. You didn't survive years of hustle and homelessness unless you had a certain amount of street smarts.

"Tell me, Plim, it's important."

Plimberley plonked herself back down on the sofa and drained the last of her coffee cup. "Den came to the flat one day."

"Your flat with Moneypenny?"

"Yeah. It was an afternoon and I'd been out all night. When I got home I could hear voices in the kitchen. So, you know, I had a little listen. It was Den and he was asking Moneypenny for money, to *borrow* money."

"How much money? Did he say what the money was for?"

"No, nothing, but seemed like he'd been doing the rounds asking people. He was pretty desperate, begging her."

"What did Moneypenny say?"

"She told him to sling his hook. Well, nicer than that. She said she didn't have any spare money at the moment and he left pretty swift."

"When was this?" asked Joe, thinking back to last night when Moneypenny had said she thought Mandy was the murderer, not Den.

"A few months ago now, and I haven't heard about him asking for money since, so I guess he got it all sorted. But, you know, being desperate enough to go door-to-door looking for a loan, you've got to be in a bad spot to end up there."

"Did you talk to Moneypenny about it afterward? Did she say anything?"

"Oh yeah"—Plimberley nodded—"I told her right off that I'd been earwigging and asked her what was going on. It was gossip, you know."

"And what was going on?"

"Moneypenny said that Den was in a bit of a financial pickle and needed a loan. She said she didn't know more than that, but just ask her, tell her I told you. I'm sure she won't mind." Plimberley stood up. "Right, I really had best be off. Thanks for letting me kip on your couch."

"You're very welcome," said Joe, thinking already, *I must find out more.*

ONCE PLIMBERLEY HAD glugged down half a carton of juice from the fridge, she left, heading back to her and Moneypenny's flat. Joe checked the time. It was still early. They still had time for breakfast before getting into drag.

As soon as Plimberley left, Miles emerged from the bedroom

rubbing his head. For breakfast, he made muesli from jars of seeds and dried fruits. It was something that Joe would never do; they simply didn't have the energy for food preparation in the mornings. Especially not when this hungover. If it were left to Joe, breakfast would be a daily serving of Pop-Tarts and instant coffee. But Miles prided himself on making a different breakfast every day and said he didn't understand people who had the same thing day in and day out. "It should be like dinner," he'd said. "You wouldn't have the same thing for dinner every day, would you?"

As Miles prepared the breakfast, Joe filled him in on everything Plimberley had said—Den's visit to Moneypenny to ask for money.

"You shouldn't jump to conclusions," said Miles. "That could have been completely innocent."

"But it's something, isn't it? It's another piece to the Den puzzle," Joe replied. And then, thinking aloud, "I should speak to Moneypenny."

"What?"

"I was just saying I should speak to Moneypenny now, see if she knows more than she told Plimberley."

Miles thought for a second, bringing two bowls of muesli to the table. "But Moneypenny can't have thought the Den asking for money thing was suspicious, else she'd have said that Den was her prime suspect, but she didn't. She said she thought Mandy was the murderer."

"I'm just going to call her," said Joe, pulling out their mobile.

"Eat your muesli first," said Miles. "It'll go soggy otherwise, and no one likes soggy muesli."

Joe smiled. "*No one* likes soggy muesli."

As they ate, Joe flicked through the pages of their Moleskine, reassessing the notes they'd made on their investigation so far.

"So, what did we learn yesterday?" asked Miles, interrupting Joe's pondering.

"Not much," replied Joe, taking a mouthful of cereal. "That the Judy Garland dress is worth more money now."

"Yes," said Miles, pointing at the notebook. "Add Anna Bowman to the suspect list."

"She didn't do it," said Joe. "She was a posh tea drinker. I can't imagine her sneaking into a nightclub dressing room to stash a poisoned chocolate. She'd have to have been working with someone who had access to the corridor anyway."

"You never know," said Miles.

"No," Joe said, "I know it's not her, I just know it."

"Detective instinct, is it?" asked Miles, clearly a little upset that Joe was writing off his Anna Bowman theory.

"Something like that, I guess. I just think it's too much effort—staging burglaries, killing someone—to increase the value of a dress. And I really didn't think she seemed the type."

"I suppose I didn't either. She didn't have the muuurdery vibes."

Joe laughed. "You know what I mean. Besides, we have two much more obvious suspects to investigate."

"Den and Mandy," said Miles.

"Exactly. And we need to get to the bottom of what was going on with Tess. She's the other one with a possible motive."

"We didn't learn too much from Moneypenny and Plimberley, did we?" said Miles.

"Just that we shouldn't mix gin and vodka and whiskey in the afternoon."

"Well, yes, that."

"We did learn that Plimberley thinks Den did it and that Den was short of money," said Joe. "And that Moneypenny thinks Mandy did it. Which kind of makes sense, because they're our top two suspects."

"We also learned that a lot of people seem to think you did it," said Miles quietly.

"Yes," said Joe, feeling a rush of butterflies in their stomach. "I remember that much. Shit. I can hardly remember any of it. Were we watching Joe McElderry videos?"

"This is why police officers aren't allowed to drink on the job," said Miles. "But how do you feel, knowing people think it's you? Are you okay?"

"I'm fine, Miles, honestly. Let them talk. *I* know I didn't do it." Joe tried to sound blasé about it, as though they didn't care at all, but they did. They really did.

There was a pause between them, and Miles stared at Joe quizzically.

"Truly, Miles, I'm not bothered about it. It's just gossip."

"Okay . . . so, what's next in the investigation?"

"Well, I'm seeing Tess this morning before my brunch. And I need to talk to Moneypenny and Den today too. Tomorrow I'm doing emails at Lady's Bar again, so I'll see if I can find out anything more about Mandy then," said Joe.

"You need to call your mum," said Miles. "You didn't do it yesterday, did you?"

Crap. With all the detecting and drinking they'd completely forgotten. They sent her a text instead, letting her know that everything was okay and that she didn't need to worry.

"Call Moneypenny now," Miles suggested, noticing that Joe had almost finished their muesli.

Joe scooped the last mouthful from the bowl and ate it, chewing as they spoke. "On it."

Miles cleared the bowls from the table and washed up at the sink while Joe called Moneypenny. She answered with a groggy voice that you didn't have to be a detective to know meant she was still sleeping.

"Sorry to wake you, Money," said Joe.

"No worries," said Moneypenny. "Is everything okay? Is Plimberley okay?"

"Yes, yes," said Joe, "she just left. She should be nearly home."

"Misty, I am so so sorry for vomming in your bathroom," said Moneypenny.

Joe chuckled, "Don't worry about it! We were all out of it."

"Well, I'm sorry anyway. My head hurts."

"Mine too. Listen, Money, I'm just about to head out to brunch—"

"Booked and blessed."

"Ha! If only. But Plimberley mentioned something this morning before she left. She said Den had been round asking for money. She said to ask you about it."

"God, she's a gossip," laughed Moneypenny. "That was ages ago."

"What happened?" asked Joe.

"Oh . . ." Moneypenny paused and Joe heard the clicking sound of her opening and putting on her glasses. "It was February, not sure which week, but it was a Thursday afternoon—I know because I'd done my Wednesday gig at Lady's Bar the night before. I was doing the tight wash in the kitchen when the doorbell went. I opened it and Den was standing there. I was really surprised because he'd never been to our place before."

"How did he know where you lived?"

"No idea!" exclaimed Moneypenny. "But anyway, he asks if I've got a minute to talk, so I invited him in for a brew and he launches into this big speech, how he's behind on his rent, and he's really sorry to ask, but could I lend him some money. He was proper upset, like he was about to cry."

"Why would he come to you?"

"Apparently he'd heard that I get paid a lot of money for my IT job, which I don't, but he thought that I might have some spare cash. I might have lent him a couple of hundred quid or something, but he asked me for a *grand*. I said to him I didn't have that kind of money to spare."

"A grand! That's a lot of money to be begging off friends."

"I felt bad for him, and he was upset when I said I couldn't help. He asked me not to tell anyone because he was so embarrassed. Anyway, it was all over and done with quite quickly, because I saw him the following week, and he said he'd sorted it all out."

"So, he got the money from somewhere?" asked Joe.

"I guess so. No idea where though. It's a bold move, doorstepping people for a grand."

"Did he say anything else while he was there? Anything about why he was behind with his rent?" Joe knew that the receptionists at the Empire Hotel got paid less than the back-office staff, and while nobody had had a pay rise there for years, London rents were getting more expensive by the day.

"No, nothing. It's hard times, Misty, cost of living crisis and all that. People are falling behind all over the place."

"True," said Joe.

"Why are you so interested in this, Misty? Not because of this rumor that Den's the murderer?"

Joe hesitated, unsure whether to confide in Moneypenny about their investigation but ultimately deciding not to. "I'm just curious, that's all," said Joe. "You know me, Money. I'm a nosy bitch."

Moneypenny snorted a little laugh down the phone. "Ow, even laughing hurts."

"I'll let you go," said Joe, realizing the time and that they needed to be getting into drag already. "Sleep it off."

"All right, speak to you soon, Misty, love."

Joe ended the call and immediately told Miles everything, though he'd grasped most of it from listening to Joe's side of the conversation.

"I still don't know, Joe," said Miles. "It doesn't seem suspicious to me. Moneypenny's right, lots of people are falling behind right now. Could be nothing."

"But could be something."

Miles rubbed his temples. "Do you mind if I don't come to brunch today?" he said. "I'm feeling a bit delicate."

Miles usually came to as many of Misty's shows as he could, and it was unusual for him to stay at home. "You're really feeling it, hey?"

Joe washed the coffee cups and tidied up the muesli ingredients while Miles retreated to the bedroom to lie down. They watched as rogue oats swirled down the plughole and thought about the previous day and the phone call they'd received from Lady Lady's solicitor in the middle of it all.

What has she left me in the will? they thought.

Joe assumed it was costumes. Lady Lady had a whole room full of costumes in her Greek Street flat and rails of them in her dressing room. She had, on rare occasions, let Misty borrow accessories from the collection for special gigs. *Yes*, Joe thought, *she's left me the costumes.*

It would be an amazing gift, if so. Hundreds of dresses, most of them bespoke and handmade. Of course, the majority of them would be too small for Misty, but she could make adjustments.

And the shoes, oh, the shoes. They would definitely fit, and there were so many shoes. An entire wall in Lady Lady's costume room was dedicated to them.

What if they're stolen? thought Joe, suddenly panicking. *What if you're about to inherit a whole closetful of Judy Garland dresses?*

No, no, no. Joe couldn't believe that Lady Lady would have knowingly worn that dress if she'd been aware of what it was.

She wasn't a thief, she just wasn't.

Once Joe had showered and shaved, they returned to the bedroom and apologized to Miles for needing to turn on the light. Miles lifted the duvet over his head, and Joe slipped on a vest and a pair of Calvin Klein boxers and sat down at the dressing table to get into drag.

Eyebrow glue, primer, foundation, blush, eyebrows . . . the makeup went on quickly today.

Before they knew it they were standing at the mirror about to put a giant blond bobbed wig on.

Say goodbye to Joe, they thought.

17

✶✶✶✶✶✶✶✶✶✶

TESS MUSGRAVE, LADY'S Bar's head of security, lived in a tiny terraced house near Mile End. Misty got out of the Uber and took it in. There were garden gnomes everywhere! Lined up along the little wall that surrounded the tiny front yard and then covering the entire yard like a brightly painted terra-cotta army. There was a garden gnome sitting atop the doorbell and three on the windowsill inside the front room. Misty double-checked the address to make sure she was in the right place. She was.

There were gnomes fishing, hugging, digging, kissing, and peeing. There were gnomes baring their cheeky pink bottoms.

Who knew, thought Misty, *that Tess had such a thing for garden gnomes.*

Misty was struck, not for the first time this week, by how you didn't really ever fully know someone. She had worked with Tess for five years. Week in, week out. And never, not once, had Tess mentioned that she was a secret gnome hoarder.

Misty was glad to be in drag. Going to see Anna Bowman yesterday had been nerve-racking, even with Miles by their side.

Joe was an impostor, but Misty belonged almost everywhere. And even now, approaching Tess's front door alone, she didn't feel afraid, not like Joe would. She felt ready, confident, and sure of herself. She was going to ring the doorbell, go inside, and find out all about Tess's suspension. That's simply how it was going to go, Misty Divine had decided.

As she walked up the little path to the front door she ran through what she knew about Tess already: a trusted mother hen type, she was well loved in the drag community and in Soho in general. But despite her soft nature with the drags she was rough as toast with the customers. Nobody messed with Tess. Nobody.

Misty pressed the doorbell with a pointed nail, and it sounded a little tune inside the house. The door swung open and Tess was standing there. She looked so different out of her security uniform, less intimidating. She was wearing a pair of jeans and a plain white T-shirt, her shaved head more prominent in casual clothes.

"Hello, Misty, love!" she said. "You look gorgeous!"

Misty had paired the blond bobbed wig with a hot pink A-line cocktail dress with cascading ruffles. She already knew she looked gorgeous, but it didn't hurt to be told.

"Thanks, Tess!"

"Come in, come in."

Misty stepped inside and realized instantly that Tess's collecting wasn't limited to garden gnomes but instead seemed to include any type of miniature figurine. The walls of the house were covered in little statues. There was everything from ornamental cats to Disney characters. A lot of the models appeared to be the kind of thing you'd order from an advert on the back of a magazine.

"Wow!" said Misty. "This is quite a collection."

"Thank you," said Tess, beaming. "It's a nightmare to dust, but I love them."

Tess led the way to the living room, also covered in tiny statues.

"Thanks for taking the time to see me, Tess," said Misty.

"Oh, no problem. Anything for you, my love. And with the club closed it's not like I'm up to much else."

"You're not picking up extra shifts until Lady's Bar reopens? I saw Jan at the RVT."

"No, love. Mandy's paying me anyway, so I'm just taking the time to process everything." Tess burst into tears. "I just can't believe she's gone, you know?" Her face crinkled into an ugly scrunch and tears sprung from the corners of her eyes.

Misty wasn't sure what to do. This hadn't been quite what she was expecting. Of all the people she'd have thought could hold it together, Tess was the one. The big strong bouncer. But this sobbing Tess, this was a surprise. Misty put her arms around her and pulled the grieving security guard into a hug, hoping that she wouldn't get tearstains on her cocktail dress before brunch.

"It's awful, Tess. Just awful."

Now Misty felt bad. Tess was clearly grieving, just like she should be. And here was Misty Divine, the greenest detective in Soho, trying to interrogate her. They comforted each other for a while longer until Tess pulled away and said, "Let me make us each a nice cup of tea."

Cups of tea in hand, they headed to a sitting room crowded with stuff: ornaments, of course, but DVDs, mugs, and a shelf full of African carvings as well. Tess's enthusiasm for collecting had no bounds, it seemed.

"I just feel so guilty," Tess was saying. "It's my job to protect you all, to protect the club. I just feel so so guilty that there was a murder on my watch. And Lady Lady of all people. My friend."

"You can't blame yourself, Tess. There's nothing different you could have done. It's not like she was killed with a knife that you could have stopped at the door."

"I know," said Tess. "I know that logically. But it's hard to come to terms with. Every time the police question me, I feel judged. The shit head of security who let a murder happen."

Misty paused. "What do you mean 'every time' they question you?" she asked. "How many times have they questioned you?"

"Once at the club and three times since. I guess it's 'cause I'm security, they expect I should know things. But I don't even remember seeing the chocolates. I searched every bag that came into the club that night, and I don't remember anything."

"You can't be expected to see or remember everything, Tess. You did the best you could. Nobody blames you."

But she's been questioned four times. She's clearly a suspect.

Tess sniffed and took a sip of tea. "Thanks, Misty. I appreciate you saying that."

"It's true. What kind of things do they ask you? The police?" asked Misty.

Tess rubbed her hand over her shaved head. "All sorts of things. They wanted to know every detail I could remember from Wednesday night, every interaction with every patron. Then they asked a lot about the dress, about whether I'd ever seen anything else stolen coming in or out of the club, which I haven't, ever. And they were asking a lot of questions about Den. I got the impression they thought he might have done it."

She paused and took a sip of tea before saying in a whisper, "They also asked me about *you*."

"Me?" said Misty, feigning ignorance but only really semi-surprised. After all, she had gone to the dressing room before the chocolates were found, and apparently accusations on the scene were pointing in her direction. It was no real shock the police were asking about her, but she didn't like it—just as she hadn't liked it when Plimberley had announced her friends on the drag scene suspected her. She wondered what her drag colleagues might be saying about her to the police, what kind of gossip they might be sharing. No, Misty didn't like this one bit. "What did they ask about me?" she said.

"Oh gosh, I don't know, Misty. My head's a total muddle from it all."

"Please remember, Tess. It's really important."

Tess heaved a great big sigh, and Misty got a waft of what had clearly been scrambled eggs for breakfast.

"They asked about your relationship with Lady Lady, whether I knew much about it, and I said I didn't but that you seemed close. They asked if I knew about your finances, your relationships, your work outside of drag. Erm . . . I think that's it."

"Okay," said Misty, processing it all, trying to settle the idea that she might be one of the police's top suspects. "And did they ask about Mandy too?"

"Oh yes." Tess nodded. "They asked about her. Apparently Mandy and Lady Lady were having some sort of row on the night of the murder, but I was on the door all night—didn't even go to the dressing rooms."

Ask her now, said a voice inside Misty's head. *Ask her about her suspension. She's a suspect too.*

Not yet.

She knew she had to ask—that was why she came, after all. If it was true, what Jan had told Misty about Tess being suspended by Lady Lady, that might have given Tess a motive. But she had to ease into it. She didn't want Tess to feel like she was being grilled. Especially not when she was already so upset.

"What do you make of this dress business?" said Misty with a tone she hoped was casual and easy. "The Kensington Catburglar and all that?"

"I don't know, to be honest. It was a surprise to me. I could never have imagined Lady Lady being involved with a thing like that. Fifteen years I've worked for her, and I've never known anything like it."

"I was wondering where she might have got that dress from . . ." said Misty, hoping that Tess might have a new line of inquiry for her to pursue.

"I think that's what the police are wondering too," said Tess. "They asked me about it constantly. But I didn't know. I don't know. I'm not involved with anything like costumes. I said to them, they need to talk to Florentina, the costume lady. She's the one out of all of us who would know where Lady Lady got the dress. But Florentina seems so gentle. I can't imagine her having stolen a Judy Garland dress, can you?"

Of course! I need to talk to Florentina.

Matthew Gray Gubler would have thought of that ages ago.

Florentina was one of the most in demand designers in the business, and Lady Lady got most of her outfits from her. If Joe's theory about the will was correct, Misty was about to inherit a huge collection of Florentina's work. She made a mental note to get in contact with Florentina as soon as possible.

"Can I ask," said Misty, approaching the subject carefully,

"did you and Lady Lady have a . . . thing? A couple of weeks ago? I talked to Jan and he said that you'd been . . . suspended."

Tess took a sharp intake of breath like she'd been kicked in the tit and then burst into a wild sob that nearly spilled her tea. Misty took the cup from her and placed it among a set of Sylvanian Families on the coffee table. They appeared to be rabbits, and Misty noted that one of them was a doctor.

"I'm sorry, Tess. I didn't mean to upset you."

"Waaaaaa!" Tess wailed like a baby.

Misty felt almost panicked—Joe would have definitely panicked. She'd never seen a person so upset before.

"I'm . . . I'm . . . so embarrassed, Misty." Tess could barely even catch her breath.

Embarrassed?

"Why, Tess? What happened?"

Tess took a few deep breaths and Misty waited patiently, knowing that she was about to learn something new.

"I skived three days last month and I got busted. I told them I was sick but I wasn't. I've never done it before, and Lady Lady said she was . . . disappointed in me." She crumpled again, covering her face with her hand. "I'm so ashamed, Misty. I got tagged in a post on Facebook at the Hamburg Garden Gnome Festival, and Mandy saw it."

Is this it? All this fuss and tears for a few skived days at a garden gnome festival?

"And things still weren't right between us when she died. I could tell she'd lost trust in me and that I'd really let her down. I told myself I'd make it up to her, I was so sure that I would. And then . . . and then I didn't stop the chocolates coming into the club, and now she's dead. It's my fault, Misty. It's all my fault."

Misty put her hand on Tess's knee and gave it a squeeze that she hoped was reassuring and not creepy.

"It's not your fault, Tess. It's really not."

And as Tess folded in on herself and sobbed on the sofa, one thing was abundantly clear to Misty:

Tess was not the killer.

A S THEY REACHED the front door and were about to say their goodbyes, Misty said, "Tess, is there something happening behind the scenes at Lady's Bar? Are Mandy and Lady Lady involved in something they shouldn't be?"

"You know," said Tess, "before all this I'd have said absolutely not. But you don't end up in a stolen dress by accident, do you?"

"I suppose not," said Misty.

"It's been nice to see you, Misty. I'm sorry I cried so much."

"Oh gosh, don't worry about that. If you need to talk anytime you know where I am."

And Misty left none the wiser about who had killed Lady Lady but pretty certain she could cross Tess firmly off the suspect list.

18

★★★★★★★★★

MISTY WAITED OUTSIDE the house for an Uber to come and collect her. She was still hungover and Tess's screeching hadn't helped the headache. As she stood on the pavement she thought about what she should do next. Clearly, talking to Florentina was a priority—a conversation she should have thought to have already. And she needed to talk to Den, who still hadn't replied to her text asking for a chat. This wasn't like Den. Normally he was there for her, and Misty would have expected a speedy response.

A young mother with a wobbly toddler in tow passed by and the woman looked up at Misty with a sort of awe.

"You look amazing," she said. "Amazing."

Misty smiled because she knew it was true.

"Thank you," she said, and the woman and child went on their way.

After a seven-minute wait, the Uber arrived. It pulled up alongside her, and just as Misty was about to open the back door, the driver sped off, leaving her alone on the pavement.

"Bastard," she said.

It was a common occurrence, sadly, that drivers would often see the drag and then drive off. Was it homophobia? A result of the culture war against drag performers? Who knew? Either way, Misty would spend twenty minutes of her evening complaining to Uber customer services, again.

She restarted the app and booked another car. Three minutes away. This driver stopped to let her in and was lovely, complimenting her hair and her dress. Funny how someone else's attitude can change your perspective.

Misty thought back to Tess's house and began feeling regretful about her questioning. Maybe she'd gone too far, asking too many questions too quickly. Tess had been very upset, and maybe that wasn't an ethical approach to investigating.

I'm not an FBI profiler, she thought. *I can't be expected to get all of it right.*

She replayed the conversation in her mind, wondering if there was a way it might have gone differently, if she could have phrased her questions more carefully. She didn't think so. She'd been polite, delicate, with a light touch. Tess was clearly just a very emotional person.

A S SHE SAT in the back of the car she thought about Den and how almost everyone she'd spoken to seemed to think he was the murderer. What did she really know about him? she wondered. They'd first met at the hotel and become firm friends before Den encouraged Joe to try drag for the first time. Den performed mostly with Len, acting out hilarious comedy sketches and lip-sync routines, and he worked four nights a week at the Empire. He was behind on his rent, desperate enough to go door-to-door asking for a loan, and he'd had a row with Lady Lady about drag king representation on the Lady's Bar lineups.

Just call him.

She whipped out her phone and scrolled through her contacts, pressing the call button when she reached Den's name.

Misty Divine means business.

The phone started to ring.

The business was short-lived as three quick beeps told Misty that Den had rejected her call.

S HE ARRIVED AT Dalston Superstore just in time for the running order chat with the host, an Italian drag king called Caesar Theday. She air-dropped Caesar her backing tracks and talked him through the order in which she wanted to perform them. She was doing rowdier numbers today than she would usually— less lounge music, more pop. She was performing two sets of two songs and had chosen nineties pop icons: Aqua, B*Witched, the Sugababes, and Shania Twain. All songs that would get the crowd going and hopefully have them singing along over their scrambled tofu.

Just as she'd finished talking to Caesar, Amour arrived, rushing through the doors in a bustle of sequins and crystals, her long dark hair down to her waist.

"Hey, Misty," she said. "Hey, Caesar."

Amour handed over her tracks: she was dancing and fire-eating today, apparently, before turning to Misty.

"How've you been?"

"I'm doing okay," said Misty. "Just working it all out."

Amour nodded wisely. She was a few years older than Misty and had a grandeur about her, a dignity that was so strong it was almost physical.

"Are you sure you're okay to be here?" asked Amour, with a great deal of care in her voice.

"Oh yes," said Misty, "I'm fine, really."

DALSTON SUPERSTORE WAS a little place, and it was packed with customers by the time brunch started. The audience seemed to be mostly gay men, though Misty knew better than to assume.

Caesar performed first, moving between the tables like a tiger, dressed in a pair of black leather trousers and a red harness. He was sexy and certainly knew how to move. Misty wished she could dance like Caesar.

Misty was up second. She belted out her first two numbers and the crowd loved them. They danced in their seats, sang along, and took videos of her performing. She was gorgeous today, she knew that much.

By the time Amour came to perform the audience was well and truly alive and the room felt electric. Misty watched in astonishment as Amour set alight two twirling batons and stuck them down her throat. How did one even begin to learn to do this? Were there fire-eating classes one could go to? Misty assumed there were. Maybe one day she'd try it, just for fun.

People think you're a murderer, Misty, and you're sitting here thinking about fire-eating classes. It made her feel sick, and if she thought about it for too long she knew her hands would tremble. *People think you're a murderer.*

She tried to clear her mind, forget what other people might be thinking. *She* knew she wasn't the murderer—so now all she had to do was find out who was. She let the gasps and whoops and woos of the crowd wash over her and fixed her mind firmly on the investigation.

She had two key suspects to focus on: Mandy and Den. And Florentina might know more about the dress. Tess and Jan were off the list. Tomorrow Misty would go to the will reading in the morning and then spend the afternoon at Lady's Bar, helping with Mandy's admin. Misty thought perhaps it was time to confront Mandy, to ask her once and for all about what she and Lady Lady had got themselves involved in.

Misty took a sip of sparkling water through a paper straw. Normally she'd have joined in with the bottomless prosecco at a brunch gig, but today she was still feeling the effects of yesterday's drinks with Moneypenny and Plimberley, and she wanted to remain as clearheaded as possible from now on. As long as the killer was still out there, Misty couldn't afford to let her guard down, not even for a moment.

MISTY AND AMOUR left the Superstore shortly after the brunch ended at 2 p.m. and walked a couple of doors down the street to an independent coffee shop that had piles of pastries and cookies in a cabinet in the window. Both of them were still in drag, and this meant that passersby from the non-brunch world were staring at them.

Misty knew that for people who weren't regulars at drag shows, she was a spectacle. She was already over six feet tall, and the wig and heels gave her an extra four inches on top. Her makeup was striking and colorful, bright pink blush and neon eye shadows to go with the pink ruffly dress. Amour was even more noticeable. She was wearing a purple gown and gold jewelry in her hair. She looked expensive and she probably was.

They ordered coffees and sat down in the corner of the café. Misty bought a Belgian bun though she knew she wouldn't eat all of it.

"How was your gig yesterday?" asked Misty, remembering that Amour had said she was reading at a Drag Story Hour.

"Horrible," said Amour. "We were protested. Some idiots with loudspeakers and banners calling us perverts."

"Ah, I'm so sorry," said Misty. "Don't people have anything better to do?"

"I guess not," said Amour. "It's not the first time it's happened, but it seems to be getting scarier."

"Don't let them stop you," said Misty. "They're trash."

Misty's style of act meant that she wasn't often invited to do family-friendly gigs. She'd performed a few pride shows for all ages but preferred the club scene. She could never imagine herself reading to a crowd of children in a library. That just wasn't her thing. But she knew the story time gigs were important work. Drag story time hadn't existed when Misty was little; the closest, she supposed, was panto. She wondered whether being read to by somebody like Amour would have had the power to change the course of Joe's life, and you know what, she thought, perhaps it might. Misty certainly knew that she wished she'd seen more out and proud queer people when she was a kid. The protestors of such events, Misty thought, were simply bigots.

"I know I shouldn't let it get to me, and most of the time it doesn't," said Amour, "but today there was a boy in the audience dressed as Elsa from *Frozen* and I just hope his lasting memory of the event isn't a man with a loud hailer calling us freaks."

"I'm sure it won't be."

"Anyway, how are you?" asked Amour, shaking off the stress with a jiggle that made her jewelry jingle. "How are you doing with all the Lady Lady stuff?"

"Well, it's been hard, I won't lie," said Misty. "I had a couple of days of crying and flashbacks, but that seems to have passed mostly now. I just miss her, you know? And I wish I could talk to her about what happened."

"And how are you doing with the rumors?" asked Amour. "Lots of people out there are saying they think you're the killer, I'm sure you already know." That was Amour: to the point, straightforward. It stung.

"Yes," said Misty, "I know."

"The police asked me a lot about you," she carried on, "and were especially interested in getting me to say that you might have been carrying something when you left the dressing room to go to see Lady Lady. Of course I wasn't paying the slightest bit of attention to what you might or might not have been carrying, and that's what I told them."

Listening to Amour, Misty started to feel riled up, irritated, annoyed, ready to burst like a big yellow pimple. Why were the police wasting so much time and energy asking questions about Misty? Why weren't they grilling people about Mandy and her dodgy dealings? Or Den and his financial woes?

Suddenly she felt hurried, eager to get out of this café, to stop wasting time with Amour when she should be hunting down answers and clearing her name.

"Amour," she said, interrupting a monologue about how Misty needed to be careful now that the police were on her back, "do you have a contact number for Florentina? The costume designer? I have her on Instagram but could do with calling her."

"I'm sure I do!" said Amour, getting the number and pinging it to Misty in seconds.

MISTY GOT HOME just after five, in time to find Miles taking a vegetable lasagna out the oven. It looked good, with a thick layer of crispy brown cheese on the top.

"I needed comfort food," he said, as if an excuse was ever needed for a homemade lasagna.

Misty sat at the kitchen table as Miles served up two dinners. She kicked off her heels and told him about Tess, about the house full of miniatures, the crying, the wailing.

"She was racked with guilt for letting the chocolates into the club," said Misty, taking a forkful of pasta. "And she was on the door all night and said she didn't even go to the dressing rooms."

"So, you're sure it couldn't be her?" said Miles.

"I'm sure," said Misty.

"What do you do next?"

"Well, tonight I'm going to call Florentina and see when she might be free for a coffee. I'll try calling Den again too. Tomorrow I have the will reading in the morning, and then I'm going to go and work for Mandy some more, doing emails for the club. There will have been a lot over the weekend, and maybe I'll find out what she's been up to."

"So, you still haven't spoken to Den?" asked Miles. "Are you nervous about it?"

"Yes and no," said Misty. "I'm nervous because he's my friend, you know, and yet some people seem to think he could really be a killer. *I'm* starting to think he could be. I just can't put all the pieces together yet. There's something going on there though, I can feel it."

"Spidey-senses?" laughed Miles.

Misty nodded and wagged a forkful of mushroom at him, "You've got to trust your gut in this detective business, Miles, that's what they say."

"That's what who says?" He grinned.

"I don't know, but I'm sure someone does."

AFTER DINNER, MISTY took off her makeup and changed into some comfortable Joe clothes. As they settled on the sofa their mind wandered to just how many people could be thinking that Misty was the killer. It seemed that the rumor was doing the rounds pretty widely, and it made Joe much more nervous than it made Misty. Should they tell Miles? they wondered. Perhaps talking to Miles about it would help put them at ease, but it would also make Miles worried, Joe knew—more worried than he already was. And the more Miles was worried, the less likely he was to keep helping with the investigation, and Joe needed Miles. The Anna Bowman visit would have been a disaster without him. But before Joe had a chance to think about it more or to say anything at all, Miles entered the living room with two glasses of orange juice.

"So, where's this will reading tomorrow?" he asked.

"At Lady Lady's solicitor's office. On Rupert Street."

"Of course it's in Soho."

"She never left it," said Joe, remembering how Lady Lady had conducted all of her business, where possible, with local business owners. She'd been the face of many Soho Preservation

Society campaigns aimed at limiting the corporate overtake of the West End. All of that—the charitable work, the mentoring—just didn't track with the image Joe was building of Lady Lady's last couple of weeks: arguments, shady cash deals, the stolen dress. Who was she, really? They had to find out the truth.

Joe called Florentina first, and she picked up right away.

"Hello?" she asked, her voice light and breezy.

"Is that Florentina?" Joe asked.

It was indeed Florentina. They talked for a couple of minutes, mostly about Lady Lady and the shock of what had happened to her.

"Florentina," said Joe, "I was wondering if I might pick your brain about something. Do you have time for a quick coffee tomorrow? I'm going to be about Soho all day if you're around."

"I can't tomorrow," said Florentina, "I've got a photo shoot. But I could do Tuesday. Would the morning be okay?"

Tuesday. The day after tomorrow. Joe supposed it would have to do. They agreed to meet at a little coffee shop on Old Compton Street, one of Lady Lady's favorites, at Florentina's request.

"Why didn't you just ask her everything on the phone?" asked Miles, frustrated.

"Because I need to do it face-to-face, to see if she's lying. It's easier to tell in person."

"Aah, I see."

Next Joe called Den and listened to the phone ring, hoping he would answer this time, but he didn't. Call rejected—again. Joe tried a second time, and this time it went straight to voicemail as though the phone were switched off.

"Rejected," they said to Miles.

"Weird . . ." said Miles. "Why don't you try the hotel, see if he's there?"

"I think *you* could be a detective too, Miles." Joe smiled.

Joe called the Empire.

"Empire Hotel, Julianne speaking. How may I direct your call?"

Joe knew Julianne quite well. She was one of the day receptionists, a chatterbox, younger than Joe, and fresh out of university like Joe had been when they started there.

"Hey, Julianne, it's Joe."

"Joe! Oh my God! How are you? I heard you're off work for a little while, but it's no surprise given everything you've been thr—"

"Julianne, is Francesca working tonight?"

"Hold on, let me check the roster sheet." There was a rustling sound as Julianne flicked through a stack of paperwork. "Nope. Francesca's next in tomorrow, and then the next three nights."

"Okay . . ." said Joe. "I know it's not normally allowed, but might you be able to see on the HR system if we've got a phone number for them? A landline or something, I can't seem to reach them on their mobile."

Julianne hesitated. "I don't know, Joe. I could get in a lot of trouble for that. I don't think I should."

Joe wanted to push her, to ask her again to please see if there was a number for Den, but they knew they shouldn't. They shouldn't be getting poor Julianne into trouble for the sake of their investigation.

"No worries. If worse comes to worst," said Joe, putting their phone in their pocket, "we know Den is scheduled to be at the

Empire tomorrow night. We could always go in, after I've finished with Mandy at the club, see him face-to-face."

"I think that's a great plan," said Miles. "The will reading,
then Mandy, then Den . . . Maybe tomorrow's the day you'll
catch a murderer."

Maybe so, thought Joe. *Maybe so.*

19

****

MONDAY

JOE DECIDED UPON waking that they were going to go to Lady Lady's will reading in drag. It's what Lady Lady would have done and what she would have wanted. She would have adored the spectacle of a drag queen in a solicitor's office hearing a will being read.

But what to wear? Would it be too much to go full grieving widow? Black veil and all?

"Yes, definitely too much," said Miles.

Joe opted for a black suit trouser with a shiny silver blazer. Smart, professional, but still drag. Respectful drag.

"Do you know anyone else who is going?" Miles asked.

"None of the other drags mentioned it, and I didn't tell them I'd been invited. I want to avoid the gossips."

"Sensible."

Joe got into makeup and chose a wig: a coiffed blond updo with a black streak at the front. Just as they were pinning the wig to their wig cap, Miles came in, jacket on, satchel in hand, ready for work. He was always so fashionable and wore an elegant brooch on his jacket lapel in the shape of a small horse.

"I've got meetings all day today," said Miles. "Follow-ups from the big pitch. It's a new grocery delivery company."

"Ooh, exciting," said Joe. "That's right up your street, isn't it?"

"Certainly is," said Miles. "There's loads we can do with cooking and food, and I think our strategy will be to focus on home bakers and get some baking influencers involved. It'll be really fun."

"Perfect!"

Apparently Miles had always been a good cook, ever since he was a little boy. His mother once told Joe that Miles had inherited his kitchen skills from his grandmother, a proud Caribbean woman who ruled the roost.

"She made every family wedding cake for fifty years," his mother had said. "Miles used to watch her, help weighing ingredients, that kind of thing. He loved it."

Seeing Miles excited about this new account was heartwarming for Joe, and they imagined little Miles helping his grandmother and how far he'd come since then. They were so pleased that Miles enjoyed his work and that his work was leaning toward one of his biggest passions.

"Right, I'm off," said Miles. "Call me as soon as you can. I want to know what she's left you in the will!" Joe kissed Miles on the cheek. There was something weird about kissing on the lips in drag. The idea of it gave Joe the ick: the thought of smeared lipstick, sticky gloss—it was too messy.

Miles headed out and left Joe alone in the flat, nearly in full drag first thing on a Monday morning.

Joe pulled the wig straight and pushed some pins through the hairline to hold it in place. Misty was ready to go.

———————

MISTY STEPPED OUT of the flat into the July sunshine, and her heart skipped a beat when she saw a man in a tracksuit and a baseball cap leaning against the door to the twenty-four-hour newsagents across the street, staring in her direction.

Shit.

It's the baseball cap guy from the alley, she thought.

Or is it?

She couldn't see him properly. His face was covered by the shade of his cap and the sun was in her eyes. And the lashes, the bloody lashes, meant her field of view was reduced by about thirty percent.

She felt panicked and thought immediately of the open apartment door.

Well, I have to carry on, she thought. *I can't just stop my day because I've seen a man in a baseball cap.*

She put her headphones in and hurried down the street toward Soho, her heels clacking loudly beneath her. As she reached the gardens in the center of Russell Square, she glanced over her shoulder to see if he was behind her, and yes, there he was, six or seven people back, taking the exact same path as Misty.

"Hey, Siri," she said into her headphones. "Call Miles's mobile."

The phone ringing sounded in her ears.

Miles picked up right away. "Hey, love," he said.

"Miles, I think I'm being followed," she said.

"What do you mean? Where are you?"

"I'm crossing Russell Square and there's a guy behind me. He was outside the flat." She glanced back again and saw that

Baseball Cap was still there, though he was a couple of people closer to her than he had been.

"Go in somewhere, go into one of the hotels or something."

"I can't," said Misty, panicking. "I'm in the middle of the square. I'm in the park."

"Okay, stay on the phone. Get somewhere safe as quickly as you can, Joe."

Misty picked up the pace, the heels getting louder. And then she snapped out of it.

I'm not Joe, she thought.

I'm Misty Divine.

I'm powerful and brave, and this bastard in the cap isn't going to get to me.

She stopped walking and pulled out her phone, switching open the video camera.

"I'm going to confront him," she said to Miles.

"Don't, Joe, get somewhere safe."

"I'm filming him," she said.

"Oh God . . ." muttered Miles.

Misty turned on her heel and started walking directly toward Baseball Cap. He looked up from under the peak of his hat and Misty saw the little scars on his cheek that she'd noticed last time.

It's him.

She held up the phone, recording as people rushed past.

"Hey!" she shouted.

Baseball Cap stopped and Misty strode toward him.

"Are you following me?" she called.

A few passersby stopped too, watching.

Baseball Cap looked around at the people gathering. Misty was close to him now and could make out his sharp features and wiry physique.

"What's happening, Joe?" asked Miles in the headphones.

"Who are you?" asked Misty to Baseball Cap.

"Are you okay?" asked one of the passersby.

"He's following me," said Misty, "aren't you?"

And Baseball Cap ran. He sprinted in the opposite direction, back out of the park toward Russell Square station.

Misty carried on filming until he was well out of sight.

"He's gone," she said to Miles.

"I don't like this, Joe."

M ISTY ARRIVED AT the offices of Mr. Colin McDermott at 9:55 a.m., according to her watch. She was the picture of poise, but inside she was shaky. The confrontation in the park had rattled her, she couldn't deny. How did Baseball Cap know who she was? Where she lived? It felt as though everything was getting too close to home. Literally.

From the outside, Mr. McDermott's offices were an old Soho town house, and the only indication a business resided there was a discreet bronze plaque next to a high-tech-looking doorbell with a camera and a little screen. Misty pushed the buzzer and a receptionist answered.

"I'm Misty Divine. Joseph Brown. I'm here for the Sean Fulton will reading." It felt unnatural to refer to Lady Lady as Sean Fulton, and she didn't like it. It pinched and made Lady Lady's death feel all the more real.

The door buzzed loudly and fell slightly ajar.

"Second floor," said the receptionist through the doorbell.

Misty entered the building and pushed the button to call the elevator. She wasn't walking up to the second floor in these heels. As she waited for the lift she watched the video of Baseball Cap on her phone and zoomed in on his face. She had his picture. Crisp and clear as day, a picture of the sharp little man with the scars on his cheek.

Who was he? Why was he following her? Did it mean she was getting close to the truth somehow? Had her investigation unnerved the killer?

Perhaps it was a sign that she should stop poking around, stop asking questions. She could be putting herself in danger, and Miles.

But being followed by Baseball Cap had riled her and, rather than discouraging her from investigating, it had hardened her resolve.

S HE DIDN'T FEEL any anxiety about the law offices, she felt determined—determined not to let Baseball Cap stop her with his intimidation. She also knew that the will reading might well reveal a new suspect, and she wondered whether there would be other drags here, whether Lady Lady had named lots of drags in the will. As the lift door opened, she knew Joe would have been very anxious indeed. This kind of corporate environment was always one in which Joe felt like an impostor, like they didn't belong there or shouldn't be there. But, thankfully, Joe wasn't here. It was Misty's time.

She got out of the lift on the second floor and was greeted by an exceptionally striking man in his fifties. He was a cross between George Clooney and Ross Kemp. Bald, stocky, muscly, a square jaw, deep brown eyes. He introduced himself as Colin McDermott.

"You must be Joseph," said the hunky solicitor.

"Misty, please."

"No problem. If you'd like to follow me to the conference room, you're the last to arrive, so we can get started."

"Great," said Misty.

She wondered again what Lady Lady could have left her. She'd never even mentioned her will, never mind that Misty might be in it. *Full of surprises, weren't you?*

"There are refreshments in the conference room," said Mr. McDermott as he led the way down a narrow corridor that opened into a large office with walls covered in books. In the center of the room was a long wooden conference table surrounded by tall leather chairs with chrome wheels.

There were a few people already there, but no other drag performers. Misty nodded a hello to Mandy, who was sitting near the head of the table.

DI Davies was there. He looked serious, glum almost, like a loser of a man who had failed to catch a cat burglar. Misty knew that he must be under a lot of pressure and, from Misty's perspective at least, he was getting nowhere. Perhaps he was here looking for new leads. *Just like me*, she thought. She loathed him silently from across the room.

Misty poured herself a glass of water from a jug packed with lemon and ice cubes and sat down at the far end of the table, the farthest possible seat from DI Davies.

The room was quiet, calm. As she waited for Mr. McDermott to start talking her mind flashed back to the confrontation with Baseball Cap, and the palms of her hands instantly began sweating. She wiped them on her legs and hoped nobody saw.

"Good morning, everybody," said Mr. McDermott. "Thank you for coming."

He gave a little introductory speech about why they were there, the order of proceedings, and asked if anybody had any questions. Misty had a hundred questions but didn't ask any. Nobody did.

An old woman in the corner of the room sighed heavily. "Let's just get on with it," she said. Misty recognized her as Lady Lady's mother, though they'd never met. She'd seen her photos on articles from the nineties about her public disowning of Lady Lady during the morning television years. She hadn't aged well. She had the face of a woman who'd lived a hard life and smoked too many cigarettes.

"Very well," said dishy McDermott. He started reading a very dry legal document that Misty just about kept up with. It seemed Lady Lady had appointed Mandy as executor of her will. This wasn't a surprise to Misty, as Mandy and Lady Lady had worked together a long time.

Mr. McDermott read a list of duties of the executor, which basically amounted to Mandy being responsible for carrying out Lady Lady's wishes when it came to the division and distribution of her estate.

"And now the bit everyone's been waiting for," said Mr. McDermott. "The disposition of estate."

DI Davies shuffled in his seat and leaned forward on his elbows.

Mr. McDermott read aloud.

"I direct my executor to distribute the estate as follows: all personal possessions, including the residence at 23 Greek Street, to be sold with one hundred percent of the proceeds to Jeanette Fulton for her own use absolutely. Ownership of Tuppy, Mr. Fulton's pet corgi, to also be transferred to Jeanette Fulton."

Lady Lady's elderly mother tutted as though inheriting the dog was the last thing she wanted.

Poor Tuppy, thought Misty.

Mr. McDermott continued. "All business possessions relating to the character Lady Lady, including all costumes, jewelry and memorabilia, to be auctioned with one hundred percent of the proceeds to Terrence Higgins Trust."

What? I'm not inheriting the costumes! Misty felt disheartened, disappointed. She'd been secretly imagining her life with hundreds, maybe thousands, of beautiful custom designs.

Mr. McDermott continued.

"Regarding Mr. Fulton's fifty percent stake of the business registered as Lady's Bar, eighty percent of Mr. Fulton's shares, forty percent of the total shareholding, are to go to Amanda White."

Misty knew Mandy already had a fifty percent stake in the business. *So now she owns ninety percent of Lady's Bar.*

DI Davies shifted in his seat and glared at Mandy. Surely that was a motive for murder.

"The remaining ten percent, registered in Mr. Fulton's name, to go to Joseph Brown."

"Wh-what?" said Misty.

"Mr. Fulton's remaining shares in the business, amounting to ten percent of all shares in Lady's Bar, have been bequeathed to you, Mr. Brown—Misty."

"Wh-what?" said Misty.

Misty made eye contact with Mandy, and Mandy smiled and gave a kind wink across the table.

Her head spun. She couldn't believe what she was hearing. She thought she'd come today to inherit a stash of shoes and dresses, possibly some wigs. She wasn't expecting to inherit anything like money or shares.

"There is a further stipulation from Mr. Fulton," said Mr. McDermott. He read, "It is my wish, with the approval of

Amanda White, that hosting duties at Lady's Bar be taken over by Misty Divine (Joseph Brown), remunerated on par with Lady Lady, with Misty Divine's agreement."

"Wait," said Misty, trying to take it all in. "I've inherited a job?"

"If you want it," said Mandy. "There's no rush to decide."

"Oh for God's sake," said Jeanette Fulton. "Is there anything else for me or are we all done here?"

"There's some paperwork to complete," said Mr. McDermott. He continued by explaining the process of probate: the sale of the assets could take a number of months, so she shouldn't expect any money for a while.

"Is there anyone else?" asked DI Davies, drumming his fingertips on the conference table. "Anyone else named in the will?"

"No," said Mr. McDermott, "that's everything. We'll email you a copy so you have all the necessary documents." He shuffled all his papers into a folder and stood up. "Thank you, all, for coming."

Jeanette Fulton left immediately, not stopping to talk to anybody. The others hung around for a few minutes chatting.

"Congratulations," said Mandy to Misty. "You're a club owner."

"I can't believe it," said Misty. "What does it all mean?"

"Come back to the club with me and we'll talk it all through. Looks like we're business partners now."

Misty wanted to ask Mandy about Baseball Cap. About who he was and what she was up to. How could she be standing here, being so nice and acting so normal, when she had dodgy dealings with the man who followed her this morning?

Misty noticed DI Davies staring at them from across the room. He had a serious look, almost a glare.

Misty realized what it meant.

She and Mandy had inherited Lady's Bar. Misty was the new Lady's Bar host, if she wanted to be. They had both benefited massively from the will. Though Misty hadn't yet processed everything, she knew that what Lady Lady had left her was life-changing. Joe could give up working at the hotel once and for all.

But the inheritance wasn't all good news, and that's why DI Davies was glaring at her.

Misty Divine now had a motive for killing Lady Lady.

20

★★★★★★★★★

ISTY AND MANDY got in the lift, and Misty caught sight of herself in the large mirror on the back wall. She looked beautiful, she thought. The wig with the black streak was still in a perfect state, not a hair out of place.

"How do you feel?" said Mandy, pushing the button for the ground floor.

"Bizarre," said Misty, overwhelmed. "I can't believe it. But how do you feel? You own ninety percent of the club now."

It felt strange, acting as if she didn't know about Mandy's dealings. They were both faking it, and they knew it, but now wasn't the right time to confront her. Not here, in this lift.

"Well, I knew what was coming," said Mandy. "We wrote our wills together. If I'd died first, I'd have left my shares in the same way: forty percent to Lady Lady and ten percent to you."

Misty felt shocked, surprised, pleasantly. "Why me? I wasn't expecting it at all."

"Lady Lady always believed that queer venues should be queer owned. And she thought Lady's Bar should always have a drag performer as the owner. She trusted you to carry on her legacy. You were her protégé, there's nobody else she would have chosen."

Misty was overwhelmed with emotion, with gratitude. She'd admired Lady Lady for years before she met her and had long yearned to follow in her footsteps, to become a big cabaret star just like her. And now her mentor had given her the greatest gift of all from beyond the grave: the chance to take over from her in one of London's most celebrated venues, and not just that, but to own a slice of it.

The lift arrived at the ground floor, and the doors opened just as DI Davies was arriving at the same level. He had taken the stairs, which were probably quicker, but he wasn't wearing six-inch stilettos. Upon seeing him Misty felt a gutful of panic and a wave of guilt about the inheritance.

"Hello again," he said.

"Hello," said Mandy.

"I'm going to need to arrange a time for each of you to come into the station."

Misty felt sick. She knew this meant that she was going to be interrogated about the will, that DI Davies must think she killed Lady Lady to inherit the bar. To fast-track her way to the top. *Maybe he thinks Mandy and I did it together.* She thought about what it must look like. Mandy having the argument with Lady Lady, Misty finding the body—between the two of them, they had the easiest access to the dressing room, and they were both seen going there on the night of the murder. And now, there was motive. A motive so strong that there was no doubt they must be the police's new prime suspects.

"Okay," said Mandy with a shake in her voice, surely having exactly the same thoughts as Misty.

"I'll call you both this morning to arrange a time," said DI Davies.

Misty didn't say anything. There was strength in silence, and she didn't want to say the wrong thing. Saying nothing was better.

DI Davies left through the door of the building out onto Rupert Street, and Misty and Mandy stood alone in the solicitor's foyer.

"He thinks one of us did it," said Mandy quietly.

"I know." It had been bad enough when her friends were gossiping that she was the murderer, but now she was most definitely in the sights of the Metropolitan Police. Perhaps DI Davies was suspecting that she was the Catburglar too. At the very least he thought she might be a poisoner. Her drag felt hot and her corset tight, restrictive, like she was trapped in it.

The only way out of this is to find out who really did it, she thought.

M ISTY TOLD MANDY that she needed to call Miles. She decided to go for a coffee on her own and meet Mandy at the club afterward. She walked down Old Compton Street and realized how safe she felt here. There wasn't another street in the world where she felt more at ease in drag. The tightly packed terraced buildings and wonky shop fronts always felt like home. Old Compton Street had everything: bars, restaurants, a West End theater . . . To Misty it was heaven. She turned into a little coffee shop and ordered herself an espresso. Then she sat at a table in the corner and waited for a waiter in a green T-shirt to bring her the coffee.

"Love your outfit," he said as he placed down the tiny coffee cup.

"Thanks so much," said Misty, smiling.

There was so much to think about with this inheritance, so many practicalities. Inheriting the hosting duties probably meant that Misty could leave Joe's job at the hotel without any financial worry. Could they really do it though? Would Joe be able to leave behind the security of the office they'd gotten so used to? The hosting job would be well paid. And that was before the ten percent stake in Lady's Bar.

Then she thought about Mandy. About following her through Soho and watching her take out cash with card after card. About Mandy being in cahoots with someone who had followed her just that morning. And now Mandy was her business partner. Her co-owner. Her boss? Perhaps Lady's Bar wasn't as financially secure as it had always seemed from the outside. Is that why Lady Lady was killed? Misty wondered whether she was inheriting a poisoned chalice.

If Lady Lady had been murdered because of something going on at the bar, Misty needed to know what it was, and fast. Because not only was she now the police's prime suspect, she was also possibly in danger.

She sipped her coffee. It was scalding hot and bitter. Not worth the three pounds she'd paid for it.

Misty pulled out her phone and called Miles.

"I didn't get the costumes," she said. "She left me ten percent of the club and her hosting job."

"What? Ten percent of Lady's Bar? And hosting there, every night? Joe, that's incredible! It's what you always dreamed of."

"Well, it is and it isn't."

"What do you mean? You're worried about Mandy and what-ever she's up to?"

Misty sighed. What if she was completely overthinking this? "What if this is why Lady Lady was killed?" she said. "Because of something at the club, with that guy in the baseball cap. And now I'm taking her place. With him following me this morning, I feel like I could be in real danger, Miles."

"You shouldn't panic or jump to conclusions, but just be care-ful with this investigating you're doing. Maybe it's time to let the police handle it."

Misty hummed noncommittally, knowing full well that she wouldn't be stopping her investigation, especially not now.

"What happens next?" asked Miles. "Do you have another meeting with the solicitor to talk about the ten percent? Or would you want to sell it?"

Misty wondered. It would certainly be nice to have some money. But she knew Lady Lady wanted her to carry on her legacy: the drag queen with her own bar in Soho. She'd trusted her with it over everyone else. Misty didn't think she could give that up. "I don't think I want to sell it, but I don't know. I need time to see how it's all going to work. And I need to talk to Mandy. I've got a meeting with her after this so she can talk me through everything. She inherited the rest."

"Wow, so she's done well out of it."

"Well, that's the other problem, you see. I think the police think I might have done the murder. It looks pretty bad for me. If I were the police I'd be suspicious. They want me and Mandy to go in to talk to them at the station. They're calling me today to set up an appointment."

"You should go with a lawyer," said Miles, his voice serious.

"What?"

"To the police station. You should make sure you have a lawyer with you."

"But won't that just make me look guilty? Like I've done something wrong? Surely I can just go in and tell them the truth."

The only lawyer Misty knew was Colin McDermott, the man she'd just met.

"In an ideal world," replied Miles, "you could just tell them the truth, but if they think you're a suspect you should have someone with you who can give you advice."

Eventually Misty agreed. They discussed it at length, and Misty decided that she would try to engage Mr. McDermott to help her. If Lady Lady trusted him, he must be good. And he had seemed nice. And he was a total ride.

M ISTY LEFT THE coffee shop and walked a few doors along Old Compton Street to the entrance of Lady's Bar, the door she'd walked through for years as just a performer. She took a good look around before going inside to make sure nobody was following her, that there were no baseball caps in sight.

I can't believe I own part of this, she thought as she descended the staircase to the underground auditorium. *This is mine.*

Had it really only been five days since she'd last performed here? Since Lady Lady's death on her dressing room floor? It felt like a lifetime, and like Misty's life might have changed forever in those five days.

As she arrived in the bar she looked around at the empty tables and chairs and wondered how many thousands of people had been entertained here over the years. How many had laughed and sung along and stood to applaud at the end of a show. How many had admired Lady Lady as much as Misty did.

This is where she felt closest to Lady Lady. The bar had already felt like home, but now even more so.

Mandy appeared from the dressing room corridor.

"Misty! My new business partner!"

"Mandy, it still hasn't sunk in."

"It will probably be a while before it does. Here, let me fix us a glass of fizz each. We can toast to Lady's Bar's new co-owner."

Mandy bustled behind the bar and plucked a bottle of champagne from the fridge. Misty knew it was the most expensive one they stocked. She took a seat on a barstool as Mandy popped open the sparkles. She filled two crystal flutes and handed one to Misty. She took it hesitantly, thinking about the poison that killed Lady Lady.

"To Misty," said Mandy, holding up her glass.

"To Lady Lady," said Misty.

"To Lady Lady."

They clinked their glasses together, and Misty waited to see Mandy take a sip of the drink before she drank any, just in case.

"There's so much to talk about," said Mandy. "But I suppose the first thing is, do you want it? Do you want the hosting job, the club?"

"Of course!" said Misty, but feeling like she wasn't sure. "It's a dream job. I suppose I need to know more about it, but in theory it's amazing." She didn't voice the dark part—the part that was telling her there was danger here.

"Hurrah!" Mandy smiled. "Well, I can talk you through it a bit if you like. The emails can wait."

"I'd like that," said Misty, thinking that if she could get Mandy talking about how the club operated, it might lead naturally to her asking about the money and Baseball Cap.

"What do you want to know?"

"Well, how does it work? What exactly did Lady Lady do here?"

"The hosting job has two parts, really: booking all the acts and hosting the show. It's super fun because you get to meet all the performers, give a platform to new and upcoming artists, etcetera. So it's some office work and some performing work. Once Lady Lady booked an act she passed their details over to me, and I managed the rest—the backing tracks, the invoices, that kind of thing. It's a full-time job and long, late hours."

"It sounds fantastic. And then, without being crude, I wondered how the money worked. Did she take a salary?"

"She did, and you'd take the same, not a penny less. The hosting fee is five hundred pounds per show, plus a costume and wig budget."

Misty quickly did the math. That many bookings was about four times what she earned a month at the hotel—and guaranteed nightly shows! The club must have been doing very well indeed to be paying Lady Lady such a high salary.

"And you get the dressing room, if you want it, given everything that happened in there."

"Wow," said Misty, trying to push away thoughts of Lady Lady's demise, trying to take the rest of it in.

Her own dressing room. Her own club. Her own shows with lineups that she would get to pick from the very best of London drag. It really sounded like a dream come true, but for Misty it was tainted with murder and suspicion and unanswered questions.

"I manage all the business side—the bar, the staffing, the accounting, and all that. That's why me and Lady Lady worked so well together. I love doing the admin side and she loved doing the creative side. It was a perfect match."

Misty thought about Miles, about how often he had encouraged her to leave the hotel. She thought about Joe and their endless days of paperwork there. This was what they'd been waiting for, surely. Opportunities like this just didn't come up very often. She was excited but feeling stage fright. Could she really replace Lady Lady in her own club? Did she really know enough about drag, enough about the drag scene, to take on such a position? Was it even a good idea at all given everything that was going on?

"Do you really think I can do it?" she asked Mandy.

"We wouldn't have done this if we didn't, Misty. Lady Lady loved you and so do I. We're family."

Misty supposed they were.

A writhing knot formed in her intestines. Guilt. Guilt about following Mandy, about suspecting her of murder when she was being so nice to her.

But she still could have done it. You could be sitting here sipping champagne with your new business partner, who is currently getting away with killing her last business partner.

"And what about the ownership side? Is there much to do on that front?"

"No. It's pretty straightforward and I take care of it as part of my admin roles. You'll get ten percent of the profits, which are healthy."

"So there aren't any . . . problems I should be aware of, on the financial side?" asked Misty, thinking about Mandy frantically withdrawing cash to give to Baseball Cap in the street.

"Problems? No, everything's in order. I'm sure Mr. McDermott will be in touch with you to go through everything."

"Yes, I expect so."

Ask her, ask her about the money, willed the chunk of her brain that couldn't let go of the mystery.

It's time.

Misty took a deep breath, steadying herself to admit that she'd followed Mandy and witnessed her dodgy deal.

"Mandy, the other day, when I came to get my drag bag—"

Misty's phone rang loudly in her handbag. A mobile number she didn't recognize.

Shit. DI Davies, she guessed.

"Sorry, Mandy, hold that thought." Then, answering the phone, "Hello?"

"This is Detective Inspector Davies." He got straight to the point. "I was hoping you could come to Charing Cross Police Station at three p.m. this afternoon."

"Erm, yes, that should be fine. I'll need to check with my solicitor."

"Solicitor?" said DI Davies. "Interesting that you think you need one. Please check with your solicitor and get back to me as soon as possible. We'd very much like to talk to you *today*."

He hung up, and Misty put her phone back in her bag, sealing shut the clasp with a satisfying click. Now she was starting to feel a little scared.

Mandy swallowed a gulp of champagne and immediately her own phone started ringing. She answered it and walked away from the bar, setting up her own appointment to be grilled by DI Davies.

While Mandy was on the phone, Misty looked up Colin McDermott's phone number from her call history and rang him. His voice was soothing, the auditory equivalent of swallowing a mouthful of yogurt. He explained to Misty that while his specialty was mainly family law, he would be happy to help her through the police interview. His fee was eyewatering, but with Misty's new job hopefully about to quadruple her income, she decided she could afford it. She also didn't know anyone else she could ask. They agreed to meet at 2:30 p.m. in a pub around the corner from Charing Cross Police Station. Mr. McDermott wanted to hear Misty's side of the story.

"Bastard," said Mandy as she came back to the bar. "DI Davies wants me to go in now, but I've got an errand to run first. I'm gonna have to dash."

Misty had hoped she could bring the conversation back to where they were before, with her about to tell Mandy that she knew about the dodgy deal in the alley, but Mandy was gathering up her stuff, ready to leave.

"Are you sure you have to go now, Mandy?" Misty said. "I really need to talk to you."

"Sorry, love, gotta go. Now listen," she said in a hurry. "I have to nip out for a quick meeting before this police interview. Shit. Here's a copy of the keys in case you go out. Feel free to make yourself at home in the dressing room and the office. We can talk through everything else later. What a fucking day, and it isn't even lunchtime!"

She handed Misty a key ring with three keys on it.

"The big two are for the front door, and the little one's for the corridor with the dressing rooms and office."

Misty took the keys and looked at them in the palm of her hand.

"You're really . . . you're really just giving me the keys."

"Well, what did you expect? You own ten percent of the place and you work here now. Hopefully." She grinned and crossed her fingers. "I just have to grab something from the office, and then I'll be out of here."

"Who are you meeting?" asked Misty, wondering where Mandy was going.

"Oh, nobody important. Just a little business to finish off."

She looked shifty. Her eyes darted to the office door and she nibbled on the corner of her lip. Misty knew instantly that Mandy was meeting Baseball Cap.

Mandy placed her champagne flute in the bar's sink and headed to the office. Misty stood and walked into the center of the auditorium. She looked up at the stage and felt filled with a mixture of excitement and dread. She'd never had an opportunity like this before, and likely never would again. But before she gave up the security of the hotel, she would want to know that everything was aboveboard at Lady's Bar, and she needed to know what Mandy and Lady Lady were involved in. She looked down the corridor and saw Mandy in the office. She was standing by the open filing cabinet stuffing a brown envelope into her handbag.

Full of cash no doubt. To give to a guy in a baseball cap in the street.

It was then Misty decided she would follow Mandy for a second time.

I want to see where you're going. I need to know what you're up to, once and for all.

21

****

MISTY WAITED AT the bottom of the stairs until she heard Mandy shut the door behind her and step out onto Old Compton Street. As soon as the door clicked closed Misty ran up the staircase two stairs at a time with her handbag in one hand and the bunch of Lady's Bar keys in the other.

When she reached the top her heart was already racing.

This is crazy. Following people. Following Mandy.

But was it crazy? Not really, she thought. Mandy was involved in something, surely illegal, and Misty needed to know what it was, preferably before she was interrogated by DI Davies. And seeing as Mandy wasn't sticking around to answer questions, following her now was Misty's best shot. Plus, she wanted another look at the bastard who'd tried to intimidate her this morning.

She rushed out the door into the street and fumbled with the keys to lock up. The locks were heavy and stiff, and each needed both her hands to turn the key. She glanced up Old Compton Street, looking for Mandy, and spotted her bobbed hair bouncing up toward Cambridge Circus. Once the door was locked Misty headed on up after her.

This is ridiculous. I'm in full drag—I couldn't be any more obvious.

But she carried on regardless, keeping just enough people between her and Mandy so that she could duck for cover should Mandy turn around unexpectedly. Thankfully she progressed forward without so much as a glimpse behind her. Misty held back as Mandy waited at the Cambridge Circus pedestrian crossing, lingering under the canopies of the grand Palace Theatre until Mandy started across the street.

Passersby were looking at her, a group of tourists pointed, and one took a photo of her without asking. The damn black streak in the front of this giant wig. It might as well have been a big arrow, with a sign saying, DRAG QUEEN HERE. EVERYBODY LOOK NOW.

She followed Mandy across the street and up Shaftesbury Avenue, past the theater ticket booths by Neal's Yard. In this part of London, just on the edges of Soho, Misty could always imagine what London past might have looked like: old wonky buildings and narrow winding streets.

Mandy had the strongest motive for the murder. That's what Misty thought as she followed her up toward Holborn station. She'd inherited an extra forty percent of the bar, and she obviously knew the content of the will before it was read. And then there was the argument in the dressing room.

We are all out of options now . . . Lady Lady had said.

We'll all end up regretting this, Mandy had snapped. *Mark my words . . .*

What were they talking about? Surely about this. Running around London with envelopes of cash. Whatever Lady Lady and Mandy were up to, they had surely been desperate to involve themselves in something like this. Or greedy.

Mandy turned into a big hotel. It was the kind of place celebrities might stay at after awards ceremonies. Fancy furniture was well maintained by fancy staff in smart tweed uniforms. To Misty it looked stuffy, restrictive, the type of hotel where you wouldn't want to make a cup of tea for fear of dirtying a pristine cup. Misty preferred a Travelodge.

She stood by the edge of a large window that opened onto a plush lounge and watched through the glass as Mandy went in and sat down at a table with none other than the bastard who had followed Misty that morning!

This time Misty was able to get a better look at him. He was thin but strong looking. His cheekbones were high on his face and made his eyes look small underneath his brow. The three little scars on his cheek shone like domino dots.

Mandy handed him the envelope. They had an animated but hushed conversation that Misty wished she could hear. The man tucked the envelope into his tracksuit top, and Mandy got up again, ready to leave.

Misty ducked into a narrow doorway and pressed herself flat, hoping to goodness that Mandy didn't see her on the way out. What would she say? She'd simply have to come clean, that's all there was to it.

But there was no need. Mandy exited the hotel and walked straight past Misty's doorway hiding place without so much as looking up in her direction. Phew.

What to do now? she wondered.

She wanted to know more about the mysterious man and decided the best course of action would be to give up following

Mandy and to follow him instead, only this time not to get caught. Mandy was going straight to the police station anyway, that's what she'd said.

Yes, she would follow the man in the cap. Misty looked up the street toward Soho and saw that Mandy was a safe distance away. She stepped out of the doorway and went back to the hotel window, peering round to see what the man with the envelope was doing.

He was getting up from the table to leave, talking hurriedly into a mobile phone pressed against his ear. He was heading for the door. A couple of businesspeople having a meeting noticed Misty, and one of them pointed, the other turning to look. Being the drag queen staring through the window was clearly not as discreet as Misty would have liked. She pulled back and stepped back into the doorway, waiting for the man to exit.

"I'm on my way now. I'll be there in twenty," he said into the phone as he walked out of the hotel.

He walked straight past the doorman and crossed the street, pointing a set of car keys at a BMW parked on double yellow lines. The lights flashed on with a beeping sound.

Shit, shit. I'm going to lose him.

The man headed to the driver's door, got into the car, and sat behind the steering wheel. Misty looked up the street and saw a black taxi approaching, its orange light glowing to indicate it was available.

Thank you.

She stepped quickly to the edge of the pavement and stuck her arm out to signal to the driver. He pulled over right next to her, and she clambered into the back.

"This is going to sound so stupid," she said to the driver, "but I need you to follow that car."

The driver laughed. "Ha! It's been a while since I done one of these. Livens the day up, I suppose."

He performed what appeared to Misty to be an illegal U-turn and slipped into the moving traffic, two cars behind the BMW.

"So, what you all dressed up for? You doing a show or something?"

"Yes," Misty lied. It was easier to say yes than to explain that she'd got dressed up like this to go to a will reading for her murdered drag mother.

"Hey," said the driver, spotting an opportunity to make conversation. "There was that drag queen murdered last week, wasn't there? Terrible business."

Misty nodded. *Terrible business indeed*, she thought.

"We get a lot of drag queens in the cabs, you know. Always have. I love it. Bloody love it. I had that one off the telly once. She won that show, the *Drag Race*. Then she did the ice-skating thing. Whatsername? The Vivienne. I had her in the car once. Bloody lovely."

Misty's eyes were fixed on the car ahead. They were heading east through Farringdon. Misty was excited. Her heart was pounding. This was a wild thing to be doing.

It's a dangerous thing to be doing, that's what Miles would have said.

Miles.

She should send Miles her location, just in case it was dangerous. She whipped out her phone and opened WhatsApp, enabling the location function for the next twenty-four hours. She sent him a text message.

Miles, don't be mad, but I'm currently in
a taxi following the man from earlier.
I've shared my location with you so you
can see where I'm going. I'll keep you
updated. I'm safe.

Three little dots appeared on the screen, indicating that
Miles was replying right away.

Joe, this sounds like a bad idea.

"Joe?" He's serious.

Her phone started ringing. Miles was calling. She picked up
and held the phone to her ear.

"Joe, I'm not sure you should be doing this." His voice was
worried and a bit shaky, and he was whispering like he didn't
want his colleagues to hear.

"I'm fine, Miles, I'm in a taxi—we're following at a distance.
I just want to see where he goes."

Miles sighed. "Well, don't do anything silly. Stay in the car."

"Yes, yes. You can see my location on WhatsApp, right?"

"Yeah, I'm looking at it now."

"Great. Well, you'll see, I'm just going to find out where this
guy is going next, and then I have to head back to Soho for the
interview with DI Davies."

Miles sighed. "Keep your phone on you and stay in the car. I
mean it."

"I will," said Misty.

She hung up as the car headed out of Central London, driv-
ing east.

When they got to Bethnal Green and turned onto Roman

Road, Misty realized with a jolt where they were going. She felt sick. Surely not.

The BMW took a couple of turns through residential streets and stopped outside The Plough, Auntie Susan's pub.

Why was Mandy giving envelopes of cash to Lady Lady's worst enemy? Surely Lady Lady wouldn't have agreed to this. Or maybe she had. Maybe that was the problem.

What the actual fuck?

We are all out of options now, Lady Lady had said.

THE PLOUGH WAS a wreck of a building, one that should have been razed to the ground and redeveloped years ago. It was a miracle that it was still standing in such a state. The paint was peeling off the walls, half the windows had been smashed and were boarded up with plasterboard, covered in flyers and stickers and Sharpied graffiti. Outside, two drunk drag queens, who couldn't have been a day over nineteen, tottered on heels that the venue did not deserve. They were raucous—laughing, pointing, causing a general scene on a street that was otherwise lonely and homely. The door to the pub swung open and Auntie Susan stepped out. A traditional drag queen, she was wearing a bright red wig, teased and curled to perfection, and a tight white Lycra dress. Through it you could see her black underwear. She was tall and fearsome.

"Get back inside and stop making a fuss!" she shouted at the young drag queens. They straightened themselves up, chastened. Misty thought that in that moment Auntie Susan looked like a Victorian farmer's wife calling in the dogs. "Go on, get inside," she said.

The young drag queens scattered past her and piled through the doors back into the rotten-looking pub.

"Stop here," Misty said to the driver. The driver did as she asked and pulled over.

"Boyfriend of yours, is he?" he asked as they watched the man in the tracksuit get out of the BMW and cross the street to meet Auntie Susan.

"Something like that," replied Misty, watching intently.

The man unzipped the top of his tracksuit and handed Auntie Susan the envelope that Mandy had delivered from the bar. She opened it and flicked through a stack of notes, counting it.

What is going on here? Misty wondered.

Baseball Cap and Auntie Susan went inside the pub, and Misty took a breath of relief. She hadn't been spotted, and she'd successfully found out something new for the investigation.

Her phone buzzed. Miles.

You're at THE PLOUGH?!

Yes! The money from the bar.
It's going to Auntie Susan!

Get out of there before they see you.

22

✦✦✦✦✦✦✦✦✦

ISTY THANKED THE driver profusely and gave him a ten-pound tip before getting out of the cab on Old Compton Street. Home again. She took a deep breath and walked to Poppies, the fish-and-chip shop. She bought a cone of chips and stood on the pavement eating them. They were hot and greasy, and their bellies were fluffy potato clouds that melted on her tongue.

She wondered what to do about Mandy and the money. Maybe she should ask Mr. McDermott about it. He might even know what was going on.

She finished her chips and dumped the cone in a bin, wiping her fingers on an oily napkin that shredded upon contact. Then she crossed the street and walked toward Charing Cross Police Station, to the bar where she was meeting Mr. McDermott.

She arrived at the pub early and ordered herself a Red Bull—the taurine and caffeine might help her think. She sat down at a table in the middle of the pub and waited.

There was a group of young office workers at the bar, probably on the tail end of their lunch break. They looked at Misty with unsure eyes, and one of them shouted, "Oi oi, what's this then?"

"What does it look like?" said Misty in return.

"What are you meant to be?" he said.

Misty sighed and ignored him, popping in her headphones until Mr. McDermott arrived.

He was bang on time, at 2:30 p.m., and ordered a sparkling water at the bar before joining Misty at her table. He smelled fresh, of newly laundered clothes and eau de toilette.

"Twice in one day, Miss Divine, what a pleasure," he said as he pulled up a chair.

"Thank you for seeing me," said Misty.

"So, let's start at the beginning. Tell me why the police want to see you."

"I think they think I'm a suspect," said Misty.

"And why would they think that?" asked Mr. McDermott. "Because of the inheritance?"

"Yes, that, but also I was the one to find the body."

She talked him through what had happened on Wednesday night, telling him everything that she'd told the police. Going up the corridor to check on Lady Lady, overhearing the argument, then finding the body, and Moneypenny calling the ambulance.

Should I tell him about Mandy and the money? she wondered.

No, she thought, *not yet. Nobody knows that I followed Mandy except Miles, and Miles isn't going to tell anybody.* Misty wanted to speak to Mandy before she revealed anything to the authorities.

"Ah," said Mr. McDermott, "so you were in fact the only person who went up the corridor to Lady Lady's dressing room that night?"

"Well, I went there, and I saw Mandy go there too. So, either

Mandy or somebody else must have taken the chocolates, because it definitely wasn't me."

"Of course. But to summarize, you were the last one to see her alive and the last one to go to the dressing room. Then you inherited her job hosting at the bar and a ten percent stake in the business."

"It looks bad for me, doesn't it?" She knew that it did.

"We're not dealing with what it looks like, we're only dealing with the facts. But seeing it through the police's eyes, you had both motive and opportunity. It's not a surprise to me that they want to question you."

Shit.

They left the pub and took the short walk together to the police station. Misty's heart was racing and her palms were drenched. She hoped she wouldn't have to shake anyone's hand.

"Mr. McDermott," Misty said as they strolled, "how long have you been Lady Lady's solicitor?"

"Twenty years," he replied, "since she opened Lady's Bar. I was a young graduate then, but Lady Lady trusted me, and we've been friends and colleagues ever since."

"Anything I ask you is confidential, right?"

"Of course," he replied.

"Well, is there something going on at Lady's Bar? Anything out of the ordinary? Anything weird with money, maybe?"

"If you're worried about your ownership stake, you shouldn't be. I'm happy to talk through everything with you at the office sometime, but as far as I've seen, everything at Lady's Bar is aboveboard. It's one of Soho's most successful independent businesses."

"Okay," said Misty. "Thanks."

Mr. McDermott stopped walking. "Why do you ask? Is there something I should know?"

Tell him, said Miles's voice inside her head.

"No, nothing," she said. "I just want to be sure I know what I'm getting involved in, that's all. I'd appreciate that meeting, like you suggest."

They arrived at the reception of Charing Cross Police Station at 2:57 p.m., according to a red LED clock on the wall.

"Joseph Brown to see Detective Inspector Davies," said Mr. McDermott to the officer behind the desk.

The desk officer made a quick phone call and asked Misty and Mr. McDermott to sit and wait on some plastic-film-covered seats that looked revolting. Mr. McDermott sat, but Misty stayed standing, preferring to remain on her heels than press her body and her outfit into one of the filthy chairs. She felt sick. She knew she was about to be treated like a suspect, like a murderer, and it sat very uncomfortably with her.

They didn't wait for long, as DI Davies entered the reception area almost immediately. "This way, please," he said. No greeting.

Misty felt stressed and a little nauseous. They followed DI Davies through a series of plain white corridors until they arrived at a door with a sign on the front that said, ROOM 4.

DI Davies unlocked the room with a swipe card and they all stepped inside. One wall, the wall adjacent to the table they were to sit around, was a mirror. Misty couldn't help laughing. "I didn't think interview rooms really had these mirrors," she said to everyone, to no one. "I thought it was just for TV."

On *Criminal Minds* there would be profilers behind that mirror, telling the interviewers what to ask and directing the interrogation. Misty doubted very much that the Metropolitan Police had the time or resources for such extravagances.

"Please, Mr. Brown, sit down."

Mr. Brown. Dressed like this!

Misty sat down next to Mr. McDermott, and DI Davies sat opposite. The door reopened and DS Hughes arrived, carrying four bottles of mineral water. Misty felt relieved to see her.

"Love the hair," said DS Hughes with a smile, receiving a glare from DI Davies in return.

"Thank you," said Misty.

"Can I get anyone a tea or coffee before we start?" she asked.

Is this a good-cop-bad-cop act? Or are they really like this?

Nobody wanted a tea or a coffee. DS Hughes distributed the water bottles around the table, and DI Davies said, "Let's begin."

He started a recording by stating the time and date and who was present in the room. He explained that Misty was there voluntarily, helping them with their inquiries, but stressed that she was not under arrest. The implication, Misty thought, was that if she wasn't there voluntarily, she'd be there in handcuffs.

"Talk us through what happened on Wednesday night, starting from the beginning of the night when you arrived at Lady's Bar."

"I must object, DI Davies," interrupted Mr. McDermott. "My client has already given two detailed statements about the events of Wednesday night."

DI Davies moved on. "Mr. Brown, why did you leave the dressing room to go to see Mr. Fulton after the show?"

"I was worried that she wasn't okay. She'd seemed nervy onstage and normally she didn't."

"By 'she' you are referring to Mr. Fulton?" replied DI Davies.

"Yes, Lady Lady seemed a bit nervous, that's all. So I went to her dressing room to see how she was."

"And *you* say, when you got there you overheard an argument between Mandy White and Sean Fulton? And then you went back to the main dressing room. Is that right?"

"Yes. I got to the door, heard the argument, and then Mandy opened the door and saw me. She asked if I'd been listening and I said I hadn't."

"Had you been listening? Could you hear what they were saying?"

"Not really," she lied. "Just the sound of a heated conversation."

"Did you give anything to Lady Lady?"

"No."

"Did you give Lady Lady the chocolates?"

"No."

"I've got six witnesses who saw you visit that dressing room moments before Lady Lady reappeared with the chocolates."

"Yes, but I didn't do it. Even Lady Lady said she didn't know who the chocolates were from. You can ask the others."

DI Davies folded his arms and opened a folder on the table in front of him. It was stuffed full with papers. Misty remembered seeing an episode of *Criminal Minds* where one of the agents padded a file like this with fake paperwork to make it look like they had more evidence than they did. It was an intimidation technique, and Misty wasn't falling for it.

"How often do you take the number fourteen bus?" asked DI Davies.

Misty was taken aback. It wasn't a question she had anticipated. "Erm, I don't know. How often does anyone take the number fourteen bus? Not often, I suppose."

"How often is 'not often'? Once a week, once a month?"

"Maybe once a month. Less, probably."

"DI Davies, may I ask what relevance this line of questioning has?" said Mr. McDermott.

"You may not," replied DI Davies curtly. "Mr. Brown, Mr. Fulton was wearing a stolen dress when he died. What do you know about that dress?"

"I only know what I've seen in the news about it. It was stolen by the Kensington Catburglar. It used to belong to Judy Garland, and she wore it to some red carpet gig in the fifties. I've already told you everything I know about it, which is nothing at all! And honestly, it feels like you're more interested in her dress than you are in her murder."

There was a pause in the room, a silence while DS Hughes scribbled something on a notepad.

DI Davies spoke again. "Did you visit Mrs. Anna Bowman at the Dress Collector in South Kensington this weekend?"

"Erm, yes." *Shit. Shit.*

"Why did you do that?"

"I wanted to know more about the dress, seeing as you'd asked me so many questions about it. I was trying to figure out where Lady Lady would have got it from. I thought if I talked to Mrs. Bowman it might be useful."

"I see," said DI Davies. "Mrs. Bowman tells us that you talked about the value of the dress and pried about who her clients are."

Misty didn't like this at all but wouldn't let them see it.

"I didn't pry," she said confidently. "I asked her whether Lady Lady had inquired about the dress, and she said she hadn't. Mrs. Bowman *volunteered* that the dress is now worth more money because of the murder. I certainly didn't ask her that."

"Hmm," said DI Davies. "You are aware how serious an offense intimidating witnesses is . . ."

"I wasn't intimidating her. I was just trying to figure out where Lady Lady got the dress. This is so stupid! I haven't done anything wrong. I haven't broken any laws." Misty dreaded to think how much trouble she'd be in if DI Davies also knew about her conversations with Jan, Tess, Plimberley, Moneypenny, Amour, and Len. She'd been "intimidating" witnesses all over town.

Misty opened her bottle of mineral water and enjoyed the sound of the seal snapping loose. She took a sip of water. She was in deep shit now, she knew it.

"Did you know the contents of Mr. Fulton's will before you attended the will reading this morning?"

"I did not," replied Misty.

"But you realize how this looks, right?" said DS Hughes softly. Good copping.

"Yes, I realize how it looks, but that's not how it is. You're wasting your time here when the real killer is still out there. I loved Lady Lady, she was my mentor. I would never do anything to hurt her!" said Misty. She was panicking a little now; her scalp was sweating beneath her wig.

"You were the only person to visit the dressing room, you were a beneficiary in the will—" said DI Davies.

"I wasn't the only person to visit the dressing room," interrupted Misty. "Mandy visited the dressing room as well."

"Ah yes, Mandy White, the *other* beneficiary. Speaking of Mandy White, I'd like to show you a video."

A video?

"Okay," said Misty, looking at Mr. McDermott for reassurance. None was provided.

DI Davies took out an iPad and tapped on the screen before turning it around to face to Misty and Mr. McDermott. The screen showed a shot of Lady's Bar, the bar itself, from a security camera above the till.

Misty watched as, onscreen, Mandy pulled a bottle of champagne from the fridge and popped it open. She poured it into two crystal flutes. It was a video taken this afternoon.

Oh my God.

"How did you get this?" said Mr. McDermott. "I hope you have a warrant for this."

"Is this you, Joseph Brown, raising a champagne toast with the other primary beneficiary of Mr. Fulton's will?"

"It's not what it looks like," started Misty. "This is a total waste of time! You should be out there looking for the *real* killer, not sitting here with me."

"This interview is over," said Mr. McDermott. "Unless you have grounds to arrest my client, we're stopping it here."

"Actually we're not. Because from here we're going to Mr. Brown's residence. We have a warrant to search the address." DI Davies handed a piece of paper from his folder to Mr. McDermott.

"You want to search my flat?" gasped Misty. She felt nauseous, horrified that they were going to search her home, her lovely home with lovely Miles. She was shocked that this is how things were turning out, that she was now the prime suspect, that everyone thought she killed her friend and mentor. She could see how the evidence was pointing in her direction. But she didn't do it. How was she going to get out of this?

They left Charing Cross Police Station in a police car. Misty and Mr. McDermott sat in the back in silence, and DI Davies and DS Hughes sat in the front. There were two more police vehicles following, including a forensics van.

Misty felt sweaty and, for the first time that day, wished she wasn't in drag. Miles would still be at work, and it looked like a visit to Den at the hotel was now out of the question. She felt frustrated. Annoyed that DI Davies kept getting in her way, wasting her time, wasting his own time, when what Misty really needed was to speak to Mandy and Den again.

"Can I please call my boyfriend?" Misty asked.

"When we get there," said DI Davies.

He was obviously worried that letting Miles know about the search might lead to him hiding or getting rid of evidence in the murder investigation. Perhaps he imagined Miles bent over the toilet flushing poisoned chocolates away so nobody would find them. The thought of it made Misty feel amused, though she knew there were no chocolates to be flushed away. Whatever it was the police were looking for, they wouldn't find it.

They arrived at Miles and Misty's flat near Russell Square and made their way up to the front door. Misty led the way with Hughes and Davies, and Mr. McDermott and uniformed officers followed behind.

When they got into the apartment, DI Davies allowed Misty to call Miles.

"The police are at the flat," she told him. "They've got a warrant to do a search."

Miles said he'd be there in five minutes, and five minutes later, there he was, his work abandoned and left behind in the office.

"Are you okay?" he asked her, stepping into the living room.

"Please don't touch anything," said DI Davies plainly.

"I'm not touching anything," snapped Miles. "This is ridiculous. What right do you have to search our flat?"

"We have every right," said DI Davies, before walking away to join officers searching the kitchen.

"I'm so sorry," Misty said to Miles quietly. "You had your meetings. Your big pitch."

"You don't need to be sorry," he replied. "This isn't your fault."

But she felt like it really was her fault.

They searched the apartment for four hours.

They went through everything, every drawer, every cupboard, Misty's makeup case. They slipped Joe's laptop and iPad into plastic sleeves and took them away for forensic analysis, saying they could have them back later. They seemed to pay extra special attention to the sinks, swabbing and testing, even unscrewing the drain pipes and swabbing the insides. DS Hughes explained that they were looking for traces of the poison that had killed Lady Lady.

Misty and Miles sat on the sofa waiting for them to leave.

"You can probably take the wig off," Miles said.

"Not a chance," Misty replied. "Not until they've left."

She wouldn't be in half drag in front of anyone, no matter who they were.

DI Davies looked stressed. He paced from room to room, checking on progress, but to no avail. Misty thought he looked like his little bigoted head might explode.

EVENTUALLY, AT 8:30 p.m., an officer in the kitchen called out for DI Davies, who hurried in. Misty perched on the edge of the sofa, still in her fabulous black-and-silver suit, and craned her neck to try to hear what they were saying in the kitchen.

"Photographer!" called Davies into the flat. "We need the photographer here."

What on earth . . . ?

The crime scene photographer hurried out of the bedroom, where she'd been doing God knows what, and Misty heard camera clicks and quiet discussion from DI Davies and DS Hughes.

"Is everything all right in there, Detective?" called Mr. McDermott from the armchair.

He had kindly rearranged a meeting so that he could stay for the entire search, and Misty found his presence comforting. Like having a nice dad in the room.

DI Davies and DS Hughes emerged from the kitchen, serious looks on their faces.

"What is it?" asked Miles.

Misty looked at DS Hughes's hands and saw she was holding a transparent plastic evidence bag. Inside it was a red chocolate box with a black bow, identical to the one Lady Lady had been given on the night she was killed.

"Joseph Brown," said DI Davies, "you are under arrest for the murder of Sean Fulton."

23

****

D ON'T SAY A word," instructed Mr. McDermott, and then to
Miles, "Either of you."

"You'll both be coming with us to the station," said DI
Davies.

Misty looked at Mr. McDermott, alarmed. "I've never seen
that box before," she said.

"I told you, don't say a word. Miles, I'll arrange for a colleague to meet you at the station."

Miles nodded calmly, but Misty could tell from the tension
in his jawline that he was just as worried as her. He reached out
and squeezed her hand.

T HE RIDE TO the police station felt lonely. The police had separated Misty and Miles and put them in different cars to travel
back to Charing Cross, and the imposed silence was difficult.

Misty felt awful for Miles, responsible for him being taken

away from home in a police car, for taking him away from his big pitch at work. What would his mother think? What would his work say? Misty hated everything that was happening. She knew one thing—she wasn't a murderer, no matter what it looked like.

Where did those chocolates come from?

The open door.

The night they went to the RVT. *Friday. I must remember to tell Mr. McDermott about the open door.*

Was it Auntie Susan? Clearly the man who had followed Misty this morning was connected to her. Her courier or something. And he had her address. Misty thought of the video she had of him on her phone from when she'd confronted him in Russell Square.

Would that be enough? she wondered. *Enough to convince the police that she was innocent?*

Perhaps.

But it would also mean exposing Mandy to the police for whatever she had going on at Lady's Bar and admitting that she'd followed her, twice. In turn, exposing Mandy's money business to the police would likely mean the end to Joe's dream of leaving the Empire Hotel for a life of costume and cabaret, following in Lady Lady's footsteps. Their dream life was at stake, but so was their real life.

As the car zipped through Central London, Misty looked out of the window and watched the city flying by. She was exhausted and her skin ached under the weight of the makeup. Makeup that, she thought, had held up exceptionally well under the circumstances. Oh yes, she might be under arrest for murder, but the mug shot was going to be a stunner.

What about Den?

He had been the police's prime suspect to begin with, but now, that was obviously Misty. She had hoped to speak with him at the hotel tonight but didn't think that was happening anymore. If the killer was Den or Mandy, Misty needed to find out quickly, before her own investigation was revealed to the police and she was busted for interfering with all the witnesses. Or, worse, she was actually done for the murder.

T HE CAR PULLED through the gates of Charing Cross Police Station into a yard that wasn't visible from the street. Misty was led inside by DI Davies, who explained that she'd be "booked in" and then he'd come and talk to her. The phrase "booked in" made Misty think of holidays, though she expected what lay ahead to be no holiday at all.

The booking in process took much longer than a hotel check-in.

She was ushered by DI Davies to a desk that was raised to a ridiculous height above her. Behind it was an officer in a black-and-white uniform, stripes on his shoulders. He was clicking on a computer. She tilted back her head to see him.

"Joseph Brown," said DI Davies, "under arrest for the murder of Sean Fulton."

The sergeant behind the high desk tapped Joe's details into the computer, and Misty stood, feeling small and helpless and out of context.

After the custody desk Misty was taken for photographs.

A photo shoot. How exciting, she wanted to joke, but she knew she mustn't.

"You'll be photographed in and out of your . . . costume," said

DI Davies, looking Misty up and down. It took every ounce of effort in her body not to roll her eyes at him.

"Where's Miles?" she asked.

"That's none of your concern at the moment," said DI Davies.

He could have told her something, she thought. He could have taken the opportunity to show her the tiniest shred of compassion. But clearly, he believed she was a coldhearted killer and should be treated as such.

THEY SEARCHED HER with a handheld metal detector and then by hand, putting their policey latex fingers all over her costume and through her enormous hair. Her handbag and telephone were taken away.

An officer with a kind smile brought Misty a vacuum-sealed packet that contained a plain gray tracksuit and a pair of black plimsoll pumps. They were two sizes too big, but they were at least new. She also handed Misty a packet of makeup wipes.

"For your face," she said.

Misty looked down at the makeup wipes and, as much as she'd felt tired of the drag in the car on the way here, now she felt hesitant about taking it off. She was vulnerable as Joe. Small. Misty could hold her own against DI Davies any day of the week, but Joe was intimidated by him.

"Come on," said the officer, hurrying Misty along. "Get scrubbing."

WITHOUT MILES'S HELP, it was a pain in the ass to get out of the corset, and none of the officers present offered any assistance, so Misty struggled for a couple of minutes to get it undone, conscious that there were eyes watching her every move. There were deep red grooves along her abdomen where the corset had squeezed her waist to a tiny proportion for the entire day.

"Oof." The officer watching sighed. "Looks sore."

"I'm used to it," said Misty.

Misty lifted off her wig and handed it to the officer. "Please keep it upright, if you can," she said.

The officer laughed. "Yes, madam," she said.

Eventually, lashes removed, face scrubbed clean, padding taken off, Joe stood in their boxer briefs in front of DI Davies and the kind custody officer. If this was some kind of humiliation ritual, it was working. Joe had never felt more exposed. They hurried the tracksuit on as quickly as they could.

The tracksuit was luxuriously comfortable.

Joe was taken by DI Davies to a cell where there was nothing but a hard foam mattress on a metal bench, a thin wool blanket, and a silver toilet.

"It's late," he said, "so I don't expect we'll question you until the morning. You can meet with your solicitor beforehand."

And with that, DI Davies slammed the door, locking it shut behind him.

Joe stood in the middle of the cell and looked around.

Murder, Joe. You've been arrested for murder.

They were in real big trouble.

24

****

TUESDAY

JOE ONLY MANAGED a couple of hours of sleep, or so they thought. It was difficult to know because they had no way of telling the time. But their body didn't feel as though it had had more than two hours, three at most.

All they could think about were the chocolates and who might have put them there, and how the police were wasting their time with this arrest when they should be looking into finding Lady Lady's real killer. Joe knew they were innocent and needed more than ever to prove it.

It was cold in the little cell, and the thin blanket the police had provided was no use at all for keeping warm. The bed was uncomfortable, the toilet disgusting. And there was noise. Drunks shouting, officers shouting, everybody shouting, all night long.

How did it come to this?

Arrested for murder. For murdering one of their closest friends. Miles had been taken away in a police car and was God knows where. Had he been arrested too? Was he in a cell too? The thought of it was unbearable.

This is all my fault, they thought. *I shouldn't have gone nosing around.*

How am I going to get out of this?

Everything started early at Charing Cross Police Station. The lights were switched on without warning, and the door swung open. Joe squinted. A custody officer stood in the doorway with a tray of food.

"It's seven," he said. "Breakfast."

Nothing like service with a smile, thought Joe.

He dropped the tray on the end of the bed and left again, slamming the door behind him.

Breakfast consisted of a small box of cornflakes and a carton of long-life milk. The milk was lukewarm, and they'd provided a wooden disposable spoon with which to eat it. Miles would be furious.

Joe had barely had two spoonfuls of cornflakes when the cell door reopened and DI Davies appeared.

"Your solicitor's here," he said. "Follow me."

"Now?" said Joe. "What time is it?"

"Yes, now. Five past seven," said DI Davies.

Joe got up from their bed and followed DI Davies down a corridor past all the other cells, through the custody reception area and into an interview room.

Colin McDermott was already there in suit and tie, freshly shaved, smelling delicious.

"We're ready to start when you are, Mr. McDermott," said DI Davies.

"Thank you."

DI Davies left in a cloud of body odor and Lynx Africa and shut the door behind him.

"Sit down, Joseph," said Mr. McDermott.

"Joe, please," said Joe.

"Have you slept? Eaten?"

"Barely either," they replied.

Joe sat on the opposite side of a small table from Mr. McDermott. In between them was Mr. McDermott's iPad and a file full of paperwork. Looking at the file made Joe feel sick.

"Have you spoken to Miles?" they asked. "Do you know where he is?"

"Yes, my colleague Sarah has been with Miles. He was questioned and released late last night. He went home."

"Thank God," said Joe, relieved. "I don't want Miles dragged into all this mess."

"Miles will be fine," said Mr. McDermott. "You, on the other hand, you're in a bit of a pickle here."

"That's an understatement."

"Yes," said Mr. McDermott seriously, "it is."

"I've never seen those chocolates before," Joe said hurriedly. "But we went out on Friday night. I had a gig at the RVT, the Royal Vauxhall Tavern."

"I know it." Mr. McDermott smiled.

"Sorry," said Joe. "But when we got back we found the front door to the flat wide open. Anybody could have been in and planted those chocolates."

"Miles told us, but there's no evidence of this break-in. You didn't even report it."

"No," said Joe, a little embarrassed that they hadn't taken it more seriously at the time.

"Why not?"

"Nothing was missing. Our computers, watches, jewelry, etcetera, were all still lying out in full view. We assumed we must have left the door open in our rush to leave."

"Let's start at the beginning," said Mr. McDermott, opening his file. "Let's talk through what we think they have against you and how we might strategize a defense so we can prepare properly for this interview. Tell me, how long have you known the victim, Mr. Fulton, Lady Lady?"

T HEY TALKED FOR a long time about Joe's relationship with Lady Lady, about how she'd been a sort of mother figure, a guiding light in Joe's life and career. They talked again through the details of the night of the murder, and then Mr. McDermott presented what he believed was the police's case against Joe.

Joe's motive, apparently, was money and/or fame. The police believed Joe had killed Lady Lady to inherit a stake in Lady's Bar and her job as the club's host. They would back this up with video evidence of Misty and Mandy toasting with champagne after the will reading.

Joe's opportunity to deliver the chocolates was when they visited Lady Lady's dressing room after the show, and all the other performers had given witness statements that Joe was the only one of them to go up the corridor.

The murder weapon: poisoned chocolates in a bespoke handmade box. An exact replica of which had since been discovered hidden in a box of cereal at the back of Joe's kitchen cupboard.

The police also believed that Joe had interfered with their investigation into the Kensington Catburglar by going to visit Anna Bowman at the Dress Collector.

"They're totally misrepresenting that," Joe interrupted. "I just wanted to try and find out where Lady Lady might have got the dress."

"In doing so," said Mr. McDermott, "you have acted in a way that the police believe to be suspicious, not behavior typically seen in a grieving friend, that's what they said."

"That's ridiculous," said Joe, thinking about all the other people they'd interrogated over the last five days.

"They also tell me that they found a notebook but haven't disclosed its contents."

Joe sighed. The pink Moleskine had been on the kitchen table.

"What's in the notebook, Joe?"

"Suspects," Joe admitted, embarrassed. "I made some lists of who I thought might have been the killer."

Mr. McDermott tutted, though not in a disapproving way. It was a tut that told Joe they were in deep water. "Is there anything else?" asked Mr. McDermott. "Anything you think they might have against you? I want us to go in there prepared for every eventuality."

Joe thought carefully. There was something else. There was *a lot* else. Mandy. Auntie Susan. Den. Baseball Cap. Tess. Jan.

Telling the police everything now would get Joe into trouble for the investigation, but maybe they had uncovered enough to clear their own name for the murder.

What about Baseball Cap? They could show the video on their phone to Mr. McDermott. It would be proof that Joe was being followed, that the guy with whom Mandy was up to something knew where they lived. On the other hand, telling the police about Baseball Cap and Mandy would almost definitely lead to Joe losing their new job at Lady's Bar before it had even begun.

They felt stuck.

Murder, Joe. You're about to get done for an actual murder.

They took a deep breath. "Actually, Mr. McDermott, there is something else—"

Just as Joe was about to spill the beans, to tell Mr. McDermott about Mandy and Den and Auntie Susan, DI Davies burst into the room as though he was the angriest man a Tuesday morning had ever seen.

"You're free to go," he said. "We're releasing you without charge." His round face was sweating and red.

"What?" said Mr. McDermott. "What's happened?"

Joe could hardly believe their ears. They'd been expecting to spend the whole day being interrogated, not be sent home immediately.

"Some new evidence," said DI Davies. "Would you mind stepping outside with me a moment, Mr. McDermott?"

Mr. McDermott got up from the table and went with DI Davies to the corridor, leaving Joe alone. Joe looked at themself in the mirrored wall. They looked tired and their face was streaked with makeup that the cheap police wipes had failed to remove. Their hair was out of control, spiky and all over the place from wearing a wig for the entire day yesterday. They looked a mess, Joe thought.

A few moments later Mr. McDermott opened the door and came back to the table.

"What's happening?" said Joe. "Are they really sending me home?"

"Okay," said Mr. McDermott, "they have new evidence, proving without doubt that there was a break-in at your home on Friday. It's enough to wipe out the chocolate box in court, and DI Davies knows it. Everything else they have on you is circumstantial. So they're not pressing charges, not today anyway, and they're going to let you go home to rest for now. But they will want to talk to you again soon, either today or tomorrow. They've asked for you to not leave London."

"That's fine," said Joe, "I won't leave London."

Joe wasn't leaving London, not because DI Davies had told them to stay but because there was a killer to catch. A killer who was trying to frame Joe for murder. And with the police still looking in the wrong direction Joe would have to be the one to catch them.

25

★★★★★★★★★

JOE EXITED CHARING Cross Police Station with Mr. McDermott and a plastic bag full of drag. The wig had not been stored upright so would likely need restyling. Joe felt irked by it. By the whole thing: the search, the arrest, the night in the cell, the wig.

"You're a lucky person," said Mr. McDermott. "That could have gone very differently."

Lucky?

Joe knew what he meant, but they didn't feel lucky. Not lucky at all.

"Joe!" called out a voice from across the street. Joe looked up. It was Miles. He ran over and threw his arms around Joe in one of his famous hugs. He was smiling, beaming widely. "I did it, Joe! I got you out!"

"What? What are you talking about?"

Miles was excited, lively, perhaps slightly delirious due to lack of sleep. "They questioned me last night, for ages. About those chocolates. And I remembered about the door on Friday. I told them about it, but they wouldn't believe me, so when they released me I went to the newsagents across the street from the flat. Turns out they have a CCTV camera that covers our front door. Someone broke in, Joe. Someone broke in and planted that chocolate box, and the break-in was captured on video while we were at the RVT. Your Instagram was our alibi."

"Miles!" Joe grinned. "You're the best!"

"A very lucky person indeed," said Mr. McDermott.

"So, who was it?" asked Joe. "Did you recognize who broke in?"

"No," said Miles. "The quality was dreadful and they were wearing a black hoodie in the dark."

"A baseball cap?"

"Nope, not that I could see."

"Damn."

"Joe, can I offer you some advice?" said Mr. McDermott.

"Of course," said Joe.

"You're in quite a precarious situation here. Making lists of suspects, talking to witnesses—whatever it is you're doing, you have to stop it. Stop it now."

"Thank you, Mr. McDermott. I'll take that on board." But Joe knew there was no way they could stop now: someone killed Lady Lady, someone had been in their home and planted evidence to frame Joe for the murder, and they had nearly succeeded. Joe wanted to get to the bottom of it as quickly as they could.

JOE TOOK THE gray prison tracksuit off as soon as they got home and jumped straight in the shower. Everything felt out of place since the flat had been searched. The shower gel was on the wrong shelf. What were the police doing looking at the shower gel? *What a waste of time*, they thought, *investigating me, searching my flat, when they should be out there looking for the real murderer.*

Misty had gone, packed back into the wardrobe, the messy wig stored upright on a polystyrene head. Joe felt angry, annoyed. Their stomach gurgled with it, and their heart pounded at the thought of someone invading their home to plant the chocolate box. Everything having been moved by the police made the flat feel less like home than usual, so after their shower Joe cleaned the kitchen while Miles took care of the living room. Joe scrubbed the kitchen surfaces, mopped the floors, and rearranged the cupboards, back to Miles's usual organized standards.

Joe had taken everything out of the fridge and was restocking it. "What were they looking for in the fridge?" asked Miles.

"Poison, apparently. Or chocolates, I guess," said Joe. "I'm so pissed off, Miles. Who would do this?"

Miles clicked on the kettle and set out two teacups on the counter.

"The best thing now, Joe, is to try to put it behind us. Forget about trying to work out who did it, let the police handle it like Mr. McDermott said. You don't want to get into any more bother."

"It could have been Auntie Susan," said Joe, "working with someone at the club. Maybe with Mandy."

Miles sighed. "You're not letting it go, are you?"

"Absolutely not," said Joe. "It's even more personal now. Someone broke into our home and planted evidence! I was arrested and spent the night in jail."

"What are you going to do?" asked Miles, the tone of his voice already resigned to the fact that Joe was on a nonstop hunt for the truth.

"I need to ask Mandy about the money," said Joe as Miles placed down two cups of tea and sat with Joe at the table. "I'm going to come clean about following her and ask her outright. I deserve an explanation after all this."

"I'll come with you," said Miles. "We'll go this afternoon."

"Miles, you should go to work. I don't want you pulled into this any more than you already have been. And you had your important meetings yesterday that you had to leave early because of all this. I can't ask you to do anything else."

"Joe, you were arrested last night. For *murder*. I'm taking a couple of personal days from the office. Chris will understand."

"Thanks, Miles, I really appreciate it. Everything."

Miles took Joe's hand across the table. "We're going to get to the bottom of this."

"Shit," said Joe, "what time is it?"

"Almost nine," said Miles, checking his watch.

"I need to get into drag."

"What? That's crazy, Joe. You were in drag all day yesterday, and you've hardly slept."

"We're meeting Florentina at ten in Soho, remember?" said Joe, glugging back their tea and getting up. "And I want to be in drag for confronting Mandy. Misty's scarier."

Miles laughed. "That she is . . ."

26

★★★★★★★★

"WHERE ARE WE meeting her?" asked Miles as they stood on the pavement waiting for a taxi.

"Just opposite the club," said Misty.

"Great, then we're in the right place for talking to Mandy afterward."

Misty and Miles met Florentina in a dark and gloomy café on Old Compton Street. It was a shame to be meeting indoors as it was a beautiful summer's day, and after her night of confinement Misty would have liked to spend the day outside. She had worn a bright blue trouser suit, flared at the ankles, and a blue wig that was whisked up so it looked like a Mr. Whippy ice cream. Her shoes were navy glitter platform heels and she'd even pressed on glittery nails for the occasion, white ones. Tacky, but perfect. She'd done the face quickly today: thirty minutes. And it wasn't perfect, but it was good enough.

When they arrived at 10:10 a.m., Florentina was already there, waiting for them. She was dressed in a long flowing summer dress, pink and white, with tassels around the neckline. No doubt a homemade creation, it was stylish and comfortable-looking and expertly crafted.

"Hi, Misty," she said as Miles and Misty sat down with her, "I'm so sorry about what happened to Lady Lady."

"Thank you," said Misty. "I'm sorry too. How are you?"

"I'm okay," said Florentina, tears welling up behind her deep black eyeliner. "I just can't believe she's really gone."

Misty felt a shimmer of shame. Seeing Florentina's grief made her realize again how much she hadn't been grieving for Lady Lady. She'd become so caught up in the investigating and inheritance and accusations that, for the last few days at least, she'd barely had a moment to mourn. Not behavior befitting a grieving friend, that's what Mr. McDermott had said, and she supposed it was true.

"It's really awful," she said. "How long had you worked to-gether?" Sitting across from Florentina, Misty was in full inves-tigator mode. Even more than before, now she'd spent a night in a cell she was laser-focused on finding out the identity of the real killer.

"Gosh," said Florentina, "it must be fifteen years. She came to one of my early shows, back when I was more fashion design than costume design. After the show she stayed to chat and asked me to make her a dress. I've been designing for her ever since."

"She had that way," said Misty. "She loved building people up." Misty thought of how Lady Lady had mentored her over the years, the invaluable advice she had shared. She'd done the same for Mr. McDermott, it seemed. And now Florentina. This was the Lady Lady that Misty knew, not the Lady Lady who engaged in dodgy back-alley deals and wore stolen Judy Garland dresses. *How could any of this be happening?*

"I'd never have got where I am today without her," said Florentina. A tear dropped from her eye and bounced down her cheek. "I'm going to really miss her."

"Me too," said Misty.

They reminisced for a while about good times they'd had with Lady Lady. Florentina told a story about going fabric shopping in Paris with her and how they'd spent hours choosing the perfect jacquard for a new suit. "I only wear jacquard that's been made in France," Lady Lady had announced to the shopkeeper, admitting on her way out the door that she had no idea what a jacquard was, never mind where it might be made.

Eventually Misty steered the conversation to the stolen dress and the night of the murder.

"Florentina, did she ever mention this Judy Garland dress to you?"

"No," said Florentina, "I was totally shocked by it. It wasn't what she was supposed to be wearing on Wednesday. She *never* veered from the costume schedule we put together every week."

"Do you know where the dress came from?" asked Misty. "Did you know anything about it?"

"I didn't, and I have no idea where it came from. All I can think is that she must have got the dress on Tuesday or Wednesday, because when I saw her on Monday she was planning to wear something else. She'd have told me otherwise. That's what I told the police too."

"And if you wanted to get something like that, a rare dress like that, do you know where you might start looking?"

"You're not going after one, are you?" laughed Florentina. "Not two drag queens in stolen dresses in one week!"

"No, no." Misty smiled.

"Well," said Florentina, rubbing her eyes, "there are of course dealers of rare and unusual dresses, and there's a black market in every industry, fashion included."

"Do you know of anyone in the drag scene who would be involved in that?" asked Miles. "Anyone who might connect Lady Lady to the dress?"

"Yes, actually," said Florentina with a cautious wobble in her voice. "But if I tell you, you didn't hear it from me."

"Okay . . ."

"I told this to the police too, but I don't want anyone to think I'm a snitch or anything."

"What is it?" asked Misty, thirsty for the new information that Florentina was about to reveal.

"A few months ago—and you *promise* you didn't hear anything from me—Den tried to sell me a stolen necklace."

"What? Den the drag king?"

Misty felt vindicated in her suspicions. *I knew there was a missing piece to the Den puzzle.*

"Yes," said Florentina. "He approached me on a Thursday while I was at Lady's Bar to watch a show. He said he had some inside information about a necklace that had been stolen in a burglary, and was I interested in buying it? It was before the Catburglar stuff started, so it wasn't one of *those* stolen items. I don't know where it came from. I told him I wasn't interested and not to talk to me about that kind of thing again. But it did make me wonder, maybe Den knew where the dress came from. Maybe he's the one who gave it to Lady Lady. Anyway, I told the police all about it, so I expect they must be following up on it."

Misty was shocked, but now it made sense why the police had originally thought Den might have done it. The suspicion wasn't about drag kings on the lineup at all. The police had suspected Den because of Florentina. If Florentina told DI Davies that Den was involved in some sort of black-market fashions, it made sense to look at him first.

So maybe the police had already investigated and dismissed Den as a suspect. Maybe that's why they'd turned to look at Misty and Mandy. *In any case*, Misty thought, *I'm going to have to speak to Den. Today.* And this time no rejected call or surprise search warrant was going to stop her.

They ended their chat with Florentina by telling her about Lady Lady's costumes and how her will had asked for them to be auctioned for charity.

Florentina beamed broadly. "I can't think of a better use for them now," she said.

Miles and Misty left the café and stepped out into the morning sun with Florentina. She kissed them each on the cheek.

"See you soon, I hope," Florentina said, leaving them on the pavement and walking up toward Piccadilly, her dress billowing in the summer breeze.

"Well, that's interesting," said Miles.

"Den," said Misty, thinking out loud. "If Den's selling stolen jewelry, do we think that he's the Catburglar? Maybe Lady Lady found out somehow, and then he killed her."

"Possibly," said Miles. "It's a theory that makes sense with everything else we've learned about him and would explain how he sorted out his financial mess."

"I can't put it off any longer. I'm going to have to talk to him today," she said. "Right now, in fact."

They waited for a gap in the traffic and stepped out into the street. A group of men in suits walked by, and one of them wolf-whistled at Misty.

"Bit early for that, isn't it?" he shouted, to the great amusement of his colleagues, who fell about themselves laughing.

"Get fucked," replied Misty.

BEFORE SHE UNLOCKED the doors to the club Misty stopped outside and pulled out her mobile. There were dozens of notifications. WhatsApp messages from almost everyone she knew. It seemed word was out that she'd been arrested. She didn't read them, instead dismissing the notifications and scrolling through her contacts until she found Den's number. She pressed the green call button.

The phone rang.

And rang.

And rang.

And Den didn't pick up.

"Right," said Misty, further annoyed than she was already. "I guess we're going to the hotel tonight. I need answers."

27

★★★★★★★★★

"MANDY WON'T BE here yet," said Misty. "She usually comes in at lunchtime."

The heavy locks clinked loudly as she turned the key and swung open the door. They stepped inside and Miles shut the door behind them.

"I can't believe you own this," he said, "ten percent of it."

Misty still couldn't believe it either.

They walked down the staircase to the auditorium and bar. Before they went in, Misty said, "Remember, the police had access to the CCTV cameras, so let's go straight to the office. No cameras there."

They passed quickly through the bar and the auditorium in silence. It looked so quiet in the daytime, especially the morning, and knowing it had been closed for almost a week made it feel even quieter. The chairs and tables sat empty waiting for their next guests, for their next show. Without lighting the stage looked small and underwhelming. Misty thought about how that was about to be her stage, how soon she could be hosting every show here, once this murder mess was resolved.

Misty and Miles opened the door to the dressing rooms and office corridor and stepped inside.

"It's so weird being here in the daytime," said Miles. Misty realized he had probably only been in Lady's Bar when there was a show on, and so hadn't spent a lot of time here during the downtime like she had.

"Well, welcome! I guess we'll be spending a lot more time here if I keep the inheritance."

"Of course you'll keep the inheritance!" replied Miles.

"It depends what this club is involved in," said Misty. "I'm not agreeing to anything until I've had it out with Mandy. Let's not forget someone was murdered here. I don't know what I'm getting myself into just yet."

They let themselves into the office and switched on the lights. There were three desks: Mandy's desk, a mountain of Tesco meal-deal wrappers and paperwork; Lady Lady's desk, immaculately tidy with a glistening crown atop her computer monitor; and a hot desk. When Misty had come to help with the emails she had used a laptop on the hot desk, and she was comfortable there. Were she to agree to take on Lady Lady's job at the club, that would be her desk, she knew. It would feel wrong to take Lady Lady's.

"Shall I make us some tea?" said Misty.

"Good idea," said Miles, sitting down on the gamer chair that Mandy used as an office seat. He put his hands up behind his head and the muscles in his arms flexed visibly. "What shall we do while we wait for Mandy?"

"Well," said Misty, "I was thinking we could have a look

through the files, see if we can spot anything out of the ordinary."

Miles leaned forward, interested. "Ooh," he said, "a spot of cyber-espionage."

"Ha! Well, I'm not sure I'd quite call it that, but definitely a cyber-snoop."

"Much more exciting than a day in the office," said Miles.

"Thank you," said Misty, "for taking the day off today to help me. It means everything."

"Of course," said Miles.

Misty made two cups of tea in chipped office mugs. She couldn't imagine Lady Lady drinking from one of these, and then looked at her desk to see a teapot and cup sitting primly next to the computer. The pot was pink with a gold trim and looked as though it were waiting for Lady Lady herself to come back in and pour a cup. *Next time I'll make a pot*, thought Misty, coveting the pink teapot and matching cup.

"So, how long do you think we have until Mandy arrives?" asked Miles.

"Not sure," said Misty. "I'll text her."

Misty took out her phone and sent a message to Mandy.

The telltale three dots of Mandy typing an instant reply appeared on the screen.

Will be in about 12, I think. Police
searched my flat last night, so just
putting everything back in order.

"Ooh, the police searched Mandy's place last night too," Misty relayed to Miles.

"I thought they might," said Miles.

"She says she'll be here about twelve," said Misty, looking at the clock. "That would give us an hour or so until she arrives."

"Time enough for a quick peek on the computers," said Miles. "If you're sure you want to carry on looking."

"I'm sure. I need answers."

"But if Mandy's coming in today that means she wasn't arrested like you were. They mustn't have found anything at her flat. That's reassuring, no?"

"Yes," said Misty. And it was, reassuring about the murder at least. If they'd searched Mandy's flat as thoroughly as they'd searched Misty and Miles's, then surely it meant there was no evidence against Mandy either.

Misty handed Miles a cup of tea. The mug was huge, branded with a giant Sports Direct logo on the side. If Misty took on the job here she would be replacing all of the rotten mismatched mugs with a nice set.

"We need to replace these cups," she said.

"You really, really do," replied Miles.

They decided to start on the computers. Miles and Misty sat at Lady Lady's desk and switched on her Mac. A picture of Lady Lady popped up on the screen, and Misty felt it like a punch in the chest. Oh, how she missed her. A password box appeared.

"What could it be?" asked Miles.

"Try her birthday." Misty shrugged.

They tried that and it didn't work. They tried the month, the month and year, LadyLady, LadysBar, and multiple combinations of password classics such as password1.

"Oh," said Misty, remembering the will reading, "try Tuppy."

"Tuppy?" asked Miles. "What's that?"

"Capital T, lowercase u-p-p-y. Try it. Her dog."

Miles tapped the dog's name into the password box, and the screen changed as the computer unlocked.

"Yessss," said Miles. "Nice one!"

"Ha!"

They celebrated their victory by clinking their ugly mugs together and taking a sip of tea.

"Where to start?" asked Miles.

"With the emails?" suggested Misty. "We can see if she sent anything interesting?"

"Good idea," said Miles, clicking on the mail app button at the bottom of the screen. An inbox opened, and there were hundreds of unread emails. All from the last few days.

"What are all those?" asked Misty.

Miles clicked open the first one. It was a message from a fan, expressing her sadness that Lady Lady had died.

"How strange," said Misty, "to send an email to a dead person."

"And look how many there are," said Miles.

"Is this an actual thing people do then? Send emails to dead celebrities after they've died?"

"I guess so," said Miles, clicking open message after message, all reading along the same lines. The writers had seen Lady Lady perform, or they'd watched her on television, and they felt a connection somehow. It was sweet actually, like a quiet memorial service taking place in her inbox. Suddenly she felt guilty for reading them, like an intruder.

"Maybe we shouldn't be reading these," she said.

"Don't be daft," said Miles, "of course we should. There might be something in here that gives us a clue who her killer was."

Misty nodded. It seemed even usually sensible Miles was up

for breaking the rules, possibly inspired by his midnight CCTV hunt. Once they'd read through the deluge of tribute messages and hundreds of Twitter notifications they arrived at the previous week's emails—the emails from when Lady Lady was still alive. They read the sent messages and the received ones, and it was sad to imagine Lady Lady sitting typing them at this very desk only a week ago.

But in the hundreds of emails there was nothing of interest to report and nothing that seemed out of the usual. There were many messages between Lady Lady and drag artists Misty knew, arranging bookings, following up on invoices, that kind of thing. There were quite a few messages from up-and-coming and beginner performers looking to get booked, sending their show reels or links to YouTube videos of them performing in other less-established venues. Misty made a mental promise that she would go through all of those emails when, and if, she took over from Lady Lady to give those new performers a chance like Lady Lady had given her.

Next they checked Lady Lady's calendar, but it seemed she either didn't have many meetings, or she didn't record them there. Week after week of sparsely filled diary told them nothing new about Lady Lady's business, except that she had a weekly costume meeting with Florentina and a monthly meeting with Mandy and Mr. McDermott. Nothing looked unusual or like it might be cause for murder.

"What now?" asked Miles.

"Her internet history?" suggested Misty, feeling slightly disheartened that their password-cracking skills had led to such little new information.

Miles clicked on the Google Chrome icon and opened up the history tab on the side of the browser. The most recently visited pages were listed under last Wednesday's date, Lady Lady's last day alive. Each page was stamped with the time and date, and a link to the page Lady Lady had visited. Misty looked at the times and realized that the last searches had been made during the interval of the show last Wednesday. Lady Lady must have come back to the office to use the computer during the break.

> 8:45 p.m.—Google search: how to tell if a dress is real or a
> replica

> 8:43 p.m.—HollywoodGlam.blog: Judy Garland 1953 red
> carpet

> 8:42 p.m.—FashionArchive.com: Judy Garland dress Los
> Angeles fundraiser

Misty took a breath, realizing what this meant. It meant that by the interval of Wednesday's cabaret Lady Lady knew the dress she was wearing was the stolen Judy Garland—or at least she suspected it. It meant that during the interval she had come to the office and looked at pictures of Judy Garland wearing the dress online. This explained why she had seemed off that night, why she'd appeared distracted in the second half of the show. She *was* distracted, with the quarter-of-a-million-pound dress that she was wearing.

"She knew," said Miles quietly.

"She knew."

Suddenly lots more made sense, such as why the police had been so focused on the dress. Reading about the stolen dress was one of the last things Lady Lady did.

"The police will already know about this," said Misty. "They took the computers for searching. When did she first start read-ing about the dress?"

Miles scrolled down the internet history. "During the show, at the interval," he said. "That's the first time I can see that she looked at anything to do with it."

"And if she's searching for distinguishing between real and replica dresses in the interval, do we assume that she put the dress on thinking it was a fake, then at some point during the show began to suspect it was the real deal?"

"I guess so . . ." said Miles as he carried on clicking, scrolling through the lists of all the websites Lady Lady had visited over the last week.

"That explains why she was so off in the second half."

"*And* it fits with what we know about Lady Lady. She wouldn't have knowingly worn a stolen dress." Miles stopped clicking. "But where did she get it from? There's nothing in her diary, nothing relevant in her internet history."

"Den," said Misty.

"You really think he's the Kensington Catburglar?"

"I'm starting to," said Misty.

THEY MOVED FROM looking at the internet history to going through the files saved on the computer. They looked through folder after folder of design work, performers' contracts, and invoices.

"There's nothing here," said Misty. She felt frustrated, like she could burp with frustration at any second.

"Where do they keep the accounts?" asked Miles, clicking through a series of folders of spreadsheets.

"The accounts?" replied Misty. "Well, Mandy does them, so

they must be in a shared folder somewhere. Have you looked in the iCloud?"

"Looking there next," said Miles as he tapped the mouse and navigated through to a shared drive. "There's a 'Finances' folder. Shit." He was excited, Misty could tell. His chest was pushed forward toward the screen, his fingers moving rapidly. The thrill of poking around had caught on. They both felt like detectives now, even though they knew they shouldn't.

"Wait," said Misty. "What time is it?"

Miles checked the clock. "It's eleven thirty. We've got half an hour until Mandy gets here."

"Okay, let's do it."

But just as Miles opened the Finances folder the office door swung open and Mandy walked in.

Busted.

"What do you think you're doing?" she said, her face flushing red underneath her heavy black bob.

"We were . . ."

"Misty, this really isn't on. You can't just be poking around like this. What are you even . . . ?" She stooped forward to take a closer look at the screen. "The *Finances* folder?"

Misty stood up and Miles closed the window on the computer, revealing about a hundred open folders, contracts, invoices . . . They had been caught well and truly red-handed.

"Mandy, let me explain—" started Misty.

"You don't need to explain," said Mandy. "I see what's happening here! You've inherited ten percent of this place, and you want to know how much money that is. Is that right? That's all you're interested in? And you're so interested you just let yourself in here and hacked into the computers."

"'Hacked' is a bit strong," muttered Miles.

"Well, I don't know what you'd call it," a flustered Mandy said. "Breaking and entering, corporate espionage, something like that maybe. But it's definitely not on, Misty."

"We should have asked you first," said Miles.

"Damn right you should have," said Mandy. "I'm happy to show you whatever it is you want to see, but you should have fucking asked."

There was an awkward silence that seemed to last for an eternity. Miles broke it first, saying, "Shall I make us all a cup of tea?"

"Good idea," snapped Mandy, off-loading her bursting handbag from her shoulder onto her cluttered desk. Miles got up and moved to the fridge, switching on the kettle above it and taking out the milk.

"Which mug do you prefer?" asked Miles.

"The Sports Direct one is my favorite," replied Mandy, then noticed the mug in question on the desk where Miles had been sitting. "But I see you've helped yourself to that too."

Miles raised his eyebrows and made a face to Misty that almost made Misty laugh. "I'll give it a wash now." Miles took the mug and left the office, heading to the bar to wash it.

"I'm sorry, Mandy, okay?" said Misty once the two of them were left alone, wondering how she was going to approach the subject of Baseball Cap. "I wasn't thinking right. Of course I should have asked you and waited for you to show me everything. I didn't mean to pry."

"Yes, you did."

"Well, yes, I did, I suppose."

"Misty, I need you to answer something for me honestly."

"Okay . . ."

Mandy took a deep breath, and Misty noticed her glasses slip

forward a little down her nose. The large frames perched peril-
ously on the tip of her little button nose, and Misty imagined
them sliding right off, like an egg off a hot pan.

"Did you kill Lady Lady?" Mandy asked. Outright, just like
that.

"No, I didn't," said Misty. "Did you?"

"No, I didn't," said Mandy, and then, collapsed into a sobbing heap. "But the police think I did it, Misty. They think one
of us did it because of the champagne we had yesterday. Maybe
they think we did it together!"

"Yes, I spent the night in a cell. That's why I'm here," she
said, deciding that telling the truth to Mandy now was the best
policy. In this moment, despite all of Misty's suspicions, Mandy
didn't seem to be the killer. She didn't have the murdery vibes
and seemed genuinely upset, just like Tess had done. But Misty
didn't know what this meant for everything else she knew about
Mandy. She might not be the killer, but she was certainly up to
something. "I'm trying to find out who did it, because I'm worried that that DI Davies has it in for me. I thought that there
might be something in Lady Lady's computer that told me more
about what she might have been involved in."

"She wasn't 'involved' in anything," snorted Mandy.

Misty felt annoyed with her now. Irritated by Mandy crying
and taking a moral high ground when she was running around
London doing dodgy deals with envelopes full of cash.

"*You're* involved in something though, aren't you? There's
something going on here that shouldn't be."

"I don't know what you're talking about."

The door opened and Miles walked back in, holding the
Sports Direct mug, his fingers still slightly wet from the sink.

"You do know what I'm talking about," said Misty, unable to

stop herself now, mad at Mandy for all her lies. "The cash. The cash that you've been giving to the guy with the scar on his face."

"How do you—have you been following me?"

"Just tell me the truth, Mandy. What are you involved in?"

Misty made eye contact with Miles, who was standing with his mouth wide open by the door. She felt relieved to have asked Mandy about the money, like a weight had been lifted from her shoulders.

"I own part of this club now, Mandy, and I've just spent the night in a jail cell. Your friend with the baseball cap has been following me, and someone planted murder evidence in our apartment. Was that you? *Auntie Susan?* I have a right to know what's going on."

Mandy sighed heavily and sat down with a thump on an office chair that didn't look as though it would be capable of withstanding such a force. She looked like she'd been beaten, bested, and had no choice but to come clean with the truth. Somehow, Misty knew just by looking at her that Mandy was about to be honest.

"It's a long story," said Mandy to Misty, and turning to Miles, "You'd better make us that tea."

ONCE MILES HAD made the tea, the three of them sat down around Mandy's desk. Misty watched Mandy closely as she rubbed her face and thought about how to begin.

"What do you already know?" asked Mandy. "Let's start with that, then I can fill in the rest."

"I followed you," said Misty. It was a relief to tell her this, to confess to her secret stalking, and the relief reminded her who Mandy had been to her before all this: her friend. "I saw you

give the money to the guy in the baseball cap, and then I followed him. I saw him go straight from meeting you to The
Plough to see Auntie Susan. It's obvious that you're paying
money to her for something, but I don't know what. And I really
don't know why you would be doing this with someone who was
Lady Lady's enemy!"

"Wow, you've really overstepped here, Misty. You don't know
what you're getting involved in."

"Overstepped?" said Misty, outraged. "Someone broke into
my apartment and planted evidence to try and frame me for
murder, Mandy. Was it you? Was it Auntie Susan?" Misty felt
her heart racing, and her face begin to flush as days of pent-up
frustration rose to the surface. "Tell me what's going on here.
Because if I'm going to own ten percent of this club, if I'm going
to take over from Lady Lady, I need to know what's going on!"

Miles shuffled uncomfortably and Mandy brushed her fringe
out of her eyes. She sighed heavily and sank into her chair. She
looked done in.

"Oh, Misty," she cried. "What have I done?" Mandy lifted
her hands to her face and began to sob.

It took Mandy a few minutes to stop crying and start speaking, and when she did she let it all out, like a military horse
emptying its bowels outside Buckingham Palace.

"It started three years ago. There's a company, an investment
company called Atrax, trying to buy up independent businesses
all across London, taking over leases that are coming up for re-
newal. They submitted a redevelopment proposal to the council
suggesting that they take on this whole building, raze it to the
ground, and rebuild it. Probably so they can turn this place into
a PizzaExpress or something.

"We didn't want that. Lady Lady didn't want that. We had

no choice but to go to Auntie Susan. She knows people, you see. She calls herself a 'fixer.'" Mandy paused. "How much do you know about The Plough?"

Misty's mind was furiously trying to put the pieces together. Someone was trying to force Lady's Bar to close? Auntie Susan was a "fixer." What did The Plough have to do with anything?

"All I know is that there's shows there and they don't pay very well, sometimes not at all. It's not a good place to work, that's for sure," said Misty.

"Yes, but beyond that," said Mandy, "The Plough is the center of Auntie Susan's operations. It's not just the bar that she runs but a whole network of activity. It's well known among the venue owners across London that Auntie Susan is into all kinds of dodgy stuff. And she knows people, people in high places. She has . . . influence."

"Influence?" asked Miles. "You mean blackmail?"

Mandy readjusted herself in her chair. "I don't like to call it that. And it's not quite blackmail. It's more . . . bribery." She said this last word quietly, as though it were the most shameful of words to say out loud. "There's a woman on the council. Auntie Susan coordinates a payment from us to her that has been keeping her from progressing the Atrax proposal for the block. I don't know how she's doing it, but she is, for now. We're hanging on by the skin of our teeth. Atrax can afford to pay a lot more than we can, and we're squeezing cash out of the bar to cover the bribes. Oh, we're in such a mess."

"How much are you paying this woman at the council?" asked Misty.

"Two grand a week," said Mandy, full of shame.

"And how long have you been paying her?"

"Two years already."

Misty did some quick math. "So, you've paid this woman hundreds of thousands of pounds?"

Mandy burst out a little sob, and a string of saliva flicked from her upper teeth to her top lip. She wiped it away with the back of her hand.

"We had to," she said. "What choice did we have? We would have lost the club otherwise."

"How do you account for it?" asked Miles. "That's a lot of money to disappear in cash."

Mandy sighed. "We take it from the bar sales. Every night before we do the final cash-up, we skim ten percent of the cash out of the bar sales and separate it out in the safe. Then we account for the ninety percent and save the ten percent to give to Auntie Susan. That's why we push for cash sales and haven't switched to card only like everyone else."

"Is this what you were arguing about? On the night of the murder? I overheard you arguing when I came to Lady Lady's dressing room."

"Yes," admitted Mandy. "I've been wanting to stop the payments, to try to make it all aboveboard. I wanted to go to Mr. McDermott, to see if there was a way to fight the investment company in court or something. But we couldn't. Auntie Susan says we're not allowed to stop."

"Surely you can stop whenever you want," said Misty. "Just stop paying."

"It's not as simple as that, Misty, love. Once you're involved with something like this, once you've already crossed the line, it's never as simple as just stepping back over it to where you were before."

"What do you mean?" asked Misty.

"You see, Auntie Susan takes a cut of the money we give her, twenty percent. She protects her own interest by keeping the arrangement going."

"I still don't understand why you can't just stop paying her," said Misty.

"Don't you see? Oh, Misty."

Miles interrupted, realizing what Mandy was trying to say. "She's blackmailing you now, isn't she? Auntie Susan? She's threatening you so that you carry on making the payments."

Mandy nodded sadly. "Yes," she said. "We're absolutely up to our necks in it, and I don't know how to make it stop."

28

★★★★★★★★★

MILES TOLD MANDY and Misty that he thought they all needed to take a break.

"Why don't we get some lunch and then regroup this afternoon to talk some more? This has been a lot."

It had been a lot, Misty knew. She felt exhausted. Confronting Mandy had been both easier than she expected and more difficult. She hadn't been prepared for all the crying, for the admission that the club was in trouble. And not just a little bit of trouble but life-threatening, club-closing-down kind of trouble. Not just Lady Lady's legacy down the drain but all of Misty's hopes for her future career too.

But now she knew that Mandy wasn't the killer; Mandy and Lady Lady had simply been trying to keep the bar alive. And the police hadn't arrested her or found any evidence against her that Misty was aware of. So where did that leave her investigation? Den? Auntie Susan? Were they working together?

"Good idea," said Mandy. "I could do with a few minutes alone."

Miles and Misty gathered their things and left Mandy by herself in the office, then walked through the auditorium and up the stairs out into the July Soho sun.

Misty took a deep breath of fresh air. She felt overwhelmed. There was too much new information for her brain to process alongside everything else.

"What do you think of all that?" asked Miles.

"I'm not sure yet," said Misty. "I just need a minute to think."

She was tired from lack of sleep after her night at the police station. She thought back to how vulnerable Joe had felt standing in their little boxers in front of DI Davies. Standing on the pavement of Old Compton Street now, seeing the reactions of the passersby to her bright blue outfit, Misty was reminded that she was a drag queen. A powerful mystical creature who could do and say whatever she wanted. She'd become so many new things over the last few days: a bar owner, a club hostess, a murder suspect. And now it turned out that the bar in which she suddenly owned a stake was engaged in illegal activities. She felt as though she'd almost forgotten who she really was. She closed her eyes and felt the midday sun on her makeup-covered face.

Does any of this matter? Does any of this help me clear my own name? she wondered.

Yes, she thought it might.

The new information from Mandy gave her a new lead that the police didn't have: Auntie Susan.

Misty had wondered about Auntie Susan from the beginning, but now she had what looked like motive: Lady Lady was paying Auntie Susan thousands of pounds a month and wanted to put the arrangement to an end.

Yes, Misty thought, *I'm ahead of you now, DI Davies.*

"Let's go to Balans for lunch," said Misty, turning to Miles, who had himself turned to checking his emails on his phone while Misty cleared her mind. "I want that walnut pesto thing they do and to google these Atrax people. I need to know more about them before I have it out with Auntie Susan."

"You're going to have it out with Auntie Susan? Are you sure? After everything Mandy's just told us."

"I've got no choice, Miles."

"Let's at least talk about it first," said Miles. "Balans sounds good to me."

It was a Soho institution. Open all night long and serving great food and nice cocktails, it was often where the cast of a cabaret might go for a late bite to eat after a show. Misty had been there many times with Lady Lady, chatting and laughing till the early hours. It was also, conveniently, just a few doors away from Lady's Bar. They started walking in that direction.

"What time does Den start at the hotel?" asked Miles as they passed along the busy pavement.

"Seven," said Misty.

"Are you still planning on talking to him today?"

"Absolutely."

THEY ARRIVED AT Balans to an outrageously enthusiastic greeting by Anthony, one of the long-standing waiters. Anthony was a huge fan of drag, drag queens in particular, and mostly the ones who had been on the telly. But he knew Misty well and greeted her with open arms.

"Misty Divine!" he called above the dining patrons. "It is wonderful to see you." Anthony made his way quickly across the restaurant as customers turned to look at Misty, to see who could have created such a commotion. As he reached them standing in the doorway, he performed two large air-kisses, one on each of Misty's cheeks. "Mwah. Mwah. You look fabulous, as always," he said. "Miles, darling"—he took Miles's hands in his—"so good to see you."

"Thank you, Anthony," said Misty. "It's lovely to see you too."

"Come, follow me," he said. "I have a private booth for you."

He walked them through the restaurant to the booths at the back of the establishment. Misty smiled as a tourist snapped a photo of her, one of the joys of being out and about in Soho in drag.

Anthony whisked back a white curtain and revealed a large round table that could have seated eight people. Misty had sat there before, many times after a show. Lady Lady was always given the private-booth treatment.

"Please, sit down. I will return with the menus." Anthony rushed away, and Miles and Misty sat down next to each other.

"Well, this is nice," said Miles.

"The Lady Lady effect," replied Misty.

"Menus!" Anthony appeared between the white curtains, holding two large menus. He handed one to Misty and then one to Miles. "Misty, I hope you don't mind me saying, I heard what happened. That you were, you know, the one who found her. I'm so sorry, my love. I want you to know that lunch is on us today, whatever you want."

"Oh, Anthony, you don't have to do that . . ." started Misty.

"Please, Misty. It's on us. It's the least we can do."

"Thank you. That's very kind of you."

"I'll be back in a few minutes to take your order."

Misty stared blankly at the menu and thought about Mandy. She already knew what she was going to eat: the walnut pesto thing. She pictured Mandy just minutes before—a sobbing heap in the office, spit hanging off her top lip. Misty had been really wrong about her. Since the night of the murder, and especially since following her, Misty had built up an image of Mandy as a villain, a bad egg who could have murdered her friend. But now she saw something else, something she wholeheartedly believed to be the truth: Mandy was innocent. She might be involved in a blackmail scheme with a criminal fixer, but she wasn't a murderer. In fact, even in the blackmail scenario, Mandy was kind of the victim. A local business owner being forced out of her community by a big-city investment firm. It was the kind of story Meg Ryan might have made a film about in the nineties.

"Do you think we should tell the police?" asked Miles, interrupting Misty's chain of thought. "About Mandy and the blackmail?"

"I don't think so," said Misty. "Do you?"

"I don't know," he replied, playing with the menu in his fingertips. "On one hand I don't want to tell them anything because they're, you know, the police. And that DI Davies is a bastard. But on the other hand it would take you out of the firing line a bit. There are new leads now, maybe ones that the police should know about."

Misty placed her menu down on the table. Miles was right, of course. For most people, she thought, the natural thing to do would be to go to DI Davies and tell him everything: about Auntie Susan, the bribery that turned to blackmail, the money stolen from the bar sales. But doing that would lead to Mandy being arrested, to her losing the club, and to Misty losing her chance at a new life.

"I can't, Miles. It would be the end of Lady's Bar and the start of this Atrax company turning it into a PizzaExpress. Think of how many people would lose their jobs. Imagine what the West End would be like without Lady's Bar, how many performers would lose regular income if it closed. If Mandy's told us the whole truth, which I think she has, going to the police would lead to her losing the bar, whether they pin Lady Lady's murder on her or not."

"I get it," said Miles. "It just feels like . . . I guess telling the police feels like what we're *supposed* to do."

"Telling the police has a bigger impact than on just us, Miles. Telling the police about Mandy will cost the drag scene a venue, a safe space. It would turn everything Lady Lady built into just another sad story about queer venues being forced out of the market. We have to protect it, Miles. Not for me, but for Lady Lady and future generations. We have to protect what she created."

"And that means protecting Mandy," said Miles.

"That means protecting Mandy."

ANTHONY RETURNED AND took their lunch order. Miles ordered a beetroot salad, and Misty ordered the walnut pasta. They sat quietly for a while. Miles took Misty's hand. "Is Joe okay in there?" he asked.

"Joe's just fine," said Misty.

The pasta was as delicious as Misty had hoped it would be. Layer upon layer of creamy, cheesy, vegan béchamel sauce, and hundreds of pinenuts that melted in her mouth. All topped with crunchy roasted walnuts. It was too hot to eat at first, but once it had cooled down a little it was perfection.

"So, who's this Atrax company?" Misty asked Miles. "You ever heard of them?"

"No, I never have. Hold on." He pulled his phone out of his pocket and opened up Google, searching for Atrax. "Ugh, gross," he said, holding up his screen to show Misty a picture of a giant black spider.

"Miles! What the hell is that?"

"An atrax, apparently. It's a type of venomous spider from Australia."

"Oh great," said Misty. "So, the company we're up against in the fight for Lady's Bar named itself after a venomous spider. Doesn't feel at all ominous."

"Here we go," said Miles, scrolling through some new Google results. "Atrax Solutions. They've got a website." Miles tapped on the screen to open the Atrax home page. A plain black page appeared. At the top was the company name in a crisp pristine white font. And underneath were just two sentences.

**Atrax Solutions supports clients with investments
   and security.**

Contact is by referral only.

Misty read the website over Miles's shoulder.

"Well, that doesn't tell us much," she said.

"Very mysterious," said Miles. He went back to Google, searching again. "Hold on, there's an article here about them. It's from the *Guardian*, written six months ago."

WHO IS THE MOST ELUSIVE DRAGON IN THE CITY
AND WHO CAN TAME THEM?
Finance. Politics. UK Politics.
Written by: Jessica Gethyn

To anyone outside of the finance and private security industries, these worlds can feel closed, inclusive, stalwarts of capitalism with little to no public profile and zero accountability or scrutiny.

The latest company to raise concerns is "solutions-provider" Atrax. Founded by two German entrepreneurs in 2016, Atrax are notoriously secretive about their affairs but are believed to provide consultancy services and representation for investors, as well as private security and, rumor has it, private military.

For almost a decade Atrax have been silently operated, accepting clients on a referral-only basis, and reporting huge profits, even throughout the country's economic difficulties. But last weekend, founder Stefan Weber appeared at a conference in San Francisco, where he gave a speech about the future of blockchain technology and cryptocurrencies. During this speech, to a carefully selected audience, Weber is reported to have said of Atrax, "The clients want what the clients want. But sometimes they need a bit of help to truly understand what they need. That's where we come in."

"Wait a minute," said Misty, "Atrax is rumored to provide military? Like mercenaries? This is ridiculous. What could they possibly want with a drag bar on Old Compton Street?"

"Who knows? Sounds like they'll do pretty much anything their client asks for. I'd assume that it isn't Atrax themselves who are looking to buy up Old Compton Street but one of their clients." Then Miles looked as though he'd remembered something important. His eyes flashed. "Wait." He dove back into his phone, tapping away, bringing up Lady Lady's obituary. "I knew it."

"What?"

"The writer of Lady Lady's obituary, it's the same writer as the Atrax article. That can't be a coincidence, right?" Miles showed Misty his phone. He was right. Both articles were written by Jessica Gethyn. It was strange, Misty supposed, for a journalist who specialized in politics and finance to write the obituary of a dead drag queen.

"Oh my God, they knew each other," said Misty. "Lady Lady and Jessica Gethyn. They knew each other, they must have."

"Then we should talk to her," said Miles. "We should try and talk to Jessica Gethyn."

"I'll email her now."

Dear Jessica,

My name is Misty Divine and I worked closely with Lady Lady. I read your obituary and found it both moving and sensitive. I also read your article about the company Atrax, and I wondered whether we might be able to meet or have a phone call to discuss it?

Best wishes,
Misty Divine

29

✱✱✱✱✱✱✱✱✱

WHEN THEY GOT back to the club after lunch Misty felt heavy, weighed down by pasta, and worried that the nightclub she'd just inherited might be dodgy as fuck.

Mandy was waiting for them in the office. She looked much better than she had when they'd left. Her face was back to its normal color, no longer blotchy from crying. Mandy had had a burger delivered, and its empty papers sat on top of a pile of paperwork on her desk, and a smell of gherkins lingered in the air.

"Listen, Misty," she said. "I want you to know that I've told you everything there is to know. All the cards are on the table. I'd still love for you to come and work here, step into Lady Lady's role, and help me to run this place, but I understand if you can't now."

Misty spoke up in reply before she'd even really thought about it. "I'm taking the job, Mandy. I've decided that I'm taking the job. But I need to know more about this situation with Auntie Susan. What do you know about her?"

Mandy sighed and sat back in her chair. "The truth is, she's awful. She'd always lurked on the edges of criminality, that's what broke up the double act. Lady Lady told me that Auntie Susan had been involved in some drug dealing, and that's why they fell out. After the double act crumbled Auntie Susan struggled to find work of the same profile, so she invested everything she had in buying The Plough. Since then, she's become involved in all sorts—drugs, burglaries . . . I heard a rumor she was running a gang of mobile phone thieves. You know, the ones on bikes who snatch your phone out your hand and then cycle off."

"And now it seems she's into blackmail," said Misty.

"Indeed," said Mandy, her face tightening into a scowl. "I wish we'd never asked her for help."

"Why did you?"

"When we found out that Atrax had submitted their proposal for the building, we weren't sure what to do. Lady Lady was worried, more worried than I'd ever seen her. She didn't want Soho to lose another independent. She didn't want the queer scene to lose another space. And of course she didn't want the club to close. It was her baby, her life."

"So, it was Lady Lady's idea to go to Auntie Susan?" asked Miles.

"Yes. She was panicked. She thought Auntie Susan might know somebody, someone we could talk to. We weren't expecting her to propose a financial arrangement with someone at the council."

Misty was surprised by all this. For months she'd been meeting Lady Lady for coffee and dinner and drinks, they'd worked together countless times, and Misty had had no idea any of this was happening. Lady Lady clearly knew how to keep a secret.

"And who is the woman at the council?"

"We don't know," said Mandy, popping a Polo mint into her mouth and crunching it. "All we know is that we pay her two K a week to keep the redevelopment proposal at the bottom of the pile. We don't know what department she's in, her name, anything."

Misty's brain felt full.

It was still complicated, and too open, like a thousand loose threads waiting to be stitched together.

"I'm sorry to do this," said Mandy, "as I know we've all got a lot going on with police searches and arrests and whatnot, but I do need to talk to you about something work-related."

"What's that?" asked Misty, her tone perhaps a little snappy. The last thing she wanted to do was talk about work.

"We have to reopen the club. We can't afford to stay closed much longer."

"But Lady Lady's only been dead a week!" said Misty. "Isn't it too soon?"

"Not if we want to pay the bills," said Mandy. "But listen, I was thinking we should reopen with a big celebration of Lady Lady—some sort of memorial. On Friday. We'll invite back everyone who performed last Wednesday, if they want to come, and Lady Lady's nearest and dearest. What do you think?"

"Sounds good," said Misty, an idea beginning to take root. "Want me to start putting together a lineup for the show?"

Mandy winked. "That is kind of your job now."

AFTER AN HOUR of brainstorming names with Mandy, Misty and Miles left her alone in the office and headed to the bar, where Misty opened them both a bottle of beer.

"Are you allowed to just take a beer like that?"

"Well, ten percent of it is mine." Misty smiled. "And I'll pay for it obviously."

"You seem very keen about this reopening on Friday," said Miles.

"I am," said Misty. "I think it's a great idea. And . . . it gives me the perfect way in with Auntie Susan."

"And . . . ?"

"It'll bring back all the suspects," she whispered. "Back to the scene of the crime. Everyone who was here when the murder happened. Maybe it'll be an opportunity to see which of them is the killer."

They sat down at one of the cabaret tables in the auditorium when Misty's phone started ringing.

Is it Den? Answer it quickly! she thought as she struggled to get the phone out of her jacket pocket.

"Who is it?" asked Miles, in a whisper.

"I don't know," said Misty, pulling out the phone and revealing the screen.

Plimberley. A video call.

"Answer it," urged Miles. "See what she wants."

Misty picked up the call and, after a second of Wi-Fi connection bother, Plimberley's and Moneypenny's faces appeared onscreen, crowded round Plim's phone.

"Hi, loves," said Misty.

"Holy shit," said Moneypenny. "You look amazing! What are you doing in drag?"

"You know me, bab"—Misty winked—"can't resist the glamour."

"Cut the shit, everyone," said Plimberley. "We're calling for the goss, Misty. Everyone's talking about it."

"About what?"

"About *you*! Getting arrested and spending the night in prison."

"Well, technically it wasn't prison . . ."

"Oh my God," said Plimberley. "It's true? It's actually true?"

"Yes, Plim, it's true," said Misty. "But it was a misunderstanding."

"So, what happened?" asked Moneypenny. "Why did they arrest you?"

"I guess I was in the wrong place at the wrong time a couple too many times," said Misty, "and they got suspicious. But it's all been cleared up now, ladies. You can tell anyone who asks, Misty Divine didn't kill anybody."

"I told you!" said Plim, turning to Moneypenny. "I told you she didn't do it."

"I never said she did!" replied Moneypenny, glancing at Misty on the screen.

"Yeah you did, all right," said Plim, digging Moneypenny's hole even deeper. "You said you reckoned if the police had enough to arrest her that she must have done it."

Moneypenny laughed, embarrassed. "Well, I was wrong, all right. Sorry, Misty."

"That's okay," said Misty. But it felt very much not okay. These were her friends, her colleagues, and if she was taking over from Lady Lady she'd likely have to be their manager too. She tried to brush it off, to not show that it had bothered her. "Listen, while I've got you, have either of you heard from Den the last couple of days? I'm having trouble getting in contact with him."

Neither of them had.

Misty hurriedly closed the conversation and ended the call, not wanting to add fuel to the gossip fire but glad she was able to get the word out that she'd been released. Plimberley would see to that.

"So," said Miles. "What's next, in the investigation? What do we do now?"

"Den. We'll talk to Den tonight at the hotel and go to see Auntie Susan first thing tomorrow. I want some time to prepare myself for that one."

"Sounds good," said Miles.

"Shall we get out of here and have something to eat at home first?" said Misty, feeling like she needed some time away from Lady's Bar after the day's intense conversations.

"Great idea."

MISTY POPPED BACK to the office to say goodbye to Mandy and pick up the laptop, promising to clear a few emails from the Lady's Bar inbox this evening.

She was about to leave, to rejoin Miles, before she turned back to her new co-owner.

"Is there anything else, Mandy?" she asked, her voice low and serious and possibly a touch threatening. "Anything else going on here that you haven't told me about?"

"No, no . . . I've told you everything, Misty, honestly." Mandy's little face wobbled in the middle of her giant black bob.

Misty stepped back into the room. "Because if I don't go to the police with what I know about this bribery scheme, I'm an accessory. This inheritance you and Lady Lady planned for me, it's a criminal record. So, I need to know, right now, is there anything else?"

"I promise, Misty. There's nothing else. I don't know any-thing about any dress or chocolates. What me and Lady Lady were arguing about on the night she was killed was this . . . business . . . with Auntie Susan."

"If I find out you're holding back on me, Mandy . . ."

"You won't. I promise. I'm an open book."

"Okay," said Misty, "I guess I'll see you tomorrow."

30

★★★★★★★★★

MILES AND MISTY walked through the apartment door into their little flat and Misty sat straight down at the kitchen table, kicking her heels onto the lino floor. So much had happened since she had last made a suspect list at this table: her arrest, her night at the cells, the truth about Mandy and Auntie Susan.

Miles flicked on the kettle and set about taking out mugs, sugar, and milk, ready to make early evening tea.

"Miles," said Misty, "do we have any of that whiskey left?"

THEY WERE BOTH taking their first sip of the good stuff when Misty's phone rang. It took her a second to wriggle it out of her handbag, but when she did she saw it was a call from Mr. McDermott. She answered.

"Hello, Mr. McDermott."

"Hi, Joe," he said. "How are you feeling? How's your day been?"

Eventful, thought Misty.

"I'm fine, glad I'm not in that cell, that's for sure."

"I bet," said Mr. McDermott. "I'm calling with an update. I spoke with DI Davies earlier. The chocolate box they found in your apartment—it's been analyzed. No trace of poison. No fingerprints and no DNA. There's no physical evidence that you or Miles ever touched it."

"That's great news," said Misty. "Miles, the police believe us, that the chocolates were planted."

"In any case," continued Mr. McDermott, "they'd still like to talk to you. They don't have enough evidence to charge you with anything now, but seeing as you seem to be connected to the case, they want to take another statement."

"What else could I possibly tell them? Well, I'm not doing it tonight. I've had enough of DI Davies for one day," said Misty.

"No, not tonight. But they'll call you tomorrow to set something up."

Misty thanked Mr. McDermott for the update and ended the call, taking a swift gulp of whiskey.

"That's good news then," said Miles.

"Yes," said Misty, "very good news." It was a relief that the police didn't have a strong enough case against her, but Misty couldn't rest easy until the real killer was behind bars and her name was cleared once and for all.

THEY ARRIVED AT the Empire Hotel just after 8 p.m. The hotel was a miserable-looking place, and Misty found it all the more so now that she had her new position as host of Lady's Bar—if she could save it. The hotel's exterior was grimy with

Central London pollution, as though the whole building was overdue a go-over with a power hose. Misty was glad to be there after-hours to be able to avoid Joe's boss, Jane. She was such a sour face. Misty was there for one reason and one alone: to ask Den if he knew anything about Lady Lady's dress.

As they walked through the doors Misty was disheartened to see an enormous coachload of tourists filling the reception area. Den was behind the desk, busily assigning rooms and printing magnetic key cards. He always looked shorter out of drag, and Misty thought his eyes seemed tired. The "Francesca" name badge on his blazer was the sparkliest thing about him. He looked up and saw them, and his mouth fell open in surprise.

"Got a minute?" Misty mouthed.

Den held up his hand to indicate that he needed five minutes to clear the waiting coach party. Misty nodded, and she and Miles took a seat in the hotel's two-star reception area.

ARE YOU NERVOUS?" asked Miles quietly. He sank his face into his hands and whispered, "*I* feel nervous. Oh God, Joe, maybe we shouldn't be doing this. Maybe it's time to just go to the police with what you've already found out."

"No, Miles. We can't trust the police! And I have to know for myself. I have to know if it was Den who killed Lady Lady and tried to frame me."

"And if it is him? If you get him to confess for your secret recording, you promise that's it?"

"Yes, if I can get him to admit it I'll take that evidence to the police and they can work out the rest without ever needing to know about Mandy's deal with Auntie Susan. If it's Den, there's a way we can catch the killer *and* save the club." And Misty thought there could be no better justice for Lady Lady than that.

She whipped out her phone and switched on the voice recording app before stashing it back in her handbag. She was ready.

They approached the reception desk, and Den seemed on edge. He was fidgeting with his blazer pocket and chewing his lip. Maybe he was nervous from having avoided her for days.

"Hi, Misty, Miles," he said. "What are you doing here? I heard from Jane you were taking some time off."

"I wanted to talk to you about something," said Misty. "I've been trying to reach you."

Den shifted his bodyweight from foot to foot and tinkered with his nose ring. "Yeah, sorry about that, Misty, love. Just been trying to keep a low profile. *You* know how it is."

He knows I was arrested, thought Misty.

But is he the one who set it up?

"Have you got a minute for a cuppa?" she asked, trying to sound friendly.

"Yeah, that's the last of my coach parties checked in. Let me make us a brew."

MISTY AND MILES leaned on the reception desk with steaming cups of tea in their hands. The cups themselves were an upgrade from Mandy's selection at the Lady's Bar office. These ones were lovely hotel crockery and were clean and unchipped. No Sports Direct logos here. Den stood on the other side of the desk, the computer and maps of London between them.

"Sorry again that I didn't reply to your messages or calls," said Den. "You must be having a dreadful time. I know how close you were to Lady Lady. I'm a terrible friend, I'm sorry." Den's head fell so far forward Misty couldn't tell if he was crying or not, but he made a little sniffle like he might be. It smelled like manipulation in here.

"Don't worry about it," said Misty. "It's been a horrible week."

"It really has," said Miles.

This was difficult for Misty. Looking at Den appearing so sad, her friend whom she'd known for years, she mostly wanted to reach her arms over the reception desk and pull him into a tight hug. But she had to remember, this was the same Den who was selling stolen jewelry out of Lady's Bar. The same Den who might have poisoned Lady Lady and planted evidence in Misty's flat. The same Den who had too much evidence pointing toward him for Misty to ignore. Misty had a right to know what was going on—she'd been arrested, for heaven's sake.

"Den, I need to ask you something," said Misty, placing her handbag on the reception desk between them to give the phone inside the best chance of capturing what was said.

"Okay . . ." His eyes darted from Misty to Miles, perhaps looking for support or reassurance.

"I heard on the grapevine that you've been selling jewelry."

"Misty . . . I don't know what you're talking about."

"Stolen jewelry," said Misty. "And maybe stolen dresses . . ."

"I said I don't know what you're talking about."

"Did you give or sell that Judy Garland dress to Lady Lady? I need to know, Den."

Den was angry. His cheeks flushed red, and a bead of sweat popped up directly between his eyebrows.

He leaned forward, whispering, "You've no right to come here, while I'm at *work*, and accuse me of this. What the fuck, Misty?"

His angry response irritated Misty, who in turn began feeling a bit angry herself. "I've got every right," she hissed. "Someone broke into my flat to try to frame me for murder, and I spent last night locked up in Charing Cross Police Station. Lady Lady was wearing a stolen dress when she died, and you've been selling stolen jewelry in her club. I'm trying to connect the dots."

"You're out of line, Misty."

"Do you know where she got the dress?" asked Misty. "Are you the Kensington Catburglar?"

"The Kensington Catburglar!" scoffed Den. "Are you serious? You've lost it, Misty. One night in prison and it's done you in." His voice was raised enough to attract the attention of the night security guard in the back office, who poked his head out and asked if everything was all right.

"We're fine!" snapped Den, waving the security guard away.

Miles put his hand on Misty's shoulder. "Come on, Joe, let's go."

"I never sold any stolen jewelry, never sold any stolen dresses. How dare you! How dare you come in here and accuse me like this. While I'm at work!"

Misty's internal lie detector was scribbling lines wildly all over the page. Den's sudden rage and his profuse denials were serious red flags. He might as well have outright admitted to selling the stolen jewelry.

"I know you've been having financial problems. Is it so crazy to think you might be doing something desperate to make money? I had to ask, Den."

"No, you didn't. You didn't have to ask anything at all. I'm here, at work, trying to keep my head down and stay out of all this drag scene murder bullshit, and you bring it right to my desk. It's not on, Misty."

The security guard stepped out of the back office, fully into the reception. "Come on, guys, whatever's going on here, it's definitely not work-related. Francesca, you know better than this. Rowing where the guests might see you. Take it outside. Tsk. Unprofessional."

Den reached forward with both hands and took back Misty's and Miles's cups of tea. If ever there was a sign that a conversation was over, it was the snatching back of tea.

"Go on," he said. "Get out."

A S THEY STEPPED out into the street Miles turned to Misty.

"So, we didn't get a confession," he said. Then, laughing, "Did we really think we were just going to walk in and ask him and he'd confess?"

Misty felt hot, defensive. Yes, that was kind of what she'd hoped would happen. But now, standing on the pavement, turning off her phone's secret recording app, she did feel like a bit of a plonker.

"Well," said Misty, trying to shine a bright light on what had otherwise been a failure of an interrogation, "we did learn one thing. Den is definitely selling stolen jewelry. He was too defensive about it, too angry. I'm sure of it."

"Yes, but was he involved with the Judy Garland dress?" asked Miles, pointing a finger. "Does this mean he's the Catburglar?"

"I don't know," said Misty. "But there's got to be a way to find out."

W**HEN THEY GOT** home, and after Joe had de-dragged, they un-packed the Lady's Bar laptop and opened the inbox. There were lots of messages. From reporters, from customers, from performers. Joe supposed Mandy was right, the club did have to reopen eventually, and it made sense to do it with a memorial show for Lady Lady.

Joe went through the emails and labeled them all. Green for performers. Blue for customers. Red for reporters. Then they set about replying to them. Joe decided to answer the performers first, because there was nothing to say to patrons yet. Mandy was planning to announce the reopening tomorrow apparently. In the meantime, Joe sent emails to Moneypenny, Plimberley, Amour, and Len, asking them all if they could return to per-form at the reopening show on Friday. They decided to hold off on inviting Den. They just weren't in the mood to write that email yet and needed to think about it carefully. Den was pissed off with them, but he was also a major suspect.

Mandy was right. Aside from assessing them all as suspects and witnesses, it would be nice, Joe thought, for the acts who had been through the trauma of the death together to be the ones performing at the reopening. But perhaps the killer would reveal themselves. Perhaps someone would remember some-thing. Joe thought back to the night in the dressing room, the foaming mouth, the panicked drags in the corridor. Was it really less than a week ago? It already felt like a lifetime. They missed Lady Lady and longed to talk to her about everything that was going on. It felt shocking to think they'd never talk to her again. But that was grief, they supposed, the blunt realization that death was permanent and irreversible. They needed to think about something else.

"What am I going to wear on Friday?" they asked Miles, hoping that starting a conversation about costumes might subdue their grief and lift the mood. "For the reopening."

Miles put down his book. "Ooh, interesting question. What are you thinking?"

"Well, the press will be there, so I need to look good. And I want to make Lady Lady proud, to show everyone she was right to choose me as her successor."

"Do you think Florentina would have time to make you something new?"

"I don't know. Maybe it's worth asking her."

Yes, Joe thought, a new dress for the reopening was an excellent idea. They sent a text message to Florentina, asking her if she'd have time to make a new gown and inviting her to come to the reopening at the same time.

"So, are you resigning from the hotel?" asked Miles once Joe had put their phone down.

"Yeah, I guess I am," said Joe. "I *have* to. Taking over for Lady Lady is a dream gig. I'd be a fool not to do it, right? I just want all this murder business out of the way . . ." Joe sighed and rubbed their eyes, picking a fleck of dried eyelash glue from their lashes. "I feel like I'm so close, Miles, to having everything I ever wanted, but I've also never felt so in danger."

"I know what you mean," said Miles.

"The flat being broken into, being followed, the arrest, the fact that there's a murderer on the loose."

"It's a lot. It's been a hell of a week."

The truth was, Joe felt at a crossroads. They longed for safety and security, hence staying for so long at the hotel in the first place. And taking the job at Lady's Bar was the opposite of safe and secure. The last post holder had been poisoned in her dressing room, and the co-owner was running a bribery scheme to keep the place open. But wasn't the potential thrilling? More exciting than sitting in the windowless hotel office processing paperwork that they simply didn't care about. Wasn't it everything they'd been working so hard toward for so long? Joe knew what Misty would do and what they wanted to do themself. It was the right thing to leave the hotel, to take a leap of faith.

"Are you worried about this business with Atrax and the bribery?" Miles had his sensible head on, and it was clear that he was worried himself.

"Well, of course I'm worried about that. If Mandy gets caught for this scheme with Auntie Susan, we'll both be in trouble now that I'm the co-owner, but I had a moment today. In the office, when Mandy said she'd understand if I didn't want to do it, it just felt impossible to *not* do it. I don't know, something about Lady Lady going to such desperate lengths to keep the club makes it feel more worthwhile than spending my days doing invoices in that hotel."

"I can't stop thinking about Auntie Susan," said Miles. "About her being a criminal mastermind. What a wild career shift."

"Hardly a mastermind, more of a ringleader by the sounds of it."

"What are you going to say to her tomorrow?"

"I'm going to invite her to the reopening," said Joe. "That'll be my way in, and then I'm just going to ask her about Mandy and Baseball Cap. And maybe, if she's really so well connected in criminal circles, she'll know something about the Kensington Catburglar or the Judy Garland dress."

"Perhaps she knows something about Den," suggested Miles. "Is that what you're thinking?"

"I'm not sure," said Joe. "I still don't see how it all fits together. If we're assuming that it was Auntie Susan's Baseball Cap who planted the chocolates, why? And where did Lady Lady get that bloody dress? It must have been Den, right?"

"I guess so . . . You'll have to go in drag," said Miles, "to see Auntie Susan."

"Oh yes, of course. I think it's better that Misty meets Auntie Susan anyway. Lady Lady would have gone in drag, for sure."

"That she would," said Miles.

THEY WENT TO bed early, both exhausted from the day and from the stress of everything that was happening. As Joe lay in bed, waiting for their brain to switch off so they could fall asleep, they felt slightly as though they were in a strange, foreign place. The search of the apartment, the police rifling through every corner, had disrupted Joe's comfort in their own home. It had been invaded, violated, searched from top to bottom. Everything had been touched. Everything had been moved. Joe lay in bed looking at the ceiling, listening to Miles's breathing, who had fallen asleep instantly. They knew the flat would feel like home again eventually.

They thought of Auntie Susan, of The Plough, and how intimidating a place it was. Were they really going to go to see her tomorrow? Auntie Susan, the fixer, the ringleader behind the Lady's Bar bribery-for-survival scheme.

The very idea of it was enough to keep Joe awake, and they lay in their bed racked with nerves about tomorrow. Eventually they drifted off to sleep, dreaming fitfully of murder and mystery.

31

WEDNESDAY

JOE WOKE WITH a start. In their dreams they'd been with Lady Lady, and she was trying to tell them something that Joe couldn't understand. It was as though she were speaking a language that Joe had never heard before. Lady Lady had reached out and grasped Joe's hand, her fingers cold like hard frozen metal on a winter's day. Joe woke up and felt their own fingers, discovering they were still chilled from Lady Lady's ethereal touch. They were sweating, their forehead was clammy against the pillow, and their bare chest prickly from the summer heat and the warmth of the duvet.

They looked at the clock—6:37 a.m. Miles was still sleeping. Joe got out of bed quietly and went to the bathroom to shower and brush their teeth. Once they were ready for the day they settled at the kitchen table with a fresh pot of coffee. They took a sip, longing for the energy and vitality it would bring. Coffee. The drink of the gods.

Joe ran through the previous day while they drank the coffee. After yesterday's revelations and confrontations, things were becoming clearer. Either Den or Auntie Susan was the killer, that's what Joe thought. Mandy, Tess, and Jan were all off the hook.

JOE HEARD MILES stirring at about 7:30 a.m., and when he emerged from the bedroom he was already showered and dressed. He was wearing a red shirt and a pair of sky blue chinos.

"You look so handsome," said Joe as Miles stepped into the kitchen.

"So do you," Miles replied, leaning over to plant a kiss on Joe's lips.

Joe poured Miles a cup of coffee and they sat at the table together.

"Thinking about Auntie Susan?" Miles asked.

"Yeah," said Joe. "I'm a bit scared to meet her. She's got a fierce reputation."

"You don't have to, Joe. You can stop now, if you want."

"Not yet," said Joe. "Auntie Susan's got questions to answer about why she's been following me. I want to know if she planted the chocolates. I need to know if she's the killer."

Joe got into drag slowly, spending more time than usual drawing on individual eyebrow hairs with a fine brush, while Miles watched TV in the living room. Becoming Misty Divine usually took about an hour, but today it took a bit longer. Joe wanted to impress Auntie Susan, and they also wanted to look intimidating, all business, like the owner of a Soho cabaret club might look. Once the makeup was finished and eyelashes glued on, Joe selected a suit from the drag wardrobe. It was pink sequin with a rhinestone-encrusted collar and lapels. The shoulders were huge and the skirt was tight and short. Joe got dressed, careful not to smudge their face as they pulled a light blouse over their head.

Once the costume was on it was time for hair, the final step. Joe looked at the wig shelf and picked out a neon pink updo. They fixed the wig with pins and glue and slipped on a pair of pink stilettos. The transformation was complete.

MILES AND MISTY arrived at The Plough shortly after 11 a.m. The taxi pulled up outside the pub and Misty realized again how filthy it looked. Half the windows were boarded up with plasterboard, and the white walls were stained and filthy from rain and grime. A tattered and shredded dirty rainbow flag hung limply above the front door, the only external sign that this was a gay venue.

Misty and Miles got out of the car and looked at the pub.

"Jesus Christ," said Miles. "What a dump."

"Is it even open?"

It didn't look open. The windows that weren't boarded up were dark and covered in cracks and curling posters.

"Let's ring the bell and find out."

They walked to the front door, and Misty reached out and pushed it, just to see. It swung open easily.

"I guess it's open after all," said Miles. "You ready?"

"As ready as I'll ever be," replied Misty.

The inside of The Plough was worse than the outside. The floor was made of worn boards that once had been painted black, but the paint was long overdue for a refresh. The whole place smelled of vinegar and stale cigarette smoke, as though they had allowed indoor smoking late into the previous night. Straight opposite the front door was a long bar, and to the right were three pool tables. There were men here playing at the tables. As Misty and Miles stepped inside the men turned to look, putting down their pool cues.

"What can I get you?" asked a woman behind the bar, whose hair was cut into a short bleached mohawk.

"Two lemonades, please," said Miles, sitting down on a stool at the bar.

The server busied herself filling two scratched pint glasses from a lemonade pump. No ice. She slid them across the bar to Miles, and lemonade sloshed over the edges onto the wooden surface, pooling in little puddles under the glassware.

"Four pounds, please," she said.

Miles got his phone out to pay and held it toward the bar.

"Cash only," said the barmaid.

Miles dug in his pocket and pulled out a five-pound note, handing it over. She snatched it off him and put it into the till, slamming the pound change down in return.

"I'm here to see Auntie Susan," said Misty to the server. "Where is she?"

"She's in the back," she replied, disinterested, pointing toward a pair of saloon doors that looked as though they opened onto a bigger room.

"Okay," said Misty. She was trying to show confidence, assertiveness, but she felt apprehensive. Even the force field of dressing as Misty wasn't enough to shake the feeling that they shouldn't be here, that this was a dangerous place and that she could be about to confront her mentor's killer. But she knew she had to do this, she had to speak to Auntie Susan and get closer to understanding what had happened between her and Lady Lady. "Shall I just go back then?" she asked the server.

"It's your life," said the barmaid. "Do what you want." She

disappeared into a stockroom behind the bar, leaving Miles and Misty alone.

"Shit," said Misty to Miles under her breath.

"Do you want me to come with you?"

"No, I think it's better that I go alone."

Miles smiled, but she could tell he was worried too. "You've got this. And I'll be right here."

Misty pushed open the saloon doors and stepped into the back room of The Plough. It was a big square space, filled with mismatched chairs and tables, and at the far wall was a small stage with a scrappy glitter curtain behind it.

To the left there was a white door with the word "office" written on it in marker pen. The paint was peeling and the door hung half open. Misty walked over to it and looked through. There was a short corridor and then a second door, which must have been Auntie Susan's office. Outside it stood a young man in a tracksuit who was scrolling on his phone. He looked up.

"Can I help you?" he asked.

"I'm here to talk to Auntie Susan. Is she here?"

"She's busy."

Misty tutted with what she hoped was an air of importance. "Tell her it's Misty Divine. She'll want to see me."

The man looked Misty up and down and sighed. Then he knocked on the second door and opened it, letting himself in. He stepped inside and closed the door behind him. Misty waited.

After a few minutes the tracksuited man emerged, saying, "She'll see you."

"Thank you," said Misty.

She felt sick with nerves. She was about to meet with an actual criminal. She took a deep breath and walked into Auntie Susan's office.

The office was huge. Much bigger than Misty expected, and at least double the size of the Lady's Bar office. It was actually beautifully decorated, unlike the rest of the pub. It was gaudy, but in a draggy way that was camp and elegant. At the far end was a gold-and-white marble desk, and in front of that was a leopard-print chaise longue. On the wall were portraits of Auntie Susan, a drag queen with flame red hair. And Auntie Susan herself was there, sitting behind the desk with a small white Chihuahua on her lap. The room smelled of cigarettes and perfume.

Auntie Susan stood up to greet Misty, dropping the little dog onto the floor. It scampered onto a luxurious deep green velvet dog bed and glared at her with beady eyes.

"Misty Divine," said Auntie Susan. "We finally meet."

"Finally," said Misty. "Thank you for seeing me."

Auntie Susan stepped around to the front of the desk. She was wearing a white Lycra minidress, with no corset, and Misty could see her belly button through it. Her hair was huge and scarlet and her makeup bold but rough. She was a traditional English pub drag queen, and her style hadn't changed since the nineties. She looked perfectly at home with the leopard print and marble.

"I hear that you're the new co-owner of Lady's Bar," said Auntie Susan. She was cold and to the point. "Condragulations."

How did she know? Nobody on the drag scene knew about the inheritance yet, not that Misty was aware of anyway. She hadn't told anybody apart from Miles. It felt strange to be confronted with it so abruptly, and she didn't like it. "Thank you," she replied.

Auntie Susan smiled, her red lips curling up into a grin that was almost a snarl. "Word travels fast. So, what can I do for you?"

This is it, thought Misty. This is what she came for.

"We're organizing a memorial for Lady Lady this Friday, and I wanted to ask if you'd be interested in performing or saying a few words. There will be lots of press and invited guests, and as Lady Lady's former partner, we thought it might be nice for you to be involved."

Auntie Susan leaned back and sat on the edge of her desk. She crossed her feet in front of her, and Misty noticed her shoes for the first time: giant heels covered in red sequins that matched her hair and lips.

"A memorial, you say?"

"Yes. To reopen the club after the murder. Given your very public falling-out I thought this could be the perfect opportunity to lay the past to rest once and for all. The whole world still sees the two of you as enemies. This could be an opportunity for you to make things right."

"Interesting . . ." Auntie Susan scratched her makeup-clad face.

"It's on Friday at eight p.m. and we thought that—"

"That's not why you're here. In fact, given that you know of mine and Lady Lady's history it makes it ridiculous that you would come here proposing this. Why would you want me there on a night like that?" Auntie Susan's smile had dropped completely, and suddenly her face was terrifying. Her long paper eyelashes were like spiders, and there was a tension in her lips that Misty found unsettling.

"It is," she said feebly. "I'm here to invite you to—"

Auntie Susan kicked her legs forward and stepped off the desk, walking back round to her chair behind it and sitting down. The Chihuahua growled.

"I don't like liars, Misty. We're both adults, so let's talk like adults. You're here about the murder."

Admit it, thought Misty. She paused, unsure what to say next. Eventually she spoke, deciding honesty here was the best policy.

"Okay. Fine. I'm here about the murder."

Auntie Susan sighed. "Your flat was searched the night before last, and you've just spent a night locked up at Charing Cross Police Station. Seems *you're* the one everybody wants to talk to about the murder."

How did she know about the flat search? How did she know about the inheritance? Was Baseball Cap still spying on her, unnoticed? Misty felt as though she were on the back foot, as though Auntie Susan already knew everything there was to know about her. *Play her at her own game.*

"I know about the two grand a week," she said. "About Atrax and the woman at the council. Mandy told me everything."

Auntie Susan laughed, but not in a joyful way, in a condescending and patronizing tone. "Everything . . . ha! Oh, sweet, innocent Misty, you don't know anything at all."

"Okay, then why don't you tell me?" said Misty, thrusting her shoulders back, irritated now at Auntie Susan's superior attitude. "Why don't we put all our cards on the table and see where we stand at the end?"

"You didn't kill Lady Lady," said Auntie Susan plainly. "You wouldn't be here if you did. So I think Mandy's told you about our arrangement, and now you're here to find out whether *I* killed her, and I can tell you now, I didn't. Why would I?"

Misty was taken aback. For Auntie Susan it seemed discussing whether or not you'd killed someone was as casual a conversation topic as what you're having for dinner. "Well, if you didn't kill her," said Misty, "who did? Come on then! If you know everything, as you claim to, why don't you tell me who did it."

Auntie Susan tutted and opened a silver box on her desk. Inside it was a row of perfectly aligned cigarettes. She lifted one to her lips and lit it with a match, blasting out a plume of smoke and sulfur. "That much I don't know, but it wasn't anything to do with me. A long time ago, Lady Lady was my friend, and we may have fallen out, but there was always a respect between us, you know. Venue owner to venue owner, queen to queen."

"And I suppose it helped that she's been giving you thousands of pounds," said Misty, trying to steer the conversation. If Auntie Susan wouldn't, or couldn't, tell her the identity of the killer, she could at least shed some light on the blackmail scheme.

A hint of a smirk appeared on Auntie Susan's face. "That too."

"Tell me," said Misty, feeling more confident with Auntie Susan now, as though they had found some kind of even ground, "who does the money go to? Who is the woman at the council?"

"I'm not giving you my contacts," she replied, puffing on her cigarette. "So, what? You can cut me out and go to her directly? I don't think."

"Well, what can you tell me about Atrax? Is it Atrax themselves or one of their clients who's trying to take over the bar?"

Auntie Susan straightened her back and inhaled deeply. "Atrax . . ." she said. "Lady Lady asked me the same thing, but I've only been involved on the council side. All I know about

Atrax is that they're secretive. I tried to use my contacts to find out who their clients are, but I didn't get anywhere and that's the truth."

Misty felt as though it was. At least they were being frank with each other now, even though it was tense. "So, you really don't know anything about who it is that's trying to take over the club?"

"Nothing. All I know is that for the time being I'm stopping them. You *need* me, Misty." She stood up behind her desk and leaned forward, placing both hands down on the marble surface. She glared at Misty and Misty's heart raced. She looked terrifying: her eyes were sharp and bore into Misty's. "Without *me*, Lady's Bar is finished, and both Mandy and Lady Lady knew it. That's why they came to me. And don't think that you can come here now with your ten percent share and change our agreement."

"That's not why I'm here."

"You're up to your neck in shit, Misty Divine."

"I know you've been following me," Misty retorted, unafraid. "Your guy in the baseball cap, but why? What do you want from me?"

"What do you take me for, Misty? Some kind of fly-by-night amateur running a tin-pot pickpocket operation? I'm Auntie goddamn Susan. And you, you're new on the scene, an intruder in an arrangement that was running perfectly smoothly until Lady Lady wore that bastard Judy Garland dress and got herself murdered. I needed to know who I was dealing with."

"So, you've been spying on me?"

"I told you, I needed to know who I was dealing with."

Misty put her hands on her hips. "And the break-in at my apartment? The chocolates?"

Auntie Susan smirked. "I'll claim the break-in. Get yourself a better lock. My guy said he picked it with a goddamn hairpin."

"Funny."

"But I don't know anything about any chocolates."

"When your guy broke into my apartment he left behind a box of chocolates, identical to the ones that killed Lady Lady. That's why I was arrested."

"Not my guy," said Auntie Susan. "I've no interest in framing you, Misty. I wanted to know who you are. We searched the place. We read your bank statements, your paperwork, your cute pink notebook with your lists of 'suspects.' That's how I knew you hadn't done it. You see, I didn't frame you, because if you go down for murder there will be eyes all over the Lady's Bar finances, and it won't take thirty seconds for a decent interrogator to get the truth out of that wimp Mandy. I don't want the police poking around my arrangement with the council."

"Then help me," said Misty, believing the criminal before her and wondering now if there was a way she could help. "If you're telling me the truth, and you're really not involved in Lady Lady's murder, help me find out who did it before the police find out about the bribery."

"And how exactly do you think I can help?" asked Auntie Susan, leaning up off the desk and folding her arms across her padded chest. "To get you out of the shit you're in?"

Misty decided the best approach now was to be honest, to tell Auntie Susan why she was there and what she needed. It was the only way she'd gain her respect.

"I need to find out who killed Lady Lady and why. *We* need to. To honor her properly and to get her justice."

"And you think I can help you find out who killed her? You

really think you're going to be better at finding the killer than the police?"

"Yes," said Misty. And she was sure of it with every cell of her being. Saying it out loud, she realized she was more determined than ever to find out the truth. "I've heard that you're . . . well connected in certain circles, and I wondered if you might have heard something. About the dress, the Catburglar, anything."

"And what makes you think I'm going to help? Why should I share any information I might have with you?"

Looking at Auntie Susan now, listening to her being so tricksy and evasive, made Misty feel annoyed. She could feel her hackles rising, her blood boiling. "You'll help me because you *should*. Because despite it being good for both of our businesses for us to solve this as quickly as possible, Lady Lady was your friend once, and you cared about her. And do you know who doesn't care about her? The police officer in charge of finding out who did this. Queen to queen, as two people who loved her, help me. Help me find out who killed her."

Auntie Susan pushed back a loose strand of hair, tucking it into the top of the wig. She paused, thinking. Maybe she was shocked by Misty's front, the confidence with which she had demanded help. She sat back down, and it looked to Misty as though her anger was fading. "There was something that might be of interest to you . . ." Auntie Susan looked like she was thinking about how, or whether, to share something real. "But there's a price."

"What price?" asked Misty, her interest piqued.

"If I tell you what I know, our agreement about the bar stays in place. You don't tell the police, anyone, about it, under any circumstances."

"Understood," said Misty. Though she was uncomfortable with the bar staying stuck in its dodgy arrangement with Auntie Susan, it did seem as though it was working, and she knew she needed to deal with one problem at a time. First things first, she had to find the killer. "I agree."

Auntie Susan played with a silver pen that was in front of her on the desk. "Have you heard of the Red Egg?" she asked.

32

★★★★★★★★★

MISTY HAD INDEED heard of the Red Egg. She'd read about it a few days ago. She racked her brain to remember the details. It was a ruby in the shape of an egg, and it had been stolen by the Kensington Catburglar, the same as the Judy Garland dress. It was the most valuable item stolen by the Catburglar to date—apparently the second most valuable ruby in the entire world.

"Yes," she said, "I've heard of it."

"I know who has it."

"You know who the Kensington Catburglar is?" Misty was excited now but also scared. Scared to know what Auntie Susan had to tell her.

"I didn't say that," said Auntie Susan. "I said I know who has the Red Egg. I can't tell you whether or not they're the Catburglar."

"Who?" asked Misty. "Who is it?"

"If I tell you this, you didn't hear it from me. I have a certain reputation to uphold, and confidentiality is part of that. This is for Lady Lady—to do my part."

"I won't tell anyone," said Misty, desperate for the information, desperate to know who it was that had the Red Egg. "I promise I won't tell anyone."

"The drag king. Den."

Den. I knew it! I knew he was lying, the bastard!

"How? How do you know this?"

"He came to me," said Auntie Susan. "He told me he had it and asked if I knew anybody who would be interested in buying it."

"How did he get it? Is he the Catburglar?"

"I don't know," said Auntie Susan. "I sent him packing, quickly. I probably could have helped him, but I don't want my hands on an eleven-million-pound ruby, not one that's been all over the news. I wanted nothing to do with it and I told him so."

"When was this?" asked Misty.

"A few days before the murder," said Auntie Susan.

"And you didn't tell anybody? The police?"

Auntie Susan tutted. "You don't do what I do and tell the police about it, Misty. Of course, I thought about him when I read that Lady Lady had been wearing that dress. But whatever's going on with that burglar, I want no part of it. It's too high-profile for me. I like my business profitable but quiet. Now that's your lot. I don't know anything else and I've got a busy day." She clicked her fingers and the Chihuahua jumped up from its bed and ran to Auntie Susan's feet. She leaned down and scooped it up, cradling it in her arms like Dr. Evil. "It's time for you to go."

"Is there anything else? Anything else you know that could help?" begged Misty.

"I've told you what I know," said Auntie Susan. "Now go on, get out of here. You've got a club to run, haven't you?"

Misty started to leave when Auntie Susan spoke up again. "Do you know what, Misty?"

"What?"

"I think I will come to that memorial."

"That's great," said Misty, though slightly unnerved at the thought of having to see her again. "Do you want to perform or say a few words maybe?"

"No," she replied. "I don't want to. But I would like to attend."

"Very well," said Misty. "It will be great to have you there."

"Now go on," said Auntie Susan, "off you go."

Misty stepped out of the smoky office and into the little corridor. The lad in the tracksuit was still there guarding the door.

"Thank you," Misty said to him. He grunted something that could have been "You're welcome" in response. She hurried past him and back into the big performance room. Her head was spinning. Den had the Red Egg. The Red fucking Egg!

So, did that mean Den was the Catburglar? Did it mean he'd given the dress to Lady Lady? Did it mean that he'd *killed* her?

There were so many questions, and the only person who could answer them was Den himself.

She paced through the tatty furniture and pushed open the saloon doors back into the bar area. Miles looked up at her as she walked over to him sitting at the bar. The barmaid was nowhere to be seen.

"So," said Miles, "how did it go?"

"It was interesting," said Misty quietly. "Very interesting. I'll tell you about it when we get outside."

Misty took a sip of lemonade. It was cool and refreshing.

"Where are we going next?" asked Miles.

"The bar," said Misty.

"Okay, let's go," said Miles.

THEY GOT INTO the back of an Uber and Misty noticed the driver looking at her in the rearview mirror. He wasn't smiling and had a disdainful look on his face. She knew she'd get a one-star rating on the app for being in drag. She rolled her eyes at him and he looked away.

"So, tell me, what did she say?"

"Not here," she said, her head nodding toward the driver.

"WhatsApp it to me?" asked Miles.

"I can't. I'll explain when we get somewhere safe."

Misty knew she couldn't have any trace of her conversation with Auntie Susan in her phone. What she knew was too big, too dangerous. Den had the Red Egg, and that was something the police surely didn't know. If they did Den would have been arrested. It would have been in the news.

She needed a plan. She was bursting to talk to Miles. To tell him everything. But the drive in silence was probably useful too. It was giving her time to think.

She thought about her bargain with Auntie Susan. That she'd agreed to keep paying the bribery money. *One thing at a time*, she told herself.

She was worried about the bribery, obviously, but she had some deniability there, she thought. She could always argue she didn't know, that the arrangement predated her inheritance of the bar. But what she knew now, about the Red Egg, *that* worried her. This was serious information that in the normal course of things the police should definitely be told.

But Misty couldn't tell the police.

She couldn't betray Auntie Susan's confidence.

Should she even tell Miles?

By telling Miles she'd be putting him at risk too. If the police found out they knew and didn't report it they'd be accessories or something. They could both be arrested. Again. Miles could lose his job. She looked at the Uber driver's phone in the stand on the dashboard. They were seventeen minutes away from Lady's Bar. She had seventeen minutes to decide what to do. Should she carry on alone? Cut Miles out of the investigation from now on to protect him? Or did she need him too much?

It was clearly Miles's decision to make.

THEY ARRIVED AT Lady's Bar as Old Compton Street was busy with lunching office workers and summer tourists. When they got out of the car Misty was greeted with a gasp of oohs from a passing group of women. She smiled at them and waved, and they waved back. One of them clicked her fingers and shouted, "Work, queen!" and Misty nodded back.

The door to Lady's Bar was locked, which meant that Mandy hadn't arrived yet. Misty was glad. She needed to talk to Miles. She unlocked the doors and let them in.

"What's going on?" said Miles as they walked down the stairs. "What's the big mystery?"

"Not here," said Misty.

She switched on the lights in the auditorium, and the polished tables shone and sparkled. It was beautiful here. So very different from The Plough. She didn't want to talk to Miles in the bar. After the CCTV incident with the champagne she didn't feel safe discussing anything where there were cameras.

"Follow me," she said, leading Miles through the tables toward the toilets on the far side of the auditorium. *Definitely no cameras in there*, she thought.

She opened the door and they stepped inside.

"This is a bit much," said Miles. "What's happening?"

Misty spoke in a whisper, concerned about telling him what she knew.

"I know something," she said. "Auntie Susan told me something. But it's something big, very big. The kind of thing you'd lose your job over if the police find out we knew and didn't report it."

"Right . . ." said Miles.

"Do you understand?" said Misty. "If I tell you this, you're risking a lot." She felt torn. "I don't think I should tell you."

Miles paused, thinking, processing. "You're telling me that just knowing what you know, and not going to the police about it, would be breaking the law?"

"Yes," said Misty, "definitely." And she was sure it was true. Knowing the identity of the person who had the eleven-million-pound ruby and not reporting it would definitely be breaking the law. Misty felt shocked by the whole thing. She wasn't surprised because she'd had her suspicions about Den for a while. But the money involved! That's what was shocking—the value of the stolen items. How had he gone from begging for a thousand-pound loan to dealing with millions of pounds, in just a few months? If it wasn't so deadly it would have been impressive.

"Then why aren't you going to the police?" said Miles. "Surely it's a no-brainer. This investigation, Joe, you shouldn't get yourself in more trouble for it. Maybe it's time to talk to that nice

officer, Hughes, the one who came for tea. Or Mr. McDermott—
he was great the other night."

"I can't talk to the police. I can't talk to anyone. Only you, if
you want to know."

Miles looked at his hands. "Of course I want to know, Joe.
I'm with you. I'm with you one hundred percent. And I don't
want you doing this on your own."

"Thanks, Miles."

"So, tell me, what did she say?"

"She told me who has the Red Egg."

"The Red Egg? The ruby the Catburglar stole?"

"Yes," said Misty.

"Well, who has it?"

"Den."

"No fricking way. I knew it. We knew it!"

"Yes! Florentina told us he was selling stolen jewelry, but
Auntie Susan said that he's been trying to find a buyer for the
Red Egg."

"Shit," said Miles, suddenly realizing the gravity of the situation. "This is really serious. Does it mean that Den's the murderer?"

"I don't know. What should we do?"

"Wait a minute," said Miles, studying Misty's face carefully.
"There's something else, isn't there? Did she want something
from you in exchange for this information?"

"Yes," admitted Misty. She felt embarrassed now, and maybe
a little ashamed that she'd made an agreement with Auntie Susan on her own. "I agreed that Lady's Bar would carry on paying
the bribes to the council."

"Joe!" Miles was annoyed. "So you've put yourself in the

middle of a bribery scheme that you were no part of? You weren't involved at all in that, and now you're smack bang in the middle of it. This is the kind of thing I was trying to stop you from doing at the start—getting yourself in trouble. What were you thinking sticking your nose in that? What will Mandy say?"

"I had to, Miles! She said she had information that might be useful. And it is, isn't it? We've found a direct connection from Lady Lady to the Catburglar. Den *must* have been where she got the stolen dress. Which means that surely Den is the murderer too!"

"For fuck's sake," muttered Miles. "This is a mess, Joe. We could have some real problems now."

"What are we going to do?" she asked.

"I don't know," he said. "I need to think. I need to go for a walk."

"You're not going to tell anyone, are you?" said Misty.

"Of course I'm not going to bloody tell anyone!" said Miles. "And put us both in the shit? I just need time to think."

Misty couldn't shake how disappointed in her he looked, like she'd done something really wrong. "I'm sorry, Miles, if you think I've done the wrong thing. I just did what felt right in the moment. I thought we should try to sort out this murder stuff before we deal with the bribery."

"I just need some air. I'll come back soon. *Try* not to get in any more trouble until then," he said. He was cross, Misty knew. For the last couple of days he'd been suggesting going to the police instead of continuing the investigation themselves, and now, maybe, it seemed he could have been right. Now they had uncovered something so dangerous it could put their reputations and lives at risk. Perhaps he was right to be cross.

MISTY LET HERSELF into the office, switching on the lights to reveal the three unoccupied desks and Mandy's mountain of sandwich wrappers. Her heart was racing and she didn't know what to do next. She felt guilty about Miles. She couldn't tell anyone what she knew about the Red Egg, and she couldn't go to the police. Besides, she didn't have any actual evidence, just the word of a drag queen criminal.

She sat down at her desk and switched on the computer, her brain full of thoughts of Den. Last night's confrontation at the hotel had been difficult. As Den's friend, Misty didn't like seeing him upset. But as Lady Lady's friend, she couldn't let him get away with murder.

Mandy walked in, bustling past the fridge with her handbag.

"Hi, Misty, love," she said. Then, looking at her desk, "God, this desk is a mess." And then she sat down behind it with a grunt, making no effort to clean it at all.

Misty smiled. "Hi, Mandy," she said.

Don't tell her anything, she thought. *Don't tell her anything about Auntie Susan.*

She didn't want Mandy to know about her deal to keep up the bribes, not yet anyway. Her head was swirling with thoughts of Den and the Red Egg, but she tried not to let on that anything was wrong to Mandy. She needed time to think. And the only person she could really trust was Miles.

"I've got the lineup sorted for Friday, by the way," she said. "We've got the performers from the night it . . . well, you know, the night it happened, as well as some big names from the drag scene, people who've worked here a lot. It's going to be a good show."

"That's great," said Mandy. "I'm working on the press list, but we have a lot of TV and film crews interested already, as well as most of the national papers. Getty's sending someone."

"Wow, it's going to be packed."

"I hope so," said Mandy. "It's what Lady Lady deserves." She took a sandwich out of her handbag and began to unwrap it. "I'm opening up ticket sales today. I'm putting half on general sale and setting half back for invites. I take it your Miles will be coming?"

"Oh yes," said Misty, anxiety pooling, "he wouldn't miss it."

And then an idea came to her head that was so mad she couldn't believe she was considering it. Miles would be furious.

"Mandy," she said, "have we got Den's home address? On his last invoice maybe?"

"Yes, I'm sure we do," said Mandy, rustling through a stack of wrappers and paperwork.

"Here it is," she said, handing over an invoice.

Misty copied down the address onto a piece of paper. "Thanks, Mandy."

33

✶✶✶✶✶✶✶✶✶

SHE SHUT THE laptop and hurried out of the office up to the street, where she hailed a black cab, reading the driver the address. It was in South London, near Vauxhall. She quickly switched open her phone settings and turned off all location services. She didn't want any trace of this journey on her devices. Then she texted Miles and said she was taking a walk to think and that she'd meet him at home later. *A white lie*, she thought.

A big lie?

A lie nevertheless.

After she'd sent the text, she switched off her phone before the cab even reached Cambridge Circus. Nobody should know she was visiting Den. It would look very bad for her later if he was found out to be involved in the murder.

As the car drove over the river, Misty wondered what kind of a reaction she would get. She would feign a welfare call, that she was just checking in to see how he was, that she was sorry for their argument at the hotel. She'd take it from there.

The taxi pulled up outside a small terraced house on a road

of small terraced houses. There was a nonbinary pride flag hanging in the living room window, and Misty felt thrilled, as always, to see it.

She paid the cabdriver in cash and got out of the taxi. She could have been less conspicuous than the pink-haired drag queen, she supposed. The driver would definitely remember this journey if the police ever asked him, but at least there was no electronic trace of it.

She approached the front door and knocked on it. It creaked open an inch. It was unlocked. Open and unlocked.

Her gut told her that something was wrong. She knew it. She was dreading it already, but she pushed open the door and stepped inside.

"Den?" she called out.

There was no reply.

"Den? Are you home? It's Misty."

The house was filled with silence. Misty looked around and took it in. Either there had been a raging party here or the place had been burgled. It was a mess. There were clothes, books, and belongings all over the floor. Misty stepped delicately inside, careful not to tread on anything that might be valuable.

"Den?" she called out again.

She turned through a doorway into what she guessed was the living room and was met with the most awful surprise.

Lying on the floor in the middle of the room, with his mouth contorted open and full of foam, Den. Dead. Den was dead.

Misty gasped and put her hands over her mouth instinctively.

Shit.

Shit.

Shit.

Den's dead. Poisoned. *And I'm the one who found the body.* Again.

Part of her wanted to run, to sprint out of the house and never look back. But she couldn't. He'd be found at some point, and then there would be CCTV, the taxi driver . . . she'd be caught out eventually.

No, the only thing she could possibly do this time was call the police. She couldn't even call Miles first. She was finally in over her head.

She pulled out her phone and switched it back on. It seemed to take forever, and Den's open and terrified eyes stared at her with a cloudy gaze. She stepped out of the living room and back into the cluttered hallway. Once her phone flickered back to life she opened it and scrolled until she found the number for DS Hughes. She called her.

"DS Hughes," said the officer answering.

"DS Hughes, it's Misty Divine. I've found a body. I need your help."

DS Hughes explained that Misty was not to touch anything, not to move anything. She agreed. She'd follow the rules. The last thing she wanted was to raise any more suspicion.

Poor Den. What on earth had happened to him?

Misty ended the call with DS Hughes and called Miles. "Miles," she said as soon as he answered the phone. "I did something stupid."

"What now?" he said.

"I came to see Den. I'm at his house."

"Joe! No! What were you thinking? I think we're going to need to have a serious talk, Joe. I'm really worr—"

"He's dead, Miles. He's been poisoned, just like Lady Lady.

He's dead in his living room, and I'm waiting for the police to arrive."

"Oh fuck." Miles exhaled. "Oh, that's awful."

"I hate this," said Misty. "I never should have started investigating this. I'm making everything worse at every turn."

"Just don't tell the police what Auntie Susan told you about the Red Egg. They'll discover that by themselves, and we'll act as shocked as everyone else. We can deny we ever knew."

Misty stayed quiet, thinking. Miles was right, she knew.

"Joe, are you there? Don't tell the police anything about Auntie Susan. It's not worth the risk, for all of us."

"I won't say anything."

"Okay, keep me updated with what happens, and come home as soon as you can. No more investigating until we know what's going on."

Misty ended the call with Miles and looked around the living room doorway at Den.

"I'm sorry this happened to you," she said, "whatever's happened. You didn't deserve this."

Then she left the living room and picked her way back through the hallway to the front door. She wanted to wait outside and not spend a second more in that house.

On the doorstep she thought about all the good times she'd had with Den over the years, all the banter they'd shared in the dressing rooms and the chats they'd had at the hotel reception. She felt awful that their last conversation had been an argument, that they'd rowed together and ended on bad terms. It was devastating to lose another friend this week, whatever he was involved in.

Within a few minutes a police patrol car arrived, its blue lights flashing and sirens blaring. Misty lifted her hand to shield

her eyes from the light. One of the officers gave Misty a cigarette, telling her they weren't supposed to. She didn't smoke
often, usually only socially, but now it felt necessary.

W HEN DS HUGHES and DI Davies arrived they said they were
going to look at the crime scene and that Misty should
wait in the back of their car. She agreed. She wasn't enjoying
standing in the street, and the growing number of police cars
meant that curtains were twitching. In the back of the car, she
texted Miles.

> I'm still here. Looks like he's been dead
> since this morning. I'm waiting to give a
> statement.

And then she put her phone in her lap and waited, waited for
DI Davies to come back, to talk to her and quiz her and accuse
her of murder. But it was DS Hughes who arrived. She was
holding a sheet of paper that had been slipped inside a clear
plastic evidence bag. She opened the car door and got in alongside Misty.

"He was your friend, right?" said DS Hughes.

"He was," said Misty.

"I think you need to read this." She handed Misty the sheet
of paper. The handwriting was scrawled, barely legible, like it
had been written in a hurry. And every "i" was topped with a
slanted circle that looked like a teenager had written it. Misty
read it, and as she did, her mouth hung open in utter disbelief.
Den, she thought, *what have you done?*

To Whoever finds this,

Firstly, I'm sorry. It can't be nice to find me dead, but someone's got to do it. I'm sorry it's you, whoever you are.

Secondly, I need your help. I need you to make sure the police get this letter so that everybody can know the truth.

I killed Lady Lady.

I'm the criminal known in the press as the Kensington Catburglar.

Lady Lady found the dress in my dressing room and tried it on—she thought it was a replica. When she wanted to wear it for the cabaret I couldn't stop her, and in the interval of the show she realized it was real—that it was valuable. She told me she was going to call the police. I didn't have any choice.

But now I'm riddled with guilt. It's all I can think about.

I'm sorry to take this way out, but I'm poisoning myself to balance the score, cosmically speaking. To die in the same way as Lady Lady to make up for what I've done. I hope it works.

Thank you, for helping me,
Den

Just as Misty had finished reading the letter there was a tap on the front window of the car. DI Davies opened the front door and sat in the driver's seat.

"We're going to the station," he said.

"I'll call my solicitor," said Misty. She didn't want to go to the station again—not with DI Davies. She didn't want to be searched and photographed and stripped and put in the cold hard cell again. She needed Mr. McDermott, and she needed him urgently.

"You're not under arrest. Not yet," said DI Davies.

"I know," said Misty. "I'd just be more comfortable with Mr. McDermott present."

M R. MCDERMOTT ARRIVED, not in his usual suit and tie, but in a gym workout outfit that Misty honestly found to be a little gratuitous in the pectoral area.

"Sorry," he said, "I came straight over."

"No need to apologize," said Misty. "Thanks for coming."

"Okay," said DI Davies with a deep, serious tone. "Let's get started."

Misty squeezed her fingertips beneath the table to keep them from trembling. Lady Lady, Auntie Susan, the Red Egg, Den's twisted poisoned face . . . and here she was, right in the middle of all of it.

M ISTY TALKED THROUGH a version of events that was as close to the truth as possible. That she was worried Den might have been involved with the Kensington Catburglar because she'd spoken to Florentina and that she wanted to ask him face-to-face.

"You do know what this is starting to look like, don't you?" said DI Davies.

"What's that?" asked Misty.

"A pattern."

"A pattern?"

"Well, how often does a person find a poisoned body? And

to find two in a week? You're either very unlucky or very very clever."

"Are you accusing my client of something, Detective Inspector?" said Mr. McDermott. "Because you certainly better have some evidence. My understanding is that there was a suicide note at the crime scene, a confession?"

"Yes," said DI Davies. "Looks like the case is closed. Unless your client happens upon another body."

Misty sighed with relief.

34

★★★★★★★★★★

DS HUGHES OFFERED to drive Misty home after she'd given her statement, and she accepted.

"I'm really sorry, by the way, for DI Davies," said Hughes. "He's a bit of a prick, but he's been doing his best to find the murderer, I promise. If you ever need to talk about what you've gone through this week, please call me. I'm here for you, Misty."

"Thank you," said Misty, thinking that she would never, ever, call her.

Misty got out of the car and walked up the stairs to the flat. It was a warm evening and the breeze felt good on her face. Her mouth tasted of cigarette and she wanted another one.

She got to the front door of the flat and let herself in. Miles came rushing out of the kitchen and wrapped his arms around her.

"What the fuck? What happened?"

"He killed himself, Miles. *Den*. He killed Lady Lady and then he killed himself."

"Oh my God, how do you know?"

"He left a note explaining everything. That Lady Lady had found the dress in the dressing room and wanted to wear it. He poisoned her when she realized what it was."

"Oh my God. That's awful. I'm so so sorry."

He leaned forward and hugged her tightly.

"I need to take this drag off," she said.

"Of course. Go get changed and I'll make us something to eat. Sandwiches okay?"

"Sounds good," said Misty. "Thanks, Miles."

Misty got out of drag and felt relieved. Relieved to be taking off the costume, relieved to have solved the mystery, to have followed the clues to Den's house. She was also angry—with Den. So incredibly angry that somebody who she thought was her friend could do such a thing. How could she trust anyone again if someone as unsuspecting as Den could be a mastermind cat burglar and a murderer?

She was angry about Lady Lady, that he'd killed her, taken her life away forever, because of a stolen dress. What a pointless and stupid reason for two people to die.

As Misty rubbed the makeup off her face, she felt furious.

JOE STEPPED INTO the shower to try to wash the day away. The meeting with Auntie Susan; the argument with Miles in the toilets; the cloudy, lifeless gaze of Den's dead eyes . . . It all swam around in Joe's brain as they washed their hair with soft, silky shampoo and scrubbed their face.

They still couldn't process it properly. That Den had been capable of all that. But there it was, in black and white. It was over.

They dried off and then put on some jogging bottoms and a

T-shirt. Miles had made curried chickpea sandwiches, with salt and vinegar crisps. They sat at the table to eat.

"So, that's it," said Miles, taking a bite of sandwich.

"That's it," said Joe.

"I can't believe it," said Miles. "Den. Gone. I know we were suspecting him, and he seemed so defensive the other night, but I wasn't expecting him to turn up dead."

"Me neither," said Joe. "In a morbid kind of way, the investigation was weirdly fun when we were making the lists in the notebook and whatnot—like an episode of something. It was strangely hypothetical, but now it feels real. One of my friends was a murderer and killed himself. It's too much to think about."

"Yeah," said Miles, "it's awful."

They ate in silence for a while before Miles spoke again.

"Shall we just watch some TV after this? Try to take our minds off it all? Are you up for a *Criminal Minds*?"

"Honestly, Miles, I think I might just need to sleep."

There was no more investigating to do. The mystery was over.

35

✱✱✱✱✱✱✱✱✱

THURSDAY

JOE WOKE AT 9 a.m. and rolled over to find Miles was already up. The bed was empty. Joe stretched out their long arms and legs like a starfish in the middle of the duvet.

They felt lighter this morning, brighter, as though an enormous weight had been lifted from their shoulders. They were no longer a murder suspect, they were no longer in danger at the club, Lady Lady's killer had been found . . . It was only good news. Well, not for Den.

They almost bounced out of bed.

"I want Pop-Tarts, Miles. I just want Pop-Tarts for breakfast today," they said as they walked into the kitchen.

Miles laughed as Joe went to the junk food cupboard—the one where they kept the crisps and the Party Rings—and grabbed a box of apple Pop-Tarts. They ripped off the foil wrappers and dropped them into the toaster. They felt almost giddy.

It was the shock, surely, they thought. It wasn't normal to feel happy after you had just found your friend's body. It was the shock. And the relief that justice had finally been found for their beloved drag mother. They'd really done it. They'd really found Lady Lady's killer.

"How are you feeling?" asked Miles.

"I feel relieved mostly and sad. Is that weird?"

"I don't think so," said Miles. "It's been pretty stressful. I'm not surprised you're relieved."

The toaster popped and two steaming hot pastries jumped up out of it. Joe caught them and dropped them onto a plate. They were too hot to eat yet.

"I'm just glad that we know who did it," said Joe, "and to know that we're not in any more danger. That the whole thing is over before Lady Lady's memorial tomorrow. Would have been strange celebrating her life while her murderer was still on the loose."

"I bet," said Miles.

Joe picked up a Pop-Tart by the corner and blew on it, cooling it down before taking a big bite.

"So, what's your plan for today?"

"I'm going to the bar," said Joe. "Florentina never replied, about making a new dress for the reopening tomorrow. So I think I'm going to wear one of Lady Lady's from her dressing room. They haven't been auctioned yet, and I thought it would be fitting with me taking over from her at the club."

Miles left and went to work and Joe got ready slowly, with the television on in the living room. They dressed in their most nonbinary finery, feeling confident as Joe for the first time in a long time. They put on a pair of pink jeans and a loose bright blue silk blouse. They matched it with a pair of boots that they'd spray-painted gold and a chunky gold chain and checked themself out in the mirror. They looked hot.

This confidence felt new. There was something fresh and

revitalizing about it, as though finding out who killed Lady Lady, starting a new life at the club—all these things together had boosted Joe up an extra five inches taller.

Everything made sense now. Den had been skint and had turned to stealing to pay the rent. Joe guessed he'd got greedy, progressing from the stolen jewelry he'd tried to sell to Florentina to the valuables of the rich people of Chelsea. Lady Lady had been in the wrong place at the wrong time, it seemed, discovering the Judy Garland gown in the dressing rooms and uncovering Den's secret life. He had killed her to keep her quiet. And Joe supposed they could understand why, to a certain extent. Den had had nothing—he'd been broke, begging friends for money—and suddenly he had in his hands an eleven-million-pound ruby. He'd found a new life, one he wanted to protect. Lady Lady was collateral damage on Den's path to riches.

A S THEY WALKED, they reviewed everything that had happened in the last week: the murder, meeting Anna Bowman, the new job at Lady's Bar, meeting Auntie Susan, finding Den . . . So much had happened. But everything would be different from now on. They'd be performing every day, booking the Lady's Bar lineups, meeting with Florentina once a week to discuss custom designs. It was a dream come true. The only dark blotch on this bright, new life was the bribery—the money the bar was giving to the council to keep from being taken over. Joe pushed the thought away. *One thing at a time*, they told themself.

They passed the British Museum, always astonished at the patience of those standing in the queue to get in. Then they walked down Tottenham Court Road to Cambridge Circus and turned right onto Shaftesbury Avenue, wanting to stroll a little, to take in London a bit before going to the office. They passed casinos and Chinese restaurants and famous theaters until they reached Piccadilly Circus. Joe noticed how people were looking at their clothes. The oversized silk blouse was billowing in the summer wind, and the bright blue color of it was certainly striking. They didn't care that people were looking, not today.

Piccadilly Circus was beautiful, Joe thought. Tall, grand buildings surrounded the busy junction and, on one side of the square, were covered in enormous video screens advertising everything from West End shows to Coca-Cola. They stopped for a moment and took it all in. It felt nice to have nothing more serious to think about, to have the freedom to allow their brain to think about something other than murder and stolen dresses.

As they reached the outside of the Criterion Theatre they noticed something, someone they recognized. It was Plimberley, across the street, getting off the bus with armfuls of shopping.

Plimberley wasn't in drag, and out of drag her style was fairly unremarkable. She wore a light gray tracksuit and blended in with the crowd. Joe waved as Plimberley looked in their direction, trying to get her attention.

"Plim!" they called across the street. "Plim!"

Plimberley looked up and waved at Joe.

"Misty!" she called. She rushed across the street and planted kisses on either side of Joe's face.

"How are you, love?" asked Joe.

Plimberley was so much younger than Joe, and talking to her always felt a little like talking to a younger sibling. She was skinny and fragile-looking and Joe always had the impression that she needed protecting from the world, that she was an innocent lost in a big city. Of course that wasn't true. Plimberley was young, but she was strong, and fiery. She'd survived a lot in her short life and certainly didn't need Joe's protection.

"Did you hear?" said Plimberley. "About Den?"

"I was the one who found him."

"No way! Was it gross?"

"What do you mean, gross?" asked Joe.

"Finding a dead body. Was it as gross as Lady Lady?"

"Yeah, Plim, it was pretty terrible."

"Fuck," said Plimberley. "I just can't believe it, you know. That Den did those things. It's all everyone's talking about."

They talked for a few minutes on the side of the street, and those few minutes were mostly Plimberley talking and Joe nodding along. Eventually, Joe grew tired of listening to her. She was primarily just repeating the rumors and gossip, and Joe knew that as soon as they left her, she'd be writing in her WhatsApp groups that Misty had been the one to find him. They wished they hadn't told her.

Joe tuned back just as Plimberley was saying goodbye. "I'll see you tomorrow anyway, for the reopening. I'm doing Gaga."

Joe grinned, knowing that Plimberley was planning to put on an amazing show for Lady Lady's memorial. Her Gaga number was known across the drag scene for being totally iconic. Clips of it on YouTube and TikTok had hundreds of thousands of views.

And then, unexpectedly, Plimberley pulled Joe into a tight hug and said quietly into their ear, "I'm so sorry you were the one who found the body. That must have been terrible."

36

✱✱✱✱✱✱✱✱✱

WHEN JOE ARRIVED at Lady's Bar they found the door unlocked. They walked down the stairs to the auditorium and passed through to the office.

As they stepped inside, Mandy jumped up from her desk and ran to give them a hug. "Misty, I heard about Den, that he killed Lady Lady! That you found him! I just heard."

Plimberley spread the word quickly, it seemed.

"I'm so sorry," said Mandy.

"Thanks," said Joe, allowing her to hug them for a few seconds before pulling away. "It was kind of horrible."

"Well, listen, everything's under control for the show tomorrow, so if you need to take today off, get your head straight, that's no problem." Mandy tucked the corner of her bob back behind her ear.

"I'd rather be working," said Joe. "I'm okay, really."

And they were okay. Deep inside they were devastated about Den, but they also felt a lightness, a calm feeling that danger had passed now that the murderer had been caught and they were no longer a suspect themself.

"I'll work on next week's lineups," they said, "and get the posters done."

"I'll make the tea."

Joe settled down behind the laptop and began sending out emails to finalize the lineups for the following week. They were trying to keep true to how Lady Lady had booked her shows: A combination of new and old acts, a mix of comedy and singing and cabaret. And a great headliner. Always a great headliner.

"Well, sad as it is about Den," said Mandy, putting down a pile of invoices in a huff, "and don't get me wrong, it is sad—I don't like *anyone* dying like that—but I feel so disgusted with him, Misty, for what he did to Lady Lady. And so angry with him."

"Me too," said Joe. "I don't know how to reconcile it. I can't match up the Den I thought I knew with the murderer. How are they the same person, Mandy? Right under our noses the whole time."

"I don't know," said Mandy. "I just don't know."

T HE AFTERNOON PASSED quickly, and within a few hours of emailing and texting and telephoning, they'd managed to confirm the lineups for the whole of next week. Everybody wanted to come back to work at Lady's Bar as soon as possible.

Joe decided that they'd take a break from the computer and went to Lady Lady's dressing room, which was soon to be theirs. Misty Divine's very own. They opened the door and stepped inside. They hadn't been in there since the death of Lady Lady, and seeing the room where she died was suddenly overwhelming.

Pushing back tears, Joe took a deep breath and walked across the room to Lady Lady's costume rails, looking for something to wear at the reopening.

As they slid costumes across the rail, they examined them one at a time. The craftsmanship was exquisite. Each costume had been individually made by Florentina, and rhinestones and sequins had been hand-stitched onto every one. They were all so gorgeous.

Joe settled on a silver sequin suit with a shiny black blouse underneath. The edges were lined with black embroidery, giving the lapels sharp pointed corners and clean lines. It was beautiful, and though a little small for Misty, it would be perfect for the reopening. They already knew they'd wear it with the blond hair with the black streak.

They took the hanger off the rail and carried it back to the office.

I T WAS QUIET in the club. Joe was looking forward to working the reopening tomorrow, when the bar would be filled with life again, instead of being at a desk with a great big pile of invoices, which didn't feel a million miles away from their work at the Empire Hotel. There were familiar names to be paid, and Joe went through them one at a time, settling up payments for the shows that had happened at the bar in the days before the murder.

Joe's phone buzzed in their pocket. It was a message from Miles.

Thought you should read this.

Love you x

Accompanying the text from Miles was a link to an article. Joe clicked the link and opened it.

KENSINGTON CATBURGLAR FOUND DEAD IN VAUXHALL

In the dramatic conclusion to one of London's most mysterious criminal stories, the body of the Kensington Catburglar was discovered last night by a drag queen at a house in Vauxhall.

Now identified as Francesca Ford, a drag performer who worked under the name Den Dorado, she is believed to have also been responsible for the poisoning of drag queen Lady Lady at London cabaret club Lady's Bar last week.

It has been reported by the Metropolitan Police that at least one of the cat burglar's targets has been recovered, that the Red Egg, one of the most valuable rubies in the world, was found at the same address.

Detective Inspector Davies of the Metropolitan Police gave a statement earlier today in which he said, "We are pleased to report a resolution in the cases of both the Sean Fulton murder and the Kensington Catburglar. Last night officers were called to reports of a dead body at a house in Vauxhall. Evidence collected at the scene strongly supports that the deceased individual was responsible for both the burglaries and the homicide of Mr. Fulton. We consider both cases now closed and will be releasing a further statement in due course."

The rest of the article was a rehash of things Joe already knew, the details of Lady Lady's murder, information about the other missing items, that kind of thing.

Joe turned back to the pile of invoices, trying to distract themself from thoughts of Den's cloudy poisoned eyes.

The first invoice on the pile was one for Amour. Joe set about finding Amour's account details in the payment system and then transferred the money. They stamped the invoice with a big red PAID ink stamp and moved on to the next one.

It was Plimberley's invoice. It was a silly one. There was a huge photograph of Plimberley on it and a signature with bright pink babyish handwriting.

And that was when Joe noticed something. The "i" in "Plimberley" was dotted with a little circle. A little slightly slanted circle. They recognized it. It was the same as in the handwriting Joe had read last night in the back of DS Hughes's car. The same writing that was on Den's suicide note.

37

★★★★★★★★★

MILES WAS ALREADY home by the time Joe got back. He told Joe about his day at work, how word had already got around the office that the flat had been searched by the police. The gossip groups in the corporate world obviously moved a bit more slowly than those in the drag scene. The flat search felt like a lifetime ago to Joe.

"Michael, on reception, has been asking me about it all day," Miles was saying. "Apparently it's all he's talked about."

But Joe's mind was wandering, thinking about something DI Davies had asked them. Something that didn't feel quite complete.

How often do you take the number fourteen bus?

That's what DI Davies had asked them in their first interview, the interview when he'd confronted Misty with the video of the champagne.

And today, what bus had Plimberley been getting off? Joe hadn't paid attention. They should have been paying better attention, they thought. But it could have been the fourteen. The fourteen was the bus that ran from Chelsea to Piccadilly after all. If Plimberley had been coming from home, she'd have taken the fourteen. In fact, working in Soho and living with Moneypenny at World's End, Plimberley must take the fourteen bus all the time.

But all of this was silly. Plimberley couldn't have had anything to do with Den's death, and she certainly wouldn't have had anything to do with Lady Lady's. Would she?

But there was the circle above the "i" in her signature. Almost identical to the ones Joe had read in Den's letter.

No, thought Joe, *this is crazy. It was Den. It's over.*

"Joe? Joe?" Miles's voice. "Earth to Joe!"

Joe snapped back to reality and realized they'd completely lost track of what Miles had been saying.

"What were you thinking about?"

"Plimberley," said Joe. They felt a bit stupid saying it out loud.

"Plimberley? Ha! And here's me thinking you were contemplating some deep question about life and death."

Joe smiled. "I know, I know, it's silly. But there's something I can't quite put my finger on. I feel like she could have been involved."

"In what? The murder? Surely not. She wasn't even friends with Den." Miles looked surprised, as if it was a really long stretch to think Plimberley could have been involved in anything. She had a reputation for being a bit vapid, or at least that's how she presented herself in the way that she spoke.

"I know, I know, it sounds impossible. But there were a couple of things today, weird things."

"What things?" said Miles. "Are you sure you're not just tired, Joe? The police are saying it's over. Case closed."

"Yesterday, when DS Hughes showed me Den's suicide note, there were little circles above all the i's, like teenagers often do. And on Plimberley's invoice today, I noticed that her i's were exactly the same."

"Joe," said Miles, "it's time to stop all this."

"And then I saw her at lunchtime, and I think she was getting off the fourteen bus. And do you remember? I told you, DI Davies asked me about the fourteen bus when he interviewed me."

Joe was feeling a little buzz, a kind of excitement, that they might be piecing something together. Miles looked like he clearly didn't agree. His face was serious, worried.

"Okay, I'm going to say something now that you might not like," said Miles. "I think you don't want to let this investigation be over because you've been using it to avoid grieving for Lady Lady. But it is over now. You *have* to accept that it's over."

"But it's weird, right?" said Joe, ignoring Miles completely, not wanting to think about grieving for Lady Lady. "That there would be two things like that on the same day. Two things that seem to connect Plimberley to the Catburglar."

"Joe . . ."

"You see?" said Joe. "There's something weird going on with Plimberley!"

Miles sighed heavily. "So, she takes the fourteen bus and—what?—she wrote Den's suicide note? She didn't do it, Joe. She just didn't. It was Den and it's over."

"What should we do about it though? About the handwriting?"

"Nothing, Joe. It's finished," said Miles. "You should stay away from it."

"And what's the deal with the fourteen bus anyway?" asked

Joe. "Why is that even relevant? Why did they even ask me about it?"

"What do you mean?" asked Miles.

"DI Davies, in the interview at the police station, he asked me how often I take that bus, but why?"

Miles looked stumped and exhausted by Joe's persistence.

Joe took their phone out of their pocket. They googled the fourteen bus, and a map of the route popped up on the screen. They looked at the stops along the route: Piccadilly, Hyde Park Corner, Knightsbridge, South Kensington . . . It was a nice route, thought Joe, through some of the wealthiest areas of London.

South Kensington. That was where they'd gone to visit Anna Bowman at the dress shop. A coincidence, Joe thought. But could it be possible . . . ?

"What was the name of the first Catburglar item? The something tiara?" Joe asked Miles.

"The Sunbeam Tiara," said Miles reluctantly.

"That's it," said Joe, typing "Sunbeam Tiara Catburglar" into Google.

There were tons of news articles about the tiara. Joe opened the first one that came up and scanned it quickly, looking for the details of where the tiara had been stolen from Christie's. On Brompton Road.

Also a stop on the fourteen bus route.

"Miles," said Joe. "I think I've worked it out."

They spent the next half an hour searching on their phone, matching up the locations of the burglaries to the fourteen bus route. They discovered what the police must have known all along, that the targets of all twelve burglaries were visible from the fourteen bus's windows.

"So," said Miles, "you're saying that if Plimberley takes the fourteen bus every day she'd have seen these places on her way."

"Exactly."

Joe gasped, suddenly realizing something. "And Auntie Susan said Baseball Cap didn't plant the chocolates when he broke into the flat. But Plimberley was here, in our kitchen, helping herself to things from the cupboards. She had the perfect opportunity to plant the chocolate box."

"I don't know about all this," said Miles.

But Joe knew. They knew that the investigation wasn't quite over.

38

✶✶✶✶✶✶✶✶✶

FRIDAY

JOE WOKE UP early—6 a.m. Miles was still sleeping, so Joe left him in bed and went into the kitchen to make coffee.

They grabbed their phone off the charger and saw they had a message from Len. He was dropping out of the memorial show tonight, understandably. The Len and Den double act was certainly over. Joe replied, sending condolences.

Their thoughts turned back to Plimberley and what they'd discussed with Miles the night before. Was it really possible that she was the Catburglar? That she'd tried to frame Joe for murder? How had she been involved with Den? It felt so unlikely, but there were signs she could at least be involved.

They'd see her tonight. Misty should talk to her, see if she gave anything away.

Maybe she could talk to Moneypenny first.

Moneypenny was probably the closest person to Plimberley these days, having taken her in when she was homeless. Perhaps Moneypenny had noticed something too.

Yes, Joe thought, they'd try to talk to Moneypenny before the show tonight.

Meanwhile they would need to prepare for the show, for getting ready in Lady Lady's dressing room, for hosting the whole evening. It was a big responsibility. Joe wished they could talk to Lady Lady about it, to ask her advice. She'd left behind very big shoes to fill.

Joe decided to pack up their bedroom makeup station as Miles woke and left for work, ready to move everything over to their new dressing room, putting away makeup, loose brushes, and beauty blenders. They packed it all into their big travel makeup case and fastened it shut. They'd take it to Lady's Bar later, along with the shoes and wig they were wearing for the reopening.

Once everything was ready to go, they picked up their phone, sat down in the living room, and called DS Hughes. If they were right, Den's death wasn't a suicide, and there was a killer still at large. As reluctant as they were to get the police more involved, they couldn't risk it, not with the reopening tonight.

"Misty," said Hughes as she answered the phone, "how are you?"

The fact that she'd called Joe Misty was well noted and well appreciated.

"I'm okay, thanks, DS Hughes. How are you?"

"Busy here, wrapping everything up. How can I help?"

"Well, that's why I was calling, actually. I noticed something strange and thought I should tell you in case it's relevant."

"Go on . . ." said DS Hughes.

Joe told her about the handwriting on the invoice, that it was similar to Den's suicide letter. They told her about the bus. DS Hughes listened silently.

"Listen, Misty, I appreciate you calling, but that really isn't anything to be worried about. Francesca Ford, Den, was the Catburglar and Lady Lady's murderer. The evidence is overwhelming. There's no doubt on our side. The case is closed."

"So, you don't think you should look into Plimberley?"

"Based on her handwriting and that you saw her getting off the bus? No. Not with everything we have on Francesca Ford. She was working alone. *He*, sorry. Den, he was working alone."

"Are you sure you don't even want to investi—"

"We're sure, Misty. Don't worry about it anymore. It's time for you to move on."

Joe ended the call with DS Hughes on polite terms but couldn't help feeling fobbed off. They felt as though they'd called with real information, a real lead, but that DS Hughes just wasn't interested.

Maybe she was right, maybe Miles was right, maybe it wasn't anything, and Joe should leave it all alone. But still, their spidey-senses were tingling again. Something was off with Plimberley.

THEY BOOKED A car to the bar because they had too much to carry and wanted to get there quickly. The driver was a nice one. A smiling chap called Peter, according to the app, who was very helpful with the bags.

Joe managed their way down the stairs of Lady's Bar with all their stuff and arrived in the auditorium to find it a hive of activity. After a week of it being empty, it was nice to see movement in the place again. There were bar staff working, polishing glasses, restocking refrigerators, getting everything ready for tonight. A team of cleaners worked the auditorium floor, wiping tables, arranging chairs. A florist was busy positioning chunky glass vases on every table, filled with tall lilies and shoots of fresh lavender. Joe said a warm hello to Tess, who was busying herself directing new security staff around the venue, and then headed to the dressing rooms.

"Afternoon, all," Joe said to everyone as they passed down the corridor, heading straight for Lady Lady's room, their new dressing room. They sat down behind the makeup station and opened their case, laying everything out for getting ready later. Brushes, makeup, blenders, bottles of cleanser, and pots of glitter—all lined up ready to go. Once happy with the setup of the dressing room they left and went to the office.

Mandy was already there, dressed up, ready for tonight. "Oh, don't start," she said before Joe had even said anything, "I decided to get ready first thing because I like the dress, okay?" She was flustered and stuffing sandwich wrappers into a plastic carrier bag, finally tidying her desk.

"You look lovely," said Joe. She did indeed look lovely. She was wearing a black knee-length dress that had a gold sequin floral pattern swirling up one side.

"Why, thank you," she said, smiling and performing a little curtsy. "Now, do you need time to rehearse in the auditorium this afternoon? Time to go over your tracks and notes? We've got a lot of press coming tonight," said Mandy, looking really proud of herself. "Apparently the memorial is going to be one of those closing fluff pieces for most of the news channels. Now that they know who the killer was, we're out of the main news for a while hopefully."

"Hopefully," said Joe, pausing, before blurting, "What do you know about Plimberley?"

"Plimberley?" said Mandy. "She's been through the ringer, that one."

"With her family you mean?"

"Yeah. They're a tough bunch. Didn't take kindly to the drag."

"How long have you known her?" asked Joe.

"Must be getting on five years. She was seventeen when she first showed up here, claiming to be eighteen, trying to get booked by Lady Lady, who saw through her, of course. ID'd her. Told her to come back when she was eighteen. I think Lady Lady always admired the kid for that, for her determination and gall. She's a bold one all right."

"Did Plimberley and Lady Lady ever have any . . . problems? Any fallings-out or anything?"

"Not that I know of. She's a tough negotiator, that's for sure. She managed to get her fee up much higher than most of the other girls her age. Lady Lady didn't mind paying it for such a good performer though."

Joe paused to think. Could they really be suspecting Plimberley this much? DS Hughes had told them to leave it alone, so had Miles.

"Why do you ask?" asked Mandy.

"I just thought Plimberley was acting a bit strange when I saw her the other day. I wondered if she was okay," said Joe, not willing to reveal their suspicions to Mandy just yet.

"I haven't noticed anything," said Mandy. "If anything, she seems a bit more with it than she used to be, I think living with Moneypenny has done her some good."

JOE WENT TO the dressing room and started getting into drag. It was strange to get ready in Lady Lady's space. Joe knew that eventually they'd redecorate it and that it would one day feel like Misty's, but in the meantime they felt like a visitor.

They put on their makeup, carefully making it as neat as possible, especially conscious that Misty was going to be on television. Their painted eyebrows swept up into steep arches that made Misty's nose look long and sharply pointed. They got dressed, squeezing into Lady Lady's silver-and-black suit, then buttoning it up to show off the illusion of a tiny waist. Once the blond wig with the black streak was on they felt much more confident. Misty Divine had arrived for her show.

By 6 p.m. some of the other acts had started to arrive, and the dressing rooms were starting to get busy. She felt out of place using a separate room, though the other acts were excited for her.

"Can I come in and have a look around?" asked Amour eagerly. "Lady Lady never let us in."

"Of course!" said Misty.

She showed Amour around the dressing room, and she was excited to be in there. She even opened the fridge to see what was inside: a four-pack of Red Bull that Misty had brought from home.

Talk in the dressing rooms was all about Den the cat burglar and Lady Lady. Misty ignored it and headed to the auditorium to rehearse her tracks before doors opened to the public and press.

She was opening the show by singing "Think Twice" by Celine Dion, one of Lady Lady's favorites. She knew she could belt it and that it would bring the house down, and she felt the lyrics were appropriate for a memorial. Jackson, the technician, started the track, and Misty stood in front of the empty room and sang like she'd never sung before.

As she looked at the empty chairs and tables she knew that in just a couple of hours the bar would be full, bursting with people, and she'd sing this song again to rapturous applause. Gosh, how she wished Lady Lady could see her, could watch her coming into her own, taking on her new role as host of Lady's Bar. Perhaps now, in this very moment, she missed her more than ever.

Just as she reached the end of the song the door from the staircase to the street opened, and Miles walked in. He was dressed up for the show, wearing a purple velvet shirt that Misty loved and a pair of matching purple shoes. He looked so handsome.

She finished her song and ran down from the stage to greet him, kissing him on the cheek.

"I'm so glad you're here," she said. "How was work?"

"All good! We landed the new account—the one from the big pitch! Chris said they loved my presentation."

"Miles! Congratulations!"

Miles smiled. "How about you? Feeling ready?"

"Ready as I'm ever going to be."

She looked at her watch—6:20 p.m. The doors would open at seven.

"Let's get a quick drink," she said.

They went to the bar, and Misty ordered two gin and tonics from Jan, who had returned to work at Lady's Bar now it was reopening. He was big and burly and had decorated his beard with black glitter for the night.

"How are you, Misty?" Jan asked her. "Sounding good up there." He nodded to the stage.

"Thanks!"

He handed them a gin and tonic each, and Miles took a big sip.

"Plimberley hasn't arrived yet," said Misty, raising her eyebrow.

"You're not still on this, are you?" asked Miles, sounding exhausted with her. "Try to concentrate on the show."

"I spoke to DS Hughes this morning," said Misty. "The police weren't interested in listening to me. They said the case is closed."

"Well, maybe it is," said Miles. "Maybe DS Hughes is right, and you should just leave it well alone. Seems like the evidence against Den was pretty overwhelming, and all you think you know about Plimberley is that she dots her i's with a circle and that she might have been on the fourteen bus yesterday."

"She hasn't arrived yet, her or Moneypenny. I'm going to try to talk to Moneypenny when she gets here, see if she's noticed anything weird about Plimberley."

Miles rolled his eyes. "Please, Joe, just leave it. Focus on the show, it's a big night."

39

****

JUST BEFORE 7 P.M. the door to the auditorium opened, and Moneypenny and Plimberley arrived, rushing into the cabaret space with suitcases and wig bags. Misty was rehearsing the script she'd drafted, kind words about Lady Lady and about Terrence Higgins Trust, the charity Lady Lady always supported.

Moneypenny was already in drag, dressed as a centenarian with a long pleated skirt and a padded burgundy jacket. Her hair was a short gray perm. Plimberley was out of drag: a tall lanky youngster in a gray tracksuit with crystal earrings.

"We're here! We're here!" shouted Moneypenny. "Sorry we're late."

Misty watched Plimberley carefully from the stage as she and Moneypenny crossed the floor, heading to the dressing rooms. Plim didn't look any different than normal: not anxious, not sad, not worried. There was nothing in her demeanor that indicated she was a killer.

Misty finished practicing her script before heading back to-ward Miles at the bar.

"I'm going to talk to Moneypenny now, before the show starts."

"I don't think it's a good idea," said Miles.

"I have to," said Misty. "For Lady Lady. And for Den too. What if Den was an innocent victim as well?"

Mandy appeared, carrying two clipboards. She handed one to Misty. It was full of paper: guest lists, running order, press lists . . . "Here you are, Misty, love," she said.

"Thanks, Mandy."

"Doesn't she look amazing?" said Mandy to Miles.

"She really does," Miles replied.

"It's not too short?" asked Misty, pulling her tiny skirt down. "Lady Lady was a lot shorter than me."

"It's fine," said Mandy. "You look gorgeous."

"You do," said Miles, smiling.

"Right, ten minutes till we let the bastards in," said Mandy. "Time for a quick brandy." She signaled to Jan behind the bar, who poured her a very generous brandy in a large glass.

Misty's tummy rumbled but she wasn't hungry. She was nervous now and slightly uncomfortable. She knew she had to speak to Moneypenny, that the investigation didn't feel over yet. If Plimberley had had something to do with Lady Lady's death, she needed to be held accountable.

"I'm heading backstage," she said to Mandy and Miles.

"I'll come with you," said Miles.

"Good idea," said Mandy. "You two go back there and get ready for show start. I'm all set here for opening."

They left Mandy at the bar and headed back to the dressing room corridor. The noise from the Kings' and Queens' Rooms was incredible. There were fifteen performers all crammed in, doing their makeup, and shouting and gossiping in loud voices.

Misty looked into the Queens' Room and saw Moneypenny with her coat and bag still on, happily greeting some of the others. Plimberley was already sitting at a makeup station, gluing down her eyebrow hairs with intense force.

"Moneypenny," said Misty, "could I have a word?"

"Are you sure about this?" whispered Miles. "Doing this now?"

"Yes," said Misty, "I'm sure."

"Of course!" said Moneypenny. "Are we going to your big fancy dressing room?" She grinned widely, and her old-lady makeup stretched uncomfortably across her face.

"Let's do it!" said Misty cheerfully.

Miles, Misty, and Moneypenny entered Lady Lady's dressing room, and Misty felt dead set on finding out whether Plimberley had been responsible for the death of their friends.

"Wow!" said Moneypenny, spinning around in the middle of the room. "This place is big! Get you!" Moneypenny took Misty's hands in hers. Her fingers were cold. "If anyone deserves this, Misty, it's you. After what you've been through this week: finding Lady Lady, going to prison, finding Den. You deserve your own happy ending. I'm so pleased for you." She leaned forward and pulled Misty into a hug. Then, when the hug was over, said, "So, what did you want to talk about? I brought us some booze, to toast to tonight."

"Well, it's a bit awkward," said Misty.

Miles leaned against the countertop in the corner of the room, not getting involved but listening as Moneypenny shrugged her backpack off her shoulders, pulling out so many bottles it was as if she were Mary Poppins. A bottle of whiskey, a bottle of vodka, a carton of juice. She set them on the side of the makeup counter, where there was a stack of plastic cups and napkins.

"It's about Plimberley," Misty continued. "I'm worried about her."

"Plimberley? Why would you be worried about Plimberley?" asked Moneypenny.

"I bumped into her yesterday and she seemed . . . off."

"I haven't noticed anything," said Moneypenny. "What are you suggesting here, Misty? That Plimberley's involved in something?"

"Maybe . . . No . . . I don't know."

Moneypenny looked shocked and taken aback. Her mouth hung open a little bit and her eyebrows twitched.

"You're not suggesting she was involved in all this stuff with Lady Lady and Den, are you? Because I'm sure she wasn't. And so are the police! They found the killer and he admitted it. Is that not good enough for you?" She seemed angry, upset that Misty was accusing Plimberley.

"She's not suggesting that—" started Miles, trying to defuse the situation.

"Yes, she is," snapped Moneypenny.

"Yes, I am," said Misty calmly. "And you need to listen to me, Money, because if I'm right you could be in danger."

"Right about what?" Moneypenny folded her arms and frowned, and even though she was dressed as a hundred-year-old grandma, Misty could see that she was seriously irritated.

Misty took a deep breath.

"This is going to sound a bit nuts, but hear me out. I think that Den's suicide note was written by Plimberley."

"Don't be ridiculous," said Moneypenny.

"I saw it, Money," said Misty. "I read the note, and the hand-writing was the same as on Plimberley's invoice."

"I need that drink," Moneypenny huffed. "We're supposed to be celebrating!"

"Listen, Money, please. It's not just that. The Catburglar takes the fourteen bus, just like Plimberley. Between that and the handwriting, there's definitely something that doesn't feel right. The police won't listen to me. It seems like we're the only people interested in getting to the truth."

"We already know the truth!" said Moneypenny. "Look, let's just all calm down and try to enjoy the night, for Lady Lady." She turned her back to Misty and Miles, pouring vodka and juice into the plastic cups on the side.

"I can tell you don't believe me," said Misty.

"It's not that we don't believe you," said Miles, seemingly taking Moneypenny's side, "it's just that it's not enough. It's not enough to be accusing somebody of something as serious as murder."

"Listen to your boyfriend," said Moneypenny, wagging her finger.

She handed a cup to Miles and a cup to Misty. Vodka and orange juice dripped over the edge onto her fingertips. It smelled strong.

"Listen, if you're so stressed about it, maybe you *should* just ask Plimberley," said Miles, giving up, finally. "Just ask her out-right and put your mind at rest so you can focus on what you really need to be doing tonight—the show."

"Don't ask Plimberley," said Moneypenny. "Just have a drink, forget all about it, and let's have a great night tonight, okay?" She lifted her cup up for a toast and looked at Miles and Misty expectantly.

Misty didn't raise her cup. *Ask Plimberley.* That's exactly what she should do. It was the only way to get to the bottom of it once and for all.

"I'm going to go get her," she said, placing her cup down on the side.

"Don't, Misty," said Moneypenny. "Just stay and have a drink."

But Misty was fixated, and she knew that if she didn't confront Plimberley now, she wouldn't be able to concentrate on anything else all night. She turned to leave as Miles took a sip of his vodka and flung herself through the door into the dressing room corridor, leaving Miles and Moneypenny behind in the dressing room.

She marched down the hallway, the sound of her shoes echoing against the starkly painted walls. Caesar Theday, dancer extraordinaire, had arrived and was holding court loudly in the middle of the Queens' Room. He was a huge presence and wore an incredible red fur coat and a pair of sunglasses. His hair was pristinely coiffed and set into chestnut brown waves. Misty greeted him warmly with air-kisses and a brief hug.

"Caesar," she said, looking over his shoulder at Plimberley behind him. Plim was still painting her foundation and had half contoured her face with dark broad stripes. "Thank you so much for coming tonight," said Misty.

"Of course, my love, of course," said Caesar.

Misty pulled away from Caesar and moved around him, approaching Plimberley. She was within touching distance when a voice called from behind her.

"Misty!" Mandy's voice. "Misty!"

Misty turned to look at her. Mandy was stressed, clearly in a bit of a panic.

"The BBC are here. They want to talk to you when you get a sec."

"I'll be there in a couple of minutes."

Mandy fiddled with her clipboard and sighed, walking off down the corridor back toward the bar. There was muffled noise coming from the bar now, like people had started to arrive. But Misty's mind was set on one thing and one thing only: talking to Plimberley.

She walked over to her, where she was sitting at the makeup station, and leaned into her ear. "Plim, could I have a word? Would you come to my dressing room?"

"Oh, I'm really behind here, Misty. I'm never going to be ready for the opening number at this rate." She was busily brushing blush onto her pointed cheekbones.

"It'll only take a minute," said Misty.

Plimberley let out a gust of breath and smacked the blusher brush down onto the surface of the station. "Fine. But really quick, Misty, you promise? I want to be ready on time if there's telly people filming."

Plimberley stood up, and the two of them walked through the Queens' Room to the corridor, leaving Caesar telling a joke about King Charles's sausage fingers to the others. They laughed with claps and clicks.

"What's this about?" said Plimberley, stopping in the corridor.

Misty stopped too and thought on her feet. She didn't want to confront Plimberley here—she wanted to be in the dressing room, in private.

"It's just about one of your invoices," said Misty, making an excuse that wasn't entirely untrue.

"Misty!" called Mandy from the other end of the corridor. "Misty, can you come now?"

"Just a second, Mandy!" Misty was trying not to sound snappy.

"Well, look, if it's about my invoices, there's no use asking me," said Plimberley.

Mandy was walking up the corridor toward them. "Come on, Misty, we need you now out the front," she was saying.

"What do you mean?" Misty asked Plimberley.

"I haven't done my own invoices for months."

Mandy reached them and grabbed Misty by the arm. "Come on, Misty. There are cameras waiting, we need you to do some interviews."

Misty started walking with Mandy toward the bar, leaving Plimberley standing in the corridor.

"Who does them?" she called over her shoulder. "Who does your invoices?"

"Moneypenny."

40

****

MONEYPENNY.

Moneypenny, thought Misty as Mandy pulled her farther down the corridor, farther toward the hubbub of the bar. So if Moneypenny did the invoices, then it was Moneypenny's writing with the circle above the "i."

"There's two lots from the BBC here," Mandy was saying, "and they want a shot of you on the stage and then a brief interview. Getty have arrived. They want some photos with you too, so we'll do a bit of a press call on the stage."

"Moneypenny . . ." said Misty.

"Come on, Misty. Snap out of it," said Mandy, her Scottish accent suddenly strong and abrupt. They stopped in the doorway to the bar and Mandy put her hands on Misty's shoulders. "It's too late to back out now, Misty, they're all waiting for you."

"I'm fine, Mandy," said Misty, shaking her head. "I'm fine."

Mandy took Misty by the hand and led her through the first rows of tables and chairs, toward the stage where there were photographers and film crews waiting.

Pull yourself together, Misty told herself. *Smile, for Christ's sake.*

She took a breath and smiled as far as her mouth would allow.

"Everybody," called Mandy to the room, "this is the new host of Lady's Bar, Misty Divine." There was a round of applause from the press, and a couple of cameras flashed. Mandy and Misty were making their way to the stage, pressing ahead through the tables. The whole room had been polished and cleaned to within an inch of its life. The tables shone and the displays of white lilies and purple lavender in the center of each one were beautiful.

If Moneypenny wrote the invoices, Moneypenny wrote the suicide note.

They reached the steps onto the stage, and Mandy put her hand on Misty's back, guiding her up the stairs, one at a time. "Say something," she whispered into Misty's ear.

Moneypenny could have planted the chocolates when she came to the apartment.

Once on the stage Misty turned to face the room. There must have been thirty photographers present, reviewers, journalists, and four film crews. All eyes were on her, and she felt the pressure to perform.

"Good evening, everyone," she said.

If Moneypenny wrote the suicide note, then Moneypenny's a murderer.

"Misty," called one of the journalists, "how does it feel to be taking over from Lady Lady?"

"It's bittersweet," said Misty. "Of course we all wish that the events that made this possible hadn't happened and that Lady Lady was here tonight with us, but it is an honor to be the host of one of Soho's most celebrated venues." She didn't know where the words were coming from, but she thought they sounded good, in spite of her inner turmoil.

Moneypenny's a poisoner.

"Can we get some photos, please?" called one of the photographers.

"Strike a pose!" called another.

Misty obliged, placing her hand on her hip and leaning forward with a big smile, a pose she knew would look good in the photographs. She wished she wasn't here, doing this, when all she really wanted was to think. There was something important, something Misty couldn't quite remember. It was like having a word on the tip of your tongue but not being able to say it. And then she realized.

Moneypenny made you a drink.

Oh God.

Miles.

41

★★★★★★★★★★

I'M SO SORRY," said Misty, pacing to the front of the stage. "I'll be back in a moment, I just have to go check on something."

She pulled off her stilettos and abandoned them on the edge of the stairs, quickly descending the steps onto the carpeted floor of the auditorium.

"Misty?" called Mandy.

Misty ignored her, and there was a hum of disappointment from among the photographers and film crews. As soon as she hit the carpet, she sped up, weaving through the tables, faster and faster until she was running. She reached the door to the dressing room corridor and pushed it open. The corridor was full of people. Drag kings, drag queens, everywhere. She pushed her way through the throng.

"Excuse me, excuse me," she was saying. "Coming through."

Once she was past the people, she sped into a full sprint, running to the dressing room as quickly as she could.

She reached the door and burst in, swinging the door open

so hard it bounced off the wall behind and almost closed shut on her again. The room felt different, as though something had moved. *Something's moved.* Miles wasn't there. His drink was on the counter.

Moneypenny looked up, shocked by Misty bursting in so abruptly.

"Where's Miles?" asked Misty.

"Toilet," said Moneypenny. Her face was red under all the makeup, flustered. "Misty, what's going on?"

"It was you, wasn't it?" said Misty, raising her finger and pointing it at Moneypenny.

Moneypenny stepped backward, a frightened look across her old-lady face. Moneypenny picked up Misty's cup of vodka and offered it forward. "Just have a drink, Misty," she said, her top lip quivering.

Misty took the cup and held it up to her nose. "And what have you put in it?"

She felt a little manic, confronting Moneypenny like this, but she was certain now.

It really feels like something has moved in here.

"Put in it? What are you talking about, Misty? You've lost it." Moneypenny started walking toward the door, past Misty. "I'm leaving."

Misty stood in front of her to block her path. "You're not going anywhere, not until I call the police."

"Don't be ridiculous."

"I know that it was you, that you wrote the suicide note, that you planted the chocolates."

The clothes rail.

The clothes rail had been moved. Not a lot, but it was just

slightly out of place. Misty's eye was drawn to it and then to the bottom of it where, poking out from underneath the hem of one of Lady Lady's gowns, was a purple suede shoe. Miles's shoe.

Misty rushed forward and pulled back the rail, gliding it easily out of the way. Behind it, rolled into the corner, was Miles, unconscious on the floor, his mouth oozing with white foam.

"What have you done?" she shouted, staggering forward to kneel beside Miles. She grabbed him by the shoulders and turned him onto his side. White froth slid down his cheek and pooled under his face and his eyelids flickered. He was still alive. Barely.

"I'm sorry, Misty," said Moneypenny as she reached the door. "When you told me you'd recognized the handwriting on the invoice it was only a matter of time before you and your interfering boyfriend put two and two together. And I couldn't let you get in my way."

And then she opened the door and ran.

Misty jumped up onto her feet. Time was of the essence. She needed to get help for Miles. Where was her phone?

Get help!

She flung herself out of the dressing room into the corridor and saw the back of Moneypenny disappearing into the crowd of kings and queens. At the back of the crowd was Amour, correcting the angle of her necklace in the mirror.

"Amour! Call an ambulance! Miles has been poisoned!"

"What?" said Amour.

"Not again!" someone shouted, and there was a laugh.

"Call an ambulance. Now. And the police."

People had stopped moving, stopped talking, and were all looking at Misty. "Help me!" she screamed. Realizing she was deadly serious, the drags suddenly sprung into action. Amour was dialing 999 and people started running up the corridor to help Miles. Everybody else stepped out of the way, pressing themselves against the wall as though making a path for Misty.

At the end of the path was Moneypenny, in full old-lady drag, escaping the corridor into the bar. Misty launched herself at her, running as fast as she could.

"Stop her!" she shouted as she reached the edge of the auditorium. The gathering of press turned to look. Misty noticed a camera swing around and point at her.

Moneypenny was way ahead, weaving rapidly through the tables and chairs, heading for the exit.

"Stop her!" shouted Misty again.

But nobody moved. Everybody was transfixed with the image of the sequined hostess chasing the old lady through the room.

Panicked, Misty picked up a flower arrangement in a glass vase from the middle of one of the tables and threw it toward Moneypenny. It sailed through the air as though it were made of feathers, showering the floor with lilies and lavender. And then it struck home, landing with a thwack against the back of Moneypenny's wigged head.

Misty couldn't believe it. She'd unlocked a new skill she never knew she had: throwing things at moving targets. Moneypenny staggered forward a few steps and then fell to her knees, collapsing onto the ground.

Tess the bouncer quickly arrived and helped Misty get Moneypenny on her feet, restraining her hands behind her back with a plastic zip tie.

"You've got no right, you've got no right," Moneypenny kept saying.

"We've got every right, you murdering bitch."

"She was asking for it!" screamed Moneypenny.

The cameras all turned, capturing the moment for all eternity.

"So, you admit it?" said Misty. "You killed Lady Lady?"

"Yes!" she screamed, looking absolutely maniacal in her grandma drag. "I killed Lady Lady!"

"Why? Why would you do that?"

"Because of the dress, the stupid dress! Den should never have brought it here. Lady Lady found it in the dressing room and was insistent on wearing it. She thought it was a replica—got all excited that it looked like Judy Garland's. You know what she was like, the old bitch, he couldn't stop her."

"And what? You killed her when she realized it was the real deal?"

"Yes! She was going to tell the police if Den didn't turn himself in. She'd have exposed us, ruined everything."

"I can't believe you killed her over a dress."

"It was more than a dress!" Moneypenny shouted. "I'm somebody now, Misty. I'm somebody." She turned to face the cameras and threw her head back, grandstanding, making a show of herself. "I'm the *Kensington Catburglar*!"

Misty could hardly believe her eyes and ears. She was truly shocked to see normally cute, funny Moneypenny unraveling like this before her very eyes, like she was descending into madness. "And Den? You killed him too?"

"Den should have been more grateful," growled Moneypenny, wringing her hands behind her back. "If it wasn't for me he'd have lost his flat. He was broke and desperate, and I gave him *everything*!"

"So, what? When he came to you asking for money you got him involved in your cat-burgling to help him out?"

"*I* did the cat-burgling! That was the easy part. Den was my fence, selling everything I stole for a cut of the money. But he fucked up with the Red Egg, couldn't find a buyer, and he let Lady Lady find the dress! It was one mistake too many."

The whole room was silent. Most of the drag kings and queens had emerged from the dressing room corridor to listen, and everyone was standing in total shock as Moneypenny showed herself to be an absolute monster to the world. She was ranting, raving for the cameras, struggling against Tess's viselike grip.

"When my attempt to frame you with the chocolates failed, I needed to pin the blame on someone, and Den was the obvious choice. What would you have done, Misty, if you were me? I wasn't expecting anyone to match the handwriting on Plimberley's invoices to the suicide note. Those damn invoices!"

Sirens sounded outside the club and Misty thought of Miles. She didn't want to spend a second longer with Moneypenny and needed to be with her boyfriend instead. She was disgusted by what she'd heard.

"Give her to the police," said Misty to Tess. "I need to be with Miles."

And with that she took one last look at Moneypenny. Her former friend, the Kensington Catburglar, the killer.

42

****

MISTY WENT WITH Miles in the ambulance to the hospital, so she didn't see most of the aftermath of Moneypenny's arrest, but she heard about it later. Everyone heard about it. Moneypenny had gone kicking and screaming into the back of a police car.

"I'm so sorry, Miles," said Misty as the ambulance sped through Central London. "I'm so so sorry."

Miles had an oxygen mask over his face and was already hooked up to all sorts of machines. He hadn't opened his eyes since Misty found him behind the clothes rail. A paramedic asked Misty to sit back away from the bed so they could run some tests on the way to the hospital. She did, of course, watching on in horror as her lovely Miles fought for his life.

She couldn't believe this was happening. She'd caught the murderer, but now Miles was hurt, in danger, teetering on the line between life and death.

MISTY SAT IN a small hospital visitors' room. Miles was having surgery, and the doctor had explained that his chances of survival weren't good. The poison had done some serious damage to his internal organs. Misty felt sick.

The memorial show at Lady's Bar went ahead without Misty, hosted by Amour, who stepped in at the last minute, and apparently it was a huge success. Auntie Susan had attended, as had Mr. McDermott and Florentina. After the show Mandy arrived at the hospital with a bag of clothes, a phone charger, and some face wipes. She sat down next to Misty in the visitors' room.

"How is he doing?" she asked.

"Not good," said Misty. "Not good."

Mandy said she'd stay in the visitors' room in case there was news from the doctors, and Misty went to the toilets to de-drag. She was grateful to find a gender neutral cubicle on a quiet floor so she wouldn't have to go into the men's in full drag. She whipped off the lashes, took off the blond wig with the black streak and dropped it into the bag Mandy had brought, and then she set about taking off her makeup, becoming Joe once again. Joe was who Miles needed and who Joe needed to be right now.

Mandy went home at 1 a.m. and left Joe in the visitors' room alone. It was a bleak little space. Four chairs and a coffee table and a faded painting of a nondescript beach on the wall. There was a pile of toys in the corner and a stack of magazines next to a bottle of hand sanitizer. Joe didn't touch any of it and instead sat upright in one of the armchairs, waiting for a doctor to come out of the surgery and tell them what was going on.

At around 2 a.m. Miles's family and Joe's parents arrived at about the same time.

"Joe, babe, I'm so sorry this is happening," Joe's mum said as she squeezed her arms around their neck in an awkward hug.

"What happened?" asked Miles's mother. "Tell me everything that happened to my baby."

Joe filled them in on the week, leaving out the risky and dangerous bits, but giving them an overview of what had led to them exposing Moneypenny at the club.

It wasn't until 4 a.m. when a doctor arrived to tell them that the surgery had been a success. They couldn't guarantee that Miles was out of the woods, but he had a chance at recovery. Joe asked if they could see Miles, and the doctor said they could, that they could sit with Miles in the recovery ward.

B Y SUNDAY THE hospital bed had been decorated with balloons and blankets and cushions from home, and Miles hadn't been left alone for two days. He was still unconscious. The doctors said they had induced a coma. Joe hadn't really understood all the medical details, just that it meant Miles might not be awake anytime soon. And there was also still a chance that he might not wake up at all.

But for the time being, spirits in the hospital were kept high. The damage to Miles's internal organs had been repaired with two further surgeries, and his family had prayed and sung and read to him from the bedside. They had embraced Joe, and they'd all had a cry together in the visitors' room.

W HILE JOE HAD waited for Miles to wake up in the hospital, Misty Divine had had a wild time on the internet. The film crews had captured the moment that Misty stopped Moneypenny with her impressive vase-throwing, and the video had gone massively viral. It had been all over every news station, every website, and clips and memes of it were all over the internet. Misty was the hottest name in drag. The drag queen who caught a murderer.

And while Misty rose to fame, so did Moneypenny. She was infamous. The drag queen poisoner and cat burglar who dressed as an old woman and confessed her crimes for the cameras.

Joe had observed this rise to fame like an outsider looking in, not looking at their social media or responding to any messages about it. For now they just needed to focus on Miles.

DS Hughes visited on Sunday afternoon, but Joe didn't hear anything from DI Davies. Hughes still had the patch of dry skin on the back of her hand and picked at it nervously.

"I'm sorry I didn't listen to you when you called," she said, "about the handwriting, about Plimberley."

"You couldn't have known it would end up like this, none of us could."

O N MONDAY MORNING Joe was finally alone with Miles for the first time since he was admitted. The hospital bed had been a hive of activity as they all waited for news, each day growing worse as the doctors looked more and more grave.

Joe thought about everything they'd been through together: the trip to the dress shop, the afternoon of drinking with Moneypenny and Plimberley, going to see Auntie Susan together. How could it have ended like this? Joe took Miles's hand and squeezed it.

"Come on, love," they said. "Wake up. Wake up. I need you."

And for the first time in three days Miles's eyes flickered open.

Epilogue

★★★★★★★★★★

TWO WEEKS LATER

MISTY WORE A brand-new dress, made especially for Lady Lady's funeral by Florentina. It was tightly fitted with a large
black ruffle across the front. She wore a straight loose white wig
with a wide-brimmed black hat.

The dress code for the funeral was Grieving Gods and God-
desses, and the drag performers of London had turned it out for
the occasion. Misty saw Len in a black rhinestoned suit with a
pair of silver angel wings on the back.

After everything that had happened it was good to say goodbye to Lady Lady properly, and the service had given Misty a
sense of peace that she hadn't felt since before the murder. Her
heart seemed to be beating more slowly, and her mind had
stopped racing. The memorial ended with a procession out of the
service, drag after drag making their way outside, gathering in
front of the chapel of remembrance, ready to go back to Lady's
Bar for the wake.

Misty held hands with Amour as they exited together. Amour was wearing a black silk dress with a delicate gold chain and she looked like a princess.

"I can't believe it's over," said Amour.

"Me too," replied Misty, and she really couldn't. For weeks her life had been consumed with the investigation and then the aftermath: the news reports, the television interviews, Miles's slow recovery at home. Something about being here, saying goodbye to Lady Lady with all of her friends, finally felt like closure.

As they stepped into the midsummer sun, a woman whose face was almost completely covered by a black veil grabbed Misty by the elbow and pulled her to one side away from Amour and the rest of the crowd.

"You're Misty Divine, right?" said the woman hurriedly.

"Yes. And you are . . . ?"

"You emailed me. I'm a journalist. My name is Jessica Gethyn."

It felt like so long ago that she'd sat with Miles in Balans and sent that message to Jessica. She'd had no reply at all. She had begun to think that Jessica Gethyn just wasn't interested in talking to her.

Jessica's face was tense and pale and serious. There were dark circles under her eyes, and her cheeks were sunken as if she hadn't eaten properly for a few weeks.

"You asked me about Atrax and I'm here to warn you," she said, her voice low and secretive, not wanting anyone else at the funeral to hear. "Stay away from Atrax—it's dangerous. And stay away from me. Don't contact me again."

And with that, Jessica Gethyn turned on her heel and walked

away, leaving Misty standing alone outside the chapel, Jessica's words ringing in her head.

It seemed there might just be one more mystery for Misty to solve.

ACKNOWLEDGMENTS

Firstly, thank you to Ronan, for reading more Misty Divine drafts than was reasonable and for being an unwavering voice of love and support. I couldn't do any of it without you.

Huge, enormous, wild claps of thanks to my literary agent extraordinaire Hayley Steed, who helped to shape this book in ways I had never imagined, all for the better. I have such overwhelming gratitude for my superstar editors: Grace Long at Penguin Michael Joseph, and Annie Odders at Berkley. Thank you for taking a chance on a drag queen detective and for believing in this project from the beginning. I can't wait to see where Misty takes us next!

To the entire teams at Penguin Random House, Janklow & Nesbit, and Madeleine Milburn Literary Agency, it has been a pleasure to work with you. Thank you for your time and energy and expertise.

I must also acknowledge my many dedicated friends and test readers over the years, who have supported my writing perhaps more than they realize. Mick, Irene, Rachel, Emily, Kelly B., Chesca R., Chesca C., Sally C., Megan R., Emma D. S., Lucy R., Caitlin P., Sarah P., Olivia M. . . . and everybody else who has cast their generous readery eyes across my works in progress. We did it!

Special thanks to my agent Patrick Bustin at PBJ Management for being an absolute rock star.

To Nancy G., Frankie O., and Elliot M., without whom life would be very different indeed.

And thanks to you, our reader. It means so much to me that you've picked up this book and entered the glamorous, dangerous world of Misty Divine. I hope you'll return soon.

Last, but by no means least, a delicious biscuit-shaped thank-you goes to Rex and Little Dog, the finest 4 a.m. writing companions this drag queen could have wished for.

Holly Stars

x